THE SECRETS OF THE CAVE

Betty Barnes has been largely brought up by her older sister, Kate, in a small West Country village. Betty's daydreams of the bright lights of Hollywood and becoming a movie star are one way for her to escape the realities of school life where she is cruelly bullied. Betty has inherited psychic gifts from her forebears and she experiences memories of an earlier time when she was the local Wise Woman, guardian of a nearby mystical cave. In desperation she runs away, but 1930s London is hardly a hospitable place ... and she cannot turn her back on her magic forever.

THE SECRETS OF THE CAVE

The Secrets Of The Cave

by

Phillipa Bowers

Magna Large Print Books
Long Preston, North Yorkshire,
BD23 4ND, England.

British Library Cataloguing in Publication Data.

Bowers, Phillipa
    The secrets of the cave.

A catalogue record of this book is
available from the British Library

ISBN   978-0-7505-2919-8

First published in Great Britain 2008 by Piatkus Books

Copyright © 2008 by Phillipa Bowers

Cover illustration © Berni Stevens

The moral right of the author has been asserted

Published in Large Print 2008 by arrangement with
Piatkus Books Ltd and Little, Brown Group Ltd.

Magna Large Print is an imprint of Library Magna Books Ltd.

Printed and bound in Great Britain by
T.J. (International) Ltd., Cornwall, PL28 8RW

For my mother, who encouraged me to read,
and Terry, who encouraged me to write.

Author's Note

For many generations the inhabitants of Wookey Hole in Somerset have handed down the legend of how they were saved from the curse of a wicked witch, by a monk from Glastonbury Abbey, who went into the cave in which she lived and sprinkled her with holy water, thereby turning her to stone.

I believe it is possible that, during a time when midwives, herbalists and healers were being persecuted, burned and hanged all over Europe, a local wise woman could be blamed for any misfortune befalling the community. The sickness of people and animals caused by pollution of the water supply by the lead mines on the hills above the village for example, would be understood today, but might have been seen as the work of the devil in less enlightened times.

A calcite ball, human bones and the remains of a knife found during excavations in a cave may have belonged to one who, in company with many other victims of witch-hunts, deserved better than the evil reputation for which she is still remembered.

This story is about the twentieth-century descendants of a woman living in a small village with a similar legend.

Chapter One

Oakey Vale, 1930

'I wish I could escape from this beastly place.'

Hearing a faint whistle above the birds singing in the foliage near by, Betty turned her head towards the sound. Might that train carry her away to freedom one day? She climbed down from one branch to another and jumped to the ground. Then, just to make sure the tree would grant her wish, she walked around its huge trunk three times to the right and three times to the left. 'London,' she whispered, 'that's where I, Betty Barnes, belong, where I was born – where my life will begin. Whoever heard of a film star living in a dreary little village like this one?'

Walking away from the tree she picked her way carefully between tendrils of brambles growing across the narrow path, leading to the edge of the cliff behind the cottage where she paused to listen for any sound of life in the garden below. Hearing nothing, she then climbed down the steep steps cut into the rock and stood behind the white sheets hanging on the washing line, wondering what to do next. There was no reason to fear being seen because it was the summer holidays and so she no longer had to hang around in the woods and then return home at teatime pretending to have been at dull and boring school all day, but she didn't want to go inside anyway. It was Monday and Kate would try to persuade her to wring the washing, which was really tedious and the mangle squeaked as you turned the handle and if you weren't careful you could squash your fingers in the rollers. Why should she want to see her sister and that horrid man who had ruined her life? Why should she help wash his clothes or the sheets he slept in with Kate?

The sudden sound of an outraged bird shrieking in the hedge caused her to look down the garden, where a striped tail could just be discerned emerging from a clump of lavender. Knowing the pretty little tabby cat had already caught most of the fledglings from the blackbird's first brood and, wanting to help the second late hatchlings survive, she ran towards it, hissing, 'Shoo, Pudden, shoo!'

The cat retreated and hid behind a clump of comfrey from where it could watch the nest in safety.

She walked to the large flat rock nearby and, sinking down onto it, sat with her back pressed against the ivy hanging down the sheer rocky cliff that ran the length of the garden. Next to her, behind the curtain of creepers, was the secret cave. Kate had made her swear never to tell a living soul about it, not even Billy Nelson; and she wouldn't, not ever in her whole life. She had hidden in there after running away on that terrible night when she'd had a row with Kate and couldn't think of where to go. Remembering the sudden, thick blackness when the candle went out and how, sinking to her knees, she had scrabbled desperately around trying to find the matches, she gave an involuntary shiver. She must have fallen asleep eventually because she could recall a strange dream she'd had in there of Kate being her mother, not her sister as she was now, and they were being chased by men who smelled disgusting and shouted a lot. Kate hadn't been at all surprised when told about it and explained that they had in fact been mother and daughter in that lifetime and the foul-smelling men were merely ghosts and could do her no harm in this present incarnation.

She had felt better about the terrifying experience after that, but nevertheless had kept close to her sister when they buried Gran in the tomb and had not thought of entering the cave on her own afterwards. Now, suddenly, the desire to go in again overwhelmed her.

Without pausing to think, she ran to the house and tiptoed past the scullery, where Kate was singing whilst scrubbing a shirt collar on the washboard. Cautiously peering into the kitchen she was relieved to find no sign of Charles Wallace and quickly grabbed an oil lamp and a box of matches from a cupboard, then, returning to the ivy hanging down the cliff, she pushed through it and lit the lamp.

For a few moments she stood looking around the domed interior and, remembering her grandmother saying this was where her ancestors kept their winter stores of food, she ran her hand along the flat rocks wondering if cheeses and fruit, or maybe sacks of barley, had been stored there. Then, repeating the moves she had seen

15

Kate make, she carried the lamp to the far inner wall and probed rocks with her fingers until one moved easily, revealing a narrow aperture. Carefully holding the lamp, she climbed through the space and stepped into the huge cavern. Looking up at the figure formed in the rocks above, from whose heart the water emerged then trickled over sparkling pink crystals before running down into a pool as red as blood, she felt giddy with excitement. This certainly was a secret worth keeping, and, not only that, the beautiful lady seemed to be smiling, as though pleased to see her.

Kate had explained that the colour of the pool was caused by mineral deposits on the rock, but nevertheless she felt surprised on finding the water was clear when dipping her hand into it and scooping some to drink.

Turning her back on the lady she looked down at the long slab of rock at her feet and recalled helping to place her grandmother's corpse into the chasm beneath it. Kate had said she wanted to be laid to rest there also, down among the bones of the women who had gone before, and had seemed sad when Betty retorted that she wouldn't be anywhere near this horrid place when she grew up and therefore couldn't possibly put her there. She wished now the right words had come to mind so she could have explained that no one could make a 'cut your throat and hope to die' kind of promise without knowing they would definitely keep it. That would have sounded better, and it was true, although not the whole reason, but she couldn't say she'd be in Hollywood by then and the funeral would be over and done with by the time she could get here on a luxury liner from America, could she?

The idea of being a rich and famous film star returning to grieve for her sister was appealing and she paused to imagine driving through the village in a large motor car with a handsome man at her side. Her outfit would be black, including the fox fur around the shoulders of her elegantly understated suit and the small hat with a veil draped over it which would be longer and thicker than was fashionable – but one had to make compromises when in mourning. She would be gracious and charming to the local people and throw silver coins to the children before departing to stay in a smart hotel in Bath.

Smiling at the vision of being consoled by Douglas Fairbanks junior, she sank down to the ground and placed the lamp beside her. Laying one hand on the cover of the tomb and the other on the ground, she sat gazing up at the figure which was just visible in the beam of light. Idly running her fingers over the rocky floor beside her, she found a small piece of stone and picked it up. Thinking it felt strangely warm whilst curling her fingers around it, she rubbed her thumb along its smooth surface and gasped as the surrounding patches of lamplight and dark shadows merged and then separated again to form the trunks of trees...

The sun was a scarlet circle shimmering through a gap in the branches to her right. Soon it would sink down leaving the forest in darkness. Her legs were heavy and her head ached from hunger and fatigue as she slowly trailed behind her mother along the narrow path. Thinking of the fish they would eat whilst sitting by the fire, her mouth filled with saliva and she quickened her step.

The slight figure ahead interrupted her steady measured pace and, lowering the heavy sack from her back, stood listening to the faint sounds in the distance before muttering, 'Huntsmen,' then picking up her burden and carrying on. Having taken a dozen strides she frowned as the noise grew into a jumble of shrieking curses, unintelligible exclamations and the occasional guffaw of laughter. Looking back, she gave a reassuring smile and said, 'The cider be strong this year,' adding whilst holding out her hand, 'Come, child, we'll soon be home by the fire.'

They walked a few paces together and then, hearing the vociferous yells grow louder, tightened their grip on one another.

A shout of 'Catch the witch!' was followed by raucous laughter.

Her mother exclaimed, 'They're getting closer!' Dropping the sack, she pushed her into a hollow tree and hissed, 'Stay there until I return.'

Her throat was tight and no sound came from her lips as she mouthed, 'But, wait...' Helpless and paralysed with fear, she crouched down, unable to hear anything other than the sound of blood thumping in her temples.

Eventually, when her heart had returned to its normal beat, she crawled out and stood hesitantly on the path. Although unaware of how long she had waited in the tree, breathing in the scent of yellow fungus growing on the rotting wood, she knew the sun was moving westwards. Night would soon overwhelm *the woods, turning trees into phantoms looming above fathomless caverns of shadow, in which familiar paths dissolved and disappeared until the sun rose again. Her terror of being alone in the darkness was greater than fear of disobeying her mother, and, with one hand on the knife in her belt, she cautiously followed the trail of sliding footprints to the riverbank. There, standing amidst trampled undergrowth and broken willow saplings, she knew this was where her mother had been caught and, whilst taking cautious steps through the mud, imagined her skidding and sliding helplessly. Seeing the trail of several footprints, she followed it along the path by the river and up through the wooded hillside hearing the sounds of men shouting getting louder until, knowing they were close by, she crouched down behind a bush.*

'Justice be done!'

'She'll kill no more babes!'

'We'll sleep safe this night!'

'Aye, 'tis done.'

In the following sudden absence of voices, the sound of a robin in the small oak nearby seemed abnormally loud and she recoiled from its assault on her ears. Then, wondering why the men were silent, she cautiously moved sideways until, peering through a gap in the foliage, she saw them beneath an oak tree and, despite the fading light, could recognise each one. A shepherd who had loved her mother was on his knees praying. Jan the blacksmith's son was bending over, clutching at his head and groaning. The three others were standing together by the bundle of rags hanging limply from a bough above them. The small, wiry miller, whose lascivious eyes made her shiver whenever she passed by the mill, was staring up at the tree

19

nodding his head, while the carter held onto his arm to keep upright. The farrier, who was the tallest of the trio, stepped towards the tree and, with one swipe of his knife, cut through the rope around the bough then gave a roar of triumph as the bundle plummeted to the ground.

Seeing the body land in disarray with naked limbs flung out from ragged cloth and long black hair strewn around a bloody pulp, she understood what they had done, and groaned aloud.

'Come–' the farrier bent and pulled at one bare leg lying pale as bone on the dark earth '–we can shove her in the cave by the mill.' And, dragging the corpse by her ankles, he walked away from the tree, followed by the others.

Feeling nothing, not fear nor grief nor cold nor pain, she huddled in the undergrowth for a while then followed the path the men had taken for a short distance before climbing up the hill and making her way to the cliff overlooking the cave in which she and her mother had often sheltered from the rain. From this vantage point above them she peered through the gathering gloom as the men emerged and rolled a large boulder into the opening and then placed others on top of that.

'A landslide–' the blacksmith patted a rock '–that's what it was.'

'Aye.' Jan sounded less sure than his father.

'Aye. Buried her inside. How sad!' The carter guffawed with false laughter

'Come, it's dark, we mun go home.'

She waited until they had all stumbled away along the riverbank and then, forgetting imaginary phantoms lurking in the shadows either side of the path,

20

turned with numb fearlessness towards the dwelling.

Fire burned within her chest as she ran along the path, hearing only the blood thundering in her temples. On reaching the clearing in front of the dwelling, she paused to get her breath. As the pain of breathing eased and her heart beat slowed to its normal rhythm she inhaled the odour of male sweat, then, hearing the sound of breaking twigs, knew in the instant before her head was jerked backwards as he grabbed her hair, that the miller had come for her.

Instinctively putting up both hands to free herself, she felt both wrists grabbed and was forced down under him. Throughout the ordeal she was aware of the knife-handle in her belt pressing into her side and thought only of the blade she had sharpened on a stone earlier that day while sitting by the river waiting for a fish to swim into her trap. When at last he gave a roar and momentarily relaxed his grip on her wrists, she slid one hand free, pulled the knife from its sheath and drove it as hard as she could between his ribs. When he gave a strangled piercing scream, she instantly pulled the knife out and lunged upwards, then smiled into the darkness at the gurgling sound from his throat as the warm blood gushed over her.

Pushing his slumped corpse away from her, she stood up and walked unsteadily to the dwelling built of rocks and thatch up against the cliff nearby. Once inside and having stirred the embers of the fire, she lit a small rush lamp and looked down at her garments, soaked with the miller's blood. If the other men found him then she too would be dragged screaming to her death. Her mother had tried to help the local people and they blamed her for their troubles: what would they do to someone they knew had killed one of their

21

own? She must hide the body, but where? In the secret cave, of course! She must put it with that of her grandmother and those who had gone before.

Taking the lamp outside, she walked alongside the ivy-covered cliff to a large boulder on which she and her mother had often sat together, then, parting the heavy green curtain of creepers hanging down beside it, she stepped into the cave and set down the lamp. Pausing to look around her at the collection of nuts, berries, herbs and a few cheeses stored in readiness for approaching winter, she dismissed the possibility of hiding the body there, knowing others might find it at any time. She must put it in the other, inmost, cavern, with those who had gone before.

Returning to the dead miller, she grabbed hold of his ankles and heaved him through the grass, then into the cave. Ignoring the pains in her exhausted body, she took the lamp and went to the boulder her mother had shown her. It moved sideways easily, leaving a narrow hole and, taking a deep breath, she began heaving the corpse through the gap.

When, feeling dizzy and weak, she had eventually pulled the body into the inner cave, she staggered forward and sank to her knees, looking up at the kneeling figure formed as though carved into the rocks above her. Gradually her breath returned to its normal steady rhythm as she gazed in wonder at the serene face and heard the water trickling from between her rocky breasts, down over pink crystals into the red pool, below stony thighs. Remembering her mother standing on this spot before burying her grandmother under the stone slab on the ground close by, she recalled her saying: 'Our destiny be to guard this lady as my mother, her mother and hers before *her, have done in both life and death. Long ago when invaders came who would claim her for their religion, our ancestor made a pledge that she and all her descendants would keep her safe and now, when the Bishop is enclosing the healing wells near the new big church and keeping them in his garden for his own pleasure, we must be even more vigilant. When I die thee must bury me here with my knife and—' she patted the leather pouch tied to her waist '—my scrying ball so my spirit may keep watch also and though thy sons will leave as mine have done, like me, thee must bear a daughter to bury thee and carry on.' Looking into her eyes, she then asked, 'Do I have thy word?'*

Thinking of the ancestral spirits watching her from the darkness of their rocky grave and feeling unable to imagine being brave enough to come into this burial chamber alone, she had faltered then, but now knew no fear. Bending forward she pulled the slab sideways, revealing a dark crevasse, then reached for the small lamp and held it over the hole. Looking down at a pale skull and bones gleaming in the flickering light, she paused to reflect that this should be the resting place of her beautiful mother, not a gross man who had helped murder her. But, shaking her head sadly, she knew there was nothing else to be done and so pushed the corpse into the crevasse then quickly replaced the cover.

Turning and dipping her hand into the pool as red as blood, she scooped a handful of water to her mouth where it mingled with the salt tears running down her cheeks. Then, taking her knife and holding the wooden handle, carved in the form of a man and woman entwined, she gave her pledge that she and all

23

her descendants would guard the cave and keep the sublimely beautiful lady safe from the men who would desecrate her.

Picking up a rock, she dashed it against the crystals overhanging the pool until a chunk broke loose and fell into the water. Reaching in, she grabbed it and held it up, anticipating the many hours she would spend carving it into a ball like the one her mother had used to look into the future. Then, raising her arms, with the lump of pink quartz in one hand and her knife in the other, she sang a mourning song without words for all those who had gone before. Eventually, sinking to the ground, she allowed her tired eyes to close and escaped from the horror into sleep.

How long had she lain here in the dark since burying the miller in the tomb? A whole night at least, maybe more. The fire in the dwelling would be dead by now. She could smell the food stored on the shelf beside her, but could see nothing without the light of the rush lamp that had long since died. Her head throbbed with pain and her throat was dry. She must drink. She needed water, but dared not return to the inner cave with no light to see by. Feeling her way along the edge of the rocks on which she knew were stored the nuts and berries for the coming winter, she edged slowly to the entrance and peered cautiously through a narrow gap in the ivy. All was quiet. A fox paused to sniff her scent and went on his way. A few birds were stirring; dawn would not be long.

She must go outside and find water and food or she would die. There would be dew on the grass and she could soon find a root or some berries. When she was stronger she could fetch the goats from where they were grazing up top – they would give her milk and she could kill a Billy kid and roast it on the fire. *Saliva filled her mouth. Food, she must have food.*

Pushing aside the ivy hanging outside she stepped forward, then, seeing a figure leave the shadows by the dwelling she turned and staggered back into the cave where she huddled against the rock wall, paralysed with fear.

'Caitlin, Caitlin, don't be frightened. I mean no harm.'

He knew her name. His voice was familiar; there was a cultured, foreign sound to the words. He was the man who had stayed with her mother for two whole moons while his injured horse was healed.

The ivy curtain parted, letting in the cool dawn light. The figure was a dark outline without features. 'They have killed her,' he said.

'I know.'

'I wish to help thee, child.'

She hesitated.

'I gave thee a ring for healing my horse.'

She had loved the beautiful creature and would have preferred it to the shining bauble. 'Aye, I remember,' she whispered.

'I was taken ill with a fever soon after leaving here and stayed at a convent across the marshes to recover. I was about to leave and continue on my journey when a fellow traveller told me of a witch who was poisoning crops and killing babies hereabouts. Then, when he said a woman whose child had been cursed by the witch had seen Satan with this evil creature and he was taller than a dwelling and his mighty stallion taller still, I recalled that while I was replacing the thatch on the roof a demented woman came to thy mother grieving after her dead child. Remember?'

'Aye,' she agreed, 'the poor soul came to blame my mother even though she had been warned it was too late to save the baby and there was nothing to be done. She pulled out her hair and was so mad with grief she frightened the horse.'

'Aye, poor creature. I believe that in her madness she thought I was the devil high above the dwelling and when my horse reared over her, startled by her ranting and shrieking, she must have thought it was his mount.' He shook his head sadly then went on, 'If only I had stayed longer, but I was sworn to go to the Holy Land, it was a sacred oath I have to keep.'

'It was not thy doing, Sire.'

'Aye, that is so, but what she thought she saw in her raging grief added to the foolish belief that thy mother was to blame for the local misfortune.' He shook his head sadly. 'We mortals cannot know that which is known only by God. Only He can understand why our babes die of the squits each summer and our crops fail. We cannot find the fault within one of us.'

'My mother only sought to give comfort to the woman. She knew it was too late to save it.'

'I know. It is the same every year, everywhere.' He held out his hand. 'Come with me, child, I can take thee to safety with the sisters at Glastonbury, they will care for thee.'

'My mother said I must look out for the goats.'

'God will keep watch until thy return.'

'I may come back?'

'I promise I will bring thee back.'

She pushed the piece of pink quartz onto a ledge and stood up, her head whirling with flashing, spark-

26

ling lights. 'Yes, kind sir.'

His arms were outstretched and she let herself go into their strong grasp. She would not die. His breath was warm on her cheek as he wrapped his cloak around her. She would not die. He lifted her onto a horse and they swayed in rhythm with the animal's slow progress through the woods. She would not die. They bounced a while as they gathered speed on the open track. She would not die. She would come back!

The sisters at the convent near Glastonbury welcomed her with small cooing sounds and sympathetic sighs. 'Poor little love,' one said. 'Such a sweet face but so pale, so thin,' said another. 'She's a little angel!' exclaimed a plump nun. 'A veritable angel.' When they laid her on a mattress filled with fresh bedstraw she slipped her knife under it, then closed her eyes and relaxed into their care.

She was aware of intakes of breath and mutterings whilst her bloodstained bodice and skirt were removed and heard their discussion as they fed her with a gruel of milk and barley sweetened with honey. They said the man was a brave and honourable knight who had given a promissory note for her keep that either he would pay on his return or the Mother would claim against his estate in the event of his death in the Holy Land.

Awakening later to the sound of women singing, she took the knife from under her and kissed the wooden handle. She would return to the valley one day and take her mother's place as guardian of the lady in the rocks and the tomb of those who had gone before, but for now she would bide her time and stay warm and safe and well-fed in this nunnery scented with

27

beeswax and flowers.

Opening her eyes and seeing the beautiful lady in the rocks gazing down on her, she was perplexed, until feeling the small object in her hand, she understood it was the source of the strange dream and pushed it into her cardigan pocket.

The lamp flickered and shadows around her deepened until the lady's face was no longer visible. Knowing the oil must be running low and fearful of the dark, she quickly squeezed through the narrow gap into the outer cave where, placing the lamp on the ground, she reached out and replaced the rock. The light died at that moment and she stood still to take a deep breath in order to control the fear flooding through her. Turning slowly, she peered into the thick darkness and, keeping one hand on the rocks, walked slowly and hesitantly until, after a while, a tiny flicker of light became apparent and, to her great relief, she felt the cool fronds of ivy on her face. Pushing through into the cool air she blinked in the light and sat thankfully on the large rock to her right.

Reaching into her pocket and taking out the small pebble she had picked up in the cave she looked at it lying in the palm of her hand. It was too light, too soft and too warm to be rock. It must be wood of some very special kind to have given her such a dream and, although it didn't look pretty or precious, it certainly was powerful; she would keep it with her treasures in the secret hiding place.

When the little cat appeared, purring and rubbing against her legs, she picked it up and snuggled against its warm, sweet-smelling fur. She heard the voices of people walking along the lane on the other side of the hedge and then Kate calling, 'Tea's ready, Betty.'

As though included in the summons, the cat jumped from her arms and ran up the path towards the house.

'Coming,' she replied, suddenly feeling very hungry. Then, realising the lamp had been left behind, she groaned aloud – there was another row waiting to happen when Kate went into the cave and found it!

Chapter Two

Regular consumption of nettle tea may ease rheumatism and arthritis.

All was quiet, apart from the sound of a bumble-bee in the thyme flowers at her feet and birds singing in the apple trees overhead. She had looked down the garden towards the dell, then in the privy, the vegetable patch and hen coop; but found no one. It was too early for Albert to come home from work so there was no danger of him being there, and Kate was talking to Charles at breakfast about going for a walk up top – maybe they were still out and the house was empty at last.

She walked to the back door, pushed it open and went through the glory-hole, carefully avoiding contact with the mackintoshes that might fall off their hooks and the assortment of walking sticks, umbrellas, scythes and gumboots lining the walls. Tiptoeing past the empty scullery to her right, she entered the silent kitchen and counted, one and two and three... Billy said that was what soldiers did to measure seconds, and seven and eight and nine and ten. There was still no sign of life. Only the grandmother clock standing at the foot of the stairs made any sound in the house.

Looking at the dead rabbit and some wild garlic leaves lying on the table, she wrinkled her nose. There was the making of yet another stew to set Albert humming one of his dreary hymn tunes! She hadn't teased the old man for ages, well, not much really. Actually, he was nowhere near as stupid as Kate seemed to think: he was simple, that was all. He knew what he needed to know and no more; just like his beloved cats. He probably knew his mother had left the property to Kate because she would look after him and he probably knew he'd have been sent to Saint Bernard's Hospital otherwise. In fact, now she came to think of it, he definitely knew about the loony bin because she'd told him last year when she was annoyed with Kate for not going to London after the old woman had died. She regretted that and wished she hadn't said anything. Maybe he'd forgotten by now? She had behaved perfectly in every way since the night she'd tried to run away; had even been polite and nice to Charles Wallace since he had moved in to live with Kate as though he was her husband, which of course everyone knew he wasn't and never would be. Not that he had been horrid or done anything to upset her, in fact he'd been rather friendly and talked to her as though she was a grown-up, which would be really nice if it wasn't for the fact that it was because of him that most people in the village didn't talk to her at all now. There was nothing wrong with him, except he was poor and, worst of all, married to Mrs Wallace who had sworn she would never set him free.

If only her sister had accepted the archaeologist Jim Hall, who was a rich respectable bachelor, things would be very different. He'd said he would pay for Betty to be educated with gentry so she could learn to do things like how to give elegant tea parties and whatever else the wife of a rich lord might need to know, not doing sums and suffering beastly insults at the village school for another year until she was fourteen!

Everything here was wrong. If only her mother hadn't died of influenza. If only Kate hadn't been sent here to the village in disgrace because she'd been stupid with a man, then they would both still be there, in London. They wouldn't be in this boring old village with oil lamps instead of electric lights and a privy in the garden instead of a proper lavvy. They wouldn't be outcasts, being sniffed at by silly old Mrs Nelson. They'd be the Misses Baines of London. Kate, an old maid of thirty, and her lovely young sister, Elizabeth, who was destined to captivate a rich young gentleman who looked like John Gilbert the film star and lived in a mansion, in London.

She sat on the new sofa and sneered down at the green plush; 'chesterfield' Charles called it. That other toff, the solicitor, had bought it so it wouldn't be in the auction at The Grange, because it had been in his study when he was rich and he wanted him to have it even though he'd lost everything and his wife had gone up north. There was nothing wrong with the old sofa – well, it was a bit lumpy at one end and sagged at the other – but it was usually buried under a pile of stuff needing to be ironed anyway so it didn't matter. Now he was here, the shirts and sheets were no longer left in heaps until they were so dry they had to be dampened down again – that wasn't good enough for a toffee-nosed gent like Charles Wallace, oh no, everything was hidden in a cupboard now! She made a face and poked out her tongue to emphasise her contempt.

Stroking the soft upholstery, she looked around the kitchen, feeling suddenly sad. This was the first change since the old woman died; if they hadn't taken the old sofa out and burned it, the room would be exactly as she had left it. Two bunches of lemon balm and six large bundles of nettles were all hanging from the wooden clothes dryer suspended above the range on which a stockpot simmered as usual. The plates Granfer had won at Pridden fair were still on the tall dresser, large ones on the top shelf and smaller ones beneath. The china cow and calf, each with only three legs, still leaned precariously together and next to them was the delicate porcelain cottage with windows that would light up when candle ends were burned inside it. Every inch of the lower shelves was crammed with Gran's knick-knacks and objects that might be useful one day. If Betty half closed her eyes and ignored her comfortable seat, she could imagine the back door might open at any moment to reveal the old woman standing on the threshold. She would hear her saying to Kate, 'Tell Whatsername to get ready for tea, my lover.'

Feeling the familiar ache she screwed up her eyes and bit her lip. She'd never understood why Gran had been unable to remember her name. It wasn't as if it was unusual – in fact she knew of two other girls called Betty in nearby villages. Come to think of it, the old lady used to call all the local children by their right names, even if she'd only met them once or twice. She swallowed hard and, dismissing the painful memory, resumed listening for sounds of Kate and the toff who now lived in sin with her.

After a few moments she stood up and tiptoed over the huge stone flags into the hall, where only the pendulum in the grandmother clock could be heard swinging back and forth, and waited for the two chimes to strike the hour. In the quiet that followed, she stepped onto the old red and blue rug Charles had put at the foot of the stairs and grimaced at it. There was no point in pretending to trip over it as she usually did if there was a possibility of anyone seeing her, instead she waited, absolutely still, listening to the steady tick, tock, tick, tock until the hands showed four minutes past two. They had definitely gone out. She was alone at last!

Her heart was thumping loudly as she went up

to the landing and into the little bedroom. Then, leaving the door ajar in order to hear them when they returned, she gazed around at the clothes and belongings that had been dumped haphazardly when Charles moved in three weeks earlier. A scarlet jacket with black lapels and shiny brass buttons down its front lay on the narrow bed alongside black trousers, a brown leather coat and several crumpled white shirts. Kneeling down, she looked at four suitcases and a trunk all plastered with colourful labels of shipping companies. She reached out, lifted the nearest lid and stared at a leather holster containing a handgun. 'Crikey-blimey!' she exclaimed, picking them up. 'Just like in the movies.'

As she put the long strap over her shoulder and buckled the belt around her hips, she was a rancher's daughter on the American Wild West Frontier, fighting the wicked gang who were trying to take control of the Red River valley. Pulling out the gun she killed two baddies hiding in the shadows then, staggering as a bullet caught her left arm, she fired at a third before sinking to her knees and crawling towards the crumpled figure of the sheriff, lying in a pool of blood. Sensing the last and most evil member of the gang behind her, she turned and shot him through the heart before clasping the hero to her chest and declaring her secret love to his corpse. Then, when the large brown eyes opened and white teeth were revealed by smiling lips, she knew he wasn't dead after all and that they could live happily ever after.

Smiling dreamily at the satisfactory ending of

her current favourite fantasy, she laid the gun on top of the bed and began looking through the suitcase. Taking out a large book of photographs she turned the black pages until one caught her eye and she stopped to look at Charles's wife sitting in a garden beneath a parasol and seeming very regal in her old-fashioned clothes. Peering closely beneath the wide-brimmed hat, she could see the pretty face smiling happily down at the baby on her lap whose long lacy gown cascaded down beside her elegantly crossed ankles and onto the ground.

On the next two pages there were several pictures of men wrapped in bandages and leaning on crutches alongside smiling nurses wearing long frocks and white aprons. Replacing the book she picked up a bundle of letters which looked promising, but the writing was difficult to read and the few sentences she slowly deciphered were boring accounts of the activities of a child called alternately 'my darling Edgar' or 'my dear boy'.

The little tabby cat slithered through the doorway, leaped onto the bed, and began investigating the piles of clothes, purring loudly while massaging them with her paws.

She stroked the cat and buried her face in the scented fur for a moment before kissing the ecstatic animal. 'You'd better not get locked in here, Pudden,' she whispered, then continued to search very carefully, replacing every item as she had found it. She had no intention of stealing anything, she wasn't really a thief, although she had taken a ring from Gran, there was no denying the fact. She knew the old woman was aware of it even though nothing was ever said about anything being missing. She'd wanted to put it back, but time went on and on until Gran died and it was too late. When at last she'd confessed to Kate, her sister didn't really seem bothered, which was a relief after all that anxiety.

Most of Charles's cases contained books with gold writing on their leather spines. Some looked really interesting and had pictures inside protected by tissue paper but there wasn't time to look at them now, she'd come back later. She was kneeling on the floor sorting through the trunk when scuffling on the landing made her head spin with fear and, picking up the gun, she turned towards the sound.

They were standing watching her, barefoot and obviously naked under the dressing gowns they clasped about them. Kate's dark hair was hanging untidily around her flushed face as she silently tied the belt of her blue Japanese kimono. She opened her mouth as if to speak, but evidently changed her mind and, whilst turning and knotting the cord around Charlie's waist, whispered to him and he nodded.

'Hello, Betty,' he said reaching for the door with his left hand.

'I thought you might be a burglar,' she replied, her voice sounding squeaky and unnatural.

'You're quite safe, it's only us.' He smiled and put his right arm around Kate.

Having the gun in her hand gave her courage and, looking up at the scarred stump resting on her sister's shoulder, she asked, 'Did it hurt?'

He nodded. 'Still does sometimes.'

'Did you get a medal?'

He nodded again and held out his left hand. 'May I have my revolver please, Betty?'

He seemed to be a long way off. 'Bang, bang, you're dead!' she said, aiming at his face.

Kate gasped and entreated, 'Please give it to Charlie, sweetheart. Please–' she gulped '–Please, there's a good girl.'

Her sister's face seemed far away and small, just like the time she had looked at Billy through the wrong end of a telescope at Pridden Fair. Feeling a terrible fear tighten her chest and churn her stomach, she narrowed her eyes and hissed, 'Prepare to meet your doom.'

Pudden meowed and stood up with back arched and bushy tail erect.

She turned towards the cat and gasped in horror.

The air was thick with smoke. A sudden blast of intense heat to her left caused her to stagger and a smell sickeningly like roasting pork made her retch. Figures loomed through the fog. A soldier wearing a helmet came towards her pointing a gun. She squeezed the trigger. Her arm juddered. 'Bang, bang!' she whispered, watching the man jerk up into the air, then, after he had fallen back into the mist, added flatly, 'Bang, bang you're dead.'

A myriad of stars burst in her head as an explosion threw her to the ground. Opening her eyes, she saw the cat fly across the room and skid through the doorway onto the wooden boards of the landing whilst Charles dived towards the bed and retrieved the gun from under it with his left hand. She sniffed the air, surprised to find no sign of smoke or burning meat, then, aware of Kate leaning over her, she moaned, 'Oh, the pain, the pain!'

'Are you really hurt?'

'Of course I'm really hurt!' Rubbing her head she pouted and, recalling the tragic performance in a moving picture she had seen the week before, allowed her lower lip to quiver before adding, 'He hit me!'

'I was protecting your sister, you silly little fool! For all I knew you'd found the bullets and loaded it.' Charles took a roll of canvas out of the suitcase and held it to his chest.

She sniffed. 'I thought that was just a sewing kit with cotton reels and things.'

'Things aren't always what they seem, Betty.' He looked at Kate, whose face was drained of colour. 'Don't worry, darling, I'll get rid of them.' He put his maimed arm around her. 'Come and lie down for a little, you look all in.'

'I must do something. I mean she might have...'

'But she didn't. Come along, you've had a nasty fright.'

Watching them walk across the landing and go into the room that had once been their grand-mother's Betty remembered the day Kate pre-tended to have found an opal ring in a box on top of the wardrobe in there and shouted, 'You're a beastly liar, Kate. That ring was never Gran's. He gave it to you.' Seeing the door close behind them, she poked out her tongue and crossed her

38

eyes before adding in a lower voice, 'I knew when I held it. I saw him give it to you in a place with lots of trees. So there!'

She stood up, and making the shape of a gun with her fingers, pointed it across the landing, saying, 'Yeah, I killed 'em. Shot 'em down like the beastly dirty rats they are. They won't be making no big trouble for this town no more.' Putting her hand into an imaginary holster at her hip, she hunched her shoulders and, just in case Kate was peeping through the keyhole, limped dramatically to her room.

Having locked the door behind her, she sank to her knees then pulled up a piece of loose floor board from under her bed and took out a small rectangular cardboard box that had once contained chocolates from a smart shop in Bath. After lifting the lid and placing it beside her, she looked down at four tiny parcels of blue tissue paper lying on top of a collection of glass beads and odd buttons then sighed with satisfaction. No one in the whole world, apart from Billy, knew about these treasures and how they gave her messages.

Picking up the smallest one she unwrapped the gold ring in which three small red stones were set and slid it onto her middle finger. Closing her eyes she saw logs burning under a wide chimney breast and, on one side of it, a man with brown curly hair and kindly grey eyes sat smiling contentedly at a beautiful young woman holding a sleeping baby.

Next she took out the gold pin with a single pearl at one end and, breathing in the sweet scent of privet flowers, listened to the sound of a man's voice singing in a foreign language. Then, having re-wrapped both of them in the tissue paper, she picked up the cameo brooch that had belonged to her grandmother and which Kate had given her the night Charles moved into the cottage. When touching it she felt confident and wise. Now, holding it close to her chest and remembering the horrific episode with the gun, she understood it had been a powerful experience of the 'sight', as Gran called it, and even more terrifying than the dream in the cave.

She knew she had the gift, of course, but had never admitted as much to anyone except Billy. She'd seen Gran telling fortunes and witnessed Kate's eyes going milky when reading the tea leaves often enough to understand the experience. So long as she had this secret she felt her bossy sister wasn't in complete control. It was bad enough knowing Kate had been her mother in a past lifetime and had brought her up in this one since their mother died; she didn't want her to know absolutely everything about her.

Suddenly wracked with uncontrollable shivers, she hugged her knees and, clenching her jaws to keep her teeth from chattering, ached for someone to confide in. Who would believe what had happened with the gun? Even Billy would think she was making it up, and anyway she'd hardly seen him lately. Gran would have been impressed, she might even have stopped calling her 'Whatsername' all the time, but the beastly old woman was dead!

Still shivering, she reached for the fourth little

parcel and unwrapped the sliver of wood she had found in the cave a week earlier, then climbed into bed holding it close to her chest and closed her eyes.

Awakening to the sound of the sisters singing in the chapel, she reached under the mattress and pulled out the knife. Whilst the nuns were at matins she was safe from prying eyes, but she dared hold it for only a few heartbeats before returning her treasure to its hiding place. No one must ever know of its existence or that she had taken a life with its sharp point. It must be kept in readiness for her return to the valley, for without a knife she would be helpless and, above all, it was the only link with her grandmother who had given her the blade and her mother who had carved the handle.

As the memory of the limp figure hanging from the oak tree filled her mind and she saw again her mother's beautiful face reduced to bloody pulp, she groaned aloud and wept.

The nuns were singing a hauntingly beautiful anthem that reminded her of a lullaby her grandmother had sung for her long ago.

Remembering the warmth of loving arms enfolding her as both the old woman's and her mother's had done, she ached with grief and, as usual, after thinking of them, she longed to walk again by the river or wander through the woods as they had done together. Within the convent walls she was safe and well fed and her life was easier than it had been in the valley when every waking minute was spent fetching wood or water or finding food, but she yearned to return nevertheless. Here there were large logs always

41

burning in the warming room for her to ease her
frozen hands and feet, but she longed to be in the small
dwelling huddled by the tiny fire in the evening or
sleeping beside it at night.

Chapter Three

Both tea and ointment made from the lesser
Celandine, or Pilewort as it is also known, may be
good for treating haemorrhoids.

The old man was humming his favourite hymn
tune and chewing his bacon at the same time.

Betty looked at Kate, standing by the range.
Was she deaf? How could she stand there gazing
at Charles Wallace with that soppy expression on
her silly face while Uncle Albert droned on and
on? Why didn't somebody tell him to shut up?
Why didn't Charles shout, 'Stop that damned
noise before I go insane! And, while you're at it,
stop staring at me like a white-haired sheep-
dog!'?

Kate said, 'Are you ready for school, sweetheart?'

She pretended not to have heard and simpered
whilst enquiring, 'I beg your pardon?'

'I asked if you're ready for school.'

'I haven't drunk my tea yet.' Picking up the cup
she took a sip and, seeing the old man placing the
knife and fork together on his empty plate,
nonchalantly stuck her foot out to one side.

42

Albert reached the line, 'For those in peril on the sea,' and stood up. He turned away from the table, looked down, carefully stepped over her shiny new shoe, and left the kitchen humming 'All things bright and beautiful'.

Damn! She was taken by surprise and almost choked on her tea with laughter. He was getting quite good at this!

'Betty, Betty, come along, sweetheart. Please get ready for school.'

'Alright, I'm going.'

'I'll walk there with you,' Kate said, her hand lingering on Charles's shoulder as she placed a plate of eggs and bacon before him.

Furious anger exploded within her. 'You can't do that to me! It's bad enough already, but you'd really make sure I was the laughing stock of the village. I'm one of the oldest pupils, I'm nearly fourteen!'

'You're just thirteen, Betty. There's a new teacher and I want to be sure you're there on her first day.'

'But...'

'No arguing, sweetheart. I'm walking to the school with you for obvious reasons.' Kate straightened her back. 'That's what we've decided.'

'We've decided!' she exclaimed. 'What's it got to do with anyone else?'

Charles looked up from his plate. 'We're sharing our lives, Betty, and that means problems as well as pleasures.' He smiled at Kate, who blushed.

She groaned inwardly. Ugh! Disgusting! She'd heard them laughing in the bedroom. They even

43

did it in the daytime. Truly disgusting! That's what they'd been doing when they caught her with the gun. The door had been locked ever since as though they thought she was a thief, but she'd only wanted to see what he had in the trunk and then picked up the gun out of curiosity, she wasn't going to steal it. They'd never mentioned the episode since – obviously they were embarrassed and ashamed of themselves. For one thing they were ancient! Kate was nearly thirty and he was an old man of forty-three. How could they make such fools of themselves? How could they not see they looked ridiculous walking hand in hand and leaning against each other all the time?

'It won't be so bad once you're there,' Kate said in a wheedling tone. 'I've had a chat with the new teacher and she seems very nice. I apologised–' she looked sideways at Charles '–for your absence during the summer term. She says so many children help on the farms the Attendance Officer couldn't keep up, but if you play truant now he'll be down on us like a ton of bricks.'

Feeling disconcerted, she looked down at her feet. No one had mentioned that she hadn't been to school after Charles Wallace came to live here in June. She'd assumed Kate would too busy being in love and going to bed with him to notice if she didn't go back to the beastly place ever again.

Charles said, 'It'll be nice to see your friends again, won't it?'

Focussing on the small button holding the strap of her right shoe, she replied, 'Billy's left.'

'I know the Nelson boy's out at work now, but surely there are some nice girls to play with?'

Tears filled her eyes. You don't just go and get a new best friend like you'd buy a yard of hair-ribbon from the haberdasher's in Wells. You couldn't just suddenly find someone so special you'd want to share secrets with them. And, another thing, why couldn't the stupid man see that all the nice girls had been told not to play with her because her sister was living in sin with him and that was the very reason she hadn't gone to school anyway?

Kate patted her shoulder. 'Come along, sweetheart. I know you're feeling shy but we really must go.' She gently pushed her out of the door, along the garden path and into the lane. 'What a wonderful morning!' she said brightly. 'Listen to the bees buzzing in the hedge. I think we're going to have an Indian summer.'

Betty ignored her. How could someone so foolish be of the same blood as her? How could the stupid creature not understand that the boys teased her because her sister was a fallen woman? How could she be so utterly silly and ridiculous? Albert did at least have an excuse. He was simple because he'd been born the wrong way round. She knew that because she had heard her grandmother describe his birth to Mrs Shaw, who had come to get the regular supply of pilewort ointment for her husband and, while having a cup of tea as usual, had talked about someone in the village whose baby died because it came out feet first.

Walking along the lane, deliberately keeping

two paces behind Kate, she touched her grand-mother's cameo brooch pinned to the liberty bodice beneath her cotton blouse and woollen cardigan, then smiled to herself. She'd heard lots of interesting things sitting under the kitchen table whilst the old lady listened to people's problems. She'd be ready to strike if any of the children tormented her about Kate and Charles Wallace carrying on as though they were married, oh yes, she was ready for them. She nodded with satisfaction. Daisy or Elsie Nelson would soon leave her alone if she threatened to tell everyone their mother wet her knickers because of all the babies she'd had, and the Smarts boys would smile on the other side of their faces when she described the abscesses on their father's arse.

A short distance from the school gate Kate paused and took her hand. 'I know it's not easy for you. I realise you're suffering because of me living with Charles.'

'It made it all worse.'

'After that business with the maid from The Grange?'

She suddenly wanted to hug her sister and say she loved her. Instead she blurted out, 'They all knew about it. Not what really happened, but what people said had happened.'

'What did they say?'

'That when Mrs Wallace's cousin's maid asked for some of Gran's special mixture she gave it to her and got rid of a baby.'

'But you were there with me. You know she just gave her raspberry leaves.'

'I tried to tell them but no one listened. They all

46

knew Mrs Wallace told the police about it. And they all knew you were–' she shrugged and rolled her eyes '–friends with Mr Wallace.'

'That's all I was with him then.'

'Everyone thought he got the police to hush it up 'cos you were having an affair with him. They called you names and I hated them.'

'Names like the Wallace whore?'

'And the Wicked Witch.'

'Good heavens! I didn't know about that one!' Kate held her close. 'I know what I'm doing makes life difficult for you, sweetheart. I know you wanted me to marry Jim Hall and I'm truly sorry I couldn't love him. When you're older you'll understand.' She kissed her cheek. 'Will you try and stick it out for this last year at school?'

'I suppose so,' she mumbled, then turned and, looking neither to right nor left at any of the children milling about, walked into the schoolroom and sat at a desk in the front knowing no one else would want to share it with her.

The new teacher made her a monitor and smiled benignly at her enthusiastic distribution of pencils and paper, while the assistant, who had been a pupil herself the year before, watched suspiciously, making clear she had not forgotten her absence for most of the previous term.

At mid-morning break time she walked around the playground alone until, walking past a gang of boys laughing in one corner, she saw Jimmy Slater, the biggest bully of the village, sitting astride a prostrate figure and waving something in the air. Guessing the victim must be the frail new boy she had seen arriving earlier, anxiously biting his nails, she felt anger overwhelm her. Recalling the image of facing the enemy with Charles's gun in her hand, she narrowed her eyes and strode towards Jimmy. Grabbing his hair, she jerked him backwards then banged his head on the ground. The bystanders all laughed and he burst into tears. Children appeared all around and cheered as she picked the gold-rimmed spectacles off the grass and handed them to their owner who grinned sheepishly and whispered his thanks.

'Are you new to the village?' she asked.

'We come last week ter stay with me nan 'cos me dad scarpered.'

'You from London?'

He nodded.

'Me too. I'm going back as soon as I can.'

The boy hopped from one foot to the other. 'I likes it better 'ere.'

Two of the girls came forward arm in arm. 'That were really brave,' Gladys Smith said.

'Yeah,' Daisy Nelson agreed, 'our Billy'd be proud of yer.'

This was the first time they had spoken to her for months and she responded warily, 'Your brother was my best friend before he left school.'

'Mmm, I know, he's walking out with Joan Mason.'

'That's nice.'

'Me mum don't think so, she says 'er family's ever so common.' Daisy offered her left arm. 'Want ter walk with us?'

Feeling a fizz of excitement, she nodded and joined them.

When the bell rang at midday Daisy and Gladys brought their sandwiches to eat next to her and eagerly accepted half a cold sausage each. From that moment the other children began speaking to her and by the time the teacher brought the after-noon class to a close at four o'clock, only Jimmy the bully continued to ignore her.

She ran home singing and, feeling over-whelmed with love for her sister, she rushed into the kitchen and hugged her.

'That's nice,' Kate said. Then, whilst placing a circle of pastry on top of a pie, she asked, 'How was school?'

In her head she said, 'It was wonderful. I'm a monitor. I was really, really brave and stood up to Jimmy Slater. It was like being in a film. Every-one cheered and now Daisy Nelson is friends with me and everyone's talking to me.' Whilst out loud she mumbled, 'Alright, I suppose.' Then she walked to the table, cut a slice of bread from the newly baked loaf and added with a sheepish grin, 'Yeah, not bad at all.'

Later, as she lay listening to the creaks and groans of the old house settling down for the night, Albert snoring and whistling in the room next to her and the owl hooting in the garden outside, she felt too excited to sleep. Sliding out of bed she went and fetched her treasures from their hiding place and, taking the piece of wood, returned to snuggle under the bedclothes with it and closed her eyes

'Caitlin, come to the infirmary, we are bidden to help

49

Sister Constance.'

She gave a sigh of irritation and nodded to the novice who had spoken, then, having laid the quill beside the vellum on the table, turned to the elderly nun sitting beside her and said, 'I would rather stay and finish it, Sister Elfreda, 'tis almost done.'

The old woman's eyes were warm and kindly as she replied, 'Go, child. Go now.'

'But 'tis so nearly...'

'Learn to obey without question, dear child, 'tis the first rule of our kind. Go now with Sister Isobel.'

She slid off the stool and stood for a moment looking down at the perfectly drawn letters she had copied so carefully before following the older girl out, through the warming room in which no fire was burning on such a hot day, and into the cloisters. Walking along behind the novice she thought of the copying she had done and smiled with pride. When first she had been sent to assist the elderly nun who needed help with cutting the quills and making the ink she had made no attempt to understand the marks she made, but after a few days while standing watching her gnarled fingers grip the quill, dip it into the ink and then draw on the parchment, she began to see the patterns being repeated and was fascinated.

Sister Elfreda spoke only to request a fresh quill or ink or some such matter but nevertheless, a bond had grown between them and now, especially since she had set her to copying some documents, she counted the hours spent with her as the happiest she had known since leaving the valley and each morning after matins she went eagerly to assist her.

Opening the door to the infirmary the novice reeled back from the stench and retched, while she, knowing

this was the smell from a suppurating wound, wondered why the nuns had not used maggots to cleanse
it as her mother would have done. Walking past the
old man whose leg was evidently the cause of the
sickening stink and seeing Sister Constance beck-
oning to her at the far end of the shadowy room, she
walked between the six beds lining the stone walls to
join her

'She is little more than a child and has done nothing
but weep since we found her by the gate,' the nun said,
indicating towards a figure crouching in the corner. 'I
fear she may be deaf and dumb, or lost her wits. Fetch
fresh bedstraw and make her last hours on earth as
comfortable as possible. I must look after the others,
one old lady is close to death and the man by the door
is in great pain.' She made a sign of the cross, added,
''Tis the will of God,' and bustled away.

Looking at the shivering girl hugging her swollen
belly with arms like sticks and whose scrawny thighs
revealed by the ragged skirt had so little flesh on them
they appeared to be bones in the dim light, she knew
the nun was right. This girl had little chance of sur-
viving the ordeal ahead. She also knew that the baby
within the starving body was already dead.

Since her arrival at the convent she had heard the
screams of women in travail, had attended requiem
mass for those who died and had seen the survivors
leave to make their living by begging or selling their
bodies to feed their babies, but this was the first time
she had been close to a birth since helping her mother
deliver the local women who lived around the valley.
She sighed and went to fetch the straw, then whilst
strewing it on the floor, looked at the novice who was
holding her rosary with shaking hands while kneeling

51

beside the girl and felt tears running down her face.

The girl looked up suddenly and fell forward onto her knees. 'I beg thee, sister, pray for my immortal soul. I am truly not a sinner. See this—' she opened her mouth revealing the gap in her front teeth '—that's what my father's brother did when forcing himself upon me.'

She stared down at her in horror. 'Thy uncle did this?'

'Aye. I pray he will be judged by God and burn in hell.'

She nodded. 'As do I.'

The novice gasped and exclaimed, 'Caitlin, I shall report this blasphemy!'

'Go, tell the Mother. Indeed, Isobel, go tell the Holy Father in Rome for all I care!'

Watching the novice walk stiffly out of the room, she wondered if this daughter of a merchant who had joined the nunnery a few days earlier had done so of her own volition and if so why she would do this when her life outside would be so much more comfortable with good food to eat, silk garments to wear and servants to wait upon her The hooded pale-grey eyes set within a long, un-smiling face gave her a mournful expression, but she appeared to have no defects that would have deterred a husband seeking a good dowry. Could she have incurred her father's wrath by refusing to marry a suitor of his choice and so had been sent here to repent her rebellion?

The girl whimpered, 'Do not leave me to die alone.'

She knelt down. 'What is thy name?'

'Marie.'

'I shall not leave thee and—' she put her arms around her '—nor shall I let thee die, Marie.'

Chapter Four

A tea made with angelica was used in the past as a remedy for the plague.

Standing inside the doorway she could hear the familiar sounds of the infirmary; snoring, moaning, snuffling and the unmistakable sound of a death-rattle. The air was thick with malodorous wounds, urine, excrement and, above all, there was the smell of death.

'Caitlin, my saviour.'

In the dawn light seeping through the narrow windows she could just make out the shape of the figure crouched beside a bed nearby.

Taking the few steps necessary to reach her side, she said, 'I had thought not to see thee again, Marie.'

'I brought my sister here last night.' The girl gave a small strangled sob. 'I did not know what else to do. I could not leave her to die. When I left here she took me in as a servant against her husband's wishes rather than let me beg for food. When he and their child died of the pestilence his brother cast us out.'

Bending over the recumbent woman she listened to her laboured breathing and knew the end was near. Saying nothing, she squeezed Marie's hand while thinking of the time when the girl had herself so nearly died and how, for many days, she had lain as though waiting to do so. Eventually, although seeming to have survived against her will and no longer

53

emaciated, merely very, very thin, she had left one morning without a word.

Leaving Marie to her vigil, she then walked between the people lying crammed together in the straw to the end of the room where, on finding a boy who had ceased breathing, she bent and lifted him up then carried him to the side chapel in which two other corpses already lay awaiting burial and placed him on a trestle table.

A small, middle-aged nun who had been kneeling before the altar, stood up and came to her and, reaching out to touch her arm, opened her mouth and then twisted it grotesquely as she fought to control her tears. 'Caitlin, ma chère. Sister Elfreda has...'

'Nay!' she interrupted, 'nay, that cannot be...' Turning from her she ran to the room beside the infirmary where the four nuns who had succumbed to the plague had been segregated from the other sick people. Falling to her knees beside the still and silent corpse, she took hold of the disfigured hands and kissed the gnarled fingers one by one, then, overcome by her grief, she ran to her small alcove and lay down on her bed sobbing. Once again God had allowed the person she loved more than any other to die.

'Betty, sweetheart, I've been calling you for ages. Are you ill?'

She opened her eyes and looked up. 'What time is it?'

'Half past seven.' Kate placed a hand on her forehead. 'Your colour's getting better. You were as white as a sheet when I came in.'

'I'm alright. I just overslept, that's all.'

Kate frowned and, pointing to the sliver of

54

wood on the pillow, asked, 'What's this?'

'Nothing.' She grabbed it and pulled back the bedding. 'I'd better hurry and get dressed.'

Her sister looked anxious for a moment and then, hearing Albert calling for his porridge, she turned and hurried out of the room.

While replacing the piece of wood she had taken from its hiding place in the early hours of the morning, she remembered the dream and pictured the stone walls around her and the sweet-smelling mattress beneath her. Clasped to her chest was a knife and, as she lay holding the blade with one hand, she traced the familiar carvings on the handle of a man and woman intertwined. Opening her eyes wide she gasped in recognition. She had run her fingers over exactly the same shapes on her grandmother's knife many times as a little girl, and now, if she went to the dresser in the kitchen, she would find the exact copy of it that Albert had made for Kate. Touching the little sliver of wood she shivered. Could this be a remnant of her own knife, her special treasure of that lifetime?

An hour later, Kate held a mackintosh towards her, saying, 'The clouds up top seem to have over-flowed into the valley.' Then, helping her into it, added, 'I went to see the teacher yesterday. She's really pleased with you. Says you've made good progress and you're very popular. I was surprised when she said you're friendly with Daisy Nelson.'

'Only at school, she wouldn't want her mother to know she speaks to me.'

'I see.' Kate placed a hand on her shoulder. 'I'm

so sorry, sweetheart.'

'S'alright. School's not too bad now and the teacher's quite nice.'

'Yes, she thinks you're a bright pupil.' Kate handed her a pack of sandwiches and smiled, adding, 'I won't come with you this morning.'

After leaving the house she punched the petals off a full-blown rose hanging limply in the dank air and went into the lane where she cheerfully scuffed at some leaves lying in sodden piles along the grass verge before running along the lane towards the school. On reaching the gate, she was greeting Daisy and a group of other children and then, when the sound of a horn made them all look round, she waved at Charles Wallace driving past in the direction of Wells.

Daisy said, 'I saw you in the car with him last Saturday.'

She explained that he had taken her with him when meeting his sister from the station.

A boy screwed his face into an expression of distaste. 'Ugh! That hook don't look very comfortable. Do he keep it on in bed?'

She paused with her hand on the gate, remembering him putting his arm around Kate's shoulder when she had found the gun and shook her head.

'What do it look like when he takes it off?'

Daisy pursed her lips and exclaimed, 'Ernie Blower, don't be so disgusting!'

The boy muttered, 'I only wondered.'

Betty shrugged. 'It's sort of silvery and there's leather straps on it to hold it on.'

'No. I meant, what do the bit left look like?'

56

She gazed around the semicircle of faces staring at her. 'It's, well, it's not very nice.'

Daisy wrinkled her nose. 'Ugh! Do it bleed or something?'

'No. It's just not nice, that's all.'

Several more children arrived and walked through the gate, followed by most of the group who had been loitering there, leaving Betty, Daisy and Ernie, who asked, 'How did it get cut off?'

She had seen Douglas Fairbanks in a film the week before. With shirt unbuttoned to the waist and full sleeves billowing, he had jumped from a balcony with sword in hand and fought long and hard with the evil villain. 'In a duel,' she replied.

Daisy looked puzzled. 'I thought he lost it in the war?'

'Oh, yes, of course he did.' She dismissed Douglas Fairbanks and replaced him with Ronald Coleman in German officer's uniform. 'Yes, when the count cut off his right hand, he just picked up the sword with his left and pierced Fritz to the heart.'

Ernie frowned. 'Sound's a bit like that flick we saw last month, the one about the Great War with Ronald...'

'Don't take no notice of him,' Daisy interrupted, waving her hand dismissively. 'Just 'cos his dad's working at the new Picture Palace he thinks he knows everything.'

Betty was impressed. 'What's he do?'

Ernie straightened his shoulders. 'He's the most important person there. He works what they call the projector and he has to mend the film when it breaks and he lets me help him sometimes.'

Daisy sniffed. 'It hasn't even opened yet.'

'It will on Friday night and–' Ernie tilted his head defiantly '–he's got a black bow tie to wear 'cos all the nobs are going. So there!'

'Are you going?'

'My dad said I could take a friend on Saturday to the matinee, that–' he smirked '–is French for afternoon.'

Betty's heart lurched and she held her breath.

'My dad says there's a flick in America called *Gold Diggers* or something like that and–' he paused to look at each one of them in turn '–it's in colours!'

'What?' She hiccupped.

Ernie laughed and she hiccupped again.

The bell rang and Daisy walked away.

'Is it really in colours?'

'Yes.'

'And a talkie?' Hiccup.

'Yes.'

'How wonderful!' Hiccup.

'It's the Marx brothers in *Animal Crackers* on Saturday and *The Showgirl and the Duke*.'

'You lucky thing. Lara Crowe's in that.' Hiccup.

A girl shouted across the empty playground, 'Ernie, Betty, hurry up!' and banged the door behind her.

'So Mr Wallace takes you out in the motor for a drive?'

'Mmm and–' hiccup '–my friends if I ask him.'

'Wanna come to the matinee?'

Glowing with delight, she agreed.

Walking up the marble staircase on thick red carpet the following Saturday afternoon she thought the new cinema was a palace fit for a queen such as Cleopatra or a king like Solomon. Holding the shiny brass handrail, she gazed at the handsome men and beautiful women who smiled out at her from large coloured photographs on the wall and admired their perfect white teeth, their glistening red lips and faultless skin. Best of all was the picture of Lara Crowe, with red hair overhanging a green bandanna tied around her head and a fur draped around her shoulders. This was how she wanted to be: glamorous, vibrant and ready to live life to the full. Yes, she'd definitely look like that when she went to London.

The house lights were on when Ernie led the way onto the balcony and she felt a little disappointed when the glamorous attendant had no need of her large electric torch while showing them to their seats in the front row overlooking the stalls. After pushing down the folding seat covered in red plush, she sat gazing around her in amazement at the cream walls on which golden cherubs with rounded buttocks and discreet drapery floated above cavorting nymphs wearing diaphanous tunics and garlands of flowers. The ceiling appeared to be open to a dark blue sky in which stars twinkled, and down below her bright crimson velvet curtains fell in extravagant folds to the floor of the stage.

Ernie jumped up several times to wave at a window behind them where the projectionist could be seen preparing for the performance. After ten minutes the woman sitting behind him said he was making her dizzy and please would he desist or else she would complain to the manager. Fortunately the lights dimmed just then and the huge red drapes flowed apart.

She joined with many others in the audience as they gasped in astonishment, first at the enormous screen, and then again when the voices of the actors could be heard as clearly as though they were in the theatre. She was too engrossed to reply to Ernie's whispered, 'I told you it'd be better'n the old temperance society hut, didn't I?'

When the film ended and the lights were switched on Ernie reached into his pocket and pulled out a twist of paper, saying, 'Fancy a gobstopper?'

She nodded.

'He's clever that Groucho; he's my favourite. Which one d'you like best?'

'Harpo.' Then, steadying his hand while taking an aniseed ball, she recoiled, exclaiming, 'Crikeyblimey! What's that?'

'It's only a wart.' He looked at his thumb as though perplexed by it. 'That's all.'

'It's huge.'

'I know, I keep catching it in things and then it bleeds and gets worse.'

She touched the cameo brooch under her clothes and knew what to say. 'I'll buy it from you.'

'Buy it?'

'Yes.' She delved into her cardigan pocket, took out her leather purse, opened it and, with a flourish, removed a farthing. Waving the small coin around his hand three times one way and then three times the other, she chanted, 'Here's a copper to buy your wopper. I know your wart, it can be bought, here is money, money, money. Here's a copper to buy your wopper. I know your wart can be bought. Sell me, sell me, sell me.' She gazed into his eyes. 'Well?'

He took the coin and stared at her. 'Well, what?'

'Will you sell it to me?'

He nodded uncertainly. 'What do I do with it?'

'I dunno. Spend it I suppose.'

The lights were dimming and the woman behind them 'tutted' loudly.

'I mean what do I do with the wart?'

'Nothing, it'll go.'

'Why?'

''Cos I bought...'

The woman hissed, 'If you two don't shut up I'll complain to the manager!'

They both quickly stuffed a large sweet into their mouths and stared down at the scene of a crowded dressing room filled with showgirls giggling and chatting as they applied their makeup. Then, as the camera homed in on the beautiful face of Lara Crowe, Betty was instantly engrossed.

Lara, or Vicky as she was called in the film, was one of a long line of high-kicking dancers wearing shiny shorts and brief tops with plumes of ostrich feathers on their heads that formed the chorus of a musical in a theatre on Broadway. When Vicky was waiting for a cab one day in the pouring rain she took pity on a man who had dropped his glasses in the gutter and, having helped him find them, shared the cab to his hotel. During the drive she told the young man she was a dancer and when he believed her to be a classical ballerina she, believing this was a chance encounter and she would never see him again, did not correct the misunderstanding. When they met again at a party she desperately tried to keep up this pretence and continued to do so throughout several adventures. Eventually the hero, who just happened to be a duke from England visiting friends, guessed her secret and, having watched the show, sent her a huge basket of flowers with a note pinned to the handle asking her to marry him.

Feeling overwhelmed with emotion Betty blinked back the tears when the lights were switched on and nodded dumbly when Ernie loudly announced he must go and see his father who was rewinding the film and rushed off towards the door marked 'Private' at the back of the cinema.

Descending the grand staircase as though with feet balanced on elegant high heels, her hand lightly caressing the handrail and head held high, she was Vicky the showgirl walking down the steps to where her noble admirer was waiting, gazing up at her adoringly. He had fallen madly in love with her despite her humble background and soon he would take her on a great ocean liner home to his estate in England where she would be a duchess. It was so romantic!

Unaware of the crowds around her, she fetched her bicycle from behind the building and rode homeward along the narrow lanes imagining she was behind the wheel of a large motorcar, and, when the autumn chill made her shiver, she hunched her shoulders as if to feel the fur coat draped casually around them and practised pouting her lips.

The sun was low in the sky as she approached the village. The hills above were bathed in a deep golden glow and the slate roofs of both church and surrounding cottages shone like silver. It was beautiful, yes, but it wasn't London, where she belonged.

Passing by Mrs Nelson, who was standing by the baker's talking to the vicar's wife, and remembering having told Kate she would be spending the afternoon with Daisy Nelson, she was thankful there was no possibility of the lie being discovered because the beastly gossip had not spoken to her sister since Charles Wallace had moved into the cottage.

On reaching Old Myrtles she was pleased to see there was no green car parked by the tall hedge and cheerfully pushed her bicycle through the gate and leaned it against the wall. Seeing Albert's huge scythe standing beside the step, she considered accidentally knocking against the long wooden handle, but decided it was not worth bothering, then went through the glory-hole breathing in the aroma of rabbit stew. Opening the door, she saw her uncle sitting in his chair in the corner with a cat on his lap and grimaced. Kate had only stayed in this boring village full of dreary people because of him. She had even refused to marry a rich respectable man because she'd promised Gran she would look after him. Beastly horrid little man!

'Thank goodness!' Kate was flushed as she

removed the pot from the range and placed it on the table. 'I thought we might have to start without both you and Charles.'

Albert gently removed the cat and took his seat at the table.

Betty sat in her usual place feeling relieved. It would be good to have a meal without Charles Wallace taking all her sister's attention. In fact, she could confess now where she'd been that afternoon and get it over with. 'I went to the...' She felt her face freeze as the door opened and Charles walked into the kitchen.

'Sorry to be so long.' He kissed the back of Kate's neck. 'I had to walk from the station.'

'Poor darling!' Kate's hand quivered as she spooned rabbit stew onto Albert's plate. 'You must be starving.'

She watched her sister turn and press her hand gently on Charles's shoulder as he sat down and then stroke the right forearm from which a steel hook protruded grotesquely onto the table. Poor darling indeed! Daisy Nelson said he'd sent his wife away to Scotland once all her money was gone and now he was living off Kate. He deserved to starve. Beastly man!

'I said would you like some greens?'

She looked at the bowl being offered and wrinkled her nose. Why did her stupid sister bother to ask? Even Gran had understood she'd never eat such a disgusting mess!

Albert said, 'I like they greens,' and began humming.

The silly old fool only liked them because Charles said they were good for him. The stupid little half-wit hung on his every word. Fancy liking the tops of beetroot! They were almost as bad as the nettles in May that Kate insisted on eating just because the old woman had said they were good for the blood. Film stars would never eat such disgusting muck; they sipped fizzy wine and nibbled exotic foods and delicious chocolates, not slimy swill fit for pigs. She thought of the glamorous pictures on the cinema wall. Lara Crowe had a green band around her short auburn hair and a pale fur draped across her shoulders. The fur would have to wait, but she could tie a scarf around her head

'That's kind of Mrs Faires, isn't it, Betty?' Kate asked loudly.

She looked at the three expectant faces around the table. Having been dimly aware of Charles's voice droning on about Bath and something to do with his sister, she responded cautiously, 'Ye – es.'

He smiled at her. 'They're in that suitcase.'

'Are they?'

Kate gave an irritated frown. 'That's what Charles was telling you. He's brought you a gift from his sister. She's sent you some books to read.'

She slid off her chair and unfastened the lid, then exclaimed excitedly, 'Crikey-blimey!'

Charles laughed. 'That's not very ladylike!'

Ignoring him, she looked at the titles of the books, *Bosom Friends*, *Madcap Madge*, *The Cloister and the Hearth*, and under them were several copies of *The Lady's Weekly*. Feeling happier, she returned to the table and continued to

65

eat her meal.

Kate had her right hand on Charles's arm as she said to him, 'I know it's hard for you, darling. I'm so sorry.'

'I couldn't afford to keep it any longer and my sister's friend is delighted with it, he even managed to start it on the third turn of the handle. And–' he winked at her '–there's more to life than that.'

Betty was horrified. He'd sold his beautiful motor. Damn! She'd promised Ernie a ride next week. How would she get him to take her to the Picture Palace again if she had nothing to offer in return? Then, seeing Kate's left hand resting on her stomach, she suddenly knew their secret. Her sister was going to have his baby and – what's more – she knew, just knew, it was a boy!

Chapter Five

Blackberry leaves when chewed will relieve bleeding gums and sores in the mouth.

'A traveller from the Holy Land has brought word from thy benefactor.'

She clenched her fists and closed her eyes. Would this mean she had to leave, just when she had found a friend and wished to stay in this safe sanctuary for ever, breathing in the scent of flowers, herbs, beeswax and incense and hearing the beautiful sound of the sisters singing...

'Did thee hear me, child?'

She opened her eyes, flexed her fingers and mumbled an apology to the Mother Superior sitting at her desk. 'He has been delayed through ill health. He wishes for thee to stay with us yet a while.'The woman's pale face creased into a beautiful smile as she looked into her eyes. 'I am hoping that when the time comes thee will choose to stay here with us and–' she rubbed the gold wedding ring on her left hand with her right forefinger '–join us as our sister.'

Her heart thumped erratically as she bowed her head and waited to be dismissed. Could she stay here for the rest of her days in peace and safety? Was that truly possible?

Walking back to the herb garden where she had been helping to collect the lavender flowers she anticipated the delight on Marie's face when she heard the news.

The girl who had come to the nunnery first as a starving beggar who gave birth to a dead child and then to bring her dying sister at the time of a plague, had now evolved into a gentle servant of the community, eagerly fulfilling any task given to her. She had also become her own friend and confidante and it was to her she had, at last, told most, but not all, of her story.

Speaking of that terrible time had been impossible before, even to her beloved Sister Elfreda for whom she worked diligently copying the daily accounts of the convent and letters from the Mother onto vellum. The fact that the girl had suffered so greatly herself had somehow opened a doorway for her and so, whilst collecting and storing the herbs with her, she had spoken of life in the valley with her grandmother and mother. She had ached with longing when remem-

bering the days spent collecting berries, catching fish in the river or even collecting dead wood for their fire. She had made Marie laugh when describing the antics of the goats and how a Nanny had once eaten her grandmother's hat, and her mouth had filled with saliva when describing the taste of roast kid. They had wept together when she told of the drunken men dragging her mother to the oak tree on the hill and then hanging her from one of its branches. But she did not speak of what the miller had done to her or indeed, what she had done to him, nor did she tell her of the cave wherein her ancestors were buried in a tomb close to a beautiful figure formed in the rocks above and from whose heart of pink crystals the water ran down into a pool as red as blood.

Seeing Marie look up and smile at her approach she quickened her step, eager to tell her they would not be parted just yet.

On awakening she lay for a few moments savouring the pleasure of friendship with Marie, then, seeing the book she had been reading the night before until the candle had burned out, she grimaced. That story, called *Bosom Chums* seemed rather dull when compared with her dream or the adventures she'd had with Billy playing truant together. Since he went to work at the ironmonger's in Wells she'd had no real friends. His sister Daisy was being nice to her at school these days, but she wouldn't be a really close chum because her mother said Kate was a fallen woman and a disgrace to the village and Ernie, who might have become a friend, would soon lose interest in her once he knew Charles had sold the car.

Picking up a green silk scarf she tied it around her head and pouted provocatively into the mirror, then poked out her tongue. She still resembled prissy old Mary Pickford no matter how hard she tried. The only solution would be to dye her hair red with the packets of henna she had seen in the chemist's shop in Bath.

Returning to the suitcase of books sent by Charles's sister, she pulled out a copy of *The Lady's Weekly* and opened it. Having looked at an article on how to keep one's hands white and some drawings of the latest fashions, she began reading a story and was immediately engrossed. The heroine was a poor but beautiful orphan aged eighteen who worked as companion to a rich lady and was secretly devoted to the nephew of her employer. However, being aware of the difference in their station in life, she demurely accepted his indifference to her. One day, whilst walking along the riverbank towards her favourite place in the shade of the willows, she saw a small boy fall from a narrow bridge into the water. Throwing the book of poetry she was carrying to one side, she dived in and pulled the unconscious child to the bank. The nephew of her employer happened to be riding by on his chestnut mare at that moment, and, on seeing her slender form revealed by clinging wet silk as she emerged from the water carrying the boy, he instantly fell in love with her. This was more like it. She wanted to read about rich handsome men falling in love with ordinary girls like her and then proposing marriage, not about a priggish girl and her best friend!

She turned the pages, dismissing requests for domestic staff as of no consequence to her because she would never ever be a cook, parlour maid or nanny, until one advertisement caught her attention. 'Companion required for elderly lady in Worthing. Apply to Venobles Employment Agency for this and many other similar positions for gentlewomen of good education.' Her heart raced with excitement. Now she knew how to escape from this beastly village. She would be a companion to a rich old lady in London, her birthplace and where she belonged. The old lady would have a handsome son who would fall in love with her just like in the story.

Hearing clattering sounds in the kitchen, she hurriedly pulled on her clothes and reached the door just as Kate called from the bottom of the stairs, 'Betty, come along, sweetheart. You'll be late for school if you don't hurry up.'

Almost an hour later she paused by the hedgerow, wondering whether to go for a wander in the woods, instead of facing the teacher who had become cold towards her since the detention with Ernie. But playing truant wasn't so much fun without Billy Nelson: there didn't seem much point in being Queen Romania without King Romany beside her to rule the land as far as the eye could see for ever and a day. She scuffed the fallen leaves with her foot and exposed a coin lying on the ground which, on crouching down and picking it up, she found was a penny with the profile of young Queen Victoria on one side of it. As she stood up clasping the coin her hair was caught in a rambling rose growing through the privet and, hearing the bell clang loudly, she panicked and pulled away from the hedge, feeling the thorns tear at her until she was free, then ran along the lane to school. Standing outside the door she held a handkerchief to her bleeding cheek and took a deep breath before entering the classroom, where the other children were kneeling beside their desks with heads bowed in prayer.

Miss Frome exchanged glances with her assistant then said, 'You look as though you've been through a hedge backwards, Elizabeth Barnes, is that your excuse for being late?'

Remembering the pain of a ruler on her knuckles after standing up to the previous teacher, she affected cringing dumbness.

The assistant gave a little titter of amusement and several children moved their heads to peer up at her.

'Well, if that's not the reason for your tardiness—' Miss Frome raised her upper lip and sneered '—may I enquire what is?'

Casting her eyes at the floor she shook her head.

'Speak when you're spoken to, child!'

Knowing there was no point in telling the truth, she put a hand up to her painful cheek and became Mary Pickford, acting the part of a young girl who was poetic, sensitive and beguilingly beautiful. 'I'm very sorry, Miss, I stopped to admire a rose.'

Snorts of suppressed laughter erupted from the children in the back row.

'Quiet!' Pink spots glowed on the teacher's

71

cheeks. 'You will stay in detention after school. Now kneel down and let us continue with our morning prayers, which you so rudely interrupted.'

Sinking to the floor she joined in the recitation of the Lord's Prayer with the other children and then, when they all stood up, she was surprised to find Daisy smiling at her and the rest of the class looking as though they were waiting for something to happen.

Whilst reciting their tables in unison a boy said nine times seven was sixty-four, upsetting the rhythm of the chant, and a tittering sound erupted in the back row. Miss Frome, obviously aware of the children's anticipatory air, clapped her hands and said in a shrill voice, 'I don't know what's got into you this morning.' When the giggling continued she added, 'There'll be trouble for whoever is at the bottom of this. You–' she rapped Ernie on the knuckles with a ruler '–stop smirking.'

At break time the other pupils rushed out onto the playground where they stood waiting expectantly for her.

Fear tightened her throat as she walked towards them. 'What, er...' She swallowed and began again. 'What are you all looking at?'

'We want you to do what yer done for him.' Gladys Taylor pointed at Ernie.

'What?'

'The wart.' Ernie held up his hand. 'You bought me wart. See? It's gone.'

Looking at the wide-eyed children she said, 'But it was just luck.'

Daisy pushed her foot forward. 'I've got a funny place underneath my foot, it hurts dreadful.'

She wanted to refuse, wanted to deny all knowledge of such a thing, but the children were pressing forward, proffering hands and feet.

'I've had these for ages.'

'Mine be worse than yourn!'

'Look at this then.' Gladys Taylor rolled down her thick brown stocking to reveal a large wart on her knee. 'I knock it every time we kneel for prayers, it dunnarf hurt. Please, Betty, please do what yer done for Ernie.'

Scanning the children's eager faces around her, she knew something had to be done to placate them. 'Alright, alright.' She felt in her pocket for the penny she had found earlier. 'You'll all have to hand it back each time, 'cos this is all I've got.'

'Come on then,' Daisy urged her, 'do her and then me.'

For a moment she could think of nothing to say, then, touching the cameo brooch under her blouse, the words came easily. 'I know your wart, it can be bought. I know your wart, it can be bought,' she recited, waving the coin around the girl's knee three times one way and three times the other. 'Here's a copper for your wopper.' Offering the penny and looking into Gladys's pale grey eyes, she said, 'Sell me, sell me, sell me your wart. Here's a penny for your pain. Will you sell me your wart?'

Gladys gulped and whispered, 'Yes,' as she took the coin.

'Now me, now me!' Daisy had already unbuttoned her shoe and removed her thick brown stocking. 'It's me now.'

Kneeling down and holding the grubby foot, Betty looked over at Gladys, who was pulling up her garters and said, 'You'll have to give me the penny first.' Hearing gasps behind her, she turned to see Miss Frome and the assistant staring down at her. The teacher's face was livid as she asked, 'What is going on here?'

'I, er...' She could think of nothing to say.

'Maybe you was getting a splinter out?' Ernie suggested.

'Yes, that's right...'

'Don't lie to me, Elizabeth Barnes. I saw you take money from Gladys.' Miss Frome grabbed her hair and pulled her upright. 'Get inside, you evil child! I'll not have witchcraft in my school.'

During the ensuing thirty minutes Betty stood in front of the class while the other pupils were interrogated. Separating herself from them she floated to the ceiling and looked down on the woman questioning the frightened children. They were small, distant figures who were really rather silly. How could anyone be so stupid? Why on earth was the teacher getting into such a state about a simple thing like getting rid of a wart? Could that really be witchcraft as she said? If so, maybe she could put a spell on the beastly woman. Billy said his mother had told him that Gran was a witch and the poppy-dolls kept in the chimney were for doing magic on people. Kate had plenty of sewing threads and remnants of fabrics left from her work as a dressmaker so she wouldn't miss a few bits and pieces. The teacher had brown hair and grey eyes, almost matching her skirt and a white blouse. A doll like her would be very easy to...

'Pull yourself together, child.'

The teacher's voice was a long way off. Down below her the rest of the class were writing furiously at their desks and the assistant teacher was sitting in front of them looking important.

'Elizabeth Barnes! Pay attention!'

She blinked and found herself down on the ground again. The teacher was staring into her face. 'I'm talking to you, you insolent little hussy!' She grabbed her arm and screeched, 'Come with me. I'll take you home and see what your sister has to say about all this.' Then, striding along so that Betty had to run to keep up or fall over, she dragged her out of the school, along the lane and up to the front door of Old Myrtles.

'Betty!' Kate called as she hurried up the garden towards them. 'What's happened? Are you hurt? What have you done to your face, sweetheart?'

'Not hurt, Miss Barnes.' The teacher's voice was cold. 'I would not say she was hurt. Hurtful perhaps; yes, hurtful and harmful.'

'Would you care to come inside and discuss this?'

The teacher's eyes narrowed as she carefully enunciated her reply, 'I thank you, but no, Miss Barnes. The school board will no doubt be contacting you in due course.'

'About what?'

'Your sister. She's impossible, absolutely impossible!'

Betty snorted with nervous and uncontrollable laughter. Why on earth did this happen? It was like getting the giggles in church.

The teacher's face verged on purple and her voice shook with fury.

'Wipe that smirk off your face, Elizabeth!' Turning to Kate she added through clenched teeth, 'I am informed, Miss Barnes, that your grandmother was known for certain old-fashioned country ways. Might she have charmed warts do you think?'

'She might have known how to get rid of them. Why do you ask?'

'My assistant has suggested your sister may have got the idea from her.'

Kate's lips were tight as she responded, 'My grandmother was highly respected in the village for being wise in the making of remedies from plants. She gave of her knowledge freely to all who needed it.'

'Freely!' The teacher's eyes glinted in triumph. 'I assume then she would not have approved of your sister taking money off other children for curing their warts?'

Betty felt her heart miss a beat as her sister's pale face flooded with colour.

'I heard her say, "You'll have to give me the penny first." My assistant heard her chanting about a wart...'

Kate groaned, 'Oh no!'

Betty hiccupped.

'Apparently she claims to have cured one for a boy in the new cinema on Saturday.' Miss Frome cocked her head to one side.

'In the new cinema,' Kate echoed quietly, 'on Saturday.'

'You presumably gave her money to go to the new Picture Palace?' The teacher raised one eyebrow.

'I don't remember exactly.' Kate raised a hand to her forehead and asked, 'Do you remember if I gave you money on Saturday, Betty?'

The words hung between the sisters as their eyes met.

Betty swallowed and looked down at the stone path as she responded quietly, 'No, Kate, you didn't give me any money on Saturday.'

'Well, that settles the matter, Miss Barnes.' The teacher straightened her back. 'I shall be reporting to the school board. You understand?'

Kate nodded and gripped the door handle with one hand and Betty's shoulder with the other.

'I must point out, Miss Barnes, that although I'm new to the village I am not ignorant of what has been going on.'

Betty hiccupped.

'Your family may have been able to hoodwink the local people in the past, but times have changed. Now I'm responsible for the education of these children, I'll not allow them to be fed with superstitious nonsense. The doctor will no doubt know how to remove Daisy's verruca and the school board will contact you, but in the meantime–' Miss Frome's upper lip rose in a sneer '–I suggest it would be diplomatic to...'

'Don't worry,' Kate interrupted, 'my sister will not be coming back to school.'

With a peremptory nod the teacher turned on

her heel and strode along the path to the front gate.

'Mean old cow!' Betty poked out her tongue.

Kate's tone was sharp as she said, 'Now, Betty, you tell me what this is all about.'

'It's all rubbish and lies and...'

'Lies!' Kate exclaimed, her eyes blazing with anger. 'You're a fine one to talk about lies.'

This was the last straw. Now everyone was against her. The pain was too much to bear, she wanted to lash out and make her sister hurt as she was hurting. 'Well, at least I'm not living in sin with a married man! And at least I'm not the one nobody speaks to in the village. And at least I'm not in *your* kind of trouble!' Tears streamed down Betty's face as she pushed past Kate and crashed through the glory-hole, pulling mackintoshes off hooks, kicking Wellington boots over and deliberately knocking a collection of walking sticks sideways onto the floor before running up the stairs to her room.

Throwing herself onto the bed she sobbed into the pillow. It was so unfair. All she'd done was try to get rid of a wart. Remembering her experience in the schoolroom, she turned onto her back and grimaced at the ceiling. Making a doll like the teacher would be fun and she could stick lots of pins all over her. She touched the cameo brooch under her blouse and heard her grandmother say, 'Ill-wishing is not our way, child. We gets it back threefold, remember that.'

Quickly jumping up she stood by the window feeling dizzy and shocked. She'd heard the old woman say that before when she was alive, maybe she'd imagined it? Could it be worth doing even though she might get something three times as bad happen to her? What if she wished her to do something like eat toadstools instead of mushrooms and be horribly sick like Billy's cousin was? Might poison be a possibility? Gran had pointed out several dangerous plants like the one growing by the hedge in the lane which was alright for making a healing ointment but deadly if it was eaten and she had once told them how an old woman died after mistaking daffodil bulbs for onions which had seemed very stupid considering the difference in smell. A nervous giggle erupted from her throat and tears suddenly trickled down her cheeks, then she hiccupped as usual.

Wiping her eyes she looked down into the garden and saw her sister carrying a lamp as she walked along the path towards the cave. She hadn't meant to let on she knew Kate was going to have a baby, that was a bad mistake. She should have held her tongue – blurting it out like that had made everything worse.

It was all the teacher's fault. Suddenly the desire to make a doll of the teacher and stick a pin in her head – just to give her a headache – nothing more, became overwhelming. Without stopping to think she ran downstairs to Kate's sewing cupboard and pulled out a few scraps of fabric, a needle, black thread, pins and scissors. After rummaging through a bag containing an assortment of knitting wool, none of which was light brown like the teacher's hair, she grabbed a small ball of black wool, and hurried back to her room.

Making the doll was very enjoyable and she felt more and more cheerful as the small figure in long skirt and blouse evolved from a piece of grey worsted and white silk. The head was not easy. She tried carving it from the end of a candle without success and then made it from the same fabric as the blouse and embroidered its eyes and mouth with the black thread. The hair made with the wool tied back to look like the teacher's bun was a good likeness, apart from the fact it was the wrong colour, but that couldn't be helped – the style of it was right.

She picked up a pin and stuck it into the black woolly head, then, hearing a tap on the door, quickly tucked the doll under the bedclothes.

Kate stood in the doorway, her face blotched and her eyes red and swollen. 'I had to come and talk, sweetheart. I can't bear to–' Her voice faded as she looked at the pieces of fabric lying on the floor and the discarded candle. Then, bending and picking up a few strands of black wool, she said, 'Show me what you've been making.'

Betty stared dumbly into Kate's eyes, feeling sick and unable to respond.

'Show me!'

She gulped and looked down at the bed.

Kate stepped forward and pulled the doll from under the covers. 'So that's all the thanks I get after all these years! I've brought you up since our mother died, I've put up with you playing truant and telling lies. How many lifetimes do I have to be a mother to you? I can't go on and on like this, it's too much. Gran said you were a mill-

80

stone hanging round my neck and she was right.' She placed her right hand over her stomach. 'If I lose my baby after this I'll never forgive you. I hate you, you vile, ungrateful–' She gave a loud groan and ran from the room then clattered downstairs to the kitchen.

Following close behind, Betty shouted, 'But you don't understand.' Running into the kitchen she saw Kate lift the lid on the range and throw the doll into the burning coals. 'It wasn't you–' She faltered as the tears welled up. There was no point in trying to explain that the doll had black hair like Kate's because that was the only wool in the cupboard and it was dressed in remnants from her blouse and skirt to look like the school-teacher, not like her.

Returning to her room she dived onto her bed and wept. Gran had said ages ago she was a mill-stone – whatever that meant – something bad, obviously. Kate thought she was a burden and hated her. There was only one thing to do now. She must get away as soon as possible.

Chapter Six

Raspberry leaf tea may help women in childbirth.

Albert had been humming a jumbled assortment of hymns throughout breakfast and, after pushing his plate to the centre of the table, he began pulling at his hair while rocking back and forth.

'Kate's only going shopping for the day, old fellow,' Charles said, placing his left hand on the old man's arm.

'Yes, Uncle.' Kate smiled reassuringly. 'I'll be back by six o'clock to give you your tea.'

Betty stared at the dresser, pretending to be unaware of their presence and unable to hear the conversation. How could they be so stupid? The old fool had been working himself into a state for days. Anyone with half an eye could see he'd been upset by something and unless they found out what it was he would stop Kate from going to Bath and, what was worse, upset her own plans for escape while her sister was gone. She guessed he had misunderstood what the beastly gossip Mrs Nelson had been saying when waiting for the bus on Saturday morning while he was cutting the hedge nearby. The mean horrid old bag had been aiming her remarks at her, not him, when telling two other local women that 'Old Myrtles must be rather crowded these days with so many people living there' and 'Mrs Lamcraft must be turning in her grave.' Although longing to keep the silence she had maintained during the three weeks since the episode with the doll, she turned to the old man and asked, 'What did Mrs Nelson say?'

Albert muttered a few incomprehensible words, ending in 'Didner'.

Kate, who always seemed to understand him, asked, 'Why does it matter what she said?'

Albert hung his head and mumbled a few more words, this time ending in 'Dinnum'.

'So you think I'm going to send you away

because there's not enough room here?'

Keeping her eyes on the dresser Betty counted the plates Granfer had won at Pridden Fair, four on the top shelf and six on the one below, and then counted them again very slowly. She knew Kate and Charles were giving each other meaningful looks behind her back but dare not move her head to see. The sound of Albert's agitated humming seemed as though it would drone on for ever.

'This is because Betty told you I went to look at St Lawrence's last year, isn't it?'

The old man nodded and pulled at his hair.

Anger fizzed in Betty's head. That was rich! Kate had gone to see the loony bin because Jim Hall the archaeologist wanted her to marry him and the old boy would have been in the way and now it was all being blamed on her. If Kate hadn't gone there in the first place then there would have been nothing to say about it, would there? She could hear Kate's wheedling tone as she talked to the old man but did not listen to the words. Once again it was all her fault. Thank goodness she was escaping from this beastly horrid place and her cruel sister.

An hour later, as she peered up at the figure in the rocks, her eyes felt dry and swollen from lack of sleep and Albert's humming still rang in her ears.

A droplet of water fell from the pink stalactite overhead and landed on her cheek like a teardrop. How glad Kate would be when she came home from Bath and found her gone! She would be so relieved to be rid of her 'millstone' and to know she would never have to worry again about being a mother to her younger sister in this life-time as well as in that earlier one long ago. Well, she herself would be relieved too. She didn't want to go on and on being grateful or stay where she wasn't wanted. Quickly swallowing the lump forming in her throat, she turned away from the lady and, seeing the slab of stone to her right, thought of her grandmother's corpse lying beneath it and how Kate wanted to be buried there too.

Her sister didn't really care about her. If she did she'd have stood up to that beastly horrid teacher. She wouldn't have screamed like that when she came into her room and saw the poppy-doll either. If she had listened to Betty she'd have understood that those bits of material were the best she could find and the hair was darker than the teacher's because there was no brown wool in the sewing box. If she had really cared about Betty she would have forgiven her and she very definitely had not. Well, now she would be rid of her burden, her millstone. She would never again have to say how Betty had let her down for she would not see her nor hear from her again in their whole lives.

This would be the last time she would ever stand here in the cave. Soon she would leave the village never to return. She rubbed the spot behind her left temple and, remembering the ache that had lingered there for two weeks after Kate had thrown the doll on the fire, gave a rueful smile – if Gran was right then the school-teacher's headache would have been a lot less than hers. Then, taking the small piece of wood from her pocket, she curled her fingers around it...

She stood before the Mother of the convent nervously, wondering why she had been summoned to her.

'I have good news for thee, my child.'

Her heart quickened its beat. 'Is there word from the Holy Land?'

'Aye. A pilgrim has brought word from thy benefactor. He will travel this way in spring, but–' the Mother held her hands together as if in prayer '–I wish thee to stay as a novice and prepare to take the vows.'

She mumbled her thanks and hurried to follow the lay sisters and nuns who were already processing into the chapel. Once there, standing amongst them, she looked at their faces made beautiful with joy as they sang 'Angelus domini' and was overwhelmed with love. Although she wanted to join in with them, no sound would come from her throat and tears filled her eyes. She longed to stay in this safe haven and live the well-ordered life in which there was never fear of having no food or shelter.

The sound of voices praying washed around her as she mouthed the words, 'Poverty, chastity and obedience.' The poverty as experienced in the convent was not an ordeal, she was well fed by her standards and life outside would be poorer and harder for her. Chastity would be easy when there were no men to tempt her, but outside these walls her life would be very different. She felt the tidal flow of her monthly cycle and sometimes her body longed for the touch of a man, at others she dreaded the cruel pangs of childbirth and the death it so often precipitated. The great advantage of becoming a bride of Christ was that, barring miracles, communion with Him did not involve the risk of dying in childbirth and this was a great temptation. Obedience was already a difficulty. She loved working on the manuscripts at which she excelled, she enjoyed collecting herbs and helping in the gardens, but she hated the laundry in which she sometimes worked along with other poor women and girls who had sought sanctuary in the convent. If Mother Superior dictated she should spend the rest of her days washing other people's linen once the vows were taken, what then?

She thought of her knife, still hidden in her bed, and how every night she held it and remembered. She thought of the beautiful pink and white crystalline formations sparkling as the water ran over them and down into the pool as red as blood. She thought of the burial place she had desecrated with the body of a man who stank of cider and sweat and piss. She thought of her mother being hunted like an animal and felt the longing for revenge festering deep within her soul and, as the nuns began filing out of the chapel, knew what she must do.

Opening her eyes and finding her vision blurred with tears, Betty pushed the sliver of wood into her pocket then dipped her hands in the pool and bathed her face. Feeling refreshed and strong, she held the oil lamp aloft for one last look around the cave before hurrying out into the garden where the frost, although still thick under the hedges, had melted on the sunlit path leading

86

to the cottage.

After collecting the small suitcase she had left in the glory-hole, she paused by the overgrown porch to wonder if a small bud amongst the thorny tangle would last long enough for Kate to pick a rose on Christmas day as usual. Then, without looking back at Old Myrtles, or down at the river while crossing the bridge, nor even glancing into the graveyard to her left, or the school to her right, she hurried to the small green in front of the church.

The three women already waiting for the bus to Wells exchanged glances and looked towards the shop where Mrs Nelson's unmistakable bulk filled the doorway. No one spoke. The bell rang in the schoolyard, a boy shouted with laughter, a door banged and a railway engine whistled in the distance. Then the bus arrived and she climbed aboard. She was leaving this boring place, at last!

On arriving in Wells she hurried to the iron-monger's shop in the High Street where Billy was standing behind a long mahogany counter. Greeting her with a bow, he said, 'Hello, Queen Romania, what can I get for your majesty?'

'Some black shoe polish if you please, King Romany.' While he was wrapping the small round tin in brown paper, she asked, 'D'you like it here?'

'S'alright, I suppose. The manager gets an-noyed 'cos I keep knocking into things. My mum says it's 'cos I'm still growing.' He stretched out his arms, exposing pale wrists projecting from the sleeves of a brown cotton overall. 'This was too big when I started work here.'

'Golly, your hands look enormous, and–' she peered down at his feet '–those shoes are even bigger than Charles's.'

'My dad's threatening to tie a brick to my head.' He grinned and asked, 'Will you have to go into domestic service now you've left school?'

'No, certainly not!' She straightened her back. 'Actually, I'm on my way to the station. I've come to say goodbye.'

'What! Where are you going?'

'London.'

'You lucky beggar. Why are you going there?'

'To be a rich old lady's companion.'

'Gosh! How d'you manage that?'

'Easy, I just answered an advertisement in *The Lady's Weekly.*'

'What'll you have to do?'

'Oh, things like help her have tea parties and fetch her hankies and, well, actually, I'm not absolutely certain yet, but it won't be skivvying, that's what housemaids do.'

'I wouldn't like to think of my Gypsy Queen on her knees scrubbing floors.' He looked down at her, his golden eyes wistful for a moment. 'We had such good times up top making camps and climbing trees, didn't we?'

'Mmm, much better than being in lessons and scratching away on slates with that horrid old teacher we used to have, the miserable old meadow lady!' She giggled and added, 'The new one's even worse. She expelled me from school.'

'I know, Daisy told me how you did magic on her wart. I've had this one for months.' He held his forefinger towards her. 'Can you put a spell on it?'

Touching the cameo brooch pinned to her cardigan, she agreed and bought it from him for a farthing.

Squinting down at his hand, he said, 'It hasn't worked, it's still there.'

'It'll just disappear in a few days.' She stood on tiptoe and kissed his smooth cheek. 'You won't forget we peed in the bucket so we were married like real Romanies?'

He shook his head.

'We'll never forget each other, even though we'll never see each other again as long as we live. We'll remember, won't we?'

He looked perplexed. 'Why won't we ever see each other as long as we live?'

''Cos I'm never coming back. Well, I suppose I might visit you sometime in my big motor car if I'm very, very rich.' She frowned and demanded, 'You won't tell on me will you, Billy?'

One of his sandy eyebrows rose up as he asked, 'Doesn't your sister know you're going?'

'No, I'm running away from this beastly place so I won't ever have to speak to her again in my whole life. I hate her.'

'I won't tell.'

'Not even your mum?'

'Never.' He ran his forefinger across his neck. 'Cross my heart and hope to die, cut my throat if I tell a lie.'

Relieved to know Kate would not hear of her departure through Mrs Nelson's gossip, she thanked him and enquired, 'Are you going to marry Joan?'

He blushed. 'I dunno, I'm only fifteen.' Seeing a woman walk into the shop and stand looking at the white enamel buckets at the far end of the counter, he indicated towards her, saying, 'I'll have to go and serve the customer.'

Her whole body felt suddenly cold. She'd expected him to be sad at her departure. Had thought he might try and stop her, to persuade her to stay. 'So–' her lips felt stiff as she smiled '–I'll say goodbye, King Romany.'

'Goodbye, Queen Romania.'

The furrier's shop in Silver Street was not the imposing mansion she had dreamed of finding on arrival in Ealing, but, reminding herself she had nowhere else to go and, as she had spent all her savings on train fares, no money to get there if she had, she pressed the doorbell.

A small man came towards her smoothing a long strand of hair from left to right over the shiny pink bald spot on top of his head. His eyes protruded, giving him an air of surprise as he greeted her. 'Pleased to meet you I'm sure, Miss Barnes. Shall we go up?'

He led her alongside a wooden counter on one end of which were shelves filled with fur hats and gloves, then past a grey squirrel coat displayed on a plaster mannequin with an old-fashioned hairstyle and bright blue eyes, to the back of the shop. Pushing through a door leading into a narrow hallway, he then walked up a staircase onto a dark landing with a narrower stairway continuing upwards to their right. To their left were three brown doors and, facing them, two

90

more. When he opened the nearest one and gestured that she should follow him, she walked in and was dismayed to find a small gloomy room in which the beige velvet curtains were drawn across the window to allow in only a narrow gap of light.

Mr Bradon approached the narrow bed alongside the wall and, hunching his shoulders, said, 'This is the girl I was telling you about, my love.'

Betty followed him, holding out her hand to greet the woman whose grey head she could see lying on the white pillow and, on reaching her, asked, 'How d'you do?' To her horror Mrs Bradon stared silently up at her, then suddenly reached out and gripped her hand with dry bony fingers, reminiscent of a chicken's foot. This wasn't what she'd expected at all. She'd have to escape soon.

Mr Bradon smoothed the hair stretched across his head with one hand while reaching for the door handle with the other. 'I think we should leave my wife to rest. I'll show you around the flat.' He led her into a small kitchen where she was astonished to find a sink with a water heater above it and a gas cooker such as she had seen only in advertisements and, pointing to the small square wooden table, he said, 'I eat mostly in here. My dear wife has the appetite of a bird you know, a little bird. I call her my Jenny Wren.' He opened a cupboard and pointed at the mop and white enamel bucket standing inside. 'Mrs Smith comes and does for us three days a week and—' he indicated the rectangular box beside them '—the laundry collects on Mondays and delivers on Fridays.'

She was wondering what she might send to be laundered and not listening as he continued talking whilst walking into the corridor and then, seeing him open a door opposite to reveal a gleaming white enamel bath standing on four rounded feet, she gasped with pleasure. No more heating of water in kettles and saucepans on the range or washing in the tin bath in the scullery on Saturday nights. This was more the sort of thing she'd looked forward to – maybe she could bear to stay here for a few weeks until she'd found something more suitable?

Mr Bradon then led the way up the flight of narrow stairs, ushered her into a large attic room with a brass bed and pointed at the fireplace. 'This gas fire's brand new.'

Looking at the strange contraption in wonderment she asked, 'That's a fire?'

Taking a box of matches out of his pocket, he knelt down and turned on the tap, then, having struck a match and lit the gas jet, left the room and clattered down the stairs.

Going to the window she looked out at the roofs of other buildings and the stretch of street below. It wasn't anything like the story in the magazine and these people were unlikely to have a potential husband in their family. Could she leave now? Was that possible?

If she sent a telegram to Kate asking for the return fare she could be back home in a few days, but that would mean she'd have to promise never to run away again and she'd have to go into service in one of the big houses near the village and she'd never be a film star or marry a lord. And how could she face Billy? He was expecting her to be rich and famous. No, she would stick it out. Besides, Kate wouldn't want her millstone back, would she?

Chapter Seven

A tea made with St John's wort may help with depression.

'So how are yer gettin' on, ducky?' Mrs Smith asked as she slowly pushed the mop across the kitchen floor.

'Very well, thank you,' Betty replied politely whilst closing the kitchen door, and then walked to the sink.

The cleaner paused and leaned on the mop handle. 'Makin' tea are yer?'

'Yes, it's time for Mrs Bradon's elevenses.' She filled the kettle from the tap and placed it on the gas stove.

'I wouldn't say no to a cup meself.'

'Of course, I'll get you one.'

'Ta ever so. I must say yer've settled in alright, but all the same yer must admit it's a bit of a rum do ain't it?'

'What?' Of course she knew it was, but was wary of admitting it to a stranger.

''Er in there. S'not natural, lyin' in that dark

room day after day.'

'She's not well, I suppose.'

'Barmy if yer asks me!' Mrs Smith put the mop into the bucket, eased her rounded body onto a chair and rested her bosom on the table. 'At least he's got you ter wait on 'er now, poor man. Bloody saint he is if yer asks me.' She burped loudly then shook her head whilst explaining, 'A martyr to me guts I am, absolute martyr!'

'Peppermint's good for indigestion, or fennel might be best because it gets rid of the wind better.'

'Gor blimey! How d'yer know that?'

'From my gran. People used to come to her for things.'

'What sort of fings?'

'Oh, comfrey ointment she made and all sorts of herbs for rheumatics and different things.'

'Fennel, eh? That's worth knowin' that is.' The cleaner burped again. 'You'll be sufferin' with yer guts an 'all if yer stays 'ere very long.'

'Why d'you say that?'

'Cos 'e don't eat nuffink but what gets bought from the baker.'

'I like the meat pies and the lardy cake.'

Mrs Smith sniffed. 'I'll bet that's not what yer used to is it?'

'My sis ... er ... my grandmother used to make nice rabbit stews, before she died.'

'What about yer mum and dad?'

She explained how her mother had died of influenza after the Great War and her father had been killed in a motoring accident.

Mrs Smith's eyes lit up. 'Had a motorcar did he?'

94

She nodded.

'If he were that rich it's a bit of a comedown for yer ter be emptying chamber pots and making tea fer a lunatic ain't it?'

Playing the part of a heroine in a short story she had recently read, she rested her chin on her hand and, repeating Kate's words regarding Charles and his circumstances, she replied, 'He took the wrong advice and invested unwisely, I'm afraid.' She wasn't going to admit her father was merely a chauffeur to a rich lady. Romances in *The Lady's Weekly* were rarely about lowly born, uneducated girls; true, they were often in reduced circumstances, but there was always good reason for this and it was not because they were born into poverty and ignorance.

Mrs Smith nodded sympathetically. 'That's sad that is, losing both parents, makes you an orphan that does. I know on account of my auntie what died of the 'flu epidermic, bad business it was, left three little 'uns what went in a orphanage.' She screwed up her eyes. ''Er in there could do with a bit of rabbit stew. Tea and biscuits ain't enough to keep body and soul together, if yer asks me.'

Betty described how Mr Bradon had said his wife would eat nothing else, adding, 'She seems quite happy with that, well not exactly happy, I suppose, in fact she looks utterly miserable and dejected, but you know what I mean. Actually I don't really know what she thinks 'cos she hasn't said a single word in the four days I've been here.'

'Poor soul. Mad as an 'atter and no mistake.'

Mrs Smith laughed then leaned forward conspiratorially whilst explaining, 'That's a joke that is. She was a milliner, see? Very ladylike and elegant she was once upon a time. Went strange on her wedding day and that was that. Poor man, what a carry on!' Without pausing to draw breath, she added, 'I could manage one of them biscuits, ducky.'

'Yes, of course.' She placed the tin in front of her.

Mrs Smith took two and pointed into her toothless mouth with a grimy forefinger. 'Now I needs the tea to dunk 'em in, if you'd be so kind?'

'So what happened to Mrs Bradon?' she asked while putting the cup of tea on the table.

'It was on account of her mother dropping down dead in the church. Everybody round here knows. They'll all tell yer the same thing. She's never been right since.'

'That's so sad.'

'Sad for him if yer asks me. He's been a saint, that's what he's been!'

'Maybe she'll get over it soon.' She watched in fascination as the woman's mouth puckered and her cheeks caved in whilst sucking on the soggy biscuit. 'How long ago did it happen?'

'Ten years come spring. It was soon after my Ernest had to marry his Bertha and their little Eric is over nine now.' Mrs Smith paused to slurp her tea. 'They'd been engaged for years and years before that, Mr Bradon and 'er in there I mean.'

'So she's been lying in that room ever since the wedding?'

'Took to her bed and never left it since.' Mrs

Smith belched. 'So yer've got no family?'

'That's right–' she crossed her fingers behind her back '–no family.'

'So yer'll be staying 'ere for Christmas then?'

She nodded.

'Mmm, that's sad that is, ter be all alone in the world and no home to go to is very sad.' Mrs Smith drained the cup, belched loudly and groaned whilst pulling herself upright before continuing to slowly mop the floor.

Betty felt lonely and miserable after this conversation. In the afternoon she walked to the greengrocer's shop higher up the street and bought two apples, then walked into the nearby park and sat on a bench to eat one. Closing her eyes she bit into the fruit and imagined she was sitting in the great oak on Hankeys Land. Billy was in his usual place astride a branch, whilst she perched in the fork leaning her back against the trunk. They had already shared the lunch they should have eaten at school and were now enjoying the crisp and juicy apples picked from the tree beside the chicken coop at Old Myrtles. Tears streamed down her cheeks and she was unable to swallow. It was no good pretending. She was no longer living in the village with Kate caring for her and worrying about her playing truant. Billy was in Wells working for the ironmonger and walking out with a girl called Joan. She was grown up and fending for herself. Kate was glad to be rid of her and probably already making her bedroom into a nursery for the baby. She could never go back. She was alone amongst strangers.

That night whilst preparing for bed she was still feeling sad and lonely when, thinking of Mrs Bradon lying on the couch looking pale and hopeless, she admitted the poor creature was in a worse state than herself. She could at least go out and breathe fresh air and enjoy eating an apple and, above all, look forward to getting away from this situation, whereas the tragic little woman who spent every day in that dark and silent room had no hope of any future improvement to her life. Whilst unpinning the cameo brooch from its usual place on her vest she held it in her left hand and absentmindedly traced the shape of the kneeling woman carved into its surface with her right forefinger.

'Her's feeling overcome with melancholy.' The voice was so clear she looked around expecting to see her grandmother's ghost, but there was no sign of it in the room. 'A cup of tea made with St John's wort two or three times a day, that's what her needs. It grows in the meadow up top, the one on the right hand just before the path forks left to the farm and right towards Pridden. Pick the flowers in summer on a sunny day and dry them like we always do.'

She remembered picking bunches of the yellow flowers with Kate and hanging them upside down over the stove in the kitchen, then gave a wry smile – she knew where to find the plant in the fields above Oakey Vale but had no idea where to look in a London suburb and, even if she did, there would be no sign of it now in December.

After finishing her duties for the day on Christmas Eve she went to her room and shivered whilst lighting the gas fire then, taking a heavy dark grey blanket from the bed, draped it around her shoulders and sat on the floor beside it. Kate would have lit a fire in the parlour early that morning so it would be warm and cosy by now and she would have placed sprigs of holly all around the room, including on the tops of the mirror and the frames of two pictures hanging on the wall. Closing her eyes she saw the black-and-white etching of Wells cathedral with tiny figures standing in front of it and then her favourite picture of a pretty lady wearing a long blue frock and white bonnet standing with a handsome young man and a priest in a glade with trees either side, which was entitled *The Huguenot's Wedding*. A rich lady from a big house the other side of Pridden had given this to her grandmother in gratitude for the healing of an ailment that was never described but which Betty suspected had involved a special mix of herbs that had a certain effect if taken in early pregnancy.

Charles had explained that the Huguenots were people in France who were not allowed to practise their religion and were presumably marrying in secret and when she had asked what the figure of a man in the distance would do on catching them he had looked stricken and exclaimed, 'God knows!'

Thinking of Kate and Charles and imagining them sitting in the parlour drinking tea from the best china and eating cake covered with marzipan and white icing made her ache to hug her sister and breathe in the scent of lavender whilst holding her close. Kate wouldn't want any affection from her now. That was all in the past. She had burned her boats and could never go back.

Thinking a good story would take her mind off the desperate longing and loneliness, she tried reading a library book but for once was not able to enjoy the story of a beautiful girl falling in love with a man who appeared to be poor but would in the end turn out to be a rich nobleman.

Throwing the book to one side she went to her suitcase and, taking out the green silk scarf in which she had wrapped her collection of treasures before leaving the cottage six weeks earlier, laid it on the bed. Lifting up the gold pin with the pearl set in one end she heard the sound of a man singing in a foreign language whilst the air was filled with the heavy scent of privet flowers and then, holding the garnet ring, saw the man smoking a pipe while sitting beside a big fireplace. Having replaced them and feeling comforted by the familiar messages, she curled her fingers around the piece of wood she had found in the cave and closed her eyes.

Marie's eyes looked painfully swollen as she stood forlornly at the cloister entrance. 'I shall miss thee so much, dear Caitlin. So very much.'

'I shall miss thee too, my friend. I will keep thee in my heart always.'

'Oh my dear, dear friend, ma chère, must thee leave us?'

'Yes, it is decided. I shall not take the vows.'

'Please, I beg thee to think again. We could be so content if both were wedded to our lord.'

'Dear friend, we have done with talking now. The benefactor who brought me here awaits and I must say goodbye.'

'But I may never see thee again.'

She took the shaking hand in hers. 'We shall meet again, Marie. I know it will be so. I can see us standing together by the little myrtle tree beside the wall in the herb garden and there is a great ivory cross hanging from a silver chain around thy neck.' She kissed her cheek and turned towards the sister waiting by the huge wooden door. 'I am ready now.'

She walked with steady measured strides, not daring to look back at the girl with whom she had spent such happy times. As the door swung open she could see a man beside a cart. Could this be the one who lifted her so easily onto his horse and brought her here all those years ago? Mother Superior said it was he, but this stooping old man, wearing a habit of coarse brown wool and with wisps of greying hair around a shaven pate, bore little resemblance to the picture she had held in her mind for so long.

'You are beautiful, Caitlin,' he said, giving a small bow, 'as was your mother.' Putting a large knobbly hand on her shoulder, he said, 'I am told thou will be sorely missed here. Is it truly thy wish to leave this place and return to the valley?'

'Aye, sire. I wish to return to the place of my birth.'

'So be it. I will keep my word.'

As they rode along in the jolting cart behind the large, lumbering horse, she asked timidly, 'Are thee a man of God, sir?'

'I fought Saladin in God's name and now I am in Christ's army of Saint Benedict. An itinerant preacher seeking to conquer souls and where I lay my

101

head each night is home and hearth enough.'

The horse slowly plodded through mud and over rocky lanes towards the hills. From time to time a child would look out from a shelter or a man and woman in a field would straighten their backs to see what stranger was passing by. Rooks were squabbling in the trees above their head, and pointing to them, she said, 'They are nesting high. I should have a fine spring to start my new life.'

'Thou hast not forgotten the ways of God's creatures.'

'I remember my mother's and her mother's teaching.'

When they reached the valley and were close to the path that led to her home, the friar tied the old horse to a willow and smiled when she jumped down from the cart. They walked together beside the river and then along the narrow track to the copse beside the cljff of rocks beneath the steeply sloping hillside.

'I came back to keep my promise,' he said, taking a metal token from his leather pouch. 'This bears the seal of Earl Reginald with whom I fought under King Richard. He owns the lands all around and his castle is two hours' walk to the north-west.' He looked searchingly at her 'Dost know which way that is?'

She pointed, first to where the sun would later sink from view, then to the north and back between the two.

'Aye, that will take thee there. He has granted thee the land for four hundred paces by two hundred paces around where thy mother made shelter.'

'And the cave?'

'Aye, that is well within the bounds of it.'

'Why should he do this for me?'

'For a favour owed me from when we fought at Acre.' He handed her the token. 'Thou and thy descendants have title to this land. No one may take it from thee, but if they do try then thou knows where to go for justice?'

'Aye, I thank thee.'

'I have made it known that this is so. The men who killed her, those that are left that is, will not dare trouble thee now.'

'Are some now dead?'

'Most of the evil sinners have died or disappeared. Few will come this way now, nor in the woods above, for fear of the curse thy mother put on them. Also I have heard–' he swallowed hard '–that her spirit haunts the big cave by the river and no one will go near it.'

'That is where they buried her.'

'Aye' He wiped his eyes on his sleeve. ''Tis as I thought.'

Her heart ached with the memory of her mother's screams as they turned and walked in silence along the narrow path to the place where she had lived. On arrival in the clearing and seeing the walls of their dwelling, made of rock and earth built up against the solid cliff, were mostly still sound, she exclaimed, 'God be praised! I thought they would destroy it.'

'They were too afeared of her curse to ever set foot here again.' He took a knife from his belt and handed it to her 'I found this on the day I returned to look for thee.'

'My mother's knife!' she exclaimed.

'Aye. I took it with me to the Holy Land as a memento of her and now–' he swallowed '–I must give it to thee.' He pointed to a pile of reeds. 'I collected withies yesterday to make good the roof before I depart, or would thee care to seek a goat to eat?'

'My mother's goats are still here?'

'Aye, they have multiplied and live on the hills all around. There's milk and meat a plenty for thee.'

She smiled and chose to mend the roof, for the sisters had given her food to eat.

The following day, after waving goodbye to the kindly friar, she made her way to the big cave by the river where he was sure the men had hidden her mother's body. She intended to retrieve the remains and place them with her ancestors but found the entrance, that had once been accessible from rocks above the river, was nowhere to be seen. A slope of mud and rocks in which a few gorse bushes were struggling to set their roots now covered the spot. She guessed the murderers had blocked it completely by causing a landslide.

Feeling saddened by the discovery she walked up the hill and found the fissure in the rocks directly above the cave. Her mother had said people lived in there many seasons before and the smoke from their fires had escaped through this hole. She peered into the darkness, wondering if she could climb down and admitted such a venture was impossible. Feeling despondent she sat down and wept for a long time, until suddenly realising that if she could not move her mother to the burial chamber then the next best choice would be to make that place into her tomb.

She hurried back to the dwelling, and having fetched her mother's knife and the remains of her broken pot, she carried them to the hole above the cave and pushed them down into the darkness. Next she collected sweet violets, thyme and primroses, made

104

them into a posy and, calling her mother's name, threw them into the void.

An expedition up the hillside revealed that her mother's goats, of which there had been four females and one male at the time of her death, had multiplied and their many offspring roamed at will. This uncontrolled expansion had had a dramatic effect on the vegetation of the hillside. In their need for roughage they had eaten undergrowth and smaller trees. Also, the lack of any culling of male kids had caused there to be too many aggressive rams roaming the area.

The stately oak, from which her mother's body had swung like a hideously bloody, boneless rag doll, was safe from the animals' relentless foraging, but few young shoots or bushes around it had escaped. Standing before the massive tree, she fingered her sharp knife and, although longing to slit other throats than the innocently grazing creatures, decided what must be done. She knew how to control the fully grown males by holding their horns and walking them where she willed. In this way she took them one by one to a smaller cave well away from the river where she quickly killed and deftly skinned them. When only one young ram was left, she piled rocks in the entrance and returned to the dwelling dragging the skins on dead branches. Tired and hungry from such strenuous labour, she roasted a small male kid on the fire and ate her fill before lying on the bed of sweet grasses and falling into a deep sleep.

Chapter Eight

Oil in which fresh flowers of mullein have been steeped may relieve earache.

She had wandered onto the common and picked a few wild flowers after going to the library and now, walking down the busy street in the sunshine, was looking forward to spending the rest of her afternoon off reading in her room. Whilst passing a woman pushing a large black pram in which a chubby baby lay fast asleep beneath a white canopy, she thought of Kate, who would be a mother by now. Would the people ignore her sister as she pushed her son through the village in his pram and would they talk about her when she had passed by?

Seeing her own reflection in a shop window she gave a small smile of satisfaction. Kate would be surprised at how grown-up she had become during the six months since leaving home. Turning away she remembered the application she had sent to an employment agency and, hoping there might be a reply by now, she hurried homewards.

After opening the door leading from the street to the flat, she went into the shop, which was closed as it always was on Wednesday afternoons. Finding no envelopes on the mat under the letterbox, she turned to leave. Then, seeing the stockroom door open, she peered inside. Having met Mr Bradon in the street on his way to deliver a repaired jacket a few minutes earlier and knowing she could look around undisturbed for a few minutes, she stepped inside and laid the library books and flowers on the treadle sewing machine.

Putting a fox evening cape without a lining around her shoulders, she stood idly stroking the brown fur while looking at a pile of books and papers on the windowsill beside her. There were several coloured illustrations of coats with names of suppliers, a sheaf of receipts, a swatch of brown, beige and black silk fabric, and under all that, a photograph. Her heart juddered with shock as she held the picture of a girl wearing shiny shorts and a brief top with a plume of ostrich feathers on her head – just like the costume worn by Lara Crowe when she was Vicky in *The Showgirl and the Duke*. 'Crikey-blimey!' she whispered, and read aloud the words written in copperplate, 'The Gentlemen's Relish, Gargoyle Mews, London'. She must remember that!

Repeating the words in her head, she hurriedly left and ran upstairs to the kitchen where she found a young woman with frizzy yellow hair resting her large bosom on the table while drinking a cup of tea. Seeing she not only looked like the cleaner, with the same shape of nose and wide cheekbones, but was also wearing her green overall with the belt tied tightly around her smaller waist, she guessed this was her daughter and politely wished her good afternoon.

'Pleased to meet you too I'm sure. Gerty's the

name.' She pursed her rouged lips. 'I've come instead of me mum on account of the youngest being poorly, but I've said I'll not do the mad woman's room. Nearly frightened the living daylights out of me she did, I had to come in here and sit down for a mo. Ought to be in the loony bin if you ask me, that's what me mum says an' all.'

Feeling indignant on Mrs Bradon's behalf, Betty responded, 'She's just terribly, terribly sad. She's not mad, I'm sure she's not. I actually think she's getting better. She says "thank you" to me now when I give her the tea.' She looked down at the yellow flowers, feeling eager to go and hang them to dry in her room.

Gerty sniffed, obviously unimpressed.

The door swung open to reveal Mr Bradon, his gaze fixed on Gerty as he smoothed the hair over his head.

'I was explaining to Miss Muffet 'ere that I can't be doing for...' Gerty's eyes indicated the direction of the darkened room.

Betty touched the cameo brooch pinned to her blouse and said, 'I'll clean the room for her. She's been eating more for a few days and she's been enjoying the books I've been reading to her. I really do think she's improving.'

The man's bulging eyes rolled from Gerty to Betty and back again. 'That sounds a good way to settle the problem. I'd be obliged, Miss Smith, if you'd give the shop a good clean, I'm expecting the new stock soon and I'd like everything spick and span before I invite my special customers to come and see what treats I have in store.' He gave a squeaky little laugh and added, 'Don't forget. I need you in the shop, Miss Smith.' Then, smoothing the hair over his head with one hand, he left the room.

'Yeah, I'll be down in a jiffy.' Gerty stood up and wiggled her hips as she placed the mop in the bucket before picking both up and clattering down the stairs after him on her high heels.

Betty sat at the table and stared morosely at the wall. What on earth was she thinking of? She had decided to leave and get a better post. How could she be stupid enough to say she'd clean the room when skivvying was the one thing she'd sworn never, ever to do? How had this happened? It had been bad enough emptying the chamber pot and carrying buckets of water for Mrs Bradon to wash in, but she'd reasoned that was probably the sort of thing a genteel companion would do for a ladylike invalid. Now she was becoming a housemaid and that would never do. Heroines in stories would have married the handsome nephew by now and film stars like Lara Crowe would never have got into such a mess!

Feeling utterly miserable she went to see Mrs Bradon and, finding her asleep, went up to her own room. Taking the piece of wood from the cupboard, she clasped it tightly and lay on the bed. Maybe seeing the girl living in the valley would make her feel better...

The sun shone through the leaves, dappling her bare legs and the brown wool of her skirt as she sat on the dry grass beneath the outer branches of the oak tree.

Bees hummed in purple thyme flowers. Small blue butterflies and larger scarlet ones fluttered amongst the tall grasses. On the rocks close by a young kid cried to its mother who bleated impatiently, scolding it for climbing so high. A small creature rustled in the undergrowth – a mouse perhaps, or a stoat. She turned and, looking through the shimmering heat, caught a glimpse of sudden movement in dark shadows under a thicket of hawthorns. Her heart juddered with shock. Was that an animal, or something larger? Could it be a man? She had assumed this area was safe, that no one would come here because it was cursed. 'Hangen-tree land', the local people now called it, for they knew it was the place where her mother had died.

During the first weeks she had only come here to mourn. Now, although still grieving, she could sit beneath the tree on fine sunny days and be grateful for its kindly filter of harsh burning rays. She knew it stored the memory of drunken murder because she had heard the trunk moaning, 'Get the witch!' when lashed with rain and its branches hissing, 'Catch her, now, catch her, catch her,' as they thrashed about in a gale; but, on this warm summer's day all was peace and tranquillity.

The present was now pleasanter and of greater importance than the past. Although thinking often of Marie, she no longer yearned for the comfort and friendship of the convent as she had for the first few days after her return, for she had a purpose in life. The women from nearby villages and farms had been visiting her of late, as once they had called on her mother for help with birthing, the herbs for lowering fever, easing a cough, cleansing wounds and earache.

110

This was a perfect day for collecting plants and setting them out to dry. She already had several useful ones and only planned to pick some comfrey before returning to her dwelling. A sparrowhawk emerged from the hawthorn where it had been surveying a thrush on her nest, waiting for a chance to take a fledgling. She watched the bird land on a tall tree and sit surveying its quarry. Something had disturbed it, and, pleased though she was for the victim, fear that she was the object of something's or someone's attention made her crouch, alert and ready to run for cover

'I seek thy help, maiden.'

She leaped to her feet at the sound of a male voice coming from behind the thicket and withdrew her knife from the sheath hanging at her waist. Standing with knees slightly bent, ready to defend herself with the sharp blade, she said firmly, 'Show thyself,' then gasped in horror as a young man emerged from the deep shadows and limped into the sunlight. His upper garments, although torn and muddy, were green silk, his breeches and boots were fine leather and the cloak over one shoulder was of green wool. He was more richly dressed and better shod than any man she had ever seen.

'Maiden, I beg thee, take pity.' He reached out to her and fell forward.

She looked at the prone form lying in the sunlit grass and waited a moment to be sure no other man was lurking behind him, then, slowly and cautiously, walked to stand over him. After waiting and watching for a few breaths until feeling sure he was alone, she knelt beside him. Blood was pouring through a cut in one leg of his kidskin breeches and over the top of his beautiful boot. Using her sharp knife she increased the length of cut in the leather and, seeing the heavy flow, tore a strip from his silken garment and tied it around his leg above the wound. There was a spring nearby, almost hidden by the comfrey she had come here to pick, and from this she collected a handful of water. Having bathed his forehead and poured a little into his mouth, she was relieved to see his eyes open.

'I did not intend to kill him. It was the stag at which I aimed.' His eyes were green with tiny golden flecks around the iris; and the locks of hair hanging loose about his neck were the colour of oak leaves in autumn.

'Come,' she said, 'come with me and I will give thee shelter.'

'Nay, De Vereau's men would show thee no mercy.' He looked anxiously up at the hill above them.

'Does he keep a castle to the north-west?'

He nodded.

'Earl Reginald?'

'Aye.' He sat up. 'I fear I killed his son.'

'In a fight?'

'Nay. A careless shot from my bow caught his neck and cost me dear. When I fled in panic his huntsman threw a knife at me. I rode the horse until she was lame and somehow walked until I found thee.' He shaded his eyes, looking to the horizon. 'I must get away from here. Where is the sea?'

She pulled him to his feet and placed one arm around her neck. 'I cannot let thee die here.' She looked down at the wound. 'I make no promise, but I can try to make thee well and send thee on thy way with a mended leg.'

They made their way through the copse to where

rocks jutted up through the earth and undergrowth. 'Down there–' she pointed over the edge of a steep cliff '–is my dwelling.'

Somehow, by dint of manoeuvring around projecting trees and stone, with frequent rests and slow, careful steps, they reached the grassy land outside the secret cave. A dog barked in the distance, the man looked like a hunted animal, his eyes wide with fear.

'Quickly, hide–' she pulled apart the heavy curtain of ivy hanging down the rock-face '–in there.'

He hopped through into the darkness.

'Don't come out until I say 'tis safe.' She ran to her dwelling and fetched the dead kid she had killed that morning. With deft strokes she quickly skinned it, placed the pink corpse to one side and laid the pelt out on the ground in the sun. She made a hole in the turf within which a fire slowly smouldered and added wood to it. Then, as voices and dogs could be heard approaching down through Hangen-tree land, she began strewing the nettles she had cut earlier out to dry on a rock.

The dogs came first. Two large hounds with slavering mouths bounded down the cliff path and ran straight to the goatskin, which they tore into shreds and then ran around until they found the meat and began fighting for it. Three men followed; all dressed in leather and coarse linen, each with a large knife at the hip and a bow strapped to his back. They strode to the dogs shouting and kicking at them. Eventually, after much noise and cursing, one tied a piece of rope around both dogs and anchored them with a boulder close to the dwelling.

'Thy pardon, maiden. We seek a squire who may have lost his way.'

'No one has passed by my dwelling this day.'

The younger of the three stepped closer. 'Thy father may have seen him. Is he nearby?'

'Nay, he is not.'

'Thy mother, perhaps?'

'Nay.' Looking from one to another, she realised her mistake and reached too late for her knife.

He was upon her immediately, and, bending her arm behind her back forced her to the ground. He pulled her skirt up over her head, thereby keeping both arms immobile and, whilst the others held her down, forced himself between her thighs and into her body. When taking his turn to hold her for the others he uncovered her face and laughed with each of the man's thrusts inside her.

When all three had had their fill and stood looking down at her sprawled in the grass with thighs streaked with blood, she stared defiantly into their eyes and said, 'All three of thee be thrice cursed. When each of thee lies with a woman I'll be there watching and each will wonder when lying with his wife what man has gone before him. Each will know when looking at his daughters that there be men evil enough to shame them as thee have shamed me.' She made a sign of the cross at each one of them, saying, 'I curse thee. I curse thee. I curse thee.'

The youngest one spat at her and raised one foot as if to kick her. The other two took his arms and pulled him away. None of them spoke as they took the dogs and returned the way they had come.

Ignoring the pain in her body and the desire to bathe in the river, she went to the cave wondering if the young man would be still alive. He opened his eyes when she parted the ivy, letting some light fall on his face, and muttered a few unintelligible words before closing them again. His breathing was shallow and his skin clammy to her touch.

Knowing she was unable to move him, she made a fire in the centre of the cave and fetched bedding straw for them both to lie on. She brewed strengthening and healing herbs for him to drink and also a cleansing mixture for his injuries. Then, looking at his leg, she saw the thickest part of his thigh was torn from the bone. Although she had seen her mother sew such gaping wounds with a needle and a linen thread, she had not done so herself. Now, knowing the flesh would knit together more quickly if held closed in that way, she desperately sought to remember what to do. Feeling sick with fear, she assembled the best tools she had for the task, pulled threads from his shirt and sat summoning the courage to begin.

Close by her were six clay pots containing a fermented concoction of elderberries and honey her mother had made shortly before her death. Remembering the soporific effect of similar beverages on visitors to the refectory, she broke open the beeswax seal and poured some into a small bowl. Having taken several sips to be sure it was neither unpalatable nor poisonous, she offered it to the man and, when he had swallowed the liquid, asked for more and drunk that also, she made him comfortable and began her task.

Once the ordeal was over, after she had bound the leg with strips of silk and he had sunk into a deep sleep, she felt free to leave him for a short time and emerged from the cave into the moonlit clearing.

Having stood for a while to ensure the men had not returned, she walked to the nearest bank of the river *where, after removing her clothes, she waded into the cool running water. There was a moment as she stood feeling the current swirling around her knees when death seemed preferable to a violated life and she deliberately knelt on the pebbles and plunged her head beneath the surface. When the pain in her lungs was unbearable she emerged gasping for air, realising that if death was her objective she would need to tie a boulder around her neck and jump into the deeper reaches of the river close to where her mother was buried in the big cave. This was a possibility if later she found the need for oblivion was stronger than fear of death. For now, perhaps, life could still be bearable. Already she had cleansed her body of the men's foul odour. Tomorrow she would seek the necessary plants and berries to ensure none of their seed took root, for she wanted no child to remind her of that evil deed.*

Chapter Nine

A tea made with lady's mantle may help with menstrual problems.

The summer was almost over. She had picked many elderberries and blackberries to which she had added honey and stored in the cave. Most plants that would be needed for healing were hanging in bunches ready for use and enough red hawthorn berries were drying by the fire in her dwelling. Five goatskins were cured and ready for making into shoes, water carriers and wine storage vessels.

Jerome's leg was healing well. He hobbled about the flat area around the cave and dwelling with the aid of a stick, but dared not attempt to go as far as the river nor climb the cliff to Hangen-tree Land. The young man no longer looked very different from any local inhabitant; his hair was an unruly mass of golden curls meeting the beard on his chin, his fine silk garments had been replaced with coarse linen and his breeches and boots were worn and dirty.

The three huntsmen had not returned and no others had called this way that might have questioned his presence. He always stayed hidden when local women called for healing remedies and therefore no one knew he was there. He had helped her scrape and clean the goatskins. He had also wanted to save the pelts from the few rabbits that had strayed from the warren on the glebe land beyond the river but she had dissuaded him fearing such evidence would have caused enquiries by the Bishop's Steward and she wanted no such interest in her small corner of the valley.

They had always slept separately after the first few nights. She had insisted that he stay in the cave just in case the men who sought him came back and he agreed. They had fallen into a habit of roasting some food each sundown and sitting for a while together beside her fire before he went to his bed in the cave and she fell thankfully onto hers in the dwelling. It was the best time in her life so far. These long sunlit days collecting nature's produce were much more enjoyable than any spent at the convent and she had the young man awaiting her return, eager for company. She was even happier than when her mother was alive and

117

sang with joy in her heart as she gathered wood for the hard winter to come, or milked the goats, or fetched a pail of water from the nearby spring.

The first frost came early, as she had known it would, and she was glad she had already brought the goats down from the hillside to where they could eat the fodder she had gathered and take refuge in the shelter she had made for them alongside her dwelling.

She had provided well for this dark season when food was scarce. There were bags of hazelnuts, sweet chestnuts and dried mushrooms hanging in the cave. Also, alongside her own cheese made from goats' milk were several yellow cheeses and two pieces of salted pig given by local women in return for ointments that eased boils, or herbal mixtures for a variety of ills.

There was enough to survive if she supplemented the stores with birds or fish or an occasional hare. She also knew which roots were nourishing when cooked and where they grew. All these things would keep them alive until the bright new spring, providing they kept warm and conserved their energy by sleeping in tune with the rhythm of the longer nights and shorter days.

When the dark sky portended snow they stayed beside the fire in the dwelling during the day and, as he went to leave her for the night, she stopped him with her hand upon his arm. 'Stay. It is too cold.'

He shook his head. 'I cannot lie so close and not be true to myself.'

When he had gone she lay awake with pounding heart, knowing at last he too felt the pull of nature, the force she had now been fighting for many, many days *and nights. She had thought to swear abstinence for life after the foul men had taken her just as the miller had before them, but now she ached for this beautiful man.*

The following day when the sun was low in the sky and after settling the goats in their shelter, she fetched some blackberry juice and poured it into a small bowl. Taking turns to drink as they sat by the fire, they became more and more at ease until he reached out to hold her hand and she placed it over her beating heart, making plain her eagerness for love. Then, as they lay upon the sweet bedstraw, she willingly accepted him and found unexpected and unimagined pleasure.

Awakening from the dream she lay remembering the sensation of lying with the beautiful man for a while. If that was how it felt – then no wonder Kate and Charles did it in the afternoon as well as at night!

Whilst replacing the piece of wood into the green silk scarf, she recalled the many herbs hanging in the cave and thought of her attempts in this lifetime to use them. She had spent hours searching for St John's wort on the common only to find Mrs Bradon refused to drink the tea she had made with it. The disappointment had been bad enough, but the sense of failure when the sad little woman had seemed even more withdrawn afterwards was still distressing six months later. From time to time in the interval she had touched the cameo brooch in the hope of hearing some other way of helping, but the

119

only other suggestion that came to her had been to dig up the root of a white valerian plant growing near the ruined mill at Oakey Vale and she had grown disheartened. What was the point of spending her precious afternoon off looking for a plant then take the trouble to make a tea with it only to have the woman spit it out over the bed covers again?

Suddenly remembering it was Christmas Day and she had accepted an invitation from the greengrocer's wife to join their family for a meal at midday, she groaned aloud and wished she had had the presence of mind to invent an excuse. The thought of being in the company of their son, who blushed whenever she walked into their shop, thereby making her equally embarrassed, filled her with dread. The obvious outcome would be an invitation to the cinema with the repulsive boy which would be difficult to refuse. This was another reason for leaving as soon as possible.

She went and lit the gas fire then picked up a copy of *The Lady's Weekly* and climbed back into bed. Looking at the advertisement marked with a big tick in red pencil, she read aloud, 'Well-educated and kindly companion to elderly lady needed north London. Must have good references.' The letter she had written purporting to be from Mrs Bradon had given a glowing report of herself and must surely bring results. If all went well and the lady found the highly complimentary letter to her satisfaction, then this ordeal might soon be over. She would be sad in a way to leave the poor little soul and feel guilty too, but she had to get away from mopping floors and emptying chamber pots and, above all, get into a situation where she could meet a rich young man who would marry her, or, better still, meet a film star who would take her to Hollywood. Snuggling down under the blankets, she smiled up at the stained ceiling while imagining Kate's astonishment on going to the cinema in Wells and seeing her gazing down from the screen. Feeling the familiar ache of longing when thinking of her sister, a momentary desire to go back to the village overwhelmed her – she could throw herself on Kate's mercy and beg forgiveness – but then what? There would be no room for her in the cottage now. The only work would be in domestic service and, above all, she would not be welcome.

At a quarter to twelve, dressed in the blue frock she had bought on a rare excursion to look at the big shops in Kensington High Street, she descended the narrow staircase from her room to the landing and met Mr Bradon, who cheerfully greeted her then flinched at the sound of the street door being opened below. 'Ah! I expect that's the cleaner. She said she might call, er, for the Christmas box, er, instead of tomorrow.' The door to the shop banged loudly. 'Off you go and have a nice time.' He ushered her to the stairs and followed her down.

She had crossed the road and walked a short distance along the pavement, when, looking back, she saw a postman push several envelopes through the shop letterbox. Thinking the elderly lady might have replied and, knowing she could not bear to wait until later, she returned to the side entrance then walked through the darkened shop where she found neither of the two envelopes on the doormat was addressed to her. Hearing Mr Bradon's voice from behind the stockroom door, she hesitated behind the display of gloves, collars and hats, then, just as she had decided to tiptoe out, the door was pushed open and a shaft of electric light made a bright path across the floor.

Gerty strutted to the long cheval mirror wearing a fox cape over her dark red frock and posed, turning this way and that with the air of a rich customer taking her time to make the right choice. 'I don't know...' She sighed, adding, 'I'm just not sure,' then walked slowly with an exaggerated wiggle back inside the storeroom out of Betty's view. A few moments later she called out, 'This is nice,' and reappeared carrying a long white fur coat trimmed with ermine tails. 'What–' she pouted and raised her left eyebrow '–would I have to do to earn this?'

'It's an evening coat.' He emerged and took a step towards her. 'I've been mending the sleeves. The silly cow made scrambled eggs on the gas stove.'

'Scrambled eggs!'

'That's what she said.'

'D'you mean she was cooking wearing this?'

'They'd been to some party and felt hungry when they got home in the early hours of the morning.' He laughed mirthlessly. 'Being filthy rich doesn't make you sensible.'

'I wouldn't mind being that stupid.' She pouted,

and stroking the fur, said, 'It feels so good. I wonder why we don't wear fur on the inside next to our bare skin?'

He smiled eagerly as he came close to her. 'Let me see you like that now, with it inside out over you, you know, like that, and you might get a nice surprise.'

Gerty returned to the stockroom trailing the coat along the floor behind her.

Mr Bradon stood looking around the shop and for a second his bulging eyes seemed to peer at Betty through the gap in the shelves as he unbuttoned his trousers.

Gerty reappeared wearing the coat inside out. 'Come to me, you naughty boy,' she called, opening it to reveal her naked body.

He groaned, turned, and stepped towards her.

'Not here, silly boy!' She twirled around to see herself in the mirror. 'It's warmer in there and that stupid brat might come in any minute for the post.'

'No, the silly little cow's gone to the greengrocer's. We're all alone!'

Betty closed her eyes. If they took only a few steps they'd see her standing there. Her heart was drumming so loudly it drowned out all other sounds, until, eventually, when her pulse had quietened to normal, she heard strange moans and loud grunts reminiscent of a barking dog behind the closed door. Opening her eyes she tiptoed across the brown linoleum and made her escape into the street where she chuckled whilst hurrying along in the biting wind – they'd made a lot more noise than Kate and Charles Wallace, maybe the fur made them feel more like animals?

The greengrocer opened the door and ushered her upstairs into a room in which red-faced people were sitting around a table crammed with food and making a lot of noise. 'Here's the little lass from the furrier's. Give her a sherry wine and a chair,' he yelled and guffawed as though it was the funniest joke he had ever heard before ushering her to the seat that had obviously been saved for her next to his blushing and tongue-tied son.

She was soon relieved to find the woman sitting on the other side of her talked incessantly without expecting more than a few monosyllabic responses throughout the meal, thereby saving her from the trouble of thinking what to say to anyone. She ate the food offered to her and drank the wine frequently poured into her glass and, while watching the comfortable way in which the group of relatives interacted, experienced a few moments of sudden and deep loneliness.

After a while, when a feeling of wellbeing and warmth spread through her, she imagined Kate sitting on the sofa in Old Myrtles with a small baby on her knee. What would the people in the village be saying behind her sister's back and would they speak to her face to face? Everyone had known when Billy's older sister was in love with the butcher in Wells who was married to her cousin and they knew why she left the village suddenly, but nobody spoke about her to her parents ever again, although they did of course talk about her at length in their absence. Mrs

Nelson had removed every reminder of her daughter from the house and even forbidden the mention of her name, which upset Billy because he'd loved her. Remembering his sister untying a particularly tight knot in Billy's shoelaces and showing her how to cross her eyes, she felt a great swell of emotion – how strange that such odd little memories stick in the mind!

After all the plates had been cleared away, the greengrocer shouted, 'Quiet, everyone. Queenie's gonner give us a tune on the Joanna.'

A large woman then sat at the upright piano and began playing Christmas carols. The family, apart from an elderly man who had fallen asleep in an armchair, all sang as many words as they knew to whatever tune she played for an hour and a half, after which time Betty explained she must return to look after Mrs Bradon and walked unsteadily along the pavement humming her uncle's favourite hymn.

On arrival at the shop she spent several minutes struggling to fit the key in the lock, which seemed very funny and the more she laughed the more difficult the task became. After several minutes, having at last succeeded in opening the door, she was about to ascend the stairs to the flat, when, looking through the open door to the shop, she saw a grey squirrel coat on the floor surrounded by torn wrapping paper. Stepping closer, she bent and stroked the fur, then, without any thought or knowledge of what she was about to do, walked through the open stockroom door and delved into a box. Having pulled out two fox tippets and four foxtails, she quickly stuffed them inside her coat and then, finding the room revolving around her, she staggered upstairs to the bathroom where she vomited into the lavatory. Feeling weak but less giddy, she wondered for a moment why her coat felt so tight then opened the door and went cautiously upstairs to her room where she lit the fire and sank onto the bed.

Awakening in the early hours of Boxing morning feeling very warm, she removed her coat and lay stroking the furs. How very soft they were and so comforting! Gerty was right, why did people wear the fur on the outside? The other question was how on earth was she going to put them back without Mr Bradon knowing?

She lay staring at the brown patch on the ceiling for several minutes, letting her eyes go out of focus until it looked like a fox standing on its hind legs. She slid off the bed and removed her clothes, then, taking one tippet and draping it around her hips and the other across her chest, she smiled at her reflection in the mirror. She looked much, much more glamorous than the showgirl in the Gentlemen's Relish!

Now she had this inspiration to think about, everything seemed clearer – this was the way she would become a film star! She would return the furs when the shop was closed and save up enough money to buy her own, then, and this made her heart beat faster, then she would go to the Gentlemen's Relish and pose for photographs with her furs. These artistic pictures would be as good as, better in fact, than the ones of actresses in the movie magazines. They would be seen by a film director who would be on the look-out for talent like hers, and that would be that – she would go to Hollywood.

Looking at the alarm clock she was thankful to see it would not ring for another two hours and returned to sleep.

The following morning, after giving Mrs Bradon some tea and doing the usual chores, she wrapped the furs in newspaper and placed them in a canvas shopping bag then went into the shop. All was quiet and she was about to open the stock-room door when the sound of footsteps clattering down the stairs made her turn and run to the mat under the letterbox.

'You tell her or I will, d'you understand?' Gerty said loudly.

Mr Bradon's placatory whine was quieter but clearly audible. 'It's not that easy, girlie, she's done nothing wrong.'

'You said you'd do it when me mum left, you said...'

'I will, I will, at the right time.'

'The longer yer leave it the worse it'll get, she's already got used to being waited on hand, foot and finger!'

'I'll sort it out, girlie, I promise. I've had an idea,' he said, lowering his voice to an inaudible whisper.

'Arfie! Yes! Yes! Yes! That's the answer. I've said all along she's mad and me mum says...'

Betty sneezed.

'Who's there?'

She sneezed again.

'So, surprise, surprise, look who's here!' Gerty

127

walked into the shop trailing a grey squirrel coat.

Betty forced a smile and replied, 'I was just seeing if there were any letters for me.'

Dropping the coat and folding her arms, Gerty said, 'Mr Bradon's got something ter say. Don't yer?'

He was standing in the doorway looking utterly miserable and smoothing the hair over his balding head. His Adam's apple bounced as he swallowed several times before stammering, 'Er, yes, you see, Betty, er, the thing is ... um, situations do change sometimes.'

'Exactly!' Gerty glared venomously at her.

Seeing the expression of loathing on the cleaner's face, she was perplexed. How strange to be disliked for no reason! What had she done to provoke the woman?

'What he's politely saying is, bugger off!'

She took a breath and, imitating the clipped English accent of an actress she had seen in a film the previous Wednesday afternoon, said, 'Of course I shall leave if you ask me to.' After waiting for the relieved expression to settle on her employer's face, she then asked, 'Are you requesting me to leave because I know about the way you carry on in the stockroom and fear I'll tell all the neighbours about what you do whilst poor Mrs Bradon, your dear wife...'

Gerty screeched, 'I'm not staying here to be insulted by this toffee-nosed little bitch!' and ran out banging the door very loudly behind her.

Mr Bradon looked stricken and whined, 'I'd lose all my customers.'

She glanced down at the fur lying on the floor

128

between them – that would be very useful when wanting to impress a film director. Putting one hand on her hip, she changed character and became Lara Crowe as a gangster's moll looking directly into his eyes. 'There might be a way...'

'Would you swear never to say a word?'

Bending down and picking up the coat, she replied, 'On the Bible if you like.'

'Come with me.' He led the way upstairs to the kitchen, then, indicating she should wait, went into the darkened room and quickly reappeared holding a large black Bible. 'It belongs to my dear ... er ... here it is.'

'I swear–' she put her right hand on the book '–if Mr Bradon gives me this fur coat I won't tell the neighbours what he got up to with Gerty on the white rabbit evening coat with ermine tail trimming.'

The man's face was scarlet and saliva dribbled down one side of his mouth as he said, 'And you'll go away today and never come back.'

She repeated the words.

'Now pack your things and get out.' Smoothing the strands of hair across his head, he added, 'I'm going out for half an hour and I expect you to be gone by the time I get back.'

She ran up to the attic room and hastily wrapped the fur coat in the ancient cotton bedspread and tied the corners in a bundle. Pulling the suitcase from under the bed she crammed her clothes and possessions inside and then struggled down the narrow stairs to the landing where, opening the door, she looked at the sleeping form in the darkened room. Suppose Gerty was unkind to Mrs

Bradon? Might she harm her? Oh no! What had the beastly man said to Gertie? Were they planning to murder the poor woman? 'I'm sorry,' she whispered, 'I'm sorry to let you down.'

After closing the door gently, she went downstairs and peered into the shop where, seeing the shopping bag containing the furs she had left there earlier lying close to the door, she took a step towards it and paused to listen. Knowing from the silence he really had gone out, no doubt to find Gertie and explain why he had given away her coat, she ran forward, grabbed the bag, and then stepped out into the street.

After walking away from the parade of shops she went to a bench near a bus stop and sat down to think. She had a fur coat, two fox tippets and some tails, and, thanks to her care with the small payment Mr Bradon had given her each week, seventeen pounds saved in her Post Office account, and, she looked in her purse, fifteen shilings and sixpence three farthings, and no job and nowhere to live. Things had happened too quickly. She was alone and afraid. She leaned forward holding her head. What on earth was she going to do?

A car pulled up and a melodious voice said, 'There won't be many buses today. Can I give you a lift?'

Looking up into the open window, she replied, 'I need to go into London.'

'It's a big place. Whereabouts d'you want to go?'

She fingered the blue fabric of her dress and, remembering where she had bought it, said,

'Kensington High Street would do.'

The woman behind the wheel peered from beneath the slanting brim of a small hat whilst saying, 'I'm going to a hospital not far from there. I could drop you off on the way. Throw that lot in the back and hop in.'

They drove in silence for a few minutes before the woman asked, 'So where exactly are you going?'

She breathed in the scent from the gardenia pinned to the woman's lapel and replied, 'I'm not sure exactly. I, well, I've just left a job rather unexpectedly and now I need to find somewhere to live. I've got a copy of *The Lady's Weekly* that has some rooms advertised in it. I haven't had time to look, that's all.'

'I see. So you haven't run away with your mother's fur coat wrapped in a bedspread?'

Feeling the blood rush to her face, she looked round at the bundle on the seat behind her and saw the grey fur protruding through a small tear in the fabric. 'It's not like that.'

'Is it just a bit like that?'

'No, I promise you I didn't steal the coat, it's mine, truly mine.'

'I believe you–' the woman chuckled '–thousands wouldn't!'

Betty laughed and burst into tears. Then, when the car was pulled into the side of the road and the engine turned off, she described what had happened at the flat that morning.

The woman said, 'Sounds to me like his wife will be locked up in the asylum before very long.'

'Oh no! It will be my fault for not staying and...'

'No, sweet pea, that is not so. Besides–' she took out a cigarette and lit it '–maybe she wouldn't be too unhappy there, she might like being with a lot of other loonies, don't yer know?'

'Maybe. She didn't seem mad to me, just sort of weighed down somehow.'

'Melancholic?'

'Yes, that's it.'

'And what are you going to do now?'

'I don't know, not exactly. I need a cheap room somewhere while I look around.'

'Hmm, let's look in this magazine of yours, shall we?'

Betty unpacked *The Lady's Weekly* and offered it to her.

'This sounds alright, a hostel for young ladies in Bayswater. Best tell the warden you're twenty-one, have done secretarial training, and give a posh sort of parental address, something like The Manor House, Chipping Sodding or something, she'll never check up.' She rummaged in her bag and produced a powder compact and rouge, 'Just use a little of this.'

'I could wear the coat, would that help?'

The woman looked doubtful. 'Let's see.'

She climbed out of the car, unwrapped the coat and put it on. 'And I could wear a headband, like Lara Crowe.' She opened the suitcase, removed a length of green chiffon and tied it around her fair hair.

'Absolutely lovely! Come along, I'll take you to the hostel, off we go.' As they drove through Shepherd's Bush, she asked where the woman lived.

'I'm a nurse so I live in a hostel close to the hos-

132

pital, but the family live in Wiltshire, that's where I've just been on a duty visit.' After ten more minutes she turned off the main road and parked outside a tall brick building. Taking the gardenia from her lapel, she handed it to her, saying, 'There you are, sweet pea. Good luck.' Then, holding her hand, she added, 'Send a card to your sister just to let her know you're safe and well.'

'But she hates me. I let her down.'

'Just a card, sweet pea, that's all. Promise?'

She nodded, then, having thanked her and waved goodbye, went to the entrance porch where a notice was pinned on the door saying, 'No Vacancies until the new year.' Suddenly feeling desperately hungry, she walked along the street in the hope of finding a café and soon saw a small tobacconist and confectioner's where she bought two walnut whirls and a bottle of lemonade. While standing outside the shop wondering what to do next, she looked in the window and saw a post-card on which was written, 'Basement room to let.'

Chapter Ten

A tea made with horsetail may help with the healing of men's prostate problems.

'Crikey-blimey!' Betty fingered her red curls whilst peering into the speckled mirror on the wardrobe door. 'That's absolutely perfect.'

She took the bucket of water she had used to wash the henna from her hair and emptied it into the lavatory outside the front door, then filled a kettle from the tap on the wall and shivered as she returned inside and placed it to heat on top of the black cylindrical oil stove. The room in what had obviously been the cellar of the house was a lot less comfortable than the modern flat in Ealing, but at least there was a proper lavvy – she'd be using an earth closet if she had stayed in Oakey Vale.

Determined to enjoy her freedom and not be downcast by such a mundane problem as lack of plumbing she fetched the fox tippet and tails, and, deciding the temperature was far too low to undress, draped the fur over her clothes. Turning to look at the murky remains of a mirror on the inside of the rickety wardrobe door, she peered into it. 'My word!' she exclaimed then asked, 'Is that really Betty Barnes?'

Shaking her head she sat down in the sagging old armchair. No, that wasn't Betty, but who was she now? Red-headed who? Her new name still eluded her. Should she be Lara like the film star? Or Rita? That was appealing and for several minutes she practised saying, 'Hello, my name is Rita,' before discarding it because it just didn't feel right. Anastasia was exotic – she had read the name in a newspaper report about a rumour that one of the Russian princesses had escaped when the rest of the royal family were murdered by the revolutionaries. It was a beautiful name, but she wanted to make a feature of the fur. How about

Lady Mink? Princess Mink? Minky? She leaned back and, looking up at the cracked ceiling, remembered the brown stains above her bed in Ealing. There was one in the shape of a fox. That's it! She gasped aloud. Lady Fox? Foxy Lady? Of course! It was obvious, yes, oh yes! 'My name,' she said in imitation of the lady with the gardenia, 'is Foxy, sweet pea, just plain Foxy!'

A sudden pang of guilt assailed her. She'd left poor Mrs Bradon at the mercy of Gerty. What would happen to the frail little creature? The gardenia lady had suggested she'd be sent to the Loony Bin. 'The Asylum', she called it, and thought it wouldn't be too bad or might even be good for someone in her state. Knowing in her heart that wasn't so, she ached for the sad little woman whose shocked mind had sunk deeply into melancholy when her mother died during her wedding.

When she had scrubbed her hands in the heated water and reduced the orange stain on her fingers to a pale yellow, she leaned forward to warm her hands over the oil stove and then, tracing the name written in gold on the side of it with her forefinger, said, 'Hello, Beatrice, my name's Foxy. How d'you do?'

On standing back her hand brushed the cameo brooch and she heard her grandmother exclaim, 'Brazen hussy!'

Frantically pulling at the brooch to remove it, she was horrified to find the cameo suddenly come away in her hand leaving the pin in her vest. Staring down at the carved figure framed in gold she gave a sob. If only she could put the clock back and try again, she would be so careful of her most important treasure! What would Kate say? She sank despondently onto the bed and held her head. Kate would be upset by the broken brooch, but, more than that, her sister, like Gran, would be horrified to see her red hair. Well, so what! She would never return to the village so Kate wouldn't see it anyway.

Lying back on the bed she found memories of childhood suddenly flooding her mind. She climbed the great oak in Hankeys Land, ran through the verdant woods with Billy and walked the sunlit hills with her sister looking for herbs. Looking up at the narrow window in the wall beside her she closed her eyes and imagined that, instead of the stark, darkening pavement, she could see the naked trees around the village, their branches like random lace against the sky. Some of their dead leaves might still be lying beneath them or in wet heaps in the lane outside Old Myrtles. Walking up the garden path in the twilight she would see the lamp inside the kitchen giving a soft yellow glow through the window and, breathing in, she would smell that special scent of evening when the cooling air somehow accentuated the fresh aroma of plants and earth.

Opening her eyes, she looked down at the cameo and sighed. Then, knowing she could not afford the money to have it mended, she fetched the green silk scarf and added the broken brooch to her collection. Looking at the small sliver of wood, she debated whether to hold it or not. The last few times she had held it had all been uneventful scenes in which she had been collecting

136

berries or catching fish. The other life would be comforting. It was the nearest she could get to Oakey Vale...

The bright green grass was still drenched with dew. She held her skirt up to her knees and walked to the cave, enjoying the fresh coolness on her bare feet. Winter had seemed long. This was the first morning to hint of change. A new beginning. Another miracle. The most glorious sunny optimism filled the valley. Birds were ecstatically warbling their mating songs and purposefully carrying twigs and straw to nesting sites.

The hawthorn had yet to flaunt its creamy flowers and the oaks were still barren. As yet there was neither promise of rampant summer from bare willows turning golden by the river, nor even a slight scattering of bright green haze in the brown hedgerows. Snowdrops bloomed bravely in the woods where lent lilies had bent their heads in preparation for opening their yellow trumpets of spring.

Soon pale primroses, tiny violets and delicately nodding windflowers would sparkle in the dappled sunshine. The undergrowth would rustle with a myriad of tiny creatures emerging into their cycle of birth and death.

Looking around her, she smiled with joy. Everywhere was bathed in a glow of optimism and expectancy as the earth stirred, almost awake after the long night of winter.

She had left Jerome asleep. Although tempted to stay and enjoy another coupling with him, the call of spring was too strong and she went to fetch her stave and a sack to gather what she could for food. Pulling back the curtain of ivy and fixing it so there was enough light to see into the area where she kept their winter store, she looked at the empty skins and bare rocks that had been filled with produce earlier.

Reaching for her stick, she looked at the notches she had made for each full moon with the accompanying marks alongside for her bleeding times. There were two gaps now and soon, in a few nights, there would be three moons without blood.

She had helped with birthing in the convent a dozen times. Destitute widows, poor women who had been abandoned or driven out by their husbands for suspected adultery and young girls, disowned because they had been raped like Marie, all came to the sisters in their time of desperate need. Often the poor starving women died, as did their tiny offspring, then the nuns said prayers for their souls and sang the requiem. Those that did survive might live on a few years whilst begging, or selling their bodies in order to feed the child.

If she had chosen to stay and take her vows she would not have known the ecstasy with Jerome, she would have lived and died ignorant of that special love, as many of the sisters were. Stepping out into the sunlight, she shivered involuntarily at the memory of a terrible, most horribly tortured birth when she had asked God to hasten the woman's demise and so end her suffering. For a frightened moment she admitted that, had she become a novice there would be no possibility of an agonising death when the seed of love bore fruit from between her bloody thighs.

She pulled on her goatskin boots and slung the sack over her shoulder, then, taking her staff she walked to the river and looked for fish in the burbling flow.

Having caught two small brown trout and taken an egg from the duck's nest in the reeds, she tramped through the woods and set traps for rabbits in three places. A young doe bounded past her followed by another larger female and two young males. She smiled in anticipation of catching one a little later in the season. Turning back towards the way she had come, she caught a glimpse of movement in a copse close by and paused to look and listen but neither saw nor heard any creature there. Several times whilst making her way to the dwelling she stopped and looked back, feeling uneasy, but without knowing why.

Jerome was milking the nanny when she arrived and grinned in delight on seeing the food she had brought. They made love whilst the fish baked in the fire, then fed each other morsels and giggled as they took turns to drink the egg beaten into a bowl of milk.

A woman from the nearest group of houses came when the sun was high and asked for help. Her husband had been unwell for most of the winter and now was in great pain.

She gave her dried horsetail and hawthorn berries, knowing that if the remedy worked a small cheese or loaf of bread would be brought to her in gratitude.

As the woman turned to leave she said, 'My man is a mason working on the church, he said Earl Reginald's men from the north-west were asking if a young man be seen hereabouts last fall.' Her eyes flicked to the pile of fodder beside the goats' shelter where Jerome had dived for cover when she arrived.

'I thank thee. I shall keep good watch.'

'Word has spread that he be somewhere in this valley.'

'I thank thee.'

Holding the herbs close to her chest the woman left.

Jerome emerged from his hiding place, looking young and vulnerable in his undisguised terror.

She held him close. Feeling his heart beating much as that of a creature caught in a trap, she kissed his trembling hands and reassured him that all would be well. 'Come,' she said gently, 'we must make thee ready for thy escape.'

He looked at her in horror 'I cannot leave thee unprotected, Caitlin.'

'Thy wound is healed and 'tis time to go.' Her heart was leaden as she pleaded, 'Go, please be gone. They will be here before long. I fear there was a stranger in the woods this very day.'

He made no further protestations or argument. His acceptance of her insistence hurt inside her soul, even as she praised him for his good sense in obeying her. Kissing him once on his quivering lips, she looked into his eyes. 'Follow the river southwards. The monks at Glastonbury will give sanctuary and further south-west is a way followed by the Knights Templar to the coast with places of refuge on the way.'

As he walked away from the dwelling, plainly dressed and with his unkempt beard and long hair, he now looked more like a local herdsman than the fine young squire who had limped into the valley all those months ago. 'Go with God,' she whispered, tasting the salt of her tears.

Lying awake throughout that night she heard the wind swing around to the north and wondered if Jerome had found sanctuary in the monastery. By the time birds nesting in the thatch roof celebrated the dawn she had accepted she would never see the father of her child again, nor ever know what

140

happened to him.

The following morning, whilst peering into the mirror and applying the recently purchased powder to her nose, the image suddenly changed. Although the blue eyes staring back at her were the same as usual, they were within a paler, thinner face with a high forehead from which the fair hair was pulled back tightly into a plait. Remembering the dream she was sad for a moment; then, blinking and seeing again the red hair curling around her solemn present-day face, she smiled and reached for the lipstick. That other girl belonged in dreams of the past – red-haired Foxy was preparing for her big adventure.

An hour later she stepped from a cab and thanked the driver. Then, feeling her new high-heeled shoes slip on the uneven cobbled street, Betty grabbed the handle of the door to stay upright. Thank goodness! If she'd fallen over that would have been the end of it. She'd have crept away and been too embarrassed to return. Taking a breath, she stepped towards the nearest doorway, where a very broad man in a grey overcoat and black felt hat with a wide brim was standing watching her. On the wall beside him was a brass plaque and, on getting closer, she read the engraved words: 'The Gentlemen's Relish'. Smiling confidently, she asked if she might speak with the person in charge of this establishment.

The man frowned. 'Could you tell me why yer wants ter see her, miss?'

'I'd like to work here.'

He looked astonished, then impressed, and

finally, embarrassed. 'I dunno, love, I mean all the girls is professionals, been at it for years, and the old dragon's, well, she's not an easy woman, not at all *easy* like.' He shifted uncomfortably from one foot to the other and cracked his knuckles. 'I'm not sayin' you don't look the part. You do. That barnet of yours is like a film star's. But to be honest, a shop'd be much more suitable for a nicely brought up young lady like you. I don't fink it's what you're used to, love.'

A long low car drew up near by and a smartly dressed man climbed out, called, 'Afternoon, Ricky old chap,' and gave Betty a long, appraising look.

'He'll know yer again,' Ricky muttered and raised a large hand in salute.

She watched with interest as the man went round to open the passenger door and, on seeing a beautiful woman climb out, knew this was exactly how she would like to make her arrival one day.

'See yer later.' The woman kissed the man lingeringly on the mouth, then turned, flicking her long blonde hair back, and walked towards them. 'Hi, Ricky.' She patted the man on his broad chest before greeting Betty. 'Hiya, sunshine. I'm Clancy, a little of what they fancy. What's yer moniker?'

'Pardon?'

'What's yer name?'

'I'm er, Foxy, and I'm looking for work.'

Ricky said, 'I told 'er it's no use. She'd be better off...'

'Shut up, Ricky.' Clancy grinned at her. 'Come

on, sunshine, what'yer say yer moniker was again?'

'Foxy.'

'Okay, follow me, down the apples and pears.' She pushed through the swing doors onto the red carpet of the stairs and led the way down them past a small ticket booth and on through two more swing doors into a tiny theatre with three rows of seats around a small stage. 'This is where the action is. You wait here a minute. I'll put in a word for yer with Madame La Fay. Whatever yer do, let her do the talking, don't say a dicky bird unless she asks a question and behave like a lady, even if you ain't one, okay?' She grinned. 'Actually you do sound posher'n what we're used to. The thing is we ain't had a new girl for ages and she don't know it yet, but there'll be a vacancy before long. You hang on in there, sunshine.' She knocked on a door and went in.

Betty gazed at the walls around her, admiring the photographs of beautiful women posing in various states of undress and was pleased to see none of them used fur in the way she planned.

The door opened and an older woman wearing a dark grey suit and a white blouse tied in a bow at the neck, looked her up and down, said, 'Nice barnet.' Then beckoned to her, adding, 'Come in, come in, let's 'ave a bucher's 'ook at yer.'

She walked into the room and stood in front of the desk on which Clancy was now sitting smoking a cigarette.

'Clancy thinks I should take yer on.' Madame La Faye exhaled cigarette smoke and asked, 'How old are yer?'

'Twenty-one.'

'I'll Adam and Eve yer, thousands wouldn't.' She laughed like a donkey. 'Neigh-ah, neigh-ah.' Then she gestured at Clancy, saying, 'This young lady thinks we ought to have a reserve in case she gets married.' She gave her an affectionate smile. 'Silly Miss Fitch!'

She understood that, it rhymed with bitch. It was a game with words and it would be good fun.

'I'm making no promises, and I'm not paying no more'n a few bob a week, but yer can come and make yerself useful. We could do with someone ter play the background records instead of the girls doing it fer each other and yer can brew Rosie Lee fer the staff, sell fags ter the customers, run errands, and clean up a bit, if yer not too proud that is.'

Clancy, who was behind Madame, winked and gave a slight, almost imperceptible nod.

Swallowing her disappointment, she gave the beaming smile she had practised for two days in the mirror and said, 'Of course I'm not too proud. Can I start today?'

'Take her with yer, Clancy, show her how ter wind up the gramophone, make sure she changes the needles regular.' As they were going through the door Madame La Faye asked, 'What's yer moniker?'

'Foxy.'

'Well that's a new one on me! Neigh-ah, neigh-ah, neigh-ah.'

After closing the door, Clancy asked, 'Why d'yer call yerself that?'

'I've got these foxtails I'm going to pose in.'

'Take a tip from me, sunshine, don't let on

144

about 'em until Madame La Fay offers yer the job. There's some as would 'alf inch an idea like that off of yer. Mum's the word, okay?'

'Okay.'

Clancy led the way through corridors, switching on lights as they went. 'No Jenny Linders in this place; like a dungeon it is. This filthy hole–' she threw open the door and illuminated a long narrow room lined with tables surmounted by large mirrors '–is the dressing room.' She spread her hands in the air and asked, 'Got any questions?'

'What's a barnet?'

'It's rhyming slang, Barnet Fair, hair, see?' Sounds of giggling and clattering shoes on the stone floor preceded three young women who she introduced, 'This here's FiFi, Zarina and Priscilla.'

Seeing them immediately remove their outer clothes and sit at the tables chatting and giggling while applying their makeup, she watched in amazement – this was exactly like a scene from *The Showgirl and the Duke!* A moment later, when a fourth woman, who looked older than the others arrived and raised an eyebrow at Clancy, she heard her whisper, 'Bit young isn't she?' before introducing herself as Jane.

On being given the task of playing records to provide a musical background for the acts, Foxy eagerly took up her position in the wings beside the small stage and began winding up the gramophone. FiFi the French maid appeared first and, to her amazement, slowly undressed. Zarina the princess followed, then Priscilla the bride, Lady

145

Jane the haughty chatelaine and finally Clancy the glamorous film star, all of whom removed most or all of their various costumes in front of a small audience of men.

This was not quite what she'd expected. The idea of posing with the fur draped around her for photographs had not included taking them off on a stage in front of men gawping like fishes at her. Now what should she do? Here she was in the place she'd planned to be with beautiful red hair – a film star's barnet, that's what Ricky said it was. Madame 'something or other' had said she could make herself useful for a few bob a week which was not what she'd had in mind, but, and it was a relief, that would be better than standing there on the stage with no clothes on. Kate would say to leave immediately, to not stay a minute longer, but she could just leave later and not come back – that would be the sensible thing to do. She could get a job in a shop like Ricky had suggested. This had all been a big mistake.

While picking up the litter left by the audience during the break between shows she was reviewing the acts in her mind when she realised that only FiFi and Priscilla had disrobed completely, and then only removed the final garment just as the curtain closed which meant that, despite craning forward, the men actually saw no more of their bodies than those of the others, who all wore a small triangle of pink cloth over their private hair. What a relief! She would do likewise – except she could keep a piece of fur strategically placed and tied on with string around her hips. Lara Crowe was seen in flimsy underwear and wearing shiny shorts and a little top when she was Vicky in *The Showgirl and the Duke;* a film star like her wouldn't worry about taking her clothes off, would she? Maybe it would be alright after all. She bent and picked up an empty cigarette packet with a flourish.

The door opened and a plump middle-aged woman wearing a plain grey skirt and green woollen twinset walked in and beamed at her through gold-rimmed spectacles. 'You must be Foxy.' She held out her hand. 'I'm Ethel,' then, getting closer, added, 'There'll be a few wolves after you!'

Chapter Eleven

Chamomile tea is calming and may help with the pain of childbirth.

A year later, whilst tidying the dressing room after the last show on Christmas Eve, she heard Clancy say, 'See what my young man give me last night, Foxy.' And, seeing the gold chain bracelet with a padlock shaped like a heart on her wrist, she replied, 'Oh, yes, it's lovely.'

'He's got ter go away up north fer Christmas so he give it me a bit early.'

'That's a shame.'

'When we're married I'll go too.'

'Of course.' She looked at the ring on the little finger of Clancy's right hand. 'That's nice.'

Removing it and handing it to her, Clancy said, 'It's not valuable, but I like it. I've had it since I was ten; it fitted my middle finger in them days.'

'It's a lover's knot... Oh!' She saw the small girl preening in front of a mirror. 'You look like a little bride, was it fancy dress?'

Clancy laughed. 'No, silly! I was being confirmed.'

'Really? We didn't dress up like that.'

'You obviously wasn't Catholic. Me dad give me the ring. He must've saved for months to buy it.'

Seeing a sailor knocked overboard by a huge metal hook swinging across the bow of a ship, she said, 'He died at sea, didn't he?'

'What! How d'yer know that?'

'Oh, just a guess.'

'Yer'll have to come up with sunnink better 'n that.' Clancy turned to Jane. 'Here, come and listen to this. Foxy can see things, she knew me dad drowned.'

Jane was already holding out her ring of silver with four tiny garnets. 'Please tell me what you see, Foxy.'

Taking the ring, she saw a soldier and a young girl embracing. Then, to her horror, the man's eyes gazed blindly out of a severed head lying in the mud with the rain running like tears down his smooth white cheeks. She was reeling from shock and holding onto the rickety dressing table when the terrible sight of bloody carnage faded and she saw the girl weeping and cuddling a tiny baby. Then, through a gradually clearing mist, a woman appeared wearing a white dress with a

148

bridal veil and at her side, smiling and stooping to offer her his arm, was a tall thin man with bright auburn hair. Allowing her eyes to come back into focus, she smiled. 'I don't know when or where, but you'll be married.'

'What! That's the most amazing Christmas present I've ever had, thanks, Foxy.'

Clancy was holding out her ring again. 'What about me and my boyfriend's wedding?'

She could see the pleading look in her eyes and knew what her friend wanted to hear. Overwhelmed with foreboding she said, 'I can't promise to see what you want.'

'Go on, 'ave a go, Foxy, there's a dear.'

'But I might not–' She broke off, knowing refusal was impossible. Taking the lover's knot ring again she closed her eyes and immediately saw her friend in a dressing gown, kneeling on the floor in a small room and dementedly pulling at her blonde hair. She couldn't say her mouth would be distorted and there would be lipstick all around it and on her teeth. She couldn't say there would be lines of mascara down her cheeks and, above all, she couldn't tell her she would bang her forehead with her fists and then tear out clumps of hair and throw them onto the brown lino. 'I can't–' she took a deep breath '–do any more. I don't know why. I saw your father so clearly. He looked like you, such a handsome man. It was an accident. He didn't stand a chance.'

Clancy looked disappointed. 'If yer can't see it, me wedding that is, don't mean it won't happen, does it?'

'Of course not,' she reassured her, 'I get

random pictures. I can't choose what to see and I've only done it a few times. And–' she shrugged '–I might be wrong.'

'But you've been right sometimes, haven't yer?'

'Sometimes.' This was getting more and more difficult. Why hadn't she kept her mouth shut in the first place?

'Well, I want to believe you're right,' Jane said dreamily.

Needing to escape, she went to the door, explaining, 'I'm just going out to post a card to my sister,' then ran out of the building to the nearby pillarbox. If only she had someone to confide in, but there was no one who could understand about the sight she had had of Clancy – no one except Kate, who she would never see again, not until she was rich and famous.

That night when going to bed in her damp basement room, she was still upset by the experience with Clancy's ring and, feeling in need of escape from the anxiety of this present life, she took the small piece of wood and placed it under her pillow...

She had toiled ceaselessly throughout the fresh bright springtime, and, although slower and more tired in the balmy days of blowsy summer, managed to make good provision for the winter. Huge piles of dead wood were ready for the fire, cheeses were stored and some early berries were fermented with honey. The child would be born when much of nature's bounty was ready to be harvested and, in case she was unable to collect it, she allowed three more male kids than usual to survive in order to kill them when they were needed for food.

The tide of water within her was pulled by the full moon and the baby began its perilous journey from the safety of her womb. Memories of the women suffering in the convent made her fearful for a short while and she wept for the mother who would have been with her had she not swung like a rag doll from the oak tree. She made up the fire and covered it with turf so it would burn slowly for many hours. Water for washing, linen with which to wrap the child and the newly sharpened knife to cut the cord were close at hand.

Those who had gone before had suffered like this and in time were buried in the tomb by the very child of that birthing. She had seen their bones gleaming in torchlight when her grandmother had been placed with them.

Kneeling beside the fire she asked for those dead ancestors to keep her company in this lonely travail and from the wisp of smoke out of the fire she saw a figure form and twirl around before coming to sit beside her. All through that night and on into the day beyond, the woman gave comfort with her gentle presence. When the final effort was needed to help the child break free, the quiet spirit whispered, 'Push now,' and again, 'Push now, my darling.'

The small being was blue. No! No! Not dead! This child must not die! She grasped her and watched as the small mouth opened, the baby changed colour and cried out her willingness to live. She lay back a moment, holding the warm little body whilst the source of her life within the womb slithered onto the sweet grass beneath her, and, after tying the cord with *her hair and cutting it, she placed the little mouth to her breast. She was playing her part in the dance of life just as those who had gone before played theirs.*

Remembering this dream memory whilst lying in bed on Christmas morning Foxy thought of Kate and wondered if she might be expecting a second baby by now and, if so, whether there might soon be a girl to follow on. It felt good to know she had again written, albeit briefly and with no return address, to her sister and Charles. She had been working at the club for a whole year now so this would be the second card since the Gardenia Lady made her promise to write. They might be pleased to know she had thought of them and wished them well even if they wouldn't want her back living in Old Myrtles – not that she'd wish to go of course.

That afternoon she was feeling lonelier than at any time since leaving the furrier's a year earlier when Jane arrived and threw a gold crepe evening frock onto the bed, saying, 'It's too tight for me and I thought you could wear it for the party on New Year's Eve.'

'It's wonderful! I don't have anything as glamorous as this.' She picked it up and held it against her whilst looking in the mirror. This was the best Christmas present she could wish for.

'It will suit you very well and set off your red hair.'

'My Barnet Fair you mean.' She grinned. 'I'll put a kettle on Beatrice for some Rosie Lee.'

Jane sat in the armchair and chatted until the tea was made and then, having waited for her to settle onto the end of the bed, she said, 'I'm really worried about Clancy and I don't know what to do. I'm sure she thought this bloke was going to come up with an engagement ring by now and when I called half an hour ago she was really, really drunk and had obviously been crying. Has she said anything to you?'

'No, she's been a bit preoccupied lately. I thought she was feeling sad and missing her family at Christmas.'

'Is that how you feel?'

'Yes, and I don't know why, really I don't. I wanted to get away from them and I wouldn't go back to the village for anything.' She looked enquiringly at her. 'What about you? Are you missing yours?'

'No, I don't have a family any more.' Jane rubbed the garnet and silver ring on her right hand, then said hesitantly, 'I wondered if you saw something about my past when you held this.'

'Yes.'

'Well?'

'Sometimes there's too much pain and I don't like to say.'

'Like when Clancy wanted to know about her wedding?'

She stared at the threadbare rug on the stone floor. Could she tell her about the sight of Clancy tearing out her hair? No, that was private. Gran would never divulge the secrets she had seen when reading people's hands and no more would Kate tell of the sights she saw in the tealeaves. 'I ... I can't say.'

Jane bit her lip. 'I've been a bit worried you'd

153

tell the others.'

Looking up and directly into the sad, brown eyes, she shook her head as she replied, 'Never. What I see is only for me and the person concerned.'

'Thank goodness! I've never told anyone what happened to me, not even Clancy. I had a baby when I was sixteen, did you see that?'

'Yes.'

'He'd be fifteen now. They took him away from me. My father said I'd disgraced the family and threw me out.' She took a handkerchief from her handbag and dabbed at her eyes. 'My sweetheart never knew about him. He was killed in France.'

'He had fair hair and blue eyes.'

'You saw him! He was such a handsome fellow, wasn't he?'

'Very, very handsome.'

They sat in silence for a few minutes until Jane said, 'I was wondering, you really did see me getting married, didn't you?'

'Yes, really and truly I saw you–' she grinned '–with my own mince pies.'

On the evening of the party she changed into Jane's frock and, arranging the long red curls resting on her bare shoulders as she peered into the murky mirror on the wardrobe door, revelled in her glamorous image. This was how she'd wanted to look for so long. Maybe there would be a film director in the audience who would see her wearing it and want her to star in one of his movies. If that happened then she wouldn't have to do her act, which in a way would be a bit disappointing after all the practising she'd done in her room in front of the mirror, but at least she wouldn't have to pose in front of the leering audience – that would be a relief!

After the show ended at ten thirty, Madame clapped her hands and shouted, 'Okay, the grubby macks have gone. Let's get on with the party. Fetch the champagne, girls, we're gaspin'!'

Foxy followed Clancy to a table beside the stage and watched as she opened a bottle and carefully poured the fizzing liquid into glasses, then, taking a tray of drinks, she walked around offering them to the guests who were mostly regular visitors to the club.

When a very attractive man with dark curly hair arrived and was greeted with enthusiasm by Madame La Fay, she watched with interest, wondering who he was.

Jane wound up the gramophone and the sound of a quickstep filled the room. A podgy man with a monocle hanging around his neck asked Foxy to 'Do him the honour' and she apprehensively agreed. Her experience of dancing was limited to a few lessons from Clancy when things were quiet and this was the first attempt to follow a man. To her surprise they stayed together quite well and were progressing even better with a waltz when a deep voice said, 'Sorry, old chap, this is an excuse-me.'

Turning to face her new partner, her heart missed a beat as the man who had been talking to Madame earlier pulled her towards him and enfolded her in his arms. He was like Douglas

Fairbanks senior, handsome and suave, but with darker, jet black hair and moustache. As they melded together to the music, she revelled in the scent of his sweat mingled with shaving soap and the feel of his hand on her back. This was a moment she'd dreamed of for so long. They made a perfect couple, as glamorous as in any movie, he in his dinner jacket and black bow tie and she in her gold evening frock.

'I'm told you're called Foxy.'

His voice was even better than his looks – if she closed her eyes, she could imagine he was the film actor Leslie Howard.

'And your name?'

'Gerald, Gerry to my friends, and, I hope–' he squeezed her hand and pressed slightly on her back '–to you.'

'Happy New Year, Gerry.'

A babble of conversation surrounded Madame La Fay. 'Remember that dinner at the Troc?'

'Those were the days, what!'

'I remember when she first pulled out the handkerchief singing "The boy in the gallery". Brought the house down it did. I don't know how we'd have got through the Great War without her.'

Foxy was in a swaying and swirling dream as the music came to a stop. To her surprise Madame appeared beside her, saying, 'Excuse us a moment, Gerry, I need a word in the office with my sizzling redhead.'

Oh my God! Was Madame annoyed because she had danced with her special man? As the door closed behind them she said, 'I'm sorry, I really didn't mean...'

'Shut up and listen. He's rich, he's important, he's powerful and he'll never marry yer. Understand?'

She nodded.

'Never take risks. Make sure he always uses a Johnny. Will yer do that?'

She gulped and nodded again. What on earth was a Johnny? Jane or Clancy would tell her.

'Never, ever take money for sleeping with a man. Have yer got that?'

'Yes.'

'If he offers yer diamonds or a gold bracelet like what Clancy got, that, my beautiful girl–' Madame smiled '–is a different matter entirely! Now go and have a nice time.'

At midnight he kissed her and held her very close. 'Happy New Year, Foxy. I think nineteen thirty-three is going to be a big improvement on thirty-two.'

'Oh dear, have you been suffering from this terrible depression?'

He shook his head. 'I'm thinking of other ways in which life might improve.'

They danced to three more records and then he said, 'I wonder if I might give you a lift home?'

She was too nervous to reply and nodded before fetching her coat.

He ushered her to an enormous black car and held the door open. Sinking onto the seat she closed her eyes and savoured the scents of leather and wax polish. This was the life she'd imagined whilst planning her escape to London. All her dreams were coming true. He probably wasn't a film director, but Madame said he was rich and powerful so he might know one. If only Jane and Clancy hadn't left before her she'd have asked them what a Johnny was.

When Gerry parked the car outside a block of flats and suggested a nightcap, she agreed and accompanied him up the stairs and into an elegantly furnished apartment on the second floor where she sank into a huge sofa with squashy cushions and accepted the glass of champagne he immediately poured for her.

They toasted the New Year again and then each other. There was a long pause. He rose and took the half-empty glass from her hand and placed it on a table nearby. 'I thought,' he said sitting very close to her, 'I thought I was going to be really lonely tonight, but–' he ran a fingertip from her index finger along her arm to her neck and down inside her dress '–I'm hoping this could be the start of a mutually beneficial friendship.'

This was like a scene in *The Showgirl and the Duke*. Gerry had fallen in love with her despite the difference in their age and class. This was so romantic. This was it! When he kissed her and pulled up her skirt with his other hand she put her arms around his neck, willingly offering her body to him.

Chapter Twelve

Tea made with the flower heads of red clover
may improve sore throats and coughs.

Clancy was wearing her overcoat while sitting at
the dressing-room mirror, plucking her eyebrows. Her voice was thick with cold as she
asked, 'Still seein' him are yer?'

Foxy waited whilst she blew her nose and
coughed before replying that she was.

'I hope you make him use a Johnny.'

'Of course.' Actually he called it a French letter
and she hadn't said a word to him.

'So does he come back ter your place?'

'No, he's been staying in an apartment belong-
ing to a friend who's gone abroad and says he can
use it for the next year or so. He's going to visit
his father for Easter so I won't be seeing him for
a few days.'

Jane, who was lying on the floor with her legs
up against the wall and her eyes closed, frowned
as she enquired, 'Nice to yer, is he?'

'Oh yes, a real gentleman.' He was even more
posh than Charles and much more charming, in
fact he was a toff in every way.

Clancy blew her nose then asked, 'Where's he
live?'

'I told you he's staying...'

'No, I mean when he goes home at weekends.

Madame said he's an MP so he comes up The Smoke for Parliament. He's got a nice big pile somewhere in the country I'll bet.'

'I don't know. I expect he'll tell me sometime.' Of course he would tell her and not only that, he would take her there. It would be exactly like the film she'd seen with the servants all lined up at the front door ready to curtsey to the Lord and Lady of the grand house. Madame had said he'd never marry her, but somehow, by some miracle, he'd find a way. Love conquered all obstacles in its way didn't it? He was always desperate to get her to bed so he must be in love with her. Surely he was planning and scheming how they could marry!

'When I'm a respectably married trouble and strife–' Clancy stopped to sneeze and continued, 'I'll invite you and Milord to luncheon and we can have muffins with bloater paste and caviar sandwiches and posh food like that.'

'That would be nice. So, d'you think he'll pop the question soon?'

'Oh yeah, he's been dropping hints for months.'

Jane opened one eye. 'What sort of hints, Clance?'

'Oh, like he's working extra hard 'cos he needs the money to get a house in a few months, that sort of thing.'

'Where's he live now?'

'The suburbs, north somewhere, I think.'

'Have you been to his home?'

'No, he said his landlady would object to me going there. Very strict she is and won't allow lady visitors unless they're relatives.'

160

Jane opened both eyes and suggested, 'You could pretend to be his sister.'

'I thought of that, but he said he's already had his skin an' blister to visit.'

'Have you met her?'

'No.' She blew her nose. 'Not yet.'

Foxy said, 'If he's saving money for a house, he's obviously serious. What sort of engagement ring would you like?'

'A nice solitaire diamond. What about you, Jane?'

'Don't ask me. No one's ever going to propose to me, let alone buy me a ring.'

'Yes they will, Foxy said so.'

Jane swung her legs down to the floor. 'I'll believe it when I see it. Gawd's truth! This place is a mess. The paint's peeling so bad you can see where my heels have rubbed it off.' She looked at the garnet ring on her right hand. 'I can't imagine wearing anything but this. I've no idea what I'd like.'

'You can't go wrong with diamonds–' Clancy held up her left hand and pretended to admire it '–they're classy they are.' She giggled and coughed. 'Ethel's got an enormous rock she won at cards. I wouldn't mind having that one I can tell yer!'

Foxy said, 'I've seen an emerald surrounded by diamonds in the Burlington Arcade. That's what I'd like.'

'Expecting to catch a rich bloke are yer?' Jane asked.

Clancy sniffed. 'Milord could afford the odd ring or two. She's got prospects, ain't yer, sunshine?'

Foxy grinned and pictured Gerry in a pin-striped suit opening the door as he escorted her into the jeweller's. She was wearing an elegant frock in her favourite shade of green with a fox fur draped around her shoulders and a small hat perched at an angle over one eye showing off her bright red hair. As she sat down by the counter and peeled off her kid gloves, the jeweller brought a tray of rings and set it before her. She sighed and agreed, 'Yes, I think I have.'

That night, lying awake with a tickle in her throat and a slight headache, she groaned at the prospect of suffering with a cold the following day. Then, recalling the conversation with Clancy and Jane and what she had seen in their rings, she switched on the light and took the bundle of treasures from the rickety cupboard beside the bed. The garnets in the ring were bigger than those of Jane's but they were not the emerald and diamonds she longed for and the pearl on the gold pin seemed rather small. She replaced them, feeling disappointed. Picking up the cameo she heard her grandmother say, 'That cold'll go on your chest if you're not careful. Red clover might help with the sore throat tomorrow, but sweet violet tea's what you'll need for that chest of yourn, mark my words.'

She remembered the scent of violets when picking them in the hedgerows around the village with Kate and felt a sudden deep longing for her sister. Was she picking and drying plants as she used to? She had stopped for a while after the scandal when Charles's wife accused her and Gran of giving a servant from The Grange some herbs to get rid of a baby. She smiled at the memory of looking for the jar in which the old woman had kept the special mix of herbs and how they had discovered she had given raspberry leaves to the girl instead because she guessed it was a trap.

Turning from the broken brooch, she picked up the sliver of wood and lay back on the pillow. Maybe something interesting had happened in the valley...

She salivated whilst placing a brown fish over the fire to cook. Then, as soon as the delicious aroma told her it was ready, she pulled it to her and soon devoured it.

Feeling contented now the gnawing hunger had been satisfied, she leaned back and, looking at her sleeping baby, ached with love. Seeing wisps of hair glinting in the firelight, she wondered if the child would have hair the colour of oak trees in autumn, like Jerome.

Although tired and longing for sleep, she reached for the rosary the sisters had given her when leaving them and fingered the wooden beads. Across the moors her dear friends would be sad, for this was the day Our Lord was crucified. There would have been only a thin gruel to eat all day, not even fish from the Abbot's pond in Mere as had sometimes been the case on Fridays and which she had liked and preferred to the roasted birds taken from the pigeon loft at the end of the garden. All the nuns would be weeping and grieving. On Sunday when the moon was full, everyone would be happy and greeting each other with a cheerful, 'The Lord is risen' each time they met in the garden or the refectory; and even in the cloisters where silence was usually kept, they would whisper the

163

greeting to one another and Marie would smile and reveal the gap where her uncle had knocked her teeth out. She passed a few beads through her fingers muttering the words, 'Hail Mary, full of grace...'

A tear trickled down her nose and she wiped it away. Suddenly, she was weeping uncontrollably. Her friend was in the convent. Jerome had fled the country unaware he had fathered a child. Her mother had been killed and then buried in a cave by drunken men. Sister Elfreda had said she must forgive all her enemies, but how could she forgive the murder of her mother and the violation of her own body? How could she forget that she too had taken a life and had pushed the miller's bloody corpse down onto the remains of her ancestors?

Throwing the beads to one side she lay down beside her sleeping child. She had lost mother, lover and friend, but she had Myrtle, the daughter she had named to remind her of the tree growing in the convent garden.

Awakening to find she was lying curled around her pillow, Foxy remembered the deep loneliness and her love for the baby. Then, feeling the painful swelling in her throat and the thump of blood in her temples, she groaned in misery at the realisation that she had caught Clancy's cold in the present lifetime.

Pushing through the swing doors ten days later and seeing Madame La Fay leaning against the closed office door, she put down the carrier bag containing a new frock, saying, 'You don't look well. Have you caught the cold too?'

'Ethel says we have ter keep going. Can't have bad publicity and that. I don't know, I suppose she's right.' Madame's mouth quivered and she swallowed hard before continuing, 'I thought we ought ter close fer a week at least, but no, she won't hear of it. Says we can close today and then carry on as usual.'

She frowned, wondering if her employer had been drinking the brandy she kept in the filing cabinet for emergencies.

Madame La Fay went on, 'You'll have to do her act. Can yer do that?'

'Whose act?'

'Clancy's, of course, didn't I say?'

Opening her mouth, Foxy shaped the word 'why?', but no sound came out of her throat.

'Silly little cow believed he'd marry her 'cos she was knocked up. Why don't no one listen ter me?' Madame reached into her pocket and drew out a gold case, removed a cigarette and lit it, then, while exhaling the smoke, indicated the room behind her. 'Jane's in a terrible state. Lives in the same block. A cleaner smelled gas.'

Hearing a moan from the other side of the door, she gently pushed Madame to one side and went into the office to find Jane sitting on the floor rocking back and forth. 'There was hair all over the floor,' she moaned, 'oh God! She'd pulled it out. She'd pulled it out!'

Foxy knelt down and held her and although able to feel the warmth of the woman in her arms, her own body was cold and numb as she murmured, 'Poor darling, poor darling.' She had known this would happen. She'd seen her friend tearing out her hair. Could she have prevented the tragedy? Oh God! Why had she done nothing to help her?

After several minutes Jane haltingly explained that Clancy had left a note stating she no longer wished to live and had turned on the gas cooker in the early hours of the morning.

Foxy heard footsteps thud in the corridor and a deep voice exclaiming, 'Christ almighty!'

When the door swung open Madame asked Foxy, 'Well, can yer do it?'

Looking up at her Foxy could hear Ricky in the corridor, cracking his knuckles continuously. She gulped and struggled to speak, 'Yes, yes. I'll have to go back in a taxi and collect my stuff.'

'You can do her act with her...'

'No, Madame,' she interrupted, 'I must show you my act first. If you really don't like it then I'll copy her. She knew I had my own ideas and she told me to keep them quiet until the right time. I just never thought, I mean ... I didn't expect it would be like this.'

Two hours later Foxy looked at her reflection in the dressing-room mirrors and recoiled in horror. The eyes rounded with shock stared back at her and the scarlet lips she had pouted so pro-vocatively hung open in ugly dismay as she saw her body draped in the collection of fox tails and tippets she had taken from Mr Bradon's shop. She couldn't stand in front of an audience like this and she certainly could not remove most of her furs – that was out of the question. Practising an imaginary act on her own in front of the murky little mirror that needed re-silvering had been fun, but seeing herself clearly like this was completely different. This was real, not just play-acting alone in her basement room.

She shook her head. It was no use. She couldn't do it. She must go and tell Madame La Faye immediately. Quickly slipping on her squirrel coat she ran to the office and, finding Madame and Ethel sitting either side of the desk, she stammered, 'I'm s-sorry, I can't...' then found she was weeping uncontrollably.

'There now–' Ethel hugged her '–there, there, love. We know how fond you were of Clancy and I expect you feel you're being disloyal taking her place but she'd want you to do it for her.'

'Yeah–' Madame La Faye put a glass into her hand '–take a swig of this, Foxy love. I always 'ad a bit of Dutch courage before I went on and so did Clancy. She was a real trouper that one.' She gave a sigh and added, 'What a waste of a beautiful life!'

Raising the glass to her lips Foxy breathed in the potent aroma of brandy and took a gulp of the golden liquid, then another and another until the glass was empty.

'That's a good girl!' Madame refilled all three glasses and then raised hers. 'Ter Clancy what will be sorely missed!'

'To Clancy!' Ethel and Foxy echoed and then they all drank in silence for a while.

'Come on then. Let's see this act of yours, Foxy.' Madame drained her glass and put it down on the desk. Ethel did likewise and they both walked out of the room and into the small theatre.

167

Feeling suddenly warm and relaxed Foxy followed them and stepped onto the stage. Looking down at the two women sitting in the middle of the front row she found her knees were trembling uncontrollably. What if they disliked her performance? Maybe it would be easier to copy Clancy's act, she knew every move by heart, but would she want to do that when her friend had just died so horribly – did she want to strip in front of an audience anyway? No, she didn't, but she couldn't let everyone down. They expected her to do it. She'd said she would and now there was no escape.

Madame lit a cigarette, inhaled and said, 'Come on, Foxy love, we ain't got all day.'

Focussing on the smoke wafting over Madame's head, she allowed the coat to slide slowly off her right shoulder and then, imagining she was practising in front of the patchy mirror in her dingy basement with Beatrice glowing beside her, she gave her performance.

When she looked down again into the audience she saw Ethel beaming up at her. Madame was also smiling and nodding her head, saying, 'We'll 'ave ter get some classy music ter play in the background. This girl's got style!'

Three days after her debut, Gerry, who had watched the show through the window in Madame La Faye's office, drove Foxy to the flat afterwards. On arrival, he placed a large box on the bed saying, 'That cheap grey squirrel coat of yours may be alright for performing in, but I think you should have something better to wear when you're with me.'

Lifting the lid she took out the fur jacket and gasped, 'It's like thistledown!' Mr Bradon never had anything as beautiful as this in his shop, but she couldn't tell him that. Clancy would be so impressed tomorrow... No, she would never see it. Oh God! Clancy wouldn't see it because she was dead.

'I was buying a tippet for–' He stopped and lit a cigarette.

'For who?'

He gulped smoke into his lungs and exhaled, before saying, 'My daughter, Henrietta.' He carefully tapped the ashtray on the bedside table. 'I was buying a parting gift. She's off to boarding school in Switzerland.' He removed his clothes and lay on the bed watching her.

She looked down at the fur and stroked it. So there was a daughter and presumably also a wife. This was the moment to leave. That's what her sister would do. Kate would say there was a big difference between her situation, where she was living in sin with Charles who wanted to marry her but couldn't because his wife refused to divorce him even though they were separated, and this situation where she was having a love affair with a married man who was still living with his wife. Her sister would hand back the jacket and make a dignified exit.

She began undoing her suspenders. There was still time to leave. While slowly peeling off her stockings she remembered Gerty in the shop on Christmas Day and then continued to undress. Once naked she turned the jacket inside out and put it on. The fur did indeed feel wonderful against her skin, and, as she sat astride Gerry, she said, 'It's the best present I've ever had. Thank you, darling.'

She had her own life to live, and Clancy would have understood even if Kate did not. Gerry must know rich and famous people who might have contacts in Hollywood or, better still, he would get divorced and marry her.

Chapter Thirteen

Wormwood tea may be effective in the treatment of worms in children.

Foxy was balanced on a small seat that folded down from the partition between the taxi driver and the passengers, and was therefore travelling backwards. Craning her neck sideways and peering out of the car window, she said, 'London seems to go on for ever.'

Ricky, who was facing her and sitting with his shoulders hunched between Jane and Ethel, replied, 'We're going from the West End to the East End.'

Ethel muttered, 'And, as yer can see, they're two different worlds.'

When the driver stopped the vehicle by an enormous tenement block and opened a map, several children gathered around, staring inside.

Ricky sneered. 'Scabby little scallywags!'

'Poor little buggers.' Ethel sighed. 'None of 'em looks like they've ever had a hot dinner in their whole lives.'

Jane said, 'I s'pect they've all got worms.'

Madame wound down the front window, threw a few copper coins onto the pavement and looked sad as she watched the urchins scrabble for the money.

Foxy was aware of a grubby little girl standing on the kerb staring in at her with dull, expressionless blue eyes. Looking at the thin shoulders from which a torn cotton frock several sizes too big for her hung down to almost reach the dirty bare feet, she reached into her handbag and took out a florin. Opening the window she held out the coin and watched as the child's eyes flashed into life while her small hand reached out and took it.

'Her old man'll spend it on drink,' the driver said, pressing the accelerator and revving the engine.

Foxy closed the window and, seeing two pale lines running from the girl's eyes down her grimy cheeks, gulped back her own tears. When Charles gave her two guineas on his return to the village after he'd lost all his money, she had saved them for her escape to London. This undernourished child would never have the luxury of such selfishness. 'I think she'll give it to her mother for food,' she said and blew a kiss as they drove away.

After a few minutes they arrived at the church, went inside and filed into a pew where, on looking around her at the other mourners, Foxy felt uncomfortably incongruous. When compared

171

with the family members in the front pew who were clad in obviously new, very cheap, black clothes and creaking shoes, she and the group from the club were obscenely over-dressed. If Clancy could see them, would she forgive their sumptuous display of bad taste? She might laugh and say they were done up like the dog's dinner, maybe she'd know a term in rhyming slang to describe them – done up like what? Tarts maybe – that's probably what the mourners were thinking.

Very soon a coffin covered in a large spray of white lilies was carried in by four men and placed on trestles in the aisle. Foxy breathed in the scent which overwhelmed her own expensive perfume.

When the priest told the congregation how he remembered Bridget Clancy looking like an angel at her confirmation, Foxy thought of holding Clancy's ring and seeing the pretty child dressed as a little bride and then the distraught woman kneeling on the floor surrounded by handfuls of blonde hair.

She stood with everyone else when they sang a familiar hymn, but found her throat too tight to join them. How could the God to whom these people were praying allow a beautiful young woman to suffer the pain of that demented dying? Clancy knew streets like the one where they had seen the children. She would have experienced the same poverty and humiliation. Had she preferred death to returning and bringing up a child in such deprivation and squalor? There would have been ways to make a little money, scrubbing floors for richer people in smarter, cleaner areas for example, and the most obvious, the dirtiest job of all, selling her beautiful young body at random to any man no matter how ugly, smelly or repulsive. Had she rejected those possibilities and chosen to take the leap into darkness instead?

In the still moment after the organ wheezed into silence, the sun suddenly burst through a stained-glass window to her right. A ray of exquisite pink light shone on the coffin, colouring the lilies with a faint rose blush. Seeing their fragile beauty and knowing they were separated by a thin piece of wood from the pale face that had once been so lovely and alive, she was suddenly made angry at this squandering of a bright and beautiful life. Inside her head she screamed, 'Oh Clancy, Clancy, a little of what you fancy, it's such a waste!' Overwhelmed with emotion, she ran from the church into the graveyard and, crouching behind a large Victorian sarcophagus, wept for her friend.

Madame found her after a while and said, 'Come on, Foxy, love, they've buried her and we've ter go and visit with her family.'

'No, I can't bear it.'

'Yes, yer can fer Clancy's sake.' The older woman pulled her upright and held her close for a moment, before taking her arm and leading her to where the other mourners were already walking through the lichgate onto the pavement. The procession crossed the road and soon arrived at a tiny terraced house where Mrs Clancy greeted her saying, 'My Bridget was such a good girl, Foxy. She sent me money every week without fail.' Pressing an envelope into her hand, she added, 'There was a list. She wanted you to have this.' She gulped back tears. 'I can't believe it, just can't take it in. She was a good girl. I'd have cared for her and the baby. I'd have found a way...' She turned and disappeared into the scullery.

Opening the envelope Foxy took out the familiar twist of gold and slipped it onto the little finger of her right hand. Then, feeling unable to cope with the people crowding around her, she went through the scullery and out into the small cobbled yard. Three women who were chatting and laughing while waiting by a lavatory door fell silent on seeing her and lowered their eyes when she smiled nervously at them.

Knowing these poor people in their cheap ill-fitting clothes turned their tired faces away from her because they thought Foxy was beneath them, she felt suddenly and deeply hurt for Clancy. They had judged her the same way no doubt, probably thought she was a prostitute, a loose woman who got what she deserved! They were poor but 'respectable'. They put up with their own miserable lot and had no time for the likes of Foxy with her dyed hair and expensive clothes. Well, they were wrong! She wasn't a tart. She loved one man and only one. This was probably how people would have treated the heroine in *The Showgirl and the Duke*, but she wouldn't care what people thought and the Duke didn't care either, he married her. In years to come, when these women saw pictures of Foxy in the newspapers with her husband, Gerald Mottram, they'd be sorry!

Looking through a gate hanging off its hinges, she could see a narrow alleyway running along between the back of this terrace and another. Quickly skirting the silent women she hurried out of the yard and, on reaching the other side of the wall, heard them resume their chatter once more – no doubt talking about her.

Walking along the muddy track between the two lines of houses she remembered the description her sister Kate had given of the home where she had lived when small and tried to imagine herself as a little girl and Kate as a young woman about her own age. She'd seen a photograph of her parents and knew her own face and hair resembled their father's, whilst Kate's dark beauty was the image of their mother's. There had been brothers, too, one who died and one who went to Canada and wrote occasional letters giving news of his children.

A boy called from one of the yards, 'Betty, where are you?'

She turned towards the sound – could this be a ghost?

A girl screeched, 'Coo – ee, can't catch me!'

Screams of laughter and sounds of scuffling were followed by a woman shouting, 'I told yer ter get the bleedin' washin'. It's not much ter bleedin' ast is it?'

A few yards further on she stepped past a battered pram minus its wheels and then into another alley leading back to the street. Emerging onto the pavement she was aware of two men sitting on a wall watching her, and was horrified when they jumped down and fell into step either side of her.

'Needin' company, darlin'?' one said, taking

hold of her right arm.

Her throat was dry with terror.

'We're good at that we are.' The other man grabbed her left arm and touched Foxy's patent leather handbag. 'We'll take care of yer. A nice young lady like you shouldn't be out alone.' They stopped. 'Live just 'ere we do.'

As they began dragging her into a gateway, she saw the big black car parked at the far end of the road. 'Help!' she croaked and then shouted much louder. A hand was clamped over her mouth and she bit into the flesh. The man on her right screamed with pain and let go of her arm, the other turned towards her and she grabbed his genitals as hard as she could. Someone was running. The metal tips on their shoes were ringing on the paving stone. The men let go and a door banged.

'Bastards!' Ricky shouted. 'I'll get the law on yer.'

She staggered into the bouncer's arms, blinded by tears.

The chauffeur, who was close behind, asked breathlessly, 'You alright, miss?'

'Yes.' She wiped her eyes and looked at the blank windows of the house. 'I'm perfectly alright, but I might not have been if you hadn't turned up.'

'Should we call the coppers?' Ricky asked.

The chauffeur shrugged. 'I dunno. Might cause more trouble than it's worth. What'yer fink, miss?'

'No, don't make a fuss.' She turned away. 'I shouldn't have gone along there like that. It was my own fault.'

All three walked to the car, where the chauffeur opened the door and placed Foxy's handbag on the seat saying, 'You was lucky we come out for a fag, miss.'

She sank into the leather upholstery and, remembering the rancid breath of the miller and the feeling of degradation and violation in that other life long ago, felt tears sliding down her face. These men would have made a sport of it just as Earl Reginald's men had and might have knocked out her teeth as Marie's uncle had done to her, or worse, much worse.

That night after the last performance, Madame called her into the office and said, 'I don't ever want to go through that again. No more strolling about in rough areas like that. They might not have killed yer, but you'd have been in a sorry state after they'd finished with yer.'

'Yes, I was stupid, I should've known better.'

'Ricky done yer proud, I reckon the sight of him put the fear of God into 'em.'

'I was so grateful to him.' She leaned against the desk. 'I wonder what Gerry would've done to them if he'd been there?'

Madame shrugged. 'Run a mile I 'spect. He never was an 'ero.'

'So you've known him a long time?'

'Donkey's years. Ever since he was a stage-door Johnny a long time ago.' Madame gave a kindly smile. 'I expect he'll be sympathetic when he hears about it tonight.'

'I'm not seeing him 'cos he's gone on a duty visit to an aunt. He would've defended me though,

177

wouldn't he?'

'Yeah, course he would, love. I was only joking.'
Madame lit a cigarette and added, 'There's sunnink else I want ter say. Even more important. If
yer gets in the family way yer come and tell me,
promise?'

'Yes, Madame, I promise.' It wouldn't be necessary of course. Gerry took care of her now and
one day they would have beautiful babies – when
they were married.

'Good. I know I'm regarded as an old dragon
round here but I want yer to remember I'm quite
a nice, loving sort of dragon,' and she laughed her
donkey's laugh.

Later, lying awake in her basement room and
unable to stop thinking about the experience
after the funeral, Foxy took out the bundle of
treasures. Maybe the sliver of wood could bring a
memory from that earlier life that would distract
her mind from that of the present...

*She sensed there was someone waiting for her before
coming to the point in the path where the clearing was
visible and laid down the bundle of reeds she had
collected to mend the roof, then adjusted the shawl
with which the child was tied to her back in order to
hold her knife at the ready. Walking cautiously past
the hawthorn bushes she disturbed a little wren about
to feed its young and it flew up above her with the
worm wriggling in its beak.*

'I need thy help, mistress.'

*Seeing the pretty girl of about her own age standing
by the dwelling, she pushed the knife into its sheath at*

her waist and greeted her cordially. 'How can I help thee, maiden?'

'I heard tell as thy mother gave spells and–' she opened the basket at her feet to reveal a round cheese wrapped in cloth '–I thought thee might also.'

Her mouth watered. She had caught few fish of late and no stray pigeons had walked into her traps. 'I make no ill wishes.'

'Nay, 'tis the very opposite of this I ask.'

'A man?'

'Aye.'

She had been making little dolls for the child to play with whilst collecting the withies and, remembering this, went and pulled off several thin pieces of reed and deftly bent, twisted and tied them into the shape of a man as long from the top of his head to his feet as the distance from the tip of her middle finger to her wrist. Feeling pleased with this creation, she was about to give it to the girl when another idea struck her and pointing to its head she said, 'Take a lock of his hair without his knowing and tie it here.' Handing it to her, she added, 'Keep this by thy heart by night and by thy hearth by day for three full moons and–' she crossed her fingers behind her back '–return then and tell me how thee fared.'

Awakening in the cool blue light of dawn and remembering the dream, she resolved to make a poppy-doll of Gerry like the ones her grandmother had kept in the chimney at Old Myrtles and sew a lock of his hair onto it. There was no real hearth in the basement room so she would have to put it by Beatrice for warmth and keeping it close to her heart would be impossible when

179

staying with Gerry, but nevertheless it would be worth trying. Remembering the headache endured after sticking a pin into the teacher's doll, she reassured herself this would be completely different – all she wanted was for him to love her enough to want to be with her all the time, not just two or three nights a week in someone else's apartment.

Turning onto her side she closed her eyes and, feeling the broken cameo brooch through the folds of green silk, ran her forefinger over the shape of the kneeling figure carved into the shell. Whilst drifting back into sleep she heard her grandmother's voice whisper, 'Take care, my lover. Them as is wished to love against their will may not always be kind to them what wants it.'

Chapter Fourteen

Marshmallow root and leaves may be used in ointments and poultices for swellings on the body and a tea of the leaves may be soothing to the digestive, urinary and respiratory systems.

'Are you still looking for a place to live, Foxy?' Jane asked while putting on her hat.

'Yes, I must find somewhere before the winter sets in. The two flats I looked at today were almost as damp as my basement.'

'I don't know how you've stuck it for so long.'

'I couldn't afford anything else until now. The

180

landlords all want a month in advance. I've been trying to save up since–' she swallowed, remembering Clancy '–since I started my act.'

Jane pulled on her gloves. 'That's six months ago.'

'I know–' she fingered the lapel of her new cashmere coat '–the trouble is I'm not very good at it, there's always something nice in the shops to tempt me.'

FiFi walked into the dressing room holding a bunch of red roses and announced, 'Another bouquet for our furry star,' then placed it in the corner alongside a bunch of white lilies and posy of anemones. 'That's five nights running he's sent them.' She rolled her eyes. 'Must be smitten ter spend that kind of money.'

Jane looked at the card pinned to the roses, saying, 'He wants to take you for tea at the Ritz.'

'I wouldn't say no to an invitation like that,' FiFi said, reaching down and pulling out a rose.

'He does look quite nice–' Jane looked at Foxy in the mirror '–don't you think?'

'I haven't really thought about him,' she replied. 'Is he the bald one in a dinner jacket?'

FiFi chuckled, 'That's good that is, being bald I mean. I heard that's a sign he's really randy. So–' she waved the rose towards Foxy '–what will you wear to the Ritz?'

Jane looked thoughtful. 'Needs to be something classy and sort of genteel, a nice suit with a shantung silk blouse like that one you got last week would do nicely. And a new hat, I'll come with you to choose one.'

She shook her head. 'I'm not going.' She wasn't

going to give up on Gerry yet. The poppy-doll might still work. He had come up from the country to see her twice a week throughout the summer, apart from the two weeks spent with his family in Monte Carlo, and sent flowers several times in between. 'The House', as he called it, would soon be sitting again, so he would be in town all week. She had no desire to go to tea at a posh hotel with anyone but Gerry – not that he could be seen with her in public like that at present, but one day, one day he would when they were married. 'No,' she said firmly, 'definitely not.'

'What!' FiFi exclaimed. 'You must be mad to miss a chance like that.'

Jane shook her head and gave a rueful smile. 'She's got it bad, I'm afraid.'

FiFi looked at the ceiling and sighed with exasperation. 'But Gerald Mottram's no good to her, he's–' She broke off hearing a knock on the door.

Ricky peered into the room saying, 'Milord says can he come in?'

Foxy felt her face flush while nodding agreement.

'Come on, Fi,' Jane said, picking up her handbag, 'we know when we're not wanted,' and ushered her out into the corridor.

While checking her appearance in the mirror Foxy could hear their high heels clattering on the stone floor and then their laughing greeting to Gerry before, feeling her heart lurch, she saw his reflection behind her. He looked so handsome in a black dinner suit with long-tailed coat and a

182

white tie at his throat.

'Have the others all gone?' he asked, looking at the empty chairs lined in front of the mirrors.

'Yes, Zarina and Priscilla left early.'

'I couldn't wait until tomorrow, so I escaped–' he kissed the back of her neck '–from the clutches of a boring duchess to see you.'

Turning around to hold him she saw his eyes flick towards the flowers and then, after their embrace, watched him bend to read the card attached to the red roses. 'They have no scent,' he said, then, taking her arm, led her out of the building to his car.

Whilst driving to the flat she waited for him to ask about the invitation with the bouquet, but he made no mention of it and she wondered if he expected her to go out with other men. If that was the case then the poppy-doll magic had failed. Desperately trying to hide her disappointment, she endeavoured to sound cheerful while describing the succession of dismal, damp and badly furnished rooms she had recently inspected. 'I'll have to find something soon,' she said, as the car drew to a halt. 'I really don't want my clothes smelling of mildew like last winter.'

'No.' He turned, patted the crocodile handbag he had recently given her, and said, 'We don't want that turning green.'

When she climbed into his car a week later, Gerald said, 'I have a little surprise for you, sweetie,' and then drove to the Bayswater road, turned right opposite the park and soon stopped outside a new block of flats.

She was apprehensive and then excited. Maybe he was ready to be seen in public with her, at last. 'Are we going to visit a friend of yours?'

He frowned slightly and pursed his lips before relaxing his handsome face into a smile. 'No, Foxy darling, we'll never do tedious things like that together.' He took her hand and led her up the stone steps. Having held open the large mahogany door for her, he strode across the marble floor and spoke to the man behind a small window marked 'Janitor' then, holding a bunch of keys, he led her up the staircase to the first floor and unlocked a door, saying, 'Welcome home, my sweet.'

'Home? Did you say home?' She stepped through the doorway and looked incredulously at the cream walls and parquet floor of the small hallway.

He nodded and opened the door facing them.

'I can't afford this sort of place.'

'No, but I can.'

'Crikey-blimey!' She covered her mouth in horror. 'That slipped out, sorry.' Foxy walked forward into the sitting room and exclaimed, 'It's absolutely divine! Oh, darling, shall we live here together?'

'Yes, my darling, this is our little love-nest – if you like it that is?'

'Like it! I adore it.'

He put his arms around her. 'And there'll be no outings for tea at the Ritz?'

'Definitely not.'

'Or anywhere else with anyone else, promise?'

'I promise.' She hugged him and then added, 'We'll be so happy here, together all the time.'

'Not quite all the time, little girl. I'll be here as much as I can.' He kissed her and stepped away, lit a cigarette and said, 'I've asked for a telephone to be installed.'

'Oh, Gerry, how wonderful! I can call my friends...'

'No, Foxy,' he interrupted, 'I need the line kept for me only. It's not–' he inhaled smoke and exhaled it '–not for chatting.'

Pulling aside the white lace curtain, she looked down on the black car under the street lamp below. 'I'll be able to see who's coming and going; and it's not far to the park.' She was imagining them walking arm in arm by the Serpentine in the spring sunshine when Gerry turned to her and asked, 'What surname shall I put on the lease?'

She stared at him uncomprehendingly.

'I can't put my name on the lease, and, I know it's ridiculous, but I don't know your surname.' He put his arm around her. 'A man in my position has to be a bit careful. I'll pay for it, of course, but I'll have to put it in your name, darling.' He coughed. 'Ahem, you do understand, my sweet, that discretion is necessary. I'm not being anything other than honest with you, am I? Our love is our secret and has to remain that way. You do understand?'

She looked at the Honourable Gerald Mottram, Member of Parliament for someplace or other, she forgot where, and hesitated. What did she know about him? Very little apart from which side of the bed he slept on, what he liked to eat and drink and that he was old enough to have a daughter going to a posh boarding school. She gazed around her. This could be her home if she accepted him without asking too many questions. He was so debonair, sophisticated and handsome. He made her feel like a princess when he gave her presents and like a film star when he made love. He was upper class and not like ordinary people who had to make the best of it for the rest of their lives. He'd arrange somehow to marry her. Just because Kate had said Charles's wife would never divorce him, that didn't mean Gerry's wouldn't, did it? His wife might want to marry someone else too. She squeezed his hand. 'I understand, darling, of course I do. Put the lease in my name. Elizabeth Fox.'

Gerald had to leave early for the country on the Friday a week later, and she therefore moved into number seven Grove Court with the help of a taxi driver.

On arrival she found the previously empty flat was now fully equipped and furnished with two blue sofas and a red Persian rug in the sitting room; a large double bed and wardrobe in the bedroom and a gas cooker in the kitchen which made her think of Clancy, kneeling on the floor surrounded by clumps of blonde hair. Oh, my friend, if only you hadn't turned on the gas and killed yourself. If only you could be here to share in my happiness, we would have such fun together!

After dumping her possessions in heaps on the floor she unpacked her suitcase and, placing the bundle of treasures on the bed, admitted Gerry would never understand why they were important to her. She lay down and curled around them for a few minutes, thinking first of her grandmother picking rosemary in the garden and then of Kate, who would disapprove of her present behaviour and remind her of the family duty to stay in the village and guard the cave. Remembering the beautiful figure in the rocks with water trickling down over pink crystals into the pool as red as blood, she gave a low moan and caressed the bundle, feeling the sliver of wood through the silk...

Watching her daughter playing with the withy doll she ached with love and, seeing the child's golden hair glinting in the autumn sunlight, reached out to stroke it then returned to scraping the kidskin. When the hide had been steeped with oak bark in water it would make a fine pair of boots next spring.

Thinking of the three more girls who had come seeking spells to make men love them and how each one had gone away eager to get a lock of their beloved's hair, she wondered if there could ever be a time when she would need to make a figure for herself and tie the hair of a man to it. Nay, she decided, shaking her head, there could never be another to take Jerome's place.

Opening her eyes Foxy lay looking up at the un-blemished cream ceiling. This was so different from her bedroom at Old Myrtles or the attic room above the furrier's and the damp basement in which her clothes had gone mouldy. Kate would say she should refuse this opportunity, that accepting it would mean she would definitely be Gerry's mistress, 'The Other

Woman'. But then what would she do? Her wages were much increased since becoming a performer and therefore she could afford a better room, but nothing like this beautiful flat. Thinking of Kate she wondered if a daughter had yet been born to take over from her and guard the cave. She would never go back to Oakey Vale to find out. Well, maybe when she was Mrs Gerald Mottram – she might go for a short visit then. It would be interesting to return to the village. Miserable gossipy place that it was. What would she be doing now if she'd stayed? Polishing grates and emptying chamber pots in domestic service as a maid probably, or serving in Woolworths, or that dress shop near the Cathedral, perhaps? Thank heavens she'd escaped!

Life was so much better here in London and one day when Gerry was free he would take her to tea at the Ritz and to dinner parties with duchesses. They would be seen together in restaurants and posh hotels. He would marry her, of course he would!

Sitting up she looked at the treasures lying beside her – Gerry need not know about them or her gift of seeing. Picking up the bundle she carried it to the wardrobe and pushed it into the corner behind the door and then prepared for work.

Ricky was leaning in the doorway reading a newspaper when she arrived at the club.

'Moved in alright?' he asked, looking up. She nodded.

'Nice little love-nest is it?'

'Lovely.'

'Be a bit restricting won't it?'

'Why?' She wanted to get away from his glittering eyes and smirking mouth, but could not resist responding to the question.

'S'obvious ain't it? I mean ter say, yer can't see any other blokes while yer *obliged* ter him, can yer?'

Frowning with irritation she shook her head. 'I don't want to see anyone else, stupid.' What on earth was Ricky thinking of? Why would she even think of other men while she had Gerry – especially now she was setting up a home with him?

'That's alright then.' He held the newspaper towards her, saying, 'There's a picture of him in here with that fascist bloke.'

She looked at the picture of the two men walking into a church and read the caption 'Leader of Blackshirts and Gerald Mottram attend Lord Snipe's funeral'. Then, seeing the headline in the column alongside it, she gasped.

'Sunnink wrong is there?' He looked at the page and read aloud, 'Pillar of society admits liaison with underage girl.' His eyes flicked sideways before continuing, 'Justice Gregory Jamieson-Gore has stepped down from the bench after pleading guilty to...'

'I'm going to be late,' she interrupted.

His large hand held her wrist as he said, 'No one really believes yer over twenty-one, Foxy, but there'll be a hell of a stink if yer under sixteen.'

'Keep your voice down, you idiot.' She looked around and on ascertaining no one was close enough to hear them, said, 'It's alright now, I promise.'

'Now!' He rolled his eyes. 'When was yer birthday?'

'March.'

'Gordon Bennett!' He released his grip and pointed to the date at the top of the page. 'That's only a few months ago. If anybody had found out milord would've been in big trouble.'

'I didn't think.'

'No I don't suppose yer did, but the likes of him's bound ter have enemies and they'll be watching and waiting. You mark my words. Sooner or later there'll be someone what makes trouble for yer.'

Chapter Fifteen

Rosebay willowherb tea may relieve asthma and whooping cough.

24 December 1935

FiFi walked into the dressing room and postured dramatically with one hand on her hip and the other in the air. 'You'll never believe what I've just heard, girls!'

Foxy, Jane and Zarina all looked up expectantly.

'There's two blokes in the office with pots of paint and ladders and they're actually going to decorate the theatre while we're closed!'

'Crikey!' Foxy exclaimed. 'Madame's been talking about doing it ever since I started, and this'll be my–' she counted on her fingers '–fourth Christmas here.'

Jane scraped some flaking paint off the wall with her fingernail. 'I hope they'll do this lot as well.'

FiFi nodded. 'They'll have to do that later. The front of house takes priority.' Picking up a powder puff she looked at Foxy and asked, 'What've you got for Gerry?'

'I've bought a present to both of us. I'm so excited, it was only delivered this morning and I'm longing to listen to it.'

'Whatever is it?'

'A wireless. I've been saving all year for it.'

FiFi paused from powdering her nose. 'Mmm, having no rent to pay must make a difference.'

Jane, who was about to leave, looked uncomfortable and turned back, saying, 'I'd like to see it, well, hear it I mean.'

'Come tomorrow if you like. Gerry has to go and do his duty with the family.'

'That's a shame.'

'I don't mind. I'm used to it now. We'll have our celebration tonight.'

FiFi grimaced and asked, 'Will milord be in the bosom of his family at the country seat, Foxy?'

Feeling her face flush, she replied whilst pulling on her fur jacket, 'It'll be the usual ritual. He hates it, of course.' Damn! FiFi always knew how to drive the knife in where it would hurt, but she wouldn't let her see she had succeeded.

'Of course! You'd hate all those dinner parties and champagne cocktails and all that boring stuff too, wouldn't you?'

Jane said, 'Steady on, Fi. You know she can't help...'

'It's alright, I can take a joke.' Foxy picked up her gloves and handbag. 'I've bought a hamper from Fortnum's so we can have a romantic time together before he goes.'

'That sounds nice.'

'Mmm, I've made the sitting room look like a wooded glade with oak leaves and twigs and lots of candles.'

'How lovely!'

FiFi pursed her lips and looked at the ceiling. 'The best I can hope for is a nice breakfast in the café downstairs before my boyfriend goes to stay with his mother.'

Foxy blew a kiss to each of the performers. 'Have a lovely time, everyone. See you next week.' She ran up the stairs to where Gerry was waiting in his car dressed in a dinner suit.

'I have just been to the most boring dinner party of the century.' He yawned and loosened the black bow tie at his throat. 'Can't wait to get to bed, little girl.'

She swallowed hard and said brightly, 'I've made a little surprise for you.'

He yawned again. 'Not tonight, girlie, I need sleep.'

'But it'll be Christmas Eve tomorrow and–' Seeing his jaw tighten she broke off and stared miserably out of the window.

'I said I need to get to bed.' His tone brooked

no argument and they drove in silence to Grove Court.

On entering the flat she held her breath. Behind the sitting-room door was a beautiful glade under an enchanted tree. A picnic of potted wild boar and turtledove pâté awaited them amongst the fallen leaves. A champagne bottle with a specially made label on which she'd written, 'Elixir from the source of eternal youth' was standing in a bucket of ice beside the largest part of the wireless. 'It wouldn't take long, Gerry. It's...'

He ignored her and walked to the bathroom from where she heard the lavatory flush followed by a cursory brushing of teeth. Leaning against the door she imagined him going into the bedroom and hanging his clothes on the trouser-press. No matter how exhausted, or, on occasion, inflamed with desire, he always hung up his clothes and pushed shoetrees into his handmade footwear before getting into bed. With deliberate abandonment of his standards she unfastened her frock and let it slide to the floor, then, leaving a trail of undergarments and stockings in her wake, she went into the bathroom and turned on the taps.

How could he be so unfeeling and beastly? FiFi was absolutely right. He was going to spend Christmas with lots of people and have food and drink and presents and he couldn't be bothered to see her surprise. She wallowed in the soothing hot water until it cooled and then climbed into bed keeping well away from him.

Awaking from a dream in which she was living

in an oak tree, she lay for a moment, remembering the feeling of safety up in the branches whilst she looked down on a circle of women below her. They were shouting something about fireweed, which was odd! Anyway, forget the silly dream, where was she now? Hearing the man snoring beside her, she remembered. This was her smart flat in London, far away from the drudgery in the furrier's flat and even further from the boring village in Somerset. So what if her lover hadn't seen her surprise last night! They could have a picnic champagne breakfast. There'd be something from the BBC they could listen to and he'd think she was so clever to have arranged it. She slid out of bed, picked up her clothes off the floor and made a cup of tea before awakening him.

'By Jove, is that the time?' he asked, looking at his wristwatch. 'I'll skip breakfast today. I have to be home by luncheon.'

Going into the kitchen, she sat at the little table feeling despondent until he appeared, dressed in a pinstriped suit and carrying his briefcase in one hand and a small parcel in the other. 'Must go, sweetie. Here's a small gift for a good little girl.'

She handed him the cracker she had intended they would pull in the magic glade and into which she had inserted a fountain pen as an extra little gift, saying with a tight smile, 'A small trifle for my big man.'

After escorting him to the door, then walking into the sitting room and standing at the window watching him get into his car and drive away, she opened the box and looked at the diamond earrings. They were beautiful, expensive and, although wanting to be grateful, she felt nothing. Looking down at the leaves strewn around a tablecloth spread on the floor, she was suddenly relieved that he had refused to join her picnic. Thank goodness he didn't see it! He'd have thought her really silly. She might have got drunk and told him about the oak tree in Hankeys Land and of her childish belief it was magical. She would have made a complete fool of herself, describing how she walked around it three times one way and then three times the other whilst making a wish.

Sinking to her knees she took handfuls of leaves and threw them at the wireless until, overwhelmed with a desperate longing to make contact with the girl living close to the tree long ago, she went and fetched the bundle of treasures from the wardrobe and then lay amongst the leaves, holding the tiny piece of wood.

The frost was glinting on blades of grass outside the dwelling and the sky was leaden with snow. She had tied the goatskin flap open to give her light to see by but was sitting close enough to the fire to feel its warmth and watch her daughter playing with her little dolls. She was taking pleasure in making Myrtle a new pair of boots and smiling whilst remembering her mother doing the same task when she was a small child, playing with similar little people and animals fashioned from green willow. Her mother had stressed to her that good boots in winter were important in their lives, almost as vital as fire or a knife, both of which were essential for survival.

Seeing a figure wrapped in a blue cloak walk cautiously into the clearing and take slow and careful steps towards the dwelling, as if ready to turn and run at any moment, she called out, 'Come in and be welcome.'

The girl pushed back the hood trimmed with fur to reveal a blushing young face and said, 'I seek thy help, mistress.'

'I give it when able, my lady.'

'I have heard of thy magic dolls.'

'Who told thee of this?'

'A maidservant at the manor.' She played nervously with the riding whip she was holding. 'It worked for her and now she is with child.'

She smiled. 'I make no promise and ask no payment, My Lady, but–' she rearranged the ragged remains of the cloak the nuns had given her around her shoulders '–if thy wish is granted, and only then, something to keep out the cold would be most welcome.'

The girl fingered the blue woollen fabric whilst replying, 'I will bring a cloak such as this if thy magic works.' Then, reaching into a pouch hanging at her waist, she pulled out a small silk bag. 'My maid acquired this lock of hair.'

She frowned. 'It is usual for the person making the wish to get the–'

'There is no way for me to do such a thing. She swore on oath it was cut by his manservant only yesterday.'

'Again, I make no promise, My Lady.' She went outside and fetched some thin stems of willow from the pile of withies outside and then fashioned the figure of a man from them. Taking the lock of shining brown hair from the little bag, she wove it around the head and tied it with twine made from nettles. Looking at

the finished doll she had a new idea and asked, 'What colour cloak do he wear?'

'I have seen him in both green and brown.'

'Then, take a piece of cloth of either hue and wrap it around.' She handed it to the girl. 'For three full rounds of the moon this must stay close to thy heart by night and close to thy hearth by day.'

'And then?'

'If there be love for any woman in him, then, My Lady, 'twill be for thee.'

Opening her eyes, Foxy lay remembering the poppy-dolls her grandmother had made for all the family. Kate would still carry on the tradition and keep them safe and warm in the linen bag inside the chimney breast at Old Myrtles. The one she had made for Gerry two years ago was still in her bedside table; maybe if she kept it close to her heart on the nights he was not with her it would revive his love for her?

When she walked into the dressing room two days later, Jane, who was sitting in front of the mirror, asked, 'Have you heard the latest, Foxy? They'll be doing this room next, at last!' She gestured around her. 'I can't imagine what it'll look like after all this time. I can't believe it's true!'

'They've done a good job on the front of house,' FiFi said, 'they worked all through Christmas and Boxing Day to get it done. The tall thin one's called John, he seems a nice chap, says he's the brother of some geezer Madame knew in the old days and the other's called Dave.'

Jane nodded. 'I saw them just now. The shorter

197

one with reddish hair looked rather embarrassed.' She grinned at Foxy. 'He's not as red as our "star performer" of course.'

'That's not fair. I asked Madame not to call me that, you know I did.'

'I know, silly, fold up yer wings. I was only teasing. I'm really pleased you've done so well, and Clancy would be delighted, I know she would.'

Foxy and Jane exchanged sad smiles in the mirror.

Zarina put down her newspaper and said, 'They're talking about Herr Hitler and war every day now. What does your bloke say about it, Foxy?'

'He doesn't discuss politics with me.' What he'd said was, 'I come to you to get away from all that. I need you to help me forget about it. Just don't trouble your pretty head with men's problems. There's a good girl.' She hadn't told him she was troubled or that she'd found the taxi drivers more and more convinced another war was inevitable and one had told her terrible things were being done to Jewish people in Germany.

Whilst they were alone in the dressing room later that evening Fifi said, 'There's a girl using fur in her act down at the Windmill. She's copying you. She really is.'

Foxy shrugged.

'And my boyfriend said there's a girl using leopard skin in a club not far from here.'

'I don't care,' she responded confidently. Actually she did care very much, but was determined not to let FiFi know that. Whilst pretending to be concentrating on applying her mascara, she

198

reminded herself she'd be married long before any competition became a serious threat. Sooner or later something would happen to set Gerry free. In the meantime she'd continue to be his faithful and devoted mistress and await the day when they could declare their love to the world and she'd be 'young Mrs Mottram' whose gracious manner, elegant clothes and soirées for artists and intellectuals were renowned. Her patience and devotion would be rewarded in the fullness of time. The fact that girls were copying her act didn't matter at all!

The following day as she passed Jane talking to one of the decorators in the corridor, she was shocked to hear her say, 'Foxy, listen to this. Dave's just heard from a bloke in a pub that the king's dead.' Having said she wondered if the club would close for the funeral as a mark of respect, she walked away thinking how young and pretty her friend was looking.

A few moments later, after telling FiFi the sad news, she commented on how Jane and Dave seemed to be becoming friendly and was surprised at the vehemence of her reaction.

'Can't possibly be anything in it, they're too old and he's too short and ugly, and he's actually going grey!'

'I think he looks really kind.'

FiFi snorted. 'I hope I'm never that desperate.'

Remembering the time she saw Jane dressed as a bride standing beside a tall man with bright red hair who definitely wasn't Dave, she said, 'Maybe they'll just be good friends.'

Two weeks later Foxy exclaimed, 'Engaged! How wonderful!'

Jane blushed. 'I expect you'll think it's a bit quick, but I'm sure he's the one for me.'

Having assured her she was delighted, she immediately went to tell Madame La Fay who announced there would be a party to celebrate after the show.

Gerry, who had been waiting outside, came into the club and danced with Jane, then, after demanding that Madame should give her rendition of 'There was I waiting at the church', he and everyone else joined in singing the last line, 'Can't get away to marry you today, my wife won't let me!'

Ethel burst into tears, explaining between loud sobs how it brought back the memory of all the lovely times they had and wasn't Fay wonderful? Then, as usual, everyone agreed Madame was indeed wonderful and must have brought the house down when she was Fay Morgan, the queen of music hall.

After performing, 'My old man said follow the van and don't dilly dally on the way', plus several other songs in her repertoire, Madame commanded them all to 'Bugger off to bed and be happy.' And they cheerfully obeyed her.

On the way home Foxy said dreamily, 'She'll look so lovely in her white dress and veil.'

Gerry laughed. 'She won't really wear white, will she?'

'Why not?'

'My darling, that'll be no innocent virgin

walking up the aisle. The poor fool isn't getting a brand new model, is he?'

She wanted to say, 'He's not a poor fool, he's a nice, kindly man who loves her,' but she shook her head and remained silent until they arrived at the flat.

Later, when they had made love and she could talk in a little girly, joking sort of voice to him, she asked, 'Is it so very important that men marry virgins?'

'Of course.'

'What if they're the one that took the virginity?'

'Depends on circumstances, but as a general rule a wife has to be able to wear white; that's how it is.'

'But there must be–' She stopped as he kissed her lips then said, 'I really must get some sleep, my darling. It's Friday tomorrow and I'll have a long drive. One of my filial duty visits I'm afraid. The old man will have a clutch of county bores waiting for me, not that Lydia will mind, she'll love it, silly cow.' He turned away from her and was instantly asleep. Lying awake beside him, listening to his snuffling and snoring interspersed with the occasional grunt or word, she felt cold and numb. This was almost the same as when Clancy died – like a grief that was beyond tears, too painful to bear.

Chapter Sixteen

A tea made from the flowers and leaves of valerian may ease stress and aid sleep.

Foxy and FiFi were the only ones from the Gentlemen's Relish to attend the wedding. Madame was expecting to audition a pianist that day and Ethel declined because she was needed in the ticket office, and the others, knowing the club must keep going, agreed to stretch their acts a little during the afternoon performance in order to cover for the two absentees.

Sitting on the underground train travelling towards the western suburbs where she had lived above the furrier's shop and cared for his wife, Foxy wondered how Mrs Bradon had fared in the four and a half years since she had left her. Might the poor little woman be in the loony bin? Or, even worse, might she have died of starvation?

On disembarking at Acton Town, they took a taxi to the church, where they saw the bride being helped out of a motor car by a tall thin man with a shock of auburn hair glinting in the summer sun and heard him say, 'Come on then, love, I promised me brother I'd get yer there in time.' Recalling her experience when holding the silver ring set with small garnets, she smiled with delight. The scene was exactly as on that day in the dressing room and the man beside Jane was obviously Dave's younger brother.

A few minutes later, when the stripper, whose future might well have been both impoverished and lonely, walked down the aisle and stood before the priest, FiFi leaned sideways in the pew and whispered, 'I do like a happy ending, Foxy.'

She smiled in agreement. Then, seeing a shaft of light beam through a stained-glass window turning Jane's dress slightly pink, just as the lilies on Clancy's coffin had been coloured, she wanted to weep for the friend whose dream of a ceremony like this had not come true.

Remembering the funeral and her embarrassment at the gross display of glamour by the party from the Gentlemen's Relish, she cringed and, looking around her, knew they were repeating that same mistake. The difference was not so great, or in such bad taste on this occasion. The family and guests were suffering neither from poverty nor grief, but FiFi's new lilac dress and Panama hat had probably cost three times more than the bridegroom's mother had paid for a similar outfit, and her own ensemble in emerald green crepe and lace was the most stylish and expensive of all – how could she have been so stupid and thoughtless yet again?

The congregation and choir filled the church with the sound of a joyful hymn and, as always on hearing such music, she thought of Uncle Albert singing, 'Oh hear us when we cry to thee, for those in peril on the sea,' and wondered if she would ever see him again. She used to worry about what Gerry would think of the old man when he met him after they were married. But would he marry her? He hadn't mentioned the subject of virginity and brides since their discussion six weeks earlier and appeared to have forgotten it, whereas she had thought of little else and the doubt was like a permanent ache that never went away.

The sound of FiFi blowing her nose brought her attention back to the couple making their wedding vows and she too reached for her hand-kerchief.

An hour later, while meeting Dave's relatives at the reception in a hall that was obviously used as a youth club and scout hut, she remembered peeping through the window of an identical building at similar celebrations after weddings in Oakey Vale. She was still watching other people being happy. Nothing had changed – she was still an outsider.

At the end of her performance that night, just as the curtains were closing, she caught a glimpse of the audience and felt sick. Most of them looked like Mr Bradon and all of them seemed shabby and sad.

After hurriedly changing and leaving the club, she ignored the cruising taxis, and, feeling the need for fresh air, walked homewards remember-ing how she had arrived here with a head full of impossible dreams. Stopping to look in a shop window in Oxford Street and, seeing her own re-flection, she wondered what Kate would say if she saw her now. She might approve of the under-stated elegance of the very expensive cream linen suit into which she had hurriedly changed on re-

204

turning from the wedding, but what would she think of the red hair falling to her shoulders, and would she admire the lizard-skin shoes with matching handbag? Grimacing and shaking her head, she knew her sister would be neither pleased nor proud.

A waft of cheap scent made her look at a couple walking past. The young girl was rouged and powdered and already being pawed by her older, richly dressed companion. What had happened to make her so desperate for money she would sell herself to an ugly old man? She shivered, knowing the answer to her own question; the girl might have been a little less lucky than she had been, that's all. Betty Barnes would have lasted only a few weeks if Clancy had not persuaded Madame La Fay to take her into the club.

Remembering Kate again, she turned away from the window and began walking. Her sister had chosen to live in sin with the man she loved, but, although some people in the village would say she had broken the rules by which they all abided, no one would ever suggest she was a tart. Whereas, she smiled wryly, most people outside her own little world, and even some inside it, would apply that word to her.

Suddenly a deep need for a glimpse of the cottage filled her being. The roses would be in bloom and their heady scent would hang on the evening air as one walked along the path from the front gate towards the back door. Then, knowing she could not face her sister, she dismissed the feeling of longing as sentimental and childish. She belonged here in the vibrant exciting city, not in a tiny village ruled by old gossips! She would marry Gerry, who would forget all that talk about brides being virgins when he had extricated himself from the wife he despised. While Kate's destiny was to guard the lady in the cave, hers was to be the wife of a Member of Parliament, a society hostess and, eventually, a devoted mother of beautiful, talented children.

Passing by Marble Arch, she saw a car like Gerry's and raised her hand to wave, then, remembering he was with his family, lowered it. Walking along the Bayswater Road a few minutes later, she heard a low male voice and light female laughter emanating from within the shadows of a doorway and ached with loneliness.

On arrival at the flat she smelled burning and rushed into the sitting room to find Gerry asleep on the floor with an empty decanter to one side of him and a cigar butt in the middle of a smouldering hole in the rug on the other.

After dowsing the fire, she knelt beside him. 'I wasn't expecting you. It's Saturday, you said you were going to the country.'

He opened his eyes. 'Emergency. Got to talk tomorrow. Silly bloody fool!'

'Am I? What've I done?'

'Not you. No. Nice, silly, pretty girl. No. Silly bloody king, thass who.'

'The king?'

'Silly fool wants to marry her, thasswhat!'

'Crikey! Who's he want to marry?'

'American woman, of course.'

She'd heard rumours about Mrs Simpson and the Prince of Wales before he became king but,

206

having seen nothing about them in the newspapers lately, was surprised by this information.
'She's already married, isn't she?'

He sat up. 'Whassat terrible smell?'

'The rug was burning. Never mind that. How's
he going to marry her?' She was thinking of her
own situation. If the king could sort it out, why
shouldn't Gerry?

'Can't.'

'Couldn't Mr Simpson divorce her?'

'Bloody fool's forgotten the bloody rules.'

'The rules?' She helped him to his feet.

'Number one, mosht important, by Jove!' He
swayed and almost fell.

'Yes?'

'What?'

'You were going to tell me the rules.'

He staggered to the bed and sat on it. 'Never
marry mishtress.' He wagged his forefinger at her.
'S'obvious, everybody knows. S'only a woman.
Bloody fool king.' He slid sideways, closed his
eyes and was asleep before hitting the pillow.

Picking up the poppy-doll dressed in a pin-
stripe suit from her side of the bed, she stuffed it
into the bedside cupboard and lay beside him
staring up at the ceiling. Madame La Fay had
told her at the start, right at the very beginning.
'He's rich,' she said, 'he's important, he's
powerful and he'll never marry you.'

Gerry's reaction to Jane's marriage reverberated
in her mind, 'Only marry a virgin.' Her head
throbbed out the words, 'Never marry your mistress. Only marry a virgin,' over and over again.

He was snoring loudly when she sat up to look

at her watch and found it was almost three o'clock. Leaning back against the headboard she listened to the rhythmic pattern of his snorting inhalations and whistling exhalations while repeating his words in her head, 'Never marry a mistress. Only marry a virgin.' Everyone knew that's what men believed; so why hadn't she understood? Why hadn't she accepted Madame's advice? Why had she needed him to spell out in drunken slobbering honesty what he'd assumed she knew all along?

After getting out of bed she walked to the window and, looking out at the moon, admitted that making the poppy-doll had not worked as she wished – the dream would never come true.

As sparrows outside the window began their celebration of dawn, she went into the kitchen to make tea. Sitting at the little table, head in hands, she resolved no one else must ever know how big a fool she'd been and acknowledged that, fortunately, none of her friends, not even FiFi, would have imagined she could have been so silly. Although longing to leave immediately, she needed time to think what to do next and so took two aspirin tablets and drank a cup of tea then leaned forward onto the table and fell asleep.

When he stumbled into the kitchen an hour later looking old and wan, Gerald screwed up his eyes and held his head while saying, 'I'll probably be in conference until late tonight. In fact, I don't know when I can get away again. You under-stand?'

She sighed sympathetically and handed him a cup of tea, saying, 'Yes, of course, darling.' In her head she added, 'I've grown up at last. I under-stand the rules, even if the king doesn't!'

Walking into the bedroom after he had departed she delved into the corner of the wardrobe and pulled out the bundle of treasures. Then, taking out the piece of wood, she lay on the bed longing to be in that world where no lovers complicated her simple life...

There were hoof marks in the mud by the river. She stopped still, listening for sounds of dogs or of men but heard nothing. Turning to the child she smiled reassuringly, determined not to frighten her. 'Wait here and hide in the willows, Myrtle, I shall not be long.'

Fear flashed in the girl's eyes but she nodded bravely and slipped behind the overhanging branches.

Picking up the bag of fungus they had collected in the woods she walked with measured stride towards the dwelling.

Seeing the horse tethered to a tree on the edge of the clearing she stood still, trying to sense the whereabouts of its rider.

'Good day, mistress.'

Hearing the deep voice she turned and saw the man standing by the rock outside the cave. Fear that he had discovered the cave made her stammer as she asked the reason for his presence.

'I am the groom of My Lady, the daughter of Earl Reginald.' He held a bundle towards her. 'She was married yesterday and wishes thee to share in her happiness.'

Her hand shook as she took it from him and held up the dark-grey cloak, allowing the fine woollen fabric to fall in generous folds to the ground.

She thanked him courteously.

He took a step towards his horse, then turned and, holding up a small wooden cross, said, 'I was warned that men be cursed if they come to these parts.'

She smiled. 'Aye. So I've heard.'

His hand juddered slightly but his eyes were steady as he asked, 'And shall I be cursed, mistress?'

'Not if thee goes in peace.'

Opening her eyes and looking up at the smooth, cream ceiling, she thought of Kate, who, like the girl who had left the safe life in the convent in order to guard the lady in the cave, knew this was her destiny and also, like Caitlin, would need a daughter to take over from her one day. She longed to be near her sister, to hear her beautiful laugh and see her green eyes sparkle with joy or go milky as they did when reading the tea leaves, but that was impossible. Kate had been in love herself and therefore might understand how she had become involved with Gerald, but there was no doubt at all how she would react to her little sister stripping in public – she'd be so shocked and horrified!

Suddenly she was ashamed of her act in the Gentlemen's Relish. How could she have ever done such a thing? She would have to get out of this situation, she knew that now. This way of life was suddenly no longer glamorous but had become tawdry and cheap. She would leave the flat and pay her own rent, leave the club and find other work; she might even leave London, but she could never go back to Oakey Vale and admit what a fool she'd been.

Chapter Seventeen

A tea made with hawthorn berries may help to avoid chilblains on hands and feet.

When Gerry left London early in the morning of Christmas Eve she felt relieved to be alone. On the few occasions he had visited her since the king abdicated two weeks earlier he had been preoccupied with arrangements for the Duke of York to succeed to the throne and therefore paid her little attention. This lack of interest would once have distressed her, but, since she had been wondering how to get out of the flat, it was a great relief.

Walking to the window she looked down and watched him climb into his car and drive away. He was as handsome as all the film stars of her childhood and as sophisticated and suave as every hero of romantic stories she'd ever read; it was, she knew now, the idea of him she'd loved, not the man himself.

Finding both work and somewhere else to live had proved more difficult than she had thought. Potential employers and landlords, having once asked for her occupation and references, had raised their eyebrows and said they 'would let her know' and then had sent letters regretting the post or room had been taken.

She filled a large glass with Gerry's best brandy

and drank a toast to him then to everyone she knew one by one. She was weeping for Clancy when, hearing a knock at the door, she went unsteadily to open it and found Ethel smiling anxiously whilst holding an envelope towards her.

'I was taking a little walk and thought I'd deliver this card and invite you to join us for lunch tomorrow,' Ethel said, adding, 'I don't want to intrude.'

'No, not at all, I'd love you to come in and have a cup of tea,' she replied with forced enthusiasm while ushering her into the hall. As she passed the mirror her swollen eyes stared miserably back at her and she tried to smile cheerfully, saying, 'I've been writing a few Christmas cards.'

Ethel walked into the sitting room and sank into one of the blue sofas. 'It's a lonely time for you, isn't it?'

Sitting opposite her Foxy started to say, 'I'm perfectly alright,' but the words dried in her throat and tears slid down her face. 'This is so stupid,' she moaned, 'so silly.'

'Being unhappy isn't stupid or silly, Foxy.'

'Yes it is,' she wailed, 'I knew I couldn't have what I wanted and still I went on believing in a fairy story, a romantic nonsense.'

Ethel shook her head sadly. 'Not everyone gets the happy ever after ending. You're very young, there'll be another man one day and you'll be older and wiser.'

'I feel such a fool. I really believed he would marry me in the end...' She burst into uncontrollable sobs.

After she had calmed down Ethel asked if she had lost contact with her family.

'I keep in touch with my sister, I send a card to let her know I'm alright but I couldn't let her know my address in case she came here and found out...' She paused while struggling to find words to express herself.

'That you were living here with Gerald Mottram?' Ethel asked.

'That wouldn't be so bad,' she replied, 'when I left home my sister was living in sin. The man's wife refused to divorce him and so they agreed to live together openly. The only way they can marry is if his wife dies. It caused a huge scandal in the village and lots of people wouldn't speak to her.'

'So she'd understand about you and Gerald?'

'Maybe.' She shrugged. 'I'm not sure. She might think the situation's different because I'm hidden away and he has no intention of marrying me.'

'So what's the big problem?'

How could she say that Kate would be appalled if she knew her little sister was a stripper at the Gentlemen's Relish when such condemnation would offend Ethel? She shrugged and replied, 'It's too difficult to explain.'

'I don't think it's difficult at all, Foxy dear.' The older woman removed her spectacles and polished them on her handkerchief, then added, 'I think you don't want her to know what you're doing at the club. You're ashamed, aren't you?'

She nodded and admitted this was the truth. Then, for the first time since she had confided in the lady who gave her the gardenia, the whole story spilled out, whilst Ethel sat quietly listening, nodding at intervals and making sympathetic noises or gestures until the tale was concluded.

That night, instead of lying awake for hours as she had of late, she drifted quickly into the best and most refreshing sleep since the king announced he wished to marry Mrs Simpson.

Awakening next morning she lay for a while, thinking about the village on Christmas Day. Some women who cooked on an open fire would have taken their goose or chicken to the baker for him to roast in his big oven and then fetch it after church in the same way as they collected their joints of meat or puddings on Sundays throughout the year. Kate would have stoked up the range early that morning and there would be a bird cooking in the oven by now and a pudding boiling in a saucepan on the hot plate. Uncle Albert would be humming his favourite hymns before and after going to church, and whilst eating the meal. Charles would be there and their little boy. Feeling desperately lonely she went to the wardrobe and fetched the piece of wood...

Snow had fallen in the long dark night, leaving the clearing transformed into a white wilderness. Looking through the flap she could see the line of footprints left by Myrtle, who had gone to see if the river had frozen over.

Unlike her child, who had been bored with the drab winter and therefore excited by the snow, she hated it. Wrapping her cloak around her she fetched some

214

wood for the fire and then sat huddled beside it humming the tune of a song the nuns had sung at this time of year. The sisters would all be so happy and saying, 'Jesus is born' and 'Our Saviour is on earth' to one another as they met in the cloister or stood by the fire in the warming room.

As always when remembering the time she had lived in such a different world within the safety of the convent walls, she felt a little sadness for the lost companionship of her dear friend Marie, who would now be a respected member of the community after such a long time. She reached for the stick beside her sleeping shelf on which she had made a notch when the first leaves began to unfold each spring since her return from the convent. Then, counting these, she knew it was now twelve years since she had last seen Marie and, counting from the mark next to them, knew that it was now ten years since Myrtle was born.

'Merry Christmas, Foxy love,' Madame greeted her at the door, 'welcome to our little gathering of old chums.' She kissed her on the cheek. 'Mmm, that's a nice scent you're wearing. Come along and meet the other guests.'

Feeling apprehensive, Foxy went into a room overlooking the park and was introduced to a large, attractive woman called Eva and her husband James who was a small man and neat both in body and dress. A few minutes later Meryl, a tall, attractive, middle-aged woman arrived with her friend Bryony, who was also no longer young but was still very, very beautiful.

It was apparent that all the other guests had

worked with Madame and Ethel in the music hall and when Ethel fetched several photograph albums and handed them around, they immediately started looking at the pictures, exclaiming from time to time at the sight of an old friend or their youthful selves.

'Gawd! Was I really that young?' Meryl said, rolling her eyes in amazement.

'Was I really that thin?' Eva shrieked with laughter.

Foxy was turning the pages of a book marked 1914 and admiring the costumes of the young Madame and her friends when a picture held her breathless attention. In a photographer's setting of a backdrop painted to look like Roman columns with long curtains to one side and a potted plant on the other, a young couple stood draped in sheets, and the faces beneath the head-dresses of laurel leaves were thinner and younger but easily recognisable. She stared in horror at the romantic scene, for the man gazing at Fay Morgan twenty years earlier was unmistakable and so was the enraptured adoration on his handsome face. She'd known Gerry and Madame had been friends for a long time, but not that they could have been lovers.

Taking a deep breath she quickly turned the page and studied a faded picture of Madame wearing a large hat with ribbons hanging from it and sitting on a swing, until, feeling calmer, she continued working her way through the book.

'Good, aren't they?' Eva asked.

'Absolutely fascinating,' she replied, determined not to show her feelings. Standing up, she walked to the mantelpiece and admired each ornament separately, an elegant French clock, then a chipped and badly painted plaster figurine of a girl with an Alsatian dog, after that a Meissen porcelain couple depicting Pierrot and Pierrette. On the other side of the clock was a plaster puppy holding a slipper and then a small, intricately carved object, which she picked up and cradled in the palm of her hand.

'It's oriental,' James said coming to join her. 'Quite old I reckon. Nice little thing, isn't it?'

Looking at the tiny figures of a naked man and woman side by side, she felt the pale ivory grow warm and saw it hanging at the waist of a man wearing a long robe with wide sleeves.

James grinned. 'I suppose they enjoyed a bit of rude in them days, just as we do today.'

She shook her head. 'It's not like that. People could point on the figure where they had the pain or the problem in their own bodies.'

'Gawd's truth, that's amazing, that is!' James called to his wife, 'Come and listen to this, Foxy knows all about this little carving.'

'Not all about it.' Damn! She'd opened her big mouth without operating her little brain. 'More of a guess really.'

'Sounded to me like you know.'

Meryl and Bryony put down the photographs and came to join them on the Chinese rug by the fireplace, asking, 'What's going on?'

'Nothing, it's nothing at all.'

Jim shook his head. 'That's not nothing. We've all thought it was rude, didn't we, Eva?'

At that moment Madame appeared in the

217

doorway looking flushed and saying, 'Come and eat, my friends.'

They trooped into the dining room and sat at the long table on which was arrayed a roasted goose, bowls of vegetables, jugs of gravy and bottles of wine. Everyone ate and drank until, after waiting for the pudding, they all cheered when it was carried in ablaze with blue flames.

When they had eaten their fill, despite protestations that the maid would be back the next day, Foxy helped Meryl and Bryony wash the dishes while they sang songs from their music hall days. She laughed when Meryl sang, 'D'you like my dress, just a little bit?' pretending she had a low décolletage and then wiggling her hips whilst adding, 'That's the little bit the boys admire.' And joined in, 'The boy I love is up in the gallery, there he is a wavin' of his handkerchief,' as she flapped the cloth with which she was drying the glasses.

On returning to the sitting room they all sang song after song together. James had a rich tenor voice and knew many old ballads as well as the comic ditties he had once included in his act. Ethel produced two enormous fans made of ostrich feathers and, after much persuasion and a glass of champagne, Meryl did a fan dance fully clothed. Everyone laughed, especially Madame, whose neighing turned into hiccups that made the others all laugh even more. As Ethel, rocking helplessly, removed her glasses and wiped her eyes on her handkerchief, Foxy noticed with a cold shudder of shock that the green woollen twinset was no longer stretched around her plump body but hung loosely on bony shoulders and a flat chest.

After many requests from the others and persuasion by Madame, Ethel left the room and reappeared wearing a monocle in one eye and carrying a top hat and a silver handled walking stick. 'I'm Burlington Bertie from Bow,' she sang, 'I rise at ten thirty, I'm Burlington Bertie from Bow!' then strutted up and down the Persian rug twirling the stick and executed a little tap dance on the parquet flooring by the window.

'I can't believe the time has gone so fast and it's fifteen years since the last time we all worked together,' Bryony said wistfully when Ethel was seated in the armchair once more.

'I can when I look at the photographs of how I was then.' Eva slapped her hips to emphasise the point. She looked at Foxy. 'Enjoy being young and lovely while you can, dear, it lasts for such a short time. Make the most of it; I did!' She roared with laughter. 'We had some larks. My word, what fun we had!'

When Foxy asked them all what they now did for a living she was told that Eva and James ran a pub in Hendon and the two others worked in Swan and Edgars department store.

Bryony chuckled. 'It's not so bad. I quite like selling clothes instead of taking them off!' She smiled at Foxy. 'What d'you think you'll do later on?'

'I don't know.' She felt suddenly cold and frightened.

Ethel patted her arm. 'You've plenty of time yet. Mind you, I always say it's a good idea to save some money for a rainy day.'

'The trouble is,' Eva said, 'there's always a bloody downpour just when you least expect it.' She looked at Madame. 'How long d'you reckon to keep the club going, Fay?'

'I've got the lease for another seven years. I'll try to keep going fer that long if the tapeworm don't kill me in the meantime.'

Foxy opened her mouth to ask what that meant, thought better of it and kept quiet.

Meryl said, 'I think a sensible parasite keeps the thing it's feeding off alive, doesn't it?'

'True,' Ethel agreed, 'but that bastard might get more money out of a different kind of business. If the club had a drinks licence for instance, or gambling, or more exotic shows like the stuff they do in Hamburg.'

'What do they do there?' Foxy asked.

Meryl laughed. 'Very rude things that might shock an innocent like you.'

James, who had fallen asleep, awoke and looked at the mantelpiece, saying, 'I meant to tell you, Ethel, young Foxy knows all about that little carving of yours.'

Everyone looked expectantly at her and Madame said, 'Come on, yer'll 'ave ter tell us now.'

'It's just a guess,' she said lamely.

'Like when you saw Lady Jane being married?' Ethel asked.

'I didn't know you knew about that.'

'Oh, yeah, we knew.'

Eva was pink with excitement. 'Does this mean you can tell fortunes?'

'Not really.'

'Oh go on, please do it for us.'

'Please, Foxy, do it for us.'

They clamoured and pleaded until, eventually, she agreed to try for them, and, taking the gold chain Eva was holding towards her, she closed her eyes. 'I see a young girl on a stage. She's wearing a pretty pink frock and singing.' The next sight made her hesitate. 'You're a bit older and holding a little boy in a sailor-suit. You're very upset.' Hearing the intake of breath, she paused to ask, 'Shall I stop?'

'No, please go on.'

'There's a large stone building by a road, it has a wide door and beside that I see a young soldier holding a bunch of flowers. You come out. You have a scarf tied around your head, sort of like a turban. You call out, "Danny!"'

On opening her eyes she found Eva was weeping and the rest of the party were staring at her with their mouths agape.

James said, 'That's her son. Her husband took him to Australia.'

Meryl handed her a bracelet that gave messages of a richer, more comfortable childhood and similar life on the stage to Eva's which she described. Then Foxy exclaimed, 'Crikey! I see you getting into an ambulance.'

Bryony gasped and moaned, 'Oh my God!'

'No,' Foxy reassured her, 'it's not because she's ill or injured, she's driving it.'

'What? How extraordinary!'

Madame asked, 'Can you drive?'

Meryl nodded, looking very puzzled, 'Yes, I used to drive my father's car. But why on earth would I be driving an ambulance?'

Everyone shrugged and looked at one another.

Bryony held out a ring set with amethysts around a pearl.

Foxy smiled. 'I see Meryl giving you this. You're both in a room with a large window, like a studio.'

The two friends nodded.

'I see you have great love for each other and–' she paused as the scene changed and they stood side by side both with more solid bodies and white hair '–I see you will grow old together.'

Madame turned to Ethel, saying, 'It's your turn next, love, come on.'

'No, I think there's too many of us today.' She dabbed at her eyes with a lace handkerchief. 'Foxy'll do it for me another time.'

When James handed her a gold pocket-watch she described the farm he had left as a young boy and then the hot dry place where he was a soldier and finally, with joy, she said, 'I see you, much older than now, you're near a river and there are several small houses visible between the willow trees.' Opening her eyes, she grinned at him. 'You looked very cheerful and there was a woman who looked familiar in the shadows.'

They talked on about families, mutual friends and also, to her delight, reminisced about the 'old days' until, seeing Ethel had fallen asleep, the guests all decided it was time to leave.

After kissing her goodbye, Eva said, 'If you're ever out for a spin with er–' she hesitated momentarily '–your young man, we'd love to see you.'

She was momentarily lost for words and then,

seeing Madame making a face and shaking her head at Eva, thanked her and departed.

Hurrying homewards listening to her high heels tapping on the pavement, she momentarily wished there was another heavier tread alongside hers. Then, pulling up her collar and stooping forward into the biting wind, reminded herself that not only would Gerry not walk anywhere with her, he would never drive her to a pub in Hendon either, and Madame and everyone at the club had known that all along.

Chapter Eighteen

Sage is a good antiseptic and can be used for cleaning wounds.

Foxy stared gloomily into the mirror and assured her reflection she would tell Gerald of her decision to leave him. This would be his second visit to the flat in the six weeks since Christmas. On the previous occasion ten days ago she had intended making her declaration, but, after drinking several champagne cocktails to give her courage, she woke up the next morning in bed with him. She had then tried to talk to him after breakfast but was interrupted by the telephone and knew from the tone of his voice and the occasional overheard word of the ensuing conversation that he would be in no mood to listen to her problems whilst worrying about the possibility of war with Germany. Tonight she would definitely tell him their affair was over and she would neither get drunk nor sleep with him.

After waving at FiFi, who was the only other performer left in the dressing room, she went up the stairs and emerged into the cold night air. Seeing Ricky standing by Gerald's car, parked with the engine running as usual at the entrance to the mews, she walked across the uneven cobbles towards him.

A man emerged from a doorway opposite.

Ricky shouted, 'Get in the car, quick!'

Panicking, she ran, almost fell and then, with the bouncer's help, climbed inside. The door banged and a flash of light dazzled her.

Gerry muttered, 'Bloody hell!' He pressed his foot on the accelerator as another bright flash exploded through the window beside him. 'Get down, get down!' he shouted, pushing her roughly with his left hand and banging her head on the dashboard. 'Get down, you silly cow!'

Shocked and frightened, she crouched on the floor and felt her forehead crash against the edge of the glove compartment as the car jerked forward, and again, bang, as it screeched around a corner.

'Damn! Damn! Damn!' Gerry kept exclaiming as he drove along, then, stopping the car suddenly, he yelled, 'Get out!'

'What?' she asked, feeling confused, dizzy and in pain. 'What d'you mean?'

'Get out, quickly! You don't know me, d'you understand? You've never met me before. Get out, get out before they catch up. For Chrissakes get out, you stupid little cow!' He leaned across, opened the door and pushed her onto the pavement. The door slammed as she landed awkwardly on one foot and fell to her knees. Watching through her right eye as the car roared away she was aware of a warm trickle running into the left one, then, seeing a lamppost close by, she held onto it and pulled herself upright.

A deep voice asked, 'You alright, love?'

The heel of her shoe had come off and her ankle hurt. 'I think so, thank you.' Holding a handkerchief to her eye, she tried frantically to see where she was. This looked like any other back street. She needed a cab. 'Oh my God!' Her handbag was in the car and she had no money. Maybe a cabby might trust her to pay him when they got to the flat. The pavement was moving up and down, or was she floating and it was staying still?

The man said, 'Hold onto me, love.'

A vehicle screeched to a halt, a door banged and FiFi appeared beside her screaming, 'Leave her alone!'

'I was only trying to help. She fell out of a car, I saw... Alright, no need to push me.'

FiFi grabbed her arm, saying, 'I'm her friend, I'll look after her.'

'But she's hurt. There's something not right about this.'

'Bugger off!'

'I know when I'm not wanted.' The man walked away.

FiFi pulled her towards the waiting taxi. 'Come on, quick before they find you.'

'Who?'

'Come on, get in!'

She struggled into the cab and sank thankfully into the seat. FiFi obviously knew what was going on.

The cab driver said, 'I don't like the look of 'er. I'm goin' ter the 'ospital.'

'She'll be alright.'

'I said I'm goin'.'

She said, 'My handbag's in Gerry's car.'

'That's the least of your worries,' FiFi snapped and then added more gently, 'I'll look after you.'

The cab swung into a gateway and then stopped. FiFi exchanged a few words with the driver about the fare and then hurried her into a waiting room where a few people sat on the chairs lining the walls. 'I'll do all the talking, you just keep quiet.'

'Why?'

FiFi hissed, 'Shut up! Just keep your mouth shut. You don't want to get Gerry into trouble do you?'

She agreed and held her head, then, when a nurse came and asked what had happened to her, she hesitated.

FiFi quickly said, 'She's drunk. The silly cow got into a fight with another girl she thought 'ad taken 'er customer. It's always the same. It's the drink what does it every time. A little mouse when she's sober and a screamin' maniac when she's 'ad a few.'

Other people appeared and she heard random words from the muddle of voices around her. 'Badly cut.'

'Stitches.'

'Shock.'

A woman said, 'That's an expensive fur. Are you sure she's on the game?'

FiFi snorted. 'She probably stole it.'

'Her breath doesn't smell.'

'She drinks vodka! Look 'ere – are yer goin' ter fix 'er up or not?'

A discussion followed about a bed in the hospital. FiFi kept insisting there was no need for her to stay and she would take care of her.

Starched white aprons rustled beside her ear and then a man's voice said, 'She's very lucky. Another fraction of an inch and she'd have lost the eye.' He yawned. 'I'll stitch it up – silly girl.'

Feeling too weak to speak Foxy stopped listening to the voices overhead and closed her eyes. Either they knew what they were doing and she was helpless to stop them, or, more likely, this was a dream and she would wake up soon.

Eventually, although longing to stay prone amongst the rustling, bustling nurses, she obeyed FiFi's commands to get up and went with her in a taxi to an unknown destination where, too exhausted to speak, she staggered up a staircase into a room where she sank onto a bed and fell instantly asleep.

Her mouth was dry and her head throbbed with pain. Her mother was dead, but not in the tomb beside the lady where she belonged. The men had thrown her body into the cave by the river Her fingers gripped the wooden handle of the knife and traced the shapes of a man and woman intertwined...

She opened her right eye. This was not the secret cave, it was a dingy, unfamiliar room. Why was her left eye so swollen? She gave a low moan and then, seeing FiFi sitting on a stool in front of a small dressing table alongside her, remembered the events of the previous night.

'It's almost five o'clock in the afternoon. You've been asleep for a hell of a long time.' FiFi leaned forwards and held her hand. 'I'm afraid it's all got very messy and unpleasant.'

'What has?'

'The row.'

She raised her painful head and then sat up. 'What row?'

'Gerry's threatened to have the club closed down because of what you did.'

'Because I went to the hospital?'

'No 'cos you contacted the *News of the Globe*.'

'I did what?'

'Madame La Faye says you telephoned the editor and that's why they were waiting to take pictures of you.'

'That's insane!'

FiFi shrugged. 'Her and Ethel reckon you've been miserable lately. Everyone knows you're fed up with waiting for milord to marry you and anyway, he's obviously lost interest in you. We all know that.'

'But why would I call the press?'

'Madame seemed to think you were frightened you'd lose the flat if he dumped you, so you needed money. She's convinced you've been persuaded by the left-wing press. They'd love to see him involved in a scandal. She says they've been gunning for him because of his involvement with the fascists.'

'I'd suffer more than anyone if the club was closed!' She leaned back against the headboard. 'Anyway, he hasn't actually had anything to do with the blackshirts, he's just related to the bloke who leads them, or went to school with him, I forget now.'

FiFi placed a newspaper on the bed. 'Look at this.'

Squinting at the photograph of a man lying on the ground with a crowd looking down at him, she saw the caption beneath it. 'Mosley followers injure shopkeeper.' Then, seeing a paragraph lower down the page, read aloud, 'The Honourable Gerald Mottram stated to our reporter that all such thuggish behaviour was totally reprehensible and any imitation of the German Fascist movement was not welcome in this country.' She looked up at her friend. 'He's against them.'

FiFi frowned, took the paper and read the article, then threw it onto the bed. 'You don't think that's a coincidence do you? The slippery slimy snake's pulled strings to get that in today, it's obvious!'

Putting a hand up to her swollen eye, Foxy ran her finger lightly over the line of stitches on her forehead. 'I don't know what to think.'

'The other thing is–' FiFi gave a small cough '–the bastard wanted all trace of you removed from your flat.'

'What!' she gasped. 'I don't understand.'

'Gerry telephoned Madame La Fay and said

he'd burn anything left after today, so I went and got as much as I could. The janitor was breathing down my neck. It was all very embarrassing.' FiFi pointed to the sofa. 'The suitcases are behind there.'

'Oh no!' She sank into the pillows disconsolately. 'What on earth am I going to do? Where can I go?'

'Home?'

'I suppose I could go and grovel to my sister and stay there for a week or two. Oh God. What a mess!' How would Kate react? She might forgive and forget the past but, on the other hand, she might not want a millstone around her neck again.

'You could stay here with me while you decide what to do. I spend most nights with my boyfriend anyway so we could manage. It's not the luxury you're used to, I know.' FiFi looked at the sagging sofa and small table with two bentwood chairs, and then gestured towards the door in the corner, saying, 'But I do have an indoor toilet and a water tap in there, thank goodness! It's a bit of a squash but better than nothing.' She wrinkled her nose. 'And you can heat the water on that stinking oil stove.'

'It's a Beatrice, I had one like it in my basement; she only smells 'cos she needs her wick trimmed, that's all. Could I really stay here for a while?'

'Edie, the landlady, runs the café down below and she's already said you can stay. She's a good sort and so long as she gets the rent on time she asks no questions – she wouldn't mind visitors if you're discreet about it.'

'Why should she mind me having visitors?'

'You know what I mean. I'm only stating the obvious.'

Foxy stared at FiFi uncomprehendingly.

'How else are you going to get money?'

The meaning of her friend's insinuation became clear. 'Are you suggesting I should go on the game?'

'I don't see what else you can do. You can't work in a club looking like that, can you?'

Foxy climbed out of bed and gazed at her reflection in the mirror. Seeing a line of black stitches running diagonally across her forehead from the corner of her left eye to an area of shaved scalp above the right one, she muttered, 'I see what you mean.'

FiFi opened the door. 'You must be starving. Come on, let's go and get some food.' She led the way down the stairs, walked along the pavement and then opened the door into the café. Four taxi drivers who were sitting together eating bacon sandwiches looked up and smiled at them. 'After-noon, ladies,' one said, winking at the others.

'Hello, duckies.' The voice preceded the short plump figure of a woman who emerged from a kitchen at the back of the room walking with dainty steps on tiny feet, her wide hips swaying beneath a black satin gown and white apron. 'Welcome, Foxy.' Edie held out her puffy hands. 'Any friend of Fiona is a friend of mine.'

She took a step forwards, the room moved around her for an instant and the smiling face floated in a mist. When she opened her eyes she was on the floor being cuddled like a baby against an enormous, warm bosom. A ring of faces looked down at her as voices made suggestions. 'Give her a cuppa tea.'

'Nah, it's brandy yer need.'

FiFi said, 'She's been in an accident.'

'I can see that, poor darling!' Edie gave her a kiss then gently released her. 'Come on you lot, help the young lady get up.'

The men moved chairs and tables to one side, pulled her upright and then assisted her onto a chair.

Edie rose to her feet with the aid of a taxi driver pulling on each arm, and, having thanked them majestically, pushed a few wisps of fair hair behind her ears and made a graceful exit to the kitchen. When she emerged a few minutes later carrying plates of scrambled eggs and buttered toast, the men called out, 'Gor blimey that was quick!' and 'I fink I'll faint meself if that's 'ow yer gets served in 'ere.' They all cringed in mock fear when Edie swatted them with a cloth and then howled with laughter.

After quickly eating her food FiFi said she needed to go to work and hurried out.

Foxy sat quietly for several minutes until, feeling better for the nourishment, she decided to go for short walk to get some fresh air. Leaving the café, she turned left and passed by a barber's, ironmonger's and bookseller's shops, all of which had flats above them. Walking around the block she found a line of large wooden garages attached to the back of the buildings from which several taxis emerged and, at the far end, behind the café, was a dilapidated lean-to in which, looking between loose planks, she saw an old pram beside a heap of rubbish in one corner. When a bundle of rags stirred and stood up, she recoiled in horror, realising it was an old woman with long, unkempt grey hair. Hurrying away she soon reached the café again and returned to the room.

Although tired, she decided to sort through the two suitcases FiFi had salvaged from the flat and soon found her jewellery box amongst the clothes in one. In the other she found the handbag from that terrible night which contained her wallet and, very importantly, her post office book, admittedly smelling of perfume because the bottle had leaked, but she had it and therefore would have some money to tide her over for a few weeks. Maybe there would be no need to become a prostitute after all!

A green chiffon scarf caught her eye. Picking it up and twining it around her fingers she smiled at the memory of making a headband long ago. Looking like the film star Lara Crowe had been so important when she was very young – now she was almost twenty and about to emulate her because she was in need of something to hide a hideous wound on her forehead.

She went to the mirror and tied the fabric around her head, allowing the ends to hang over to one side onto her shoulder. Feeling pleased with her camouflage, she picked up the old grey fur coat and sank onto the bed, then fell into an exhausted sleep.

Looking up at the lady she grasped the handle of her knife and, feeling the shape of two figures intertwined, vowed she would take her mother's place...

Foxy awoke with a start, exclaiming aloud, 'The piece of wood! It was the handle of a knife!' Then, remembering where it was, added, 'My treasures!'

FiFi, who was in the small room in the corner with the door open while washing her hair, raised her head from the enamel basin balanced on the lid of the lavatory and asked. 'Your what?'

'Just some things I've left in the flat. What time is it?'

'It's ten o'clock in the morning. I've just got in. I stayed with my boyfriend last night.'

Looking down at her crumpled clothes, Foxy exclaimed, 'Crikey! I fell asleep fully dressed.' She stood up. 'I have to go to Grove Court.'

'You can't.' FiFi grabbed a towel.

'I must. I've got to get them.'

'I tell you it's too late. They'll have cleaned it out and he's probably got another woman in there by now...'

Reaching the door carrying her old fur coat and handbag, she called, 'I won't be long.' Then hurried down the steps and ran to hail a taxi.

On arrival at Grove Court she saw the janitor look around shiftily as though worried someone might see him talking to her.

'I'm sorry to trouble you, Mr Wallman.' She had always given him a title despite Gerry and all the other residents calling him plain 'Wallman'.

He smiled and straightened his back, puffing

out his chest and patting the medal ribbon on his jacket pocket. 'I'm afraid the lock's been changed, Miss Fox.'

She relaxed, knowing the small gesture of respect was now going to pay dividends. 'Yes, I thought it would be. I've left something in the flat, something important to me, but of no interest to anyone else. I wonder if I could...'

'There's nothing left, Miss. I checked it myself after your friend came and collected your things for you. She said as you'd asked her to get them and wouldn't ever be coming back.' He looked at the floor a moment and bit his lip. 'She said as I could have anything what was left. I was a bit worried but she insisted and...'

'That's alright, Mr Wallman, I don't want anything like that, I expect your daughter made use of a few things?'

'Yes, thank you, Miss Fox. She's delighted, but I could get them back for you, it's no trouble.'

'No, she's welcome to anything. All I want is this one favour.'

'The cleaner's been in, Miss. And—' he gulped '—I'm sure there's nothing.'

'Could you let me look in the wardrobe? Please, please, Mr Wallman, it's so important to me.'

'I dunno, I really dunno what to do.'

'You could come with me to see I don't do any damage or take anything.'

'I wouldn't think a lady like you would do no harm, Miss, it's just that I've been told not to let nobody in, see?'

'I do see. Yes, I do see your problem, I really do.' She sighed. 'My problem is that I don't remember the lease running out, you know, the one I signed?'

The man's jaw dropped slightly and his eyes told her what she wanted to know. She smiled and looked confidently at him. 'Tell me, please, Mr Wallman, when did the lease I signed run out?'

He looked like a hunted animal as his eyes swivelled around the lobby. 'Mr Mottram's solicitor arranged it.' He gulped. 'His daughter's moving in any day now, so she can get to the parties and that, for the season and that, and sort of go to the shops and that.'

She was impressed – what a stroke of genius and so quickly, too! Gerry would be seen in his car with a young woman as before. He would tell newspaper reporters this was the one who had been with him all the time. He would certainly want to avoid a confrontation between her and the daughter and so, therefore, would the janitor. She said thoughtfully, 'I suppose I could come back when Henrietta's here and ask for my things, would that be better d'you think?'

Mr Wallman reached for his keys. 'Come along, Miss Fox, we'll have ter be quick about it.'

He hurried up the staircase to number seven, unlocked the door and led her to the bedroom.

Opening the wardrobe door, she reached into the far corner and, touching the silk, she exclaimed, 'Thank God!'

'You alright, Miss?'

'Yes, I'm more than alright, Mr Wallman.' She pulled out the bundle and quickly stuffed it into her handbag. Then, pulling out her wallet, she looked into his grey eyes, saying, 'I'm so grateful.'

He put a hand over hers. 'No thanks, Miss Fox, it was a pleasure.' He looked at her face and evidently saw the stitches revealed when the scarf slipped during her exertions. 'You been in an accident, Miss?'

'Yes, Mr Wallman, I'm afraid so.'

They walked down the stairs together and he called a taxi for her. Looking back as the car pulled away, she waved and smiled whilst he stood to attention and saluted. Sighing with relief she hugged her handbag. The flat was no longer hers and Gerry had abandoned her. She had an ugly wound on her forehead and could no longer work at the club but – and she laughed aloud – she still had her precious treasures.

On reaching the room Foxy was surprised to find the door was ajar and there was no sign of FiFi. Assuming her friend had gone to work at the Gentlemen's Relish, she sank onto the sofa. Looking at the dressing table across the room, she noticed it was no longer cluttered with jars and bottles. Standing up, she pulled open the wardrobe and found it contained an old brown overcoat with several moth holes in the front, and three pairs of shoes in need of repair. Then, looking behind the sofa, she saw an untidy heap of her own clothes and a battered leather suitcase smaller than her own, and felt as though hit by a hard cold stone in her chest.

Chapter Nineteen

Dried coltsfoot can be smoked as herbal tobacco.

'I don't suppose you've heard anything from FiFi,' Edie said, sitting down at the café table six weeks later.

Foxy shook her head.

'I reckon she went straight to Hamburg. She'd been talking about it for months.' Edie leaned on her elbows and added, 'I still think you should've reported her to the coppers. I mean ter say, taking your jewellery and furs is robbery, isn't it?'

'All the valuable stuff was given to me by my boyfriend and I don't want to get the police involved in case they drag him into it.'

'Mmm, they'd probably ask a lot of awkward questions at that club, too. Best leave well alone.' Edie gave a beautiful smile. 'Look on the bright side. You're nice and cosy upstairs and now you're working at the cinema everything's working out fine.'

'Yes, I'm really grateful you let me take on FiFi's room and I was really lucky to get the job so quickly. I can't believe I was only out of work for two weeks.' She fingered the scar on her forehead. 'This gets a bit itchy under the makeup, but apart from that it's all worked out perfectly.'

'It's been a terrible time these past ten years, what with so many people unemployed, every job

238

gets snapped up immediately. After my Sydney died I realised the best way for me to earn a living was to keep the café going. Five years I've been doing it now and apart from this–' Edie patted her generous hips '–I've never regretted it. My trouble is I can't waste food. When you've seen starving little mite with white faces and sunken eyes like I have, you don't throw it away.'

She remembered the girl on the way to Clancy's funeral and asked, 'D'you have any children?'

'No, ducky, I couldn't keep 'em any more than three months. I used to grieve for those babies. I cried myself to sleep many a night and all around me there were women crying because they were having another unwanted mouth to feed.' She looked up at the print on the wall of a child sitting on a doorstep making bubbles with Pears soap. 'My little boy would've looked like that angel. I just know it. I'd have called him Bubbles, too, like the picture. I've got over it now of course, but I was very bitter for a long time, very bitter.' After giving a deep sigh, she asked, 'What's the film like this week?'

'It's quite difficult for me.' She touched the lover's knot ring on her little finger. 'It's about a group of showgirls and the star has a happy ending but–' tears welled in her eyes '–one of the girls kills herself and it's so like what happened to my friend, I don't know how I'm going to watch it for another five days.'

Edie reached out and patted her arm. 'I'd like to hear about her, ducky.'

'The thing that upsets me most is that I knew and I did nothing to stop her. I pretended I'd only seen her father giving the ring to her and then being drowned. I've only done it once since because it frightened me so much. Last Christmas I did it for friends, but I've tried to avoid it.'

'So how did you see this, did you read her palm or the cards?'

'No, I held this.' She pointed to the ring with her left forefinger.

Edie unpinned a gold brooch in the shape of a bow from the throat of her black frock. 'I've worn this every day since my Sydney gave it me on our wedding day.' She looked beseechingly. 'Please, ducky.'

Slowly and reluctantly Foxy took the brooch and held it until, seeing a slender young woman on a beach with a broad swarthy young man, she said, 'You're holding your skirts up as you paddle barefoot in the shallow water. The man with you walks a short distance away, picks up a stick and writes Edith and Sydney in the sand, then draws a big heart with an arrow through it. He writes plus two and you add two more.'

'That's the children we wanted,' Edie whispered.

'You jump on his back and he carries you piggyback towards the buildings and a sort of stone bank with a railing.'

'The promenade.'

'The picture's changed. He's wearing a brown uniform and you watch him walk towards you. You hesitate as though unsure what to do. You go to meet him and lead him into a small dark room with a bed at one side and a square table by the

240

window. He lies on the bed and starts coughing. You fold up a blanket and put it behind his head. He goes to sleep and you sit at the table with your head in your hands.'

'He was gassed. His lungs were never right afterwards.'

'There's a strong pungent smell.'

'He smoked special herbal tobacco, it was called...'

'Sh!–' Foxy put a forefinger to her lips '–I lose the picture when you speak too much.' She watched as the scene changed and Edie, plumper, but still much thinner than at present, was kneeling with her hands clasped in supplication. 'I see a beautiful stained-glass window to one side of you and a statue of a woman holding a baby, she has a blue cloak, you are praying to her.' Several glimpses of the same scene followed, plus one of a demented woman, her hair loose about her agonised face, throwing furniture and objects at a wall patterned with blue flowers. 'I see you are desperately unhappy, you are heartbroken.' The picture switched to a plump figure silhouetted against a flickering red and yellow background before she awoke to find herself sprawled on the floor with a pale frightened face gazing down at her. 'Fire!' she cried. 'You must be careful, Edie. I saw a fire!'

That evening, while reading a movie magazine by the light of her torch during the second film, she was interested to see Lara Crowe had opened 'The Jackdaw Club' in Hollywood and, while selling ice creams and choc bars from a tray hanging around her neck during the interval, was wondering what visitors did in such a club when, looking up into the next customer's face, she gasped in astonishment. 'Ricky!'

He gestured behind him at the long queue. 'I'll see you later.'

After the national anthem had been played and all the audience had left, she went out and found Ricky waiting for her. They wandered along the pavement to a bench close to a bus stop and sat down.

'A lot's happened since yer left,' Ricky said, cracking his knuckles. 'There's three new girls.'

'But I've only been gone six weeks.'

'I know, but the whole place seemed ter fall apart, what with you and FiFi goin' and then Priscilla went a couple of weeks ago. All the ones you knew have gone apart from Zarina and she's only hanging on 'cos of Ethel.'

'Is she ill?'

'Yeah, it's really bad. She collapsed a few days after you went and she's been in hospital ever since.'

'I'd love to go and see Ethel. She was so kind to me.'

'Then go.'

'But I don't want to get her into trouble with Madame.'

Ricky looked puzzled. 'Why should she mind?'

'Because of what happened with the press photographers. FiFi said Madame thought I'd arranged it, that I was the one who told the newspaper, so I can't...'

'She what!' Ricky placed his large hands on

either side of her shoulders. 'She thought you never came back 'cos you was angry with her.'

'Why would she think that?'

'FiFi said as you thought it was Madame what called the newspapers.'

'Oh my God!' They stared at each other and then agreed that Foxy must go to see her the following morning.

'I know everyone thinks I'm a hard-nosed bitch, well I am, mostly, but she's the love of my life, and I can't bear it.' Madame La Faye lit a cigarette and went on, 'That's a stupid thing to say. I can bear it. I do bear it for her sake. I shall bear it for as long as she does.'

Foxy looked at the photographs of herself on the walls and memories of the giddy giggling years she had thought would lead to marriage with Gerry came flooding back. How could she have been so silly?

'I never did like FiFi. I reckon she put 'em up to photographing you and Gerry and, either they didn't get a decent picture, or he managed to shut them up.' Madame laughed. 'Sorry, I know it's not funny for him, but it certainly set him on the straight and narrow. He hasn't been near the club since and I've seen him in the papers several times, looking very much the family man with his trouble and strife on one arm and his didn't-oughter on the other. We won't be seeing him again, I'm pleased ter say.'

Seeing Foxy's surprised reaction, Madame smiled knowingly. 'We go back a long way, Gerry and me, but he let the side down badly that night.

243

I wrote and told him what I thought of him an' all.' She sighed and went on, 'Years ago he was infatuated with me for a while, a stage door Johnny we'd have called him, but I've never liked men much in that way. We went about together and 'ad some larks an' that. He did me a few favours and even lent me some money to start my own company. Eventually he married his lovely Lydia, the belle of the ball, you know, debutante of the year at Queen whatsit's ball.'

'So, did you arrange for me to meet him?' Immediately regretting the question, she added, 'I just wondered, I don't mind if you did. I really don't.'

'That's the first time I've been accused of being a pimp!' Madame grinned. 'I'm sorry yer thought that, love. It was just pure chance he turned up out of the blue after several years. I suppose he'd got bored of Lydia and made some excuse to be in town that night. I really don't know. Anyway, he arrived, guessing I'd be having a party, no doubt, and you two hit it off.' She leaned forward. 'I did try ter warn yer, didn't I?'

'You certainly did and I still went on and believed what I wanted to. What I don't understand is why FiFi would want to tell the papers about Gerry and me.'

'I reckon she saw an opportunity to make a few quid from my landlord. She knew the bastard's been lookin' fer a way of gettin' us out of the premises and offered to set it up with reporters and photographs so there'd be a big scandal and we'd get a bad name. We'd lose most of our regulars if they thought the press 'ad their mince pies on us. Lucky fer us it didn't work and there never was nothing in the papers. The only person what's suffered is you with that scar on yer forehead.'

Foxy fingered the silk bandanna tied around her head and then asked about Ethel.

Madame stubbed out her cigarette in a crystal ashtray and lit another. 'I don't know how long I can watch her being crucified. I just sit there with her day after day, willing her to die. I know it means I'll be so lonely without her, but I want her to go.'

'Would I be in the way if I came with you to the hospital tomorrow?'

'Oh, Foxy love, I'd be so grateful if yer would. It's bleedin' torture waiting fer someone yer love ter kick the bucket.'

That night on returning to the room after seeing the distressing film again and wanting to escape from the memory of Clancy's terrible death, she took the piece of wood and lay on the bed...

The bright sunshine of early spring was shining through the newly opened leaves of the oak tree overhead as she sat holding the ball of pink quartz.

'Is it done, Mother?'

She shrugged and sighed. 'Aye, Myrtle. At last, after all these years. Although not perfect, I thought 'twould be good enough for scrying, but now I find I can see nothing.'

'May I hold it?'

Smiling at the child she placed it into her little hands.

Screwing up her eyes, the girl peered into the cloudy crystal for a while, then exclaimed, 'There's a girl with golden hair! I see her walk with a limp and on her face—' she bent closer '—there be a red mark.'

She leaned across. 'Show me.'

Myrtle shook her head. ''Tis gone.'

Chapter Twenty

Lemon balm tea is a safe remedy for headaches and morning sickness in pregnancy.

Leaning against a huge slab of granite beside the roaring log fire, Foxy looked around the saloon bar of the old inn and, listening to past echoes of hooves clattering on cobbles in the yard outside, thought of the many travellers who had rested in this room before climbing into a malodorous coach for the next stage in their uncomfortable journey. Then, hearing the rustle of a taffeta skirt above the low hum of voices, she watched Eva walk purposefully to the mahogany bar, turn to face the sombre gathering of people, pat the ostrich feather stuck in the side of her black felt hat and shout, 'Let's give our Ethel a good send-off. The drinks is on Fay and the food's on us, so get stuck in!'

The atmosphere lightened as the barmaid pulled pints of beer into tankards and filled glasses with port and lemon, and Eva handed plate after plate of pork pie and jellied eels around to everyone, then, when faces were glowing with food and drink a man shouted, 'Come on, Eva, let's 'ave "My Old Man".'

The feather in her hat swung back and forth as Eva nodded. 'Later, Bert, I'll do that later.' She clapped her hands, and when all in the room were silent, she said, 'We give our Ethel a proper funeral back there in Edmonton, but now we're gonner have a party in her honour.' She gestured to a small, white-haired figure sitting by the bay window and called out, 'Give us a poem, Freddy.'

The elderly man held onto a chair while pulling himself upright and, balancing precariously on a walking stick, took a deep breath and then recited, 'Strew on her roses, roses and never a spray of yew. In quiet she reposes. Ah! Would that I did too!'

There was a long, still silence. The old man fought to control his mouth before eventually saying, 'I can't remember the rest of it. I think Matthew Arnold wrote it.' And he sank back onto the seat behind him.

A huge man of heavy build with enormous hands and feet stood up and sang in a sweet, boyish voice, 'Two little girls in blue, lad; two little girls in blue.'

When Foxy went to the man who had read the poem and thanked him, he patted her arm, saying, 'Don't forget her, love. The only way we achieve immortality is in the memory of those we leave behind.'

Everyone was very emotional, very loud, very jovial and, eventually, very drunk. Madame La

Fay and Meryl took their shoes off and stood on a table to sing several old music hall songs. Eva's hat slipped further and further sideways as she sang, 'My old man said follow the van and don't dilly daily on the way.' James and the large man, whose name was Teddy Baire, joined in with this and also 'Daisy, Daisy give me your answer do', and 'If you were the only girl in the world'.

Eva led all the mourners in a 'Lambeth Walk' in and out of the public and saloon bars, encouraging the other customers to dance with them, which some of them did in a good-humoured, albeit self-conscious, way.

Feeling dizzy and hot, Foxy backed away from the wildly thrashing throng and leaned against the cool wall. Jane's husband had been sensible when persuading Jane not to come here after the funeral because the baby was due very soon. She would have found the heat and the smoke all too much in her condition and wouldn't have enjoyed it at all. Clancy, on the other hand, would have loved this party. She'd have danced to 'Knees up Mother Brown', swishing her skirt to reveal lace petticoats and pink suspenders. She'd have sat on the bar with her legs crossed as she sang along with the others. Oh, Clancy, Clancy, a little of what you fancy, why are you dead? And why are all these people screaming with laughter when Ethel is dead too? Then, closing her eyes and shutting out the sight of grinning red faces, she understood. The sound of their helpless mirth was almost the same as that of distraught weeping.

Awakening the next morning with pain thundering in her head and her stomach churning, she ran to the lavatory where she swore, on her knees, never to drink alcohol ever again.

An hour later, although not wishing to speak to anyone, not even Edie, but needing to give her the rent she had forgotten to pay the day before, she walked into the café.

Edie took the money and said, 'You can't go to work in the cinema looking like that, ducky.'

'I've got two days off. I'm going to see Madame at the club.'

'Fancy scrambled eggs?'

Cold sweat formed on her forehead as she fought the nausea. 'No thanks. I'd like a piece of dry toast, please.'

Placing it before her a few minutes later, Edie asked, 'Have you had any word from the bloke you were with?'

'No, that's all over.'

'What'll you do on your own?'

'I dunno, just keep going I suppose.'

'I meant about, you know what.'

'What?'

Edie waved her hand. 'Nothing, ducky, nothing.'

Foxy was intrigued. 'What's so mysterious?'

'I just thought you looked like it, that's all. My mistake, ducky. Forget I ever mentioned it.'

'Mentioned what?' Whilst uttering the words she knew Edie was right. Nodding agreement, she conceded, 'I don't know for sure.'

'How many have you missed?'

'One.'

'Ever done that before?'

'No, I thought it might be because of all the worry, you know, the accident and...' She burst into tears.

Edie was immediately beside her, one arm around her shoulders and the other hand offering a handkerchief. 'We'll be alright, ducky. We'll stick together, everything in the garden will be lovely, you'll see, mark my words.'

Dabbing her eyes, she fought for control. 'Thanks, Edie, you're such a friend. I really do have to go.'

Leaning back whilst being driven along Oxford Street she closed her eyes. Inside her was a child fathered by a man who thought she had betrayed him to the press and who had never intended marrying her anyway. The most he might do would be to give her money for an abortion and if he denied being the father it would be her word against his.

On arrival at the club she found Madame looking very old and tired. 'I'm closing down, Foxy. I can't go on.' She held up a letter. 'The landlord's demanding more rent, but what he really wants is for me to leave so he can take it over.'

'I know you've told me that before, but why does he want it?'

'The club's already set up and if he encourages more audience participation with the girls, if yer see what I mean, and maybe gets a drinks licence, plus a few deals on the side, he'd have a nice big earner.' She waved her hand at the photographs of her earlier career. 'We're a hangover from the old music-hall way of doing things, like what I'm used to. My Ethel was right when she persuaded me to change to the Gentlemen's Relish and we done very well with it. She saw we was out of date, said we had ter move with the times. But even though we done the stripping and that, I prided myself we was never common. Always had a bit of style we 'ave.'

The telephone rang and Madame answered it. 'Yeah. Yeah, I received your note. What? I don't give a Friar Tuck about your overheads. Reasonable! There's no need ter shout, I'm not Mutt and Jeff. Yer can 'ave the lease back and stuff it up yer Khyber Pass!' She slammed the telephone down. 'My Ethel knew how to talk to him, but I can't bloody do it.' Then, pulling out a bottle from the filing cabinet beside the desk, said, 'A little medicinal is called for.' Having taken a swig she offered the bottle to Foxy and seeing her decline with a shake of the head, she nodded. 'Yer right, it's best to keep a clear loaf in this situation.'

'What will you do?'

She sighed. 'I don't rightly know. I've got our savings for the little hotel we was goin' ter run somewhere like Bournemouth or one of them seaside places with a bit of class. We talked about it endlessly and never did decide exactly where.' She stared disconsolately at the wall. 'I can't bear to be in the flat. Eva's persuaded me ter go and stay with them while I look around.' She lit a cigarette and inhaled. 'I couldn't do it on my own. Ethel was the one with the ideas, I told yer that.' She exhaled the smoke and stared at the wall for a few moments. 'I could do it with you.'

'I don't know the first thing about hotels,' Foxy replied. 'I've never even stayed in one!'

'Didn't you never go nowhere with Gerry?' Then, without waiting for an answer Fay added, 'No, that's what the flat was all about, 'cos he wouldn't want ter risk being seen with yer on account of the scandal.' She shrugged. 'You'd soon learn.'

'But what about cooking and cleaning?'

'I reckon we could manage the cooking and we'd pay other people ter do the cleaning.'

Foxy took a deep breath. 'There's something else, something I should tell you.'

'A baby?'

'Crikey! How d'you guess?'

'I've worked with women all my life and I can usually tell when they've got a bun in the oven. Sometimes, not always, the bosom gets bigger, like yours has, and just a certain look.'

'We got drunk on champagne cocktails one night when I was trying to get up the courage to tell Gerry I wanted to end it. I suppose that's when it happened.'

Madame opened the safe beside her desk. 'The offer for the hotel still stands.'

'With a baby?'

'Yer could fix that, it's been done before.'

'I need to think about it.'

Madame looked in a notebook and copied out two addresses onto the back of a used envelope. 'These might be useful.' She held out a bundle of notes. 'And this'll pay fer what's necessary, or, if yer decide ter keep it, yer'll have enough oak an' ash to keep yer going until I'm settled.' Then,

252

dismissing Foxy's expressions of gratitude with a wave of her hand, went on, 'When I've settled on something, I'll send for yer. If yer wants ter come yer can and if not that's okay too.' She laid a hand on her shoulder. 'With or without a baby, we could manage.'

They sat in silence for a few moments until Foxy voiced her thoughts, 'I wonder what Ethel would've advised me to do.'

'She wouldn't want yer ter do what Clancy done fer one thing and she wouldn't want yer goin' on the game to support it neither.' Madame frowned and asked, 'What about all them herbs yer gran used ter give people?'

'It won't be so easy to find them in London. I'll go back now and think about that.'

Madame reached into her handbag and pulled out a small parcel. 'Here's a little memento. Now, off yer go and make yer mind up.'

On arriving back in her room, Foxy untied the string and opened the brown paper to find Madame had given her Ethel's little ivory figures. For an instant she saw a strikingly pretty young woman playing cards with three men, one of whom handed her the small carving. 'Here, Ethel,' he said, 'take this, it's worth more than my shirt.' The group laughed and faded away into the past.

Remembering the conversation earlier she picked up the bundle of treasures and sat on the bed holding her grandmother's cameo brooch.

'You'm needing good nourishing food in your condition.'

'I want to know the plants to get rid of it, Gran.'

253

There was no sound in the room but the ticking of her alarm clock.

She rubbed the figure carved into the shell. 'I remember the one with flowers like a foxglove that grows by the river near Trout Bend. I'm sure I could find that one by the Thames. The trouble is, when we picked it you said it was very dangerous and could kill anyone who took too much and it should only be taken with a mixture of other herbs. Oh, Gran, I don't remember what the others were – please help me. I'm desperate, please, please help me.'

A car horn hooted in the road outside. A door banged. A man called out, 'See yer later.'

She screwed up her eyes, trying to will her grandmother's voice to come through, but there was nothing. Eventually, feeling exhausted, she replaced the brooch and picked up the little piece of wood...

She was standing in the river placing a trap for fish when she saw the movement in the willows. After turning to ascertain that Myrtle was still sitting making a basket from withies, she moved slowly and carefully towards the bank, then said, 'Come forth if thee wishes to speak with me.'

The drooping branches parted and a woman stepped forward holding a baby. 'I need thy help, mistress.'

She looked at the dark shadows under the eyes of both mother and the pale, thin child. 'I can give thee a remedy for the worms in thy little one.'

'Nay. 'Tis for that what is growing in me, mistress.'

The nuns had said this was a sin. Every time she

helped a woman in this way she thought of Sister Elfreda and of Marie who believed she would be eternally damned.

'I beg thee, mistress. There be no food for the children already born and my man be so sick with fever he cannot work in the fields.'

'Come, follow me to my dwelling and I will give thee all I can.'

Walking along the path with Myrtle skipping ahead and the woman following behind, she admitted the nuns might well be right and she would go to hell, but this woman was now in a hell on earth, and she could not bear to refuse her.

On awakening the following morning Foxy went through the dream again and again, desperately trying to remember the herbs she would have given the woman, but, although she could see the linen bags containing dried plants hanging near the fire and knew which one contained the necessary mixture, the contents of it remained a mystery. Kate would know, but she couldn't go crawling back begging for help – no, there must be a way without admitting to her sister what a mess she'd made of her life. She'd recognised lots of plants on the common near the furrier's shop and even seen some growing in the park nearby, and, if the worst came to the worst she could find the one Gran had said was dangerous and take the risk, but first she would go and visit one of the addresses Madame had given her. That would get it over and done with quickly. In fact, yes, she would go this very morning.

A few minutes later, while combing her hair

after dressing, she heard a tentative knock on the door and she hurried to open it.

'I was a bit worried, ducky.'

'Edie, how kind!'

'You won't do anything silly or illegal like, will you?'

'I don't know yet. I'll have to think about it.'

The rounded body quivered as Edie pleaded, 'Promise me, ducky. Please, promise you won't do it. I'll help. I'll look after you. We'll manage together.'

'I don't know.'

'Those women with knitting needles can make you bleed to death. And if the police catch you it's terrible. I knew a poor soul was being done and the coppers burst in right in the middle of it all. They held up her knickers in court as evidence and...'

'Please, Edie, please stop.'

'I'm only doing my best for you. I don't want you bleeding to death or going to prison.'

'I know, I know, I am grateful. I promise to think it through. I really will. Now I have to go out.'

Edie turned and left the room, banging the door behind her.

On arrival outside a dilapidated but still imposing old house in Stoke Newington two hours later, Foxy walked up the wide stone steps leading to the front door and rang the doorbell then waited, knocked on the door and waited again. Eventually, after several attempts, a window above her opened and a man said, 'Go away!'

She called up to him, 'I've been given this address for Mrs Smith.'

'She's been took. I told yer, bugger off.'

Realising what he meant, she looked about her for a possible police presence, saw no sign of anyone and hurried away feeling sick with fear and with a headache settling behind her left eye.

Having taken a taxi to a street close to the second address, she walked towards a row of houses thinking the slums seemed dirtier than ever in the bright burning sunshine. A large dog appeared from the dense shadows of an alleyway and showed her its teeth in a menacing grimace. 'Here, Bruce!' a man's voice shouted before he too emerged into the sunlight, paused to stare at Foxy while hitching up his trousers and fastening a thick leather belt under the curve of his over-hanging belly. 'Lost are yer?'

'I'm looking for number twenty-three.'

He gestured towards a house nearby before walking away, followed by the snarling hound.

Several filthy children with scabs around their mouths came sidling up to her and a face peered out from an upper window. Looking at a girl swinging on a garden gate, she saw a tiny insect crawl across her forehead and felt an itch in her own scalp, and then one on her back, then another and another until her whole body was raging with irritation. Turning without stopping to think, she hurried away, scratching frantically.

There were no cabs cruising in the area and she took the first bus going towards the West End. Choosing to sit on the lower deck because the cigarette smoke upstairs made her feel queasy, she found the only empty seat was beside a young woman holding a little girl on her lap. The child stared solemnly and unblinkingly at her for several minutes, took her thumb out of her mouth and reached forward to touch Foxy's hair, thereby knocking her hat slightly askew.

'No, naughty girl!' the mother said pulling the small hand away.

'I don't mind.' She straightened the hat and asked the child her name.

'Tell the nice lady what your name is, Susan.'

'Thoothy.' The child put her thumb in her mouth and buried her face in her mother's shoulder.

The woman looked fondly at the child and stroked her fair curls. 'She's gone all shy, silly-billy.'

She longed to hold the plump little body and touch the shining hair from which no flea was likely to emerge. This was a well-nourished child with perfect skin and bright eyes. Her daughter would be like this; an inquisitive person wanting to touch things and experience life, but still needing to wriggle into her mother's arms when feeling shy or unsure of her surroundings. 'My little girl will be called Myrtle,' she heard her voice speaking as if independent of her brain.

'That's nice,' the woman said politely.

Staring unseeingly out of the window, Foxy knew this was the right decision. A lonely un-married future lay ahead bringing up an illegiti-mate child, but – she hugged her handbag to the safe place where a tiny baby was growing – she'd manage somehow. She'd cope without a man, and anyway, there could never be a love in her life again like Gerry!

On arrival at the café she saw the building swathed in a swirling mist, and then, whilst reaching for the door, suddenly knew no more. Opening her eyes she found Edie and a taxi driver were looking anxiously down at her whilst she was lying on the pavement with a pain in her right knee.

'She's fainted.'

'Water, she needs water.'

'Should we call a doctor?'

'I'll be alright. I'm tired and thirsty. I'm–' she sat up '–I'm pregnant, that's all.'

Edie burst into tears.

They helped her into the café. 'A cup of tea, lady, that's what yer need,' the cabby said placing her handbag on the table.

Edie appeared, red in the face and bustling with excitement. 'I'll look after her now. She'll be alright with me.'

Sinking onto a chair, Foxy was relieved to be cared for by such an attentive friend.

Edie looked like a young girl as she placed a plate of scrambled eggs on the table a few minutes later. 'I'm so pleased you're back home, ducky. I've been terribly worried about you and little Bubbles.'

Looking up at the picture on the wall of a small boy playing with soap and water, she decided against arguing that she knew, just knew some-how, a little girl was growing inside her. It was good to be with Edie again, good to see the welcoming smiles of the cabbies and even good to see the tramp they called Smelly Nelly stop slurping her tea for a moment to nod a battered straw hat in her direction.

Easing herself onto the chair opposite her, Edie leaned forward resting her large bosom on the table. 'I've been thinking, ducky. They won't want yer in the cinema in your condition.'

'I'll be going to work for Madame when she's in her hotel.'

'That'll take time to organise. You can work for me until then.'

Chapter Twenty-one

Ragwort, also known as St James' wort, should not be taken internally. It is best used externally for ulcers and wounds or as a gargle for mouth ulcers and the quinsy.

Sitting on the bench beneath the naked trees in the centre of the large square she placed her hands around the baby within her and took stock of the situation. Helping in the café for the past seven months, although not always easy, had at least made the time pass quickly and now that she had stopped work and made all the arrangements for the birth all she had to do was wait for the arrival of Myrtle. She had booked a room in the maternity home in Holland Park and the cot, carrying basket and small enamel bath were all arranged in her room, as were the tiny nightdresses, nappies and woollen garments – including those knitted by Edie which were all blue in the hope of a little boy she could call Bubbles.

Hearing the sound of people singing in the church across the road, she thought of Uncle Albert. 'Abide with me' was one of his favourites and he often hummed it while sharpening his scythes outside the back door. If the old man were here now he'd be joining in, knowing every word by heart and perfectly in tune. She grinned. He'd also be singing a fraction behind everyone else – not that the inhabitants of Oakey Vale seemed to mind. A choirboy did get the giggles from time to time, but it wasn't necessarily about that.

Gazing through the metal railings enclosing the churchyard she focussed on the lines of headstones marking graves and imagined skeletons lying in coffins under the earth. A taxi driver had once told her the squares in London had been formed around pits in which the victims of the Black Death had been buried. If that were true then she was sitting above another graveyard and this oasis in the middle of tall brick and stone buildings contained the remains of hundreds of people who had once been tiny babies like the one now kicking within her.

A deep pain suddenly overwhelmed her, and, gripping the metal arm of the bench, she breathed deeply until it had washed away. This was it. Myrtle was ready to be born. Standing up she held the grey squirrel coat as far around her as it would go and then walked slowly homewards through the windswept streets, stopping from time to time to accommodate the cramping pain. Despite longing to warm herself by Beatrice, she took the longer route around the block in order to avoid passing the café where Edie might see her through the window. Her friend had been watching her every move for weeks now and, although knowing the constant offering of care and advice was given with love, it was beginning to feel like a relentless assault on her privacy. She needed time alone to prepare for the ordeal ahead.

On arrival in her room, out of breath from climbing the stairs, she reached under the bed and pulled out the old leather suitcase FiFi had left behind, which was already packed for her confinement. Knowing one of the two catches no longer worked and the other was loose, she began looking for a leather belt to strap around it but, after searching her room and unable to find one, she carried the case carefully down the stairs to the street.

Standing on the pavement to one side of the café in the hope that Edie might be busy in the kitchen and therefore unable to see her, she waited for a taxi in the biting wind. When one at last arrived, she climbed in, closed the door and sat back with a sigh of relief but then forced a smile as Edie, still wearing a large white apron climbed in and put her arm around her, saying, 'Thank heavens I saw you, ducky. You'll be alright, now. Don't worry, I'm here to look after you.'

All the way to the nursing home Edie kept asking how she felt and then not listening to her reply. On arrival outside the large house in Holland Park she quivered excitedly, fussing around her and demanding the attention of the nurse who came to greet them, urging her to hurry up, get on with it and stop dilly dallying. Once inside the hallway, while struggling to keep the one arm around Foxy, she took the suitcase from the taxi driver with the other hand and then gave a raucous screech as the loose catch slid open and all the contents fell out.

In the gap between pains Foxy watched Edie sink to her knees and frantically scrabble around picking up the safety pins that had spilled out of a cardboard container and spread across the black-and-white tiled floor. When a second nurse came and, having exchanged looks with the one who was repacking the muddle of nightdresses and nappies, led her up the stairs, she was glad to follow. On arrival in a small room directly above the hall, she heard the nurse below say loudly and emphatically, 'We will call you when your daughter is delivered. Now please leave us to look after her.'

After closing the door, thereby shutting out any further sounds from the hallway, the nurse soon assured her, in a calmly detached manner, that she had many hours of labour ahead. Then having settled her into bed said, 'We have your mother's address so we can send a telegram in case of emergency. Is there any way we can contact your husband?'

Foxy hesitated. Edie would be humiliated and heartbroken if her lie was discovered. Maybe it was unimportant? Surely no one really minded who was or was not her mother?

'Your husband?'

She wanted the woman to leave her in peace and let her concentrate on this strange and rather frightening situation. Fingering the wedding ring bought from a pawnbroker in order to look the part, she replied, 'He's in the army. My mother will let him know.'

Some time later she heard a woman moaning in the room next door. Fear gripped her as the intervals between pains became shorter. 'All things pass,' she whispered, 'this will end, it *will* end.' Then added, 'I don't have to accept this suffering. I can rise above it. I can rise *above* it.' Over and over again, as the tide of pain ebbed and flowed through her, she demanded that her brain should ignore what her body was feeling and so floated away from the agony, firstly to look down on herself curled over in travail and then away to the little dwelling in the valley.

Leaving Myrtle playing with her dolls she wrapped her cloak around her and went outside the dwelling to fetch more wood for the fire. Having picked up an armful from the stack of fuel close by, she paused to admire it and the clods of turf heaped nearby. If she was careful and managed them well then the fire would burn until spring. With a smile of satisfaction she glanced at the cave, thinking of the bounty of summer and autumn stored therein and then looked first at the nanny goats in their compound on one side of the clearing and the billy tethered on the other. The winter would be harsh and long, but she was prepared

264

for it.

Hearing the rooks give warning of someone approaching, she turned towards the path and waited to see who was coming to visit her. Then, seeing a young girl who had come last winter seeking a spell to make a man love her, she walked sadly to greet her.

The cloak which the girl was holding around her swollen belly was muddy and torn. 'My father has cast me out. I have slept in the woods these past weeks praying for death but now I am feared of dying alone. I pray thee, let me bide a while until the child be born.'

Nothing would be gained by reminding her of the warning she had given, but, inside her head she repeated, 'Those who be wished to love against their will may not be kind in times to come.' Taking the girl's arm, she simply answered, 'Aye,' then led her inside and helped her to sit close by the smouldering fire.

'I tied his hair to the doll as thee said. His passion was great and I thought as all was well—' she bit her lip '—but now he spurns me and says as any man could be the father of this child.'

Seeing the girl's face contort with pain she knew her time was come. Remembering the nuns saying prayers for the destitute mothers and their tiny offspring, she wondered what life this poor soul would have if she did survive. Then, putting her sadness aside, she smiled down into the frightened girl's eyes. ''Tis a miracle from God,' she said.

'I beg thee, do not leave me.'

'Fear not. I shall stay by thee and my daughter will tend the fire to keep us warm.' She prepared linen with which to wrap the child and tested her knife to be sure

the blade would cut the cord cleanly. Then, having sent Myrtle to fetch water for washing away the blood, she looked into the fire as always when attending a birth and asked for the ancestors to keep company with her. From the wisp of smoke out of the fire she saw two women in white arise and sit beside the girl, then settled down herself to wait for the baby to be born. These spirits looked like the sisters in the convent but with white veils over their heads instead of black which seemed odd, but, feeling safe in their loving care, she closed her eyes and dozed.

Awakening with a start, she heard the women encouraging the girl.

'Push now,' they said, and again, 'push now, my dear.' A few moments later as the tiny child slithered into life, one said, 'It's a girl. A beautiful little girl.'

Suddenly finding she was not in the dwelling but lying on a bed in a small room, she realised the two women who had kept vigil with her were not the spirits of nuns in white veils but the nurses she had met on arrival at the maternity home. 'It's a miracle!' she whispered.

'You were a model patient,' said one.

'It was a textbook delivery,' said the other.

The following day, Friday the eleventh of November, Fay arrived at two o'clock with a bunch of roses and a newspaper.

Taking the paper Foxy read the headline, '"Nightmare as brown shirts rampage." Oh my God, whatever's happened now?'

Fay answered, 'Them Germans have burned synagogues and smashed lots of Jews' shop win-

266

dows. They got no call fer doin' that just on account of them bein' four-be-twos. Disgustin' I call it!'

Foxy nodded sadly and then, gazing down at the sleeping baby in the small cot beside her, thought of her future and asked about the property in Chiswick.

'The transaction's complete,' Fay replied, 'and I'll be moving there in four weeks.'

'I can't wait to get there and take Myrtle for walks by the river.'

'It might be a bit rackety for a while, lots of work to be done. Yer could hang on fer a couple of months where yer are, couldn't yer?'

'Oh, Madame, I don't know.'

'Fay's the name now.'

'Alright, Fay. I'd really like to come as soon as possible.'

'I can see that little room up all them apples and pears would be difficult with a baby.'

'I really do need to get away.'

Fay hitched the fox fur around her shoulders. 'I'll have ter go soon, the ghost of Florence Nightingale said she'd give me an enema if I stayed a minute after three o'clock.'

'So can I come soon, please?'

'It'll be chaos, Foxy love, there'll be builders knocking down walls and taking up rotten floorboards. I'll let yer know when they're finished.'

'Our favourites from Acton?'

'Yeah. I thought that way I'd get ter see Jane as well.'

The door burst open. 'I couldn't wait any longer to see my granddaughter!' Edie exclaimed. Her face was flushed with excitement and her blue eyes flashed at Fay before focussing on the baby. Picking up the sleeping child, thereby causing her to awaken, whimper and start searching for food with her mouth, she clasped her close to her large bosom and sat beside the bed crooning to the increasingly distressed baby.

Reaching forward Fay put her hand out to touch the small face and, as two pink lips sucked at her finger, she said, 'She looks like a little bird.'

At that moment a nurse came through the doorway and placed some clean gauze squares on the bed; 'I'll come back in a few minutes.' Smiling at Edie she added, 'I expect you've changed more nappies than I have in your time.'

Fay snorted with laughter before announcing she would leave and, after kissing Foxy gave her a small card, saying, 'Here's the address.'

'The Laurels, Hardy Road,' she read out and then laughed. 'I'm not likely to forget Laurel and Hardy.'

'See yer in Chiswick. Tee tee eff enn.'

Foxy blew a kiss. 'Ta ta fer now. I'll come as soon as you say I can. I don't care what sort of a mess it's in.'

When Edie brought a recently delivered letter to her on Christmas Eve while she was feeding the baby, she opened it with one hand and read it aloud, 'Dear Foxy, Here is a cheque to buy presents for you both. The building work has been delayed. I am in a right mess what with dry rot in the floors. It will be too dirty for a small baby for months. I suggest you stay put until March when it should be finished. Will come to see you soon. Lots of love, Fay.' Looking up she smiled tentatively saying, 'This means I'd like to stay a bit longer than I thought. I hope that's alright with you.'

Edie closed her eyes for a moment. Her mouth changed from smiling to a thin line and back to smiling again. 'That place sounds unsuitable anyway, ducky. You're much better off staying here. I'd forget the whole thing if I was you.'

'No, Edie, I've decided to go. It's been delayed a bit that's all.'

'I'd have thought we were managing very well between us. I've come up and down these stairs every day to help you. I've let the business run down. I don't know what else I can do.'

'You really don't need to keep coming up like this, Edie. I can manage, I really can.'

Edie sniffed and bent down to pick up a small bootee from the floor.

Foxy moved the baby from one breast to the other. 'You could visit us often. It's quite easy to get there on the tube. We'll be able to go walking in the park and by the river. Fay says Kew Gardens isn't far away and it's so lovely when the magnolias are in bloom.'

Edie looked away. 'I hate those underground trains.'

'I think it's mostly above ground after Earls Court.'

'Sounds to me like she's having second thoughts.'

'About what?'

Edie pretended not to hear the question and

walked to the door, saying, 'I've got the plum pudding ready for boiling and the chicken's stuffed. See you at three tomorrow?'

'Looking forward to it,' she replied, wondering if Madame was indeed regretting her invitation. A small child might be an encumbrance in a guest house, especially one catering for theatrical types who led a bohemian existence.

Christmas day was a tense disappointment. Having refused wine because she was afraid of the effect when feeding Myrtle, she then anxiously watched Edie, who had obviously been drinking whilst preparing the meal, pick up the baby and dance around the room with her singing 'I'm forever blowing bubbles, pretty bubbles in the air.'

They pretended to be happy whilst eating chicken with roast potatoes and Brussels sprouts followed by plum pudding and custard until Edie, who had drunk continuously during the meal, suddenly began weeping for her dead babies. Then, after a few minutes during which Foxy tried to console her, she leaned her arms on the table and fell forward in a deep sleep.

Chapter Twenty-two

Fumitory may be helpful for problems of blood circulation, the heart, the digestion and the skin.

'I'm sorry it's took so long fer me ter come and see yer. These past four months were a nightmare,' Fay said, pushing a pile of baby clothes to one side of the sofa, then, after sitting down, added, 'There was a filthy old pram outside the café when I arrived. I thought fer an 'orrible moment it were yours.' She gave a neighing laugh. 'I weren't half relieved when I took a butcher's 'ook inside and saw it were full of rubbish.'

Foxy smiled down at the sleeping baby in her arms as she replied, 'That's Smelly Nelly's. She sleeps in a shed at the back when she's not out pushing that pram round the streets. Edie's very kind and gives her cups of tea. The poor old soul's probably the only one of the regulars who still goes there – when it's open that is.'

Looking at the nappies hanging on a rope over the oil stove, Fay raised an eyebrow. 'You'll certainly be better off at The Laurels. There's a big garden with a washing line and if it's raining we can dry things over the Ideal boiler in the kitchen.' She lit a cigarette then added, 'The flat's almost ready for yer. Jane's making some pretty curtains fer Myrtle's room and there's a surprise she made fer yer birthday last week. She's convinced the fourteenth of March was yer twenty-first, is that right?'

Foxy nodded.

'We agreed we'd have a belated party for yer. She's so excited and looking forward to seeing yer again and her Dave says he'll come and fetch yer next Sunday in his van. She's dying ter see the baby.'

'I can't tell you how grateful I am, Madame.'

'Fay's the name nowadays. We don't want the guests thinking it's a knocking shop, do we?' Hearing Foxy chuckle, she said, 'That's better. I was beginning ter think yer'd forgotten how ter do that.'

'I've been worried in case having Myrtle and me was too much and you didn't like to say so. I mean I really would understand if...'

'Don't be silly! I'm looking forward to it and so's Twankey.'

'Who?'

'He's sort of come with the property yer might say. Been stayin' there fer years 'cos the Chiswick Empire's not far away. You'll love him. He's been playing dame in the panto fer so long he's forgotten his real name.'

'The pantomime doesn't go on all year does it?'

'No, he goes round selling brushes and cleanin' stuff door ter door in between times. There's other regulars what travels from one place ter another doin' variety acts like singers an' conjurers an' that and they just stay fer a week at a time.' Fay grinned. 'He's bought a brass doorknocker in the shape of Laurel and Hardy on account of the address, The Laurels, Hardy Road.'

Foxy laughed and then found she was crying. After a few moments she explained. 'It's all getting on top of me. I'm desperate to get away. Edie's been very kind to me, but the situation is turning into a nightmare. She doesn't want me to leave and keeps trying to persuade me you don't really want us and just feel obliged to keep your word. She walks in any time from morning 'til night and acts as though she's my mother. In fact I don't suppose a real mother would take Myrtle over the way she does. If I ever try to explain I want privacy or have a view on what's right for my baby, she just makes me feel guilty. She couldn't have a baby herself and so I feel sorry for her and try to be patient and understanding. She calls Myrtle "Bubbles" and spends more time up here with her than working in the café. The business is really run down. The taxi drivers and the other regulars all go to another place that's opened round the corner. I really don't want to leave Myrtle with her, but I let her mind her sometimes just to keep the peace.' She accepted the lace handkerchief being offered to her and dried her eyes. 'Oh, Mad – I mean Fay, I can't wait to get away from here and start a new life.'

Fay shook her head sadly. 'I knew yer wasn't happy from yer letters, but I'd no idea it were that bad. It's a pity the work went on so long. I never realised how much mess there'd be, what with underpinning the foundations and dealing with the dry rot. The builders done their best, but they couldn't go no faster. The place had been let go ter rack and ruin by the old lady what ran it before, but I knew it were the right place fer me the moment I clapped eyes on it. I'd seen all these posh little hotels and realised a guest house fer theatrical types was more my style.' Seeing one of her black leather gloves on the floor, she absentmindedly picked it up, unwittingly scooping up a small blue mitten at the same time, and put them into her handbag. 'So, all's well in the end! There's a lovely garden waiting for yer. The daffodils are almost over, but the primroses and other spring flowers are coming out. And as fer the flat, well, yer'll be snug as two little bugs in a rug.' Seeing the little ivory carving tied to a bar of the cot, she exclaimed. 'Gawdstruth! Would yer Adam an' Eve it. That's my Ethel's little whatsit ain't it?'

Foxy smiled. 'Myrtle loves it. There's no sharp edges on it and teething rings are often made of ivory. I hope Ethel wouldn't mind.'

'She'd be delighted ter find a sensible use fer it.' Fay chortled. 'That was the weirdest thing she ever won at cards, which reminds me, I want Myrtle to have the diamond ring she won as well.' Bending over to kiss the baby on her head, she exclaimed, 'Gordon Bennett, there's another Smelly Nelly here!' Then, saying she needed to do some shopping in Kensington High Street and would see them both the following weekend, she departed.

Foxy placed Myrtle on the bed in order to change her nappy and then groaned on hearing a tap on the door.

'I saw that Madame woman all done up in her furs and high heels,' Edie said, walking into the room without waiting for a response to her knock.

274

'Did you tell her you wouldn't be troubling her after all?'

'No, it's all arranged. The delays were because of the work on the house and not because she didn't want me. I'm going next Sunday.'

'I see.' Edie's mouth formed a thin tight line in her plump face. 'So it's all settled without asking me is it? I count for nothing. The one who helps you the most, who closes the café so she can look after Bubbles for you, she doesn't get asked her opinion, does she?'

'Come and sit down, Edie, dear.' She patted the bed. 'Please come and talk to me.'

The ancient metal springs creaked as Edie sat down. She gave a shamefaced smile. 'I'll get you a better bed.'

'I don't need it. I'm leaving next weekend.'

Edie gave a sob.

'I don't want to fall out with you. I know you meant well suggesting she was trying to put me off because she didn't really want a baby in the guest house. But she does, she really does want us there. She's made a flat for us. There's a pretty garden where I can put Myrtle in her pram. It's just what we need. Oh, Edie, you've been a wonderful help to me and I want us to stay friends for years and years.'

'She's all my dead babies brought to life.' Edie paused for a moment before smiling and saying reassuringly, 'Don't take any notice of me, ducky. I'm just a silly, sentimental old fool who gets a bit carried away sometimes. Of course we'll be friends for years and years and I'll come and visit you as soon as you've settled in.'

The following Saturday, on hearing the familiar knock, she braced herself – this was the last day she would have to put up with the constant intrusion and she was determined to keep calm.

'This has just come for you, Foxy!' Edie rushed into the room and thrust the yellow envelope into her hands, then collapsed onto the sofa, fanning herself with a handkerchief.

Feeling perplexed, Foxy opened the telegram and read, 'Meet me Lyons Corner House Marble Arch three p.m. stop Gerald.' 'Oh no!' She handed it to Edie. 'I've no idea how he knew I was here and anyway, I can't possibly go.'

'I 'spect FiFi told him.'

'I thought she was in Hamburg.'

'No. She came here the other day when you'd gone to the library. Last Tuesday it was. I didn't like to tell you 'cos you'd be upset. She came back a month ago on account of the political situation. She didn't want to be in Germany any longer in case there's a war. I told her I think it's a lot of fuss about nothing and Mr Chamberlain said it won't happen, but she's sure they'll invade us.' Edie smiled brightly. 'I think she felt guilty and wanted to put things right for you.'

'Did she say that?'

'Not in so many words, but I'm sure that's how it is.' Edie looked down at the telegram and read it through slowly before saying, 'There'd be no harm in seeing him, would there? You've got plenty of time, ducky, it's only one o'clock now.'

'I thought I'd never see him again.' She sat down and held her head. 'Actually, I'm not sure

276

I even want to.'

'You'll never get another chance, what with you moving tomorrow. He deserves to know about Myrtle, and he ought to help provide for her. He probably wants to say he's sorry for what he did. You really should meet him. If you don't you'll regret it for the rest of your life.'

'But what shall I say?'

'Just tell him about the baby and see what happens.' Edie patted her shoulder sympathetically. 'You can leave her with me for a couple of hours and maybe bring him back to see her?'

After hastily unpacking her smartest dress and putting it on, she walked to the door. Looking back at the clothes strewn across the bed, she apologised for the mess, and, seeing the bundle of treasures had fallen onto the floor, picked it up and pushed it into her handbag. Then, looking at the stove and remembering it needed more paraffin, said, 'Beatrice is low. I'll fill her before I go.'

'No,' Edie reassured her, 'I'll deal with that, you get going.'

Thanking her again, she ran down the stairs into the street.

Having arrived with half an hour to spare, she sat at a table by the window where she could see everyone who came through the door. While sipping tea from the white china cup she wondered what had precipitated this invitation. Might Gerry now be divorced and wanting to marry her? Could that be possible? More likely he wanted to resume their relationship now the fuss had died down.

She had got over him now and could easily refuse him, or could she? She smiled at the memory of dancing with him at the club and feeling so proud to be with such a handsome and sophisticated man, then shook her head. He had kept her in the flat to avoid being seen with her in public and when he thought the press might photograph him with her and cause their affair to be known about by the public, and possibly more importantly, his wife, he had pushed her out of the car and driven away without caring what happened to her. He couldn't possibly think she would take him back. A more likely scenario would be that he'd met FiFi by chance who'd told him what had happened and he thought he should help her financially. She dismissed a momentary thought that Edie might have contacted him because in that case he would have written to her or come to see her before now. No, she was sure FiFi had engineered this meeting somehow.

Snippets of her life at the club came to her like scenes from films while watching the people come and go. Clancy and Jane and FiFi acted out their parts before her while surrounded by the hubbub of chattering voices and clattering of china. The pungent aroma of French perfume wafted to her despite the pipe being smoked at the next table and the cigarettes being puffed all around her. Eventually, when the hands of a clock on the wall had slowly moved around for an hour and a half, she looked out and, through a gap in the traffic, saw a tall man standing in a doorway opposite. He was wearing a black homburg and a dark overcoat and carrying a briefcase. It was him!

She ran out onto the pavement, waving frantically, and stepped into the road, where a taxi screeched to a halt a few inches from her. The driver waved a fist then drove off shaking his head. Ignoring the calls of a passing woman to be careful, she made her way through the cars, still waving although unable to see him because a bus had stopped at that spot. Reaching the opposite side she found no sign of him and looked frantically around her. Seeing the bus draw away, she wondered momentarily if he could have caught it, but, knowing he had never travelled on one in his life, ran towards a taxi parked further up the kerb and wrenched the door open only to find an elderly woman staring at her in surprise.

Turning back, she stood dejectedly for a while, staring across at the café where she could see people sitting beside the window as she had done. He had probably stood watching her and was shocked by the change in her appearance. The scarf tied like a bandanna around her head as usual covered most, but not all, of the scar, and she was fatter since having Myrtle. He had thought her no longer attractive and changed his mind.

While sitting on the bus back to Kensington High Street, although feeling strangely empty and numb, she consoled herself with the knowledge that tomorrow she and Myrtle would begin their new life together with Fay. She would manage without any help from Gerald Mottram.

The bus drew to a standstill several yards short of the usual stop behind many other vehicles and the conductor jumped off the platform, went and spoke to a taxi driver, then returned and announced that the traffic was stopped ahead.

She stepped down from the bus and walked along the crowded pavement towards the corner of the street leading to the café. Then, hearing a bell ringing and smelling burning, knew what had caused the hold up. On reaching the turning and seeing smoke in the distance, she remembered seeing Edie silhouetted against the flames. 'Fire!' she screamed. 'There's a fire! My baby! My baby!' and she ran towards the café.

Finding a crowd standing in her way, she paused briefly to look up at the bright orange light flickering in the windows and the smoke and flames issuing from the roof, then, screaming, 'Myrtle!' she pushed between two elderly women and ran to the steps leading to the flats. People were shouting, far away in the distance. Someone clutched at her arm as she hurried to the steps, but she pulled away and, kicking off her high-heeled shoes, ran up them. Myrtle was in there – she must be so frightened.

Her eyes streamed and she retched as the smoke filled her lungs and stomach. Reaching the top step, she grabbed the handrail on the wall in readiness to step into the dense fog on the landing. She heard an explosive thud as the door blew towards her and saw the blazing inferno behind it whilst being thrown backwards. A woman was screaming – it sounded like her own voice echoing in her head.

A man kept telling her she was safe now and would be alright. A light was flashing and a bell clanging. A bright light shone overhead and faces looked down at her. A woman asked, 'Did they find the child?'

A man's deeper voice replied, 'No, 'fraid not.'

Another man said, 'Cut the hair off here.'

The lady in the rocks seemed to smile in the flickering light as she knelt before the pool. The dark shadows in the rocks formed figures around her.

A voice echoed in her head, 'I think she's coming round.'

A long face with a big halo, no it was a white headdress, loomed into view and out again, and spectacles glinted and sparkled as another voice crooned. 'It's alright, dear, you're in hospital.'

The nurse sat down beside her, took her hand and said, 'You were in an accident.'

She remembered running along the pavement. Her lungs were burning and all she could hear was the blood pounding in her ears. Her throat hurt. She had screamed loudly; why? What made her run? The sound of her own anguish returned and she heard her voice scream, 'My baby! My baby!'

A man appeared beside the bed.

'Where's my baby?' she asked.

The nurse gave a small, strangled gasp.

The doctor stepped closer. 'You fell and hit your head.'

She had no interest in her own body. 'My baby, where is she?'

'I'm very sorry.' He gave a tiny cough. 'They were too late.'

She remembered seeing a cow tearing at the ground after its calf had been taken away and now, in her distraught, unreasoning grief, she

281

heard its bellowing cries in her head. She wanted to pull at the window blinds, to break the glass, punch the walls and kick in the doors. Her baby, her little girl, her unique and beautiful child, was dead. Was her dear friend Edie burned to death too? Had she died trying to save the baby she loved so much? Poor Edie, poor Edie! The pain was too deep to bear. Separating from the body in the bed, she floated up over the group tending to it and, hovering like a hawk hanging in the still air over its prey, felt no pain.

Below her they discussed the patient, who appeared suddenly and inexplicably comatose.

People came into the room and cared for the woman in the other bed and attended to her own silent, motionless body. A doctor scratched his head and muttered to himself. Fay placed a huge bouquet of flowers in a vase and sat for a while talking in a low voice about her new life in Chiswick and how magnificent the magnolia in the garden had been and how much Foxy would like it next year.

She wanted to respond, to tell Fay not to look so sad, but that would mean going down to where she could feel the pain.

The nurses came and went. A body was removed from the other bed in the room and a new patient was brought in.

Fay sobbed and pleaded, 'Wake up, Foxy, please. The nurse says I must talk to you. She says you need to be stimulated. I wonder if you just can't bear life; I don't know. I arranged for a grave by the church in the square near where you lived, I thought that might be acceptable. All the neighbours escaped, even the old woman called Smelly Nelly who lived in that shed at the back. A taxi driver saw her limping away pushing her pram, poor old soul. The buildings are all going to be demolished, they're beyond repair. The other terrible thing is... Oh, Foxy, maybe you're better off not knowing.' She blew her nose. 'There's going to be war, I know it's going to happen.'

After Fay had left a man walked to the other bed and cried, 'No, no. Dear God. No!'

For a moment she hovered over him as he sobbed and begged his wife to come back to life. She could go too, it would be easier. How could she exist knowing her baby died in a fire? How could she live with that agony? Life would mean learning to bear grief that never faded. It would mean hurting every day for however long she kept breathing.

Floating away from the hospital room she returned to the garden in Oakey Vale and wandered down the sunlit path between lavender and rosemary, breathing in the honeyed scents of the flowers. On reaching the ivy hanging down the cliff she pushed through it into the outer cave and, seeing light glowing through the secret opening into the larger one, tiptoed to peer through it. At first, overawed by the beauty of the lady in the rocks illuminated by many candles set around the pool, she saw nothing else and heard only the water running down into the pool, then, becoming aware of a slight movement in the deep shadows by the tomb held her breath and waited. After several minutes she climbed through the gap in the rocks and then, hearing several loud groans, walked warily towards the sound. Was this the ancestors calling her to join them in the grave? Was this to be her death?

On reaching the tomb she saw the outline of a figure kneeling beside it and heard her sister exclaim, 'Betty! You've come home at last!'

Bending to embrace Kate she saw the beads of sweat running from her forehead and cried, 'My God! Are you ill?'

'No, sweetheart, I'm going to have another baby, that's all. I wanted to come and drink from the pool first, but I've left it a bit late. My labour has started.'

Helping her to stand up, she said, 'You can't stay here. I'll walk back to the house with you.' With the sudden knowledge that the baby ready to emerge into life was a boy she felt a momentary pang of disappointment. This was not the next guardian in line waiting to be born.

They left the caves and, on stepping through the ivy, Kate groaned and almost lost her balance then sank down onto the rock nearby.

Charles appeared outside the back door calling, 'Kate, darling, where are you?'

Looking up, her sister said, 'Come home, sweetheart, I beg you, come home.'

Awakening from the dream, she saw Fay was below her again, moaning as if in pain. Desperate to show her love for this dear friend, she reached out to touch her hand and, with a sudden thump of shock in her chest, found she was back in her body once more. Her mouth felt dry as she whispered, 'I have to write to her.'

Fay gave a small sob and asked, 'Who?'

'To my sister, I must write to Kate.'

Fay let out a sigh and kissed her hand.

Chapter Twenty-three

Comfrey ointment may help heal non-infected wounds. The plant is known also as knitbone for its power to mend broken bones.

'There were men chasing a boar in the forest high on the hill,' Myrtle said as she laid down the basket of berries.

'Did they catch it?'

'Nay. It ran down into Hangen-tree Land. I heard one shout, "Leave it be." Then they all turned and went away.'

She smiled with satisfaction. It suited her well to have men believe themselves cursed if they went near the tree.

'The maid who came for comfrey salve told me 'tis well known that men will lose potence if ever they set foot this side of the hill.'

'Aye, so they say.'

Myrtle frowned. 'What does that mean?'

'I means they'd be weak and–' She struggled for the words.

'Not fit to serve like the billy goat does the nanny?'

'Aye. Exactly so.'

Myrtle nodded. 'I thought so.' She picked up an empty basket, saying, 'There's more berries by the path to the river' and walked out of the clearing, singing cheerfully.

She followed her daughter and stood watching the

slender figure skipping along swinging the basket. The day would come when this beautiful child must become a woman and bear the next in line. For now it was good that few men ever came this way and all those that did were in great fear of them both, but in a few summers from now one must be found to play his part.

Awakening in the early morning sunshine, Foxy fingered the piece of wood under her pillow. She had kept it there since coming to live at The Laurels over a year ago. Visiting the simple, quiet life of the valley had calmed her tormented spirit. Thinking of how it seemed to help her cope with the busy boarding house in which she had lived and worked since recovering from the fire, she wondered if the simplicity of that earlier existence would be preferable to the present. The difficulties of survival would be very great and, on balance, she would not change places with Caitlin, although she did envy her the child and also having a purpose in life, for, above all else, she must keep the lady in the cave safe for the generations of the future.

Remembering this was the day she would at last go back to Oakey Vale and see Kate for the first time since running away all those years ago, she slid out of bed and dressed, pinned the recently mended brooch to her blouse and then ran to the kitchen.

'None of 'em wants cooked breakfast. It's too hot,' Fay said, fanning herself with a newspaper. 'I want ter do some shopping up west so I'll come to the station with yer.' She gestured towards the portly man standing at the sink washing dishes. 'Your replacement's doin' a grand job with the washing up.'

'I prefer this to being Mr Cleany, it's better for my feet than selling scrubbing brushes door-to-door,' Twankey said, then, drying his hands, added, 'Your hair looks lovely at the front, Foxy, but I think you should get rid of the hennaed bits at the back before you go home.'

Fay shook her head. 'I reckon she'd do better goin' red again. I never seen the like of that barnet of 'ers.'

Taking a pair of scissors from his pocket, Twankey grinned and indicated that Foxy should sit down at the table.

Pay pursed her lips and warned, 'You'll be late fer the train.'

'Won't take a minute.' Twankey crossed the floor and began snipping at Foxy's hair. 'By the time you've gone and got your titfa on, Fay, it'll be done.' When she had left the room he said quietly, 'This is the last little reminder of your old life being removed, love. Maybe it's a symbol of new beginnings?'

Feeling the tears rise in her eyes, she gave a slight nod in response. Dear, sweet Twankey meant well. He had been such a good friend during the past year, always so kind and encouraging her to talk about Myrtle on their walks along the towpath by the river. But he was wrong – how could she have a new beginning when her heart still ached like this?

Two hours later Fay looked at the crowds of men

in khaki uniforms all around them. 'I never thought it could ever happen again until this moment.'

Foxy nodded sadly and, catching sight of a pigeon leaving its perch on the wrought iron archway leading to the platform, watched it fly to a metal beam high above the station, then, when steam from an engine wafted upwards, saw it swoop away to join its fellows on a windowsill above the café. She and Fay smiled at each other and continued onwards through the milling throng. Passing alongside a queue of mainly women and children, her heart lurched as her eyes met those of a mother who was wiping a sooty smut from a small boy's forehead and, for a second, caught a glimpse of pure agony.

A girl nearby said, 'It smells like when Nanna's chimney went on fire.' A little further down the line two boys squabbled over a gas mask and a small woman in black screeched, 'Behave yerselves, yer little varmints!' before cuffing both of them.

On reaching the platform, they passed by an official making a list of each child who boarded the train. Looking up she saw small faces peering out of the windows and all around her were weeping women. She and Fay climbed aboard the nearest carriage and, finding two neatly dressed little girls sitting primly upright and holding small suitcases, she looked at the labels attached to the children's blue cardigans and, raising her eyes to meet Fay's, whispered, 'The situation must be serious. They wouldn't send the children away like this if war wasn't imminent.'

Pay nodded. 'Twankey reckons it's inevitable, that's why he's volunteered for the ambulance service.' She grinned. 'It'll make a change from panto.'

'I wonder what they'll call him?'

'Twankey of course, it's his moniker, ain't it?' She gave her neighing laugh then added, 'He's got a real soft spot for you, thinks the sun shines out of yer eyes.'

'And I love him dearly. He's been so kind to me.' She squeezed Fay's hand. 'I don't know what I'd have done without both of you.'

They stood silently for a few moments until Fay said, 'It'll be strange for you, going home after all this time.'

'True. I'm really excited and apprehensive at the same time. I kept making excuses and putting it off because I just didn't feel strong enough, but I know I'll be alright now. I'm dying to see my sister and her boys.'

Fay handed her a small blue mitten. 'I found this when I was clearing out me wardrobe yesterday. I didn't know if you'd want it after so long, but I couldn't just throw it away. It was in an old handbag. I don't know how it got in there. I suppose I must've picked it up when I visited yer.' She squeezed her hand. 'Oh, Foxy love, I know how it hurts and I know how it will never go away. People say time is the healer. I don't agree, you just learn how ter live with it in time, that's all.'

Tears filled her eyes as Foxy nodded, unable to explain how she could not grieve for Myrtle in the same way as she had for Edie. The constant agony of separation from her baby had never eased, whereas she had mourned for Edie during the past months and gradually, although it was still painful, she could now accept her friend was dead.

Fay stepped onto the platform and called over the heads of several children, 'See yer next week.'

Four boys climbed into the carriage, filling the space with their jostling, giggling excitement and making plain their resentment at both window seats being already occupied by her and a little girl. They pushed the sliding door leading into the corridor to and fro several times and then the oldest, having banged the carriage door shut, hung out of the window waving and shouting.

When the guard blew his whistle the boys cheered, the little girl jammed a thumb into her mouth and her older sister, whose lower lip was quivering, put a comforting arm around the small shoulders.

Foxy sank back into the seat. Sympathy with these two frightened girls loosened her own tenuous grip on her self-control and she felt the flood of pain threaten to rise up and overcome her like a tidal wave. Looking out of the window she struggled to focus on the backs of grimy tenement blocks lining the track and breathed slowly and deeply. By the time the buildings had changed to cleaner houses interspersed with trees and green spaces, she no longer feared breaking down into hysterical weeping.

When the London suburbs had slipped away and only fields and woods were visible, she took the blue mitten from her pocket and pressed it to

290

her lips. Myrtle was twenty-two months old now and much too big for this ... no, she was dead and so was poor, dear Edie who had knitted it whilst fervently praying for a boy she could call Bubbles. Admittedly her friend had been irritating and stretched her tolerance to its limits, but her generosity and love were never in doubt. If only that telegram had not arrived and she hadn't gone out leaving Beatrice low on paraffin then Edie wouldn't have had an accident filling it and would still be alive. No one had actually said that was how the fire started, but it seemed to her the most likely cause.

Clasping the mitten, she leaned back against the upholstery and, closing her eyes, imagined herself in the park she often visited in the afternoons. *The sun was warm on her back as she walked across the grass to the bench on which she liked to sit and rest before returning to The Laurels. To her surprise, on looking down she saw a tartan rug spread out on the grass in the shade of a tree and, lying on it fast asleep, was a little boy in a blue sailor suit. She sat on the rug beside him, marvelling at the beauty of his long, dark eyelashes and short tight curls. He was the most beautiful child she had ever seen.*

Opening her eyes she smiled. It was a dream of course, but such a pleasant one, and there was just the possibility that she had seen into the future and one day a baby son would share her heart with Myrtle.

On arrival at Wells, she went to reach for her suitcase on the luggage rack and, looking in the mirror below it, paused to make sure her fringe covered as much of the scar on her forehead as possible then smiled – thanks to Twankey there was no sign of red in her fair curls. Betty had come home.

The platform was filled with children by the time she disembarked and several members of the Women's Royal Voluntary Service were marshalling evacuees into crocodiles.

'Queen Romania, is that you?'

She looked round at the man raising his panama hat to her. 'King Romany, is that you?'

He was older, broader and his hands and feet no longer seemed too big for the rest of him. His golden eyes flickered momentarily and then met hers with a steady gaze as he explained that Kate had asked him to meet her because the baby was recovering from whooping cough. Then he picked up the suitcase and led her to a car parked outside the station. Opening the rear passenger door he announced solemnly, 'The carriage, your majesty.'

Pointing to the front, she asked, 'Couldn't I sit next to you, Your Grace?'

'That's breaking with convention, Your Highness.'

'I'd have thought royalty like us would be above that sort of thing.'

Billy nodded. 'That's true, milady.' He opened the other door.

She sat inside and, when he had started the engine with the handle and was beside her, asked, 'D'you still work at the ironmonger's?'

'No, I bought this last year 'cos I wanted to be my own boss.' He patted the steering wheel. 'The idea was to start a taxi service. I've been doing quite well and if it wasn't for the war I'd be buying another car soon and going into partnership with my cousin but–' He shrugged.

While driving through Wells he made polite conversation about the new owners of the shops she had known and was then silent as they drove through the cow parsley crowding into the lane leading to the village.

Leaning forward, she waited for the bend in the road and, on reaching it, held her breath. The weather was perfect. Pridden was free of mist and the village lay beneath the sunlit hills just as she remembered.

Billy pulled into a gateway, switched off the engine and waved his hand towards the Mendips. 'I'll carry this with me wherever I go.'

'Have you been called up?'

'Your Majesty's my last passenger before I join the Royal Armoured Corps. When I've dropped you off I'll take the car to Higher Tops farm. As you know, Charlie's been running it since Kate's tenant died two years ago, and he said I can leave it in a barn until the war's over. He's been really good to me, taught me to drive and encouraged me to save up for this car.'

She remembered Billy's mother and knew she would disapprove of him being friends with Charles Wallace who was living in sin with Kate.

'I heard about the baby.' He looked ahead through the windscreen. 'I'm so sorry. It must be the worst thing that can happen to anyone.'

She touched his arm and nodded. So many people avoided mentioning the tragedy. She knew they didn't know what to say, but it was good when someone managed to find kind words. 'It's been eighteen months since I lost her and I'm trying to find a way to live without her. I've only just found the courage to come here to see Kate even though we've been writing for ages – since it happened in fact. She wanted to come and see me but I kept putting her off – I just needed more time. I don't really understand why.'

He turned and smiled sympathetically. 'She told me. We've spoken about you a lot. She's longing to see you.'

It was so good to talk to him. He understood. His eyes were extraordinary – she'd forgotten how wonderful they were. 'How's Joan?' she asked.

'She's very happy with her little girl.'

'Congratulations.'

Billy grinned. 'She realised I wasn't the right man for her years ago and took my cousin on instead.' He opened the glove compartment and took out a gardenia. 'I bought you this. I thought we should remind ourselves there's still beauty in the world.' He gave a sheepish grin. 'Are you in love with anyone?'

Breathing in the exquisite scent, she remembered the woman who gave her the same flower after driving her into London and recalled her saying, 'I'm a nurse so I live in a hostel close to the hospital. There you are, sweet pea. Good luck.'

'No,' she replied, 'I'm not in love, nor likely to be. I need to stay single, because–' she felt a sudden glow of happiness for the first time since the fire '–I've just realised what I need to do. I'm going to train as a midwife.'

294

Billy opened the door and climbed out. He stood with his back to her, looking up at the hills for a few moments before starting the engine with a handle. Then, without a word, he drove slowly into the village, where he waved outside the church at Albert who looked up and nodded without altering the rhythmic motion of his scythe as he cut the grass.

The bridge across the river seemed narrower. The dell on her right was surprisingly small and the stretch of hedge leading to Old Myrtles was shorter than she remembered. Seeing a boy hanging over the little garden gate she felt her heart quicken and was disappointed when he disappeared as the car pulled up.

Billy said, 'They're looking forward to seeing you,' then climbed out and placed her suitcase beside the gate.

Joining him, she placed her hand on his shoulder and whispered, 'Keep in touch, King Romany.'

'I'll send you a Valentine, Queen Romania.' He kissed his forefinger and placed it on her lower lip then quickly returned to the car and drove away.

Seeing her sister standing by the white roses holding a baby and with the boy leaning against her holding a posy of wild flowers, she stood in the lane holding the moment in her heart. Then whilst opening the gate with a trembling hand, she heard Kate say, 'Welcome home, sweetheart. Welcome home, at last!'

Later on she'd go to Hankeys Land and walk around the tree three times one way and then the other making a wish for peace before climbing up and sitting on the branch for a while. This evening she'd take her poppy-doll from the chimney and put it by her bed so she could remember the old woman who had called her Whatsername but nevertheless made it for her, and tomorrow she would go into the cave with Kate and sit a while with the lady in the rocks. She would tell her sister about the life she had led and the loss of her baby. She would tell her of this new and sudden revelation that she should become a midwife, but, for now, all she could do was laugh and cry simultaneously as they hugged and kissed each other.

Chapter Twenty-four

Sweet violet tea may help with respiratory tract illnesses and mouth infections.

London, 1944

'April Fool! Ha, I got yer!'

Shouts of laughter were followed by the sound of metal studs clattering on paving stones as three boys ran out of the churchyard and into the square.

Listening to the raucous noise receding into the distance, Betty ran her finger along the top of the headstone. Her life had changed completely since the fire had taken her beautiful baby six years ago this very day, but deep down inside her the pain still smouldered, ready to ignite into a secret, searing flame. No one at the hospital knew about her loss – she'd never told any of the other midwives that, unlike most of them, she had experienced giving birth or how her baby had died. Helping to bring joy to other women's lives had helped her cope with the bereavement, but talking about it still hurt too much.

April the first. She hadn't even thought about the date that day because she'd been so busy packing and then received the telegram from Gerald. It must have been the first of the month because there it was carved into the stone. That meant it was a fact and indisputable didn't it? Sister had used the words last week when a husband had persisted in demanding to know how long labour would last, 'The baby will come when it's ready, there's no set time written in stone.'

Myrtle Barnes, born 10th November 1937, died 1st April 1938. That could not be true. She'd know if her baby was here, wouldn't she? Fay had been right when she said one learned to bear the grief. She had done that, but she still wanted to scream and tear out her hair. And, above all, she could not accept Myrtle was dead.

On the previous three visits to the church she lacked the courage to visit the place where it had all happened – could she try once more? There was just enough time to go there before catching the bus to Hammersmith.

Leaving the graveyard she walked out into the square and, seeing the bench amongst the trees where she had felt her first birthing pain, stood for a moment remembering the cold November wind pulling at her old squirrel fur coat as she walked slowly back to her room.

Crossing the road, she saw a young mother lift a little boy into a pushchair and walk towards the High Street. Myrtle would be six and a half now. She wouldn't want to sit in... She must stop this! Stop thinking as though her baby was alive!

She walked along the pavement until, arriving at the smart apartment block built in place of the parade of shops that had been destroyed in the fire, she stood remembering the ironmonger's where she'd bought paraffin for Beatrice the stove and next to that the window through which the barber waved so cheerfully. Looking at the place where the café had once been, she pictured Edie emerging from the kitchen, carrying scrambled eggs on toast, her bulky figure balancing on tiny feet and her blue eyes shining with delight. Dear Edie who had loved Myrtle so much and had died with her.

Focussing on the window in front of her she saw a figure move behind the lace curtain and, realising she must appear to be staring in, turned and walked away, shivering uncontrollably. This visit had been a bad idea, just as Fay had said it would be. She must never come here again. The café and her shabby room above it were no more and the grave had given her no solace. She must carry Myrtle in her heart and live her new life as best she could, alone.

On arrival at the nurses' hostel she found a letter from Kate in her pigeonhole and walked up the stairs to her room where she lay on the bed and opened it.

Dear Betty,

Teddy Nelson was killed last week in Burma. Alice is being brave. I have said she can stay in the tied cottage for as long as she likes. His mother has taken it badly and looks very old, poor woman.

There are anemones and violets blooming in the woods. Nature pays no heed to war!

Charles is well although he gets tired these days. The boys are growing up fast and are healthy and happy. I have had some 'women's problems' lately and need an operation. I would be grateful if you could put my mind at rest before I go into hospital. Will you keep that promise you made to bury me with Gran?

We all send our love. Kate.

Oh no! How could she keep her word when she lived so far away? It was impossible.

Alice had three children to bring up alone! And his poor mother, the bigoted old hag, had lost her oldest boy. The beastly, gossipy old cow who still ignored Kate must be suffering agonies of fear for Billy, her last living son, who was driving around the desert in a tank. Billy would be sad too, having lost his older brother. Maybe she should write to him? He had sent a Valentine card every year since they met before he was called up so he hadn't forgotten her. She smiled at the memory of their childhood game when they ruled the hills up top and the dell and

Hankeys Land. Yes, a few words from her might give him a little comfort and remind him of home.

A sudden surge of anger overwhelmed her. Teddy Nelson would be alive if he hadn't been sent to fight for his king and country in a foreign land. He'd probably been no further than Weston-Super-Mare in his life before he was called up. This was what war was about. It meant ordinary people with quiet little lives being blinded, maimed and killed far from home. Teddy should be whistling to his dog as he rounded up the sheep, or mending stone walls, or digging his vegetable patch at the back of the cottage, or complaining in the pub about the struggle to make ends meet on his weekly pittance, not rotting in a steaming jungle.

She read the letter again. Poor Kate would be distraught. This would mean no more babies, no more chance of a daughter to carry on. Looking at the watch pinned to her chest she saw it was almost time to go on duty and hurriedly put on her black stockings and starched uniform, then, after putting the black belt around her waist, she fastened the silver buckle and patted it. One day she would wear a bigger one if she became a Sister as everyone was sure she would.

Picking up the stiff white cap, she placed it over her fair hair and stood back to check her image in the mirror. The face before her crumpled and became blurred by tears. Touching the cameo brooch pinned to her bra, she traced its shape through the cotton uniform and knew Kate's understated letter was a desperate plea for help.

Her sister needed her. She must hand in her notice and return as soon as possible to Oakey Vale.

Taking the dark blue cloak off the hook on the door she swung it around her shoulders. She would miss this orderly way of life controlled by a matron, a sister and babies. She would miss the company of other nurses in the hostel and hearing of their romances and heartaches, but most of all she would miss Fay and Twankey – she must go and stay the night with them before leaving. It would mean going back to Oakey Vale with a hangover, but that was a small price to pay for their friendship. And, remembering the parcel she had left in Fay's safe, she could collect her treasures and take them home with her.

One week later the station was crowded as it had been the day she went to visit Kate just before war was declared. A pigeon was again perched on the topmost curl decorating the number eight above the wrought iron archway – it couldn't be the same one, could it? Betty stood watching as the bird took off and swooped away out of sight.

There were no queues of anxious mothers and children this time, but there were many young people in military uniform just the same as before. A smart young woman with a black band on her left sleeve hurried by. Was she a war widow? An older woman wearing an ill-fitting black coat coaxed a small boy along as she struggled with a suitcase. Dear God! She definitely was!

Seeing Fay walking towards her, elegantly dressed as usual in a black suit and hat, Betty smiled at her. Her own head was still suffering the effects of too much British sherry the previous night, but her friend, who had been singing her repertoire until the early hours, showed no sign of having drunk a large quantity of alcohol and had gone in search of food for the journey.

'This is all I could find,' Fay said, offering her the sandwich in her right hand. 'I dunno what's in it but whatever it is there's not much of it.' She shook her head. 'I can't believe I left that pork pie on the kitchen table, and–' she held out the large brown envelope in her left hand '–I nearly forgot ter give yer this.'

'My treasures!'

Their eyes met as she took it and thanked her, adding, 'I'm so grateful to you for keeping them out of harm's way for me all this time.'

Fay watched anxiously as she put it into her handbag. 'I'm more worried about how the mitten will affect yer than I am about Jerry's bombs blasting it ter kingdom come. That time yer woke us all up screamin' the place down really upset everyone else so much I wished I'd never found it in the first place. It's been locked up in the safe for three years and I'm none too keen ter give it back now. You'll be alright with it, will yer?'

'Of course I will. I was still coming to terms with what had happened at that time and the mitten was the only thing I had of Myrtle's, the only souvenir. And besides, I was probably drunk–' she grimaced and rubbed her forehead '–I usually am when I visit you.'

'I couldn't let yer go without a good send-off, Foxy love.' Fay chuckled. 'And a good time was 'ad by all.' She sniffed. 'I still don't understand why yer 'ad ter burn yer boats.'

'I might still come back here when my sister's recovered. I don't know how long I'll be needed. She may be very weak for months after the operation and it would be a help if I stay in the cottage with my uncle and look after him. She's been traipsing up and down from the farm to the cottage every day to cook his meals since they moved up there. It's too much going up and down...'

'Like an whore's drawers?' Fay suggested with a grin, then shrugged, adding, 'I suppose yer know what yer doin'.'

A piercing whistle was followed by a series of bangs as doors were firmly shut on a train at a platform on the far side of the station.

She could still change her mind. It wasn't too late. Kate had said in her letter this was a big step and she would understand if she decided against it, but she had also made plain that this arrangement would be the best way of helping in the circumstances. Dismissing the possibility of doubt, she turned to Fay. 'Don't wait any longer, it's bound to be late leaving.' Then, having hugged and kissed her and promised to keep in touch, she walked to the platform.

Finding the train was already crowded with passengers she pushed her bags into a corner near the toilet, which, although bound to be malodorous before long, provided enough space to sit on the largest suitcase.

303

After half an hour a group of soldiers began singing 'Why are we waiting', to the tune of 'O come all ye faithful' and when others began a descant further down the carriage she felt a sudden joy in knowing humans could produce a sound of such beauty whilst feeling so uncomfortable and frustrated.

At the sound of the guard's whistle a good-natured cheer replaced the hymn and then only the creaking of the rolling stock could be heard as the train began to move.

Once the journey was underway, Betty leaned against the bulkhead in order to keep her balance as the suitcase swayed with the movement of the rattling carriage. Peering through the window she saw the backs of grimy buildings lining the track interspersed with spaces lined with rubble. On either side of some gaps there were savagely scarred houses with the remains of neighbours' fireplaces and bathrooms still clinging to their sides. Bomb damage was always a shock, always horrifying. Who had died there? How many children were burned? How many old ladies buried alive?

She sighed with relief on reaching the outer suburbs where cleaner houses in tree-lined streets showed only occasional signs of an incendiary bomb having destroyed a home.

A constant stream of people passed by and a queue soon formed for the toilet. A soldier leaned against the bulkhead beside her, and each time the train swayed he gave an exaggerated lurch over her saying, 'Sorry, love.' When, after ten minutes, he offered her a cigarette and she ignored him, he moved away and another man took up the same position.

Reaching for the newspaper squashed into her bag she touched the treasures in the envelope and, taking out the little mitten, held it for the first time in three years. Although having insisted she would not be upset by doing so, a frisson of fear made her shiver nevertheless as she recalled how Fay had persuaded her to put it away with the garnet ring and pearl pin after a distressing incident in which she had awakened the whole household in the middle of the night. All she'd done was hold the mitten when she couldn't sleep – just to remember Myrtle and feel close to her. When she saw the beautiful little boy toddling along behind some older children she'd been entranced at first, but then, on witnessing him trip and fall as he followed them across some railway lines, she had been distraught and her screams had awakened everyone in The Laurels.

Closing her eyes she felt her heart beat faster as a spot of light appeared and became a flashing zigzag opening into a circle that moved outwards until suddenly she found herself standing behind a woman who was reading to a group of children sitting at four rows of small desks.

The teacher closed the book. 'That's enough Peter Pan *for today. Now, we'll do ABC until the bell goes. A is for...'*

A boy at the back shouted, 'Ack-ack gun!' All the children laughed.

'B is for...'

'Baby?' a beautiful little girl with dark curly hair suggested.

A boy fired an imaginary gun. 'Bang, bang!'

Another boy bounced up and down with excitement. 'Bomber-command!'

Everyone screamed with laughter

The teacher smiled. 'Well done, children, I think you're...'

'Excuse me, miss.'

'Pardon?' Why was someone interrupting the lesson? She hadn't had time to see which of the boys was the one in the sailor suit three years ago.

'Your paper, miss, you've dropped it.'

She focussed on the elderly man holding out her newspaper and thanked him, then stared at a headline proclaiming, '4,500 tons of bombs dropped on enemy targets.' Another stated, 'Balaklava captured.' The nurses all knitted hats to keep children's ears and necks warm as part of the war effort. She hadn't realised there was a place called that before. Presumably people who lived there wore them? Vera Lynn was pictured with a group of smiling British soldiers on one page and Betty Grable waved from an American Jeep in another.

A man went into the toilet whistling and the words of the song rang in her head. 'We'll meet again, don't know where, don't know when, but I know we'll meet again, some sunny day.' Songs like that often stuck in her mind for days and she tried to dismiss it.

Only another few hours and she would be back in Oakey Vale with Uncle Albert and going up to the farm every day to help Kate. Fay had tried to talk her out of this adventure, insisting one should 'Never go back.' But then, she was also fond of saying 'Never say never!'

Recalling the school children she had seen when holding the mitten, it seemed a relief in a way not to have recognised the little boy. He might have been sent out of the room for being naughty and in that case she would have been upset and caused an embarrassing scene here on the train. Or, more likely, the whole thing was nothing to do with any child she had known – it was probably a kind of wishful dream of children the same age as Myrtle would be now if she had lived.

The man came out of the toilet, still whistling. 'Keep smiling through, just like you always do, for I know we'll meet again some sunny day.' Damn! She was stuck with the song for the rest of the journey.

On arrival at the cottage she was relieved to find very little had changed in the intervening years. Seeing Albert sitting in his corner with a tortoise-shell cat on his lap and humming his favourite hymn, she wondered momentarily if she should kiss him, decided against it and stroked the cat instead.

Kate said, 'You're making my life so much easier, sweetheart. When we moved up to live at the farm Uncle couldn't be persuaded to come with us–' she glanced at the old man '–and I don't blame him, of course, he's lived here so long now. The Land Army girl is staying here too, but she can't be expected to cook and look after him, so I've been coming in every day and it's difficult sometimes to keep going up and down all the time.'

Remembering Fay's vulgarity she said, 'Like a...' then, seeing the small boy under the table who was listening to every word, decided against repeating her words and reached for the exercise book in which Kate had written instructions for care of the old man and read out, 'Sunday, joint. Monday, cold meat and bubble and squeak. Tuesday, rissoles if there's any more leftovers and vegetables. Toad in the hole, or rabbit stew and dumplings, or rabbit pie. Crikey, I'd forgotten the routine!'

Kate looked anxious, then, pointing first at the oil lamp hanging from the ceiling and then at the range in the chimney breast, sighed. 'Oh, Betty, you're going to find it all awfully hard work.'

'I'll soon get used to it. I managed with an old oil stove for ages and I did live here before, don't forget.'

'I know, but after years of modern conveniences I think you'll find it all...'

'Stop worrying. I'll cope. The important thing is to get you into hospital and well again.'

'Alright, sweetheart, I'll say no more.' Kate went and kissed the old man, who was now humming 'Abide With Me' very, very slowly.

'Goodnight and God bless, Uncle.' While putting a cardigan around her shoulders she grimaced with pain then forced a smile at Betty. 'I'm so grateful to you, sweetheart. Olive meets up with some other Land Army girls sometimes and will probably be late, she'll lock up when she comes in.' Hearing the clock in the hall chime eight times, she walked to the door. 'I must get back to the farm. Come along, Johnny,' and when the boy emerged from under the table she led him out into the twilight.

While making a few preparations for the following morning, Betty admitted the most mundane of tasks would be difficult without electricity and the tin bath in the scullery filled with water heated on the range would be very different from the bathroom she had recently used in the nurses' hostel. Stepping out into the garden, she heard Albert humming his favourite hymn tune on his way to the privy, then the sound of an aeroplane whining in the far distance and, above them both, a robin warbled its evening song. Breathing in the scent of cool countryside, so different from the city, she walked through purple shadows to the rock close by the secret cave.

Kate was right. Returning to this way of life would not be easy. She had given up the job she loved to be here and had accepted that if her sister died then not only must she keep the promise to bury her with those who had gone before, she would never be able to leave because there was no one else to take her place. For the time being she must be strong and support the people she loved. Charles, who looked weighed down with fear, and Kate, who seemed too frail to survive the operation booked for three days hence.

Leaning back against the ivy hanging down behind her, she ran her finger over the scar across her forehead and thought of Gerald Mottram, who had pushed her out of his car and was now seen at the side of the Prime Minister whenever he was photographed for the newspapers or filmed for the newsreels in the cinema. She'd been in love with the idea of Gerry, who was so suave, so elegant and so handsome. A sob caught in her throat. He had sent her a telegram on the day their child died. It was almost as though he had known, had a premonition perhaps? Why had he not turned up to meet her? It had been a critical time in the run up to war being declared and there might have been a crisis in negotiations with Germany or Poland or Italy or Russia. Or maybe he just changed his mind. She had wondered a few times whether Fay had contacted him and told him about Myrtle, but she had never asked her. There seemed no point.

'Betty! Betty!' Albert's agitated call made her jump up.

'I'm here, don't worry, Uncle.' She hurried up the path towards the small figure standing by the back door. 'Goodnight, God bless.'

He nodded his head, muttered something unintelligible ending in 'innum', and went in search of his candlestick.

Having waited until he had climbed the stairs and gone into his room, apparently content to accept her in place of Kate, she sighed with relief and looked around the kitchen. Several bunches of lemon balm and mint were hanging from the clothes dryer above the range, just as they would have been when her grandmother was alive. The plates Granfer won at Pridden fair were still on the tall dresser, large ones on the top shelf and smaller ones beneath. The china cow and calf, each with only three legs, leaned precariously together as usual. Next to them was the delicate porcelain cottage with little windows that would light up when a candle end was burned inside it. Every inch of the lower shelves was crammed with a random selection of useful objects, plus two bowls of odd buttons and other things that could not be thrown away because they might come in handy one day.

She went upstairs to the room that had once been her grandmother's and prepared for bed, then, lying in the darkness she heard the steady hum of aeroplanes in the distance. Were they ours, or theirs? Were they coming here to bomb us or going there to wreak havoc on them? Our bombers dropped four thousand five hundred tons on them yesterday. So how much do they drop on us today?

How long was this bloody carnage going on? Hitler had to be stopped. She could see that, but it was taking so long!

The sound of a door latch clicking broke the silence, then giggling followed by a loud, 'Sh... Sh!' The staircase creaked as did the loose floorboard on the landing. The Land Army girl was evidently entertaining company in her bedroom.

Closing her eyes she remembered Albert smiling and humming his favourite hymn, which meant he was pleased to see her. 'Eternal father strong to save–' Oh no, not that one going round and round in her brain all night!

Sitting in the hospital room five days later she tried to imagine she was back in Hammersmith with a woman awaiting her baby. This dimly lit room looked the same in the early hours of the morning as those she was used to and the occasional sounds of footsteps in the corridor or a nurse doing the rounds of other rooms and wards were reassuringly familiar, as were the smell of disinfectant and the smooth feel of the neatly turned down sheets on the bed. But this situation was entirely different. She had tried to appear strong when persuading Charles to go home to be with the boys while she stayed to keep vigil through the night, but in fact she felt helpless and frightened.

The Sister had been kindly but very clear and so had the surgeon. Both had made plain there was little chance of recovery. If she looked through her nursing eyes at the patient lying in the bed she also knew the situation was hopeless. Too much blood had been lost and now it was only a matter of time before the last little drop of life drained away. But this wasn't just a patient, a woman whose name she knew by reading it on the clipboard hanging on the wall above the bed, no, she was now on the opposite side of the line between the carers and the cared for. This was Kate, her beloved sister.

Closing her eyes, Betty tried to summon up the guiding spirits who had helped her when giving birth but without success, and saw only the darkness behind her eyes. Touching the cameo brooch also had no immediate effect and, feeling despondent and exhausted, she allowed her heavy eyelids to close for several minutes until, awakening with a start she saw the figure sitting on the other side of the bed and exclaimed, 'Gran!'

Had the old woman come to ease her darling granddaughter's way into death?

As though answering the unspoken question her grandmother gave a slight shake of her head.

'But she's dying, look at her!'

The old woman leaned forward, placed her hands on Kate's chest and indicated that Betty should do likewise. On doing so their fingertips met and she felt tingling throughout her whole body, then became aware of the small irregular beat beneath her right palm. After a while she closed her eyes and dozed, half conscious of the nurse who came in from time to time while she drifted in and out of dreams of walking on the hills up top or sitting beside the pool in the cave.

'Betty!'

Awakening with a start she saw her sister looking up at her.

'I had such a wonderful dream, sweetheart. I was a little girl in that other time, long ago. I was very ill and delirious with a raging fever. My grandmother carried me to the cave and laid me on her cloak, then she dipped a piece of cloth in the water and put it on me. I wanted to die, I wanted to let go but Gran wouldn't let me. She kept on and on for hours dipping that cloth in the icy water until the fever cooled and I woke up – only I didn't wake up in that lifetime in the cave, I'm here with you in the hospital. Isn't that wonderful?'

'Oh yes, Kate. Truly, truly wonderful.'

Chapter Twenty-five

A tea made with the dried flowers and seeds of tansy may help with gout.
It should never be taken during pregnancy.

Kate placed her cup and saucer onto the kitchen table and said, 'I'm truly grateful for all your help, sweetheart.'

Betty smiled. 'I'm glad I could be of use. It's wonderful to see you here in your own home looking so well – it's like a miracle.'

'It certainly is – only four weeks since the operation and yet I feel a new woman thanks to you.'

'Thanks to Gran, you mean!' she laughingly replied, adding more seriously, 'Mind you, I agree with Charles, you shouldn't overdo things yet.'

'We're both so grateful you came home to help us, sweetheart, and now I'm so much better, I really think I can't make you stay any longer unless–' Kate swallowed nervously '–unless you want to, that is.'

'I do want to stay longer.' She hesitated – maybe this was the moment to tell Kate the secret she'd been keeping to herself for ten days. 'I'm waiting to hear from the matron at Melfont Maternity Home. I may have been a bit hasty. I said I could start next week – if they took me on that is. I'm not sure if you're well enough yet...'

'Of course I'm well enough. Oh, sweetheart, it would be so wonderful if you stayed. Melfont's not far away, only two miles or so, you could cycle there from Old Myrtles.' Kate dabbed at her eyes. 'Does that mean you won't go back to London?'

'I want to stay here, where I belong.'

Kate's lower lip trembled. 'It was worth being so ill to hear you say that!'

Seeing a sketchbook lying on the dresser, Betty asked, 'Have you started painting again?'

'I've been looking again at my illustrations for Gran's recipes. We were about to get it published when war was declared and Charles says it makes him believe peace might be possible if he thinks about trying again. I thought I'd call it *My Grandmother's Herbal Remedies,* but I'm not sure and anyway, it would probably be a waste of time and money. No one's interested in old-fashioned remedies, they seem to take M and B tablets for everything nowadays.'

Picking up an illustration of a wood anemone, Betty said, 'I think these paintings are beautiful and you should definitely get ready to publish when it's all over. Everyone thinks it can't be long now.'

Charles came into the kitchen and put his hand on Kate's shoulder, saying quietly, 'You're looking a bit pale, darling.'

Thinking they wished to talk in private, Betty went to the window and watched the boys playing with a cricket bat and ball in the yard. Myrtle and Johnny were almost the same age; she was born in November nineteen thirty-seven and he in February thirty-eight. Would she have joined in their game, or might a little girl have been shy in their company?

A short while later, when they were eating the meal Betty had cooked for them, she thanked Kate and Charles for the battery operated wireless they had recently installed in the cottage for her and, remembering the electric one she had bought for Gerald, thought sadly of the magical glade she had made for their Christmas picnic and felt again the pain of his indifference.

Peter scooped up the last spoonful of apple pie and custard from his plate and, holding it in mid air, asked, 'What's your best programme, Auntie Bee?'

Dismissing the memory of that past disappointment, Betty grinned. *ITMA*. What's yours?'

'Same here! It's smashing!'

Kate said, 'When you've finished your lunch, boys, you could go and play outside for a bit while us grown-ups talk.'

Johnny jumped off his chair. 'Can we play in the car, Dad?'

'If you promise to be careful of it. Billy won't be very pleased if he finds you've scratched it when he comes home.' Charles watched with amusement as they rushed to the door, pushing against each other and banging into the doorposts before disappearing into the yard. 'They spend hours being General Montgomery and his driver. They know Billy's with the eighth army so they're obsessed with Monty and his desert rats.' He glanced at Kate then asked, 'Do you ever hear from him, Betty?'

'I get the annual Valentine, that's all.'

'He's a good chap. He kept on seeing you despite his mother banning him from speaking to you.' Charles shook his head. 'How on earth that dreadful Nelson woman produced such nice children I really don't know.'

'He was my best friend until he left school and discovered girls.'

'They don't come much more girlie than you were, Betty. You were the best damsel in distress I've ever seen, apart from Kate of course!'

'Maybe, but I was his friend and boon companion, never a girlfriend.' Actually they'd been blood brothers to begin with and then later when they played truant together they'd been King Romany and Queen Romania who married for ever and a day and ruled all the land as far as the eye could see.

Kate said, 'Well, he's a hero to our two boys. Peter wants the war to go on long enough for him to join up and drive a tank.'

'What about Johnny?'

'He repeats whatever Peter says.'

When the sisters were alone again and Betty had finished washing the dishes, she asked, 'Do the boys know about the cave?'

'No, I managed to keep them unaware of it. You'll take care not to let Olive see you going into it, won't you?'

'Of course.'

'I hope you're getting on alright with her. I asked her to Sunday lunch for several weeks, but she never came. She seems frightened of me.'

Betty chuckled. 'Maybe she heard you're the

scarlet woman of Oakey Vale.'

'I suppose that's what I am. Mrs Nelson still doesn't speak to me, and one of the local girls told the boys they're bastards. I wasn't given any evacuees when I offered, so I was obviously deemed unsuitable to look after children.'

'People still come to you for healing and for reading the tea leaves don't they?'

'That's true, I'm accepted in that way.' Kate smiled fondly at Betty. 'And do you use your gift?'

She shook her head. 'Not often – at least, not for other people.'

'That seems a waste.'

'I've had a few bad experiences. The first was with Charles's revolver, d'you remember?'

'I'm not likely to forget, sweetheart. I thought you were going to kill us both.'

'Yes, I'm very sorry for that.' Betty hesitated, then took a deep breath before saying, 'Actually, Kate, I've got this piece of wood I found in the cave ages ago. I think it was the handle of a knife my mother carved for me. She was hanged by these drunken men...'

'That was me.'

'I know.'

They sat in silence for a few moments and then Kate said, 'I don't suppose you'd let me...'

'Be with me?' She felt suddenly very excited. 'We could go into the cave as soon as you can get down to the cottage. In a way I'd like to keep it there. That's where it belongs.'

Two days later when Charles had driven Kate to

Old Myrtles, Betty ran to greet her, waving a letter. 'I've got the job. I start on Monday.'

Kate hugged her. 'This is wonderful news, sweetheart. Just wonderful!' Then, going into the cottage, she fetched an oil lamp from the cupboard while Betty ran upstairs and took the small piece of wood from the drawer in the bedroom. They walked together down the garden, pushed through the ivy curtain and went first into the outer cave and then, having slid the rock to one side, went and stood side by side before the lady and watched the water trickle down over the pink crystals and fall into the pool as red as blood.

After a short while they sat on a rock and Betty took the tiny piece of wood from her pocket, saying, 'I hope I don't just go off into a dream and not tell you anything,' then closed her eyes and immediately continued...

'My daughter be sturdy and strong; her runs like a deer in the woods and swims like a fish in the river. In winter her hair be darker than Jerome's, but summer's sun colours streaks of it golden as oak leaves in autumn. Her green eyes shine quick and bright and her nimble fingers make the little dolls from withies for the lovelorn girls that do come for them from far and wide. Her can look into the scrying ball I made and see what will befall in time to come, whilst I see nought but the pink stone from whence it came.

'Her knows the turnings of the sun and moon and whether rain will fall or no. I have taught her all I knows of healing and birthing. I have taught her what writing I remember from the convent in my youth. I stretched a kid's skin and though 'twas not

319

fine as vellum, we made marks upon it with a feather quill, such as the nuns used, dipped in the kid's blood. But there be no need in our lives for such a task and little time for it between dawn and sunset.

'Since the day of her birthing the daughter I named for the myrtle tree in the convent garden was by my side, until now. No longer do we search for the food we eat together by the fire or the herbs for remedies we give, nor do we sleep within arm's length of each other at night.

'When her ran off into the woods alone a sennight past I left her be, for all beings must leave their mothers in time and though my heart ached I were glad to know the child was full-grown and pretended not to see the secret in my daughter's eyes when she returned from time to time.

'Yesterday whilst collecting comfrey from the large patch close by the river, just below the cave wherein my mother lies buried, I were about to cut some leaves when I saw a shelter made amongst the willows on the bank. Knowing the laugh I heard from within to be hers, I hid amongst the undergrowth and waited. After a while a naked young man came out singing merrily and dipped a pail into the water then returned into his den. His beard and hair were dark and though he were too far away for close scrutiny I know he were beautiful.

'I know this be the way of youth and love. I too have felt the craving and a calling like a young doe to the stag and, indeed, I knows there must be another born to carry on, but, she be so young.' She gave a deep groan. *'So very young.'*

Opening her eyes Betty smiled at Kate and then

placed the piece of wood on a nearby ledge of rock. 'I haven't experienced it like that before. Talking about it makes it even better than just seeing it like a dream.'

They left the cave and sat in silence on the rock outside for several minutes until Betty sighed and asked, 'Young girls don't change much, do they?'

Kate chuckled. 'I'm afraid we're all like Myrtle when young, I know I was.'

'Me too. Mind you, I really was a very difficult child, wasn't I?'

'You were pretty awful at times, but I knew you were affected by our mother's death and you turned out alright in the end.'

'D'you really think so?'

'I know so, Betty, and now I come to think of it, being a midwife means you're following in Gran's footsteps in a modern way.' She placed a hand on her arm. 'I'm very, very proud of you.'

'It's a miracle I'll never get used to,' Betty said, putting the kettle onto the gas stove in the rest room at Melfont. Turning to the older nurse, she added, 'You do look awfully tired, Mrs Hobson. Maybe you should ask Matron if you could go home early. I can cope with things now.'

'No, a cup of tea will put me to rights. Although I have to admit I'm exhausted. I haven't slept for a week. My son's due to get his call-up papers. He's not very strong, always was a delicate child.'

'Maybe it'll be over soon, before he can go anywhere.'

'That's what I'm hoping.' Mrs Hobson sank onto a chair with a sigh then looked up at her. 'I heard you have a Land Army girl living with you.' One side of her upper lip was raised in a disapproving sneer. 'She's up to no good with one of the orderlies who works at The Grange, so I'm told by Alice Nelson. Poor soul! Left alone to bring up those children. I was in service at The Grange with her sister Mary. That was a scandal! She had a child the wrong side of the blanket, but Alice says she's married a builder in Liverpool and is quite well-to-do now.'

'She could cross her eyes and get knots out of boot-laces.'

'Really, fancy you knowing that!'

'I was at school with Billy Nelson.'

'That ne're-do-well.'

'Why d'you call him that?'

''Cos he's broken his mother's heart that's why! And her still grieving for her Teddy and coping with her hubby who's had a stroke.'

'What on earth's he done?'

'The usual. Got a girl into trouble. And not content with that, oh no, it has to be foreign one doesn't it? If you ask me it's because of all these American films they see these days. The boys swagger around looking like Errol Flyn and the girls think they're Joan Crawford plastered with lipstick and forget they might get caught. And now poor Mrs Nelson's got a little heathen grandchild on the way.'

Keeping her eyes downcast while pouring water into the teapot, she made no response. King Romany was married and about to be a father – perhaps he would have a son with coppery hair and marmalade eyes like his own.

322

Mrs Hobson tightened her lips. 'They should wait until they get married, like me. That's what they should do.'

Betty silently fetched the bottle of milk from the cupboard and poured some into two cups. This woman would probably hear of her own illegitimate baby before long and might well not be so friendly afterwards.

Mrs Hobson screwed up her eyes. 'Are you related to the woman at Higher Tops Farm?'

'Yes, that's my sister, Kate.'

Mrs Hobson stood up and left the room.

That night Betty lay awake, thinking of Billy, who would one day bring a foreign wife home with their baby and eventually, having stirred up memories of Myrtle and feeling the need to be close to the only memento she had of her, went to the chest of drawers, took out the small woollen mitten and, holding it close, climbed into bed. Lying back she saw a ball of light that began to zigzag and then quickly became a flickering flame above a small candle beside a bed...

The child's face was gaunt and her eyes were glassy with fever.

She blew on the glistening forehead and, looking at the limp little body, saw several places where a red rash had merged to form dark areas like bruises. This child was close to death. Her pulse was only just discernible and her chest barely moved.

'Take my breath.' She blew gently into the small mouth. 'You must live, live, live.' On and on through the night she cooled the fever and breathed into the tiny lungs.

Soon after dawn the sunken eyes opened and looked directly into Betty's, then closed again in sleep.

Awakening and seeing the mitten lying on the pillow she decided to keep it with her all the time, just in case it might bring another vision, or fantasy, or whatever it was, of the beautiful child.

When cycling home after work that afternoon, she saw a young man in khaki uniform close the gate of the cottage behind him and walk along the lane in the direction of The Grange. On entering the kitchen she found the pretty young Land Army girl wrapped in a silk dressing gown and greeted her, 'Hello, Olive, not working today?'

'Er, no. I had a touch of the collywobbles. I've been in bed all day.'

The room smelled of pungent smoke and, looking at the flat cigarette butts in a saucer on the table, she said, 'I used to know someone in London who smoked Passing Cloud.'

Olive blushed. 'I'm usually more of a Woodbine person, but they were given to me as a present.' She pushed back her curly brown hair, causing the gown to fall open revealing her naked breasts. 'I must get back to bed.' The clock chimed and she grinned. 'Your uncle will be home soon.'

'Yes, I'll get his tea.'

'Funny little soul, isn't he?'

'Yes, he's no trouble so long as his routine isn't disrupted, and–' she picked up a knife and chopping board '–fortunately he's a heavy sleeper.'

'Oh, I see. You've heard us. You know, don't you?'

'I only know you have a visitor at night and, seeing someone leave just now, I presume that might be him?'

Olive looked anxious. 'I don't know how your sister would react. I mean, she might kick me out and I'd have to go home to Brum and I wouldn't be able to see him and I couldn't bear it...'

'Stop!' She held up her hand. 'What you get up to is none of my business. Your secret is safe with me.'

When Olive had left the room Betty turned the wireless on and heard the announcer say, 'Good afternoon on Monday the twelfth of June, nineteen forty-four. This is Alvar Lydell reading the news. The allies are advancing into Italy on all fronts...'

That meant Billy and thousands of others were fighting. King Romany might already be dead. No, please, God, no. He had a wife and a baby on the way, he must not die now. Hearing Kate walk through the glory-hole, Betty turned off the wireless and turned to greet her, and, on hearing that she had walked from the farm, said, 'I hope you're not overdoing it.'

'No, the exercise does me good,' Kate replied, then added with a frown, 'I've just met Alice, she's really upset. Apparently Billy's written to say he's married a nurse from New Zealand and she's having a baby and his mother's hopping mad. And on top of that now they've heard his regiment's in the thick of it in Italy.'

So it was true. Billy was married.

'She's very fond of her brother-in-law,' Kate continued, then shook her head sadly. 'She's having a hard time of it. What with losing her husband and now she's having all her teeth out tomorrow.'

'Poor thing.' Who did she mean, Billy or Alice, both maybe?

'Her daughter doesn't help. She wants to be a film star!'

Betty forced a smile while desperately trying to keep control. 'I think most thirteen year olds have that dream. D'you remember how I spent hours trying to emulate Lara Crowe?'

'I'm not likely to forget. I don't know why you wanted to look like her when you were the spitting image of Mary Pickford!'

'I suppose we none of us ever look as we'd like.'

'No, I suppose not.' Kate sat on the sofa. 'Alice has been cleaning at The Grange. She says there's some really sad cases there. Mostly men who are paralysed. Terrible, isn't it?'

Betty nodded. 'It's the stuff of nightmares.' It could happen to anyone. Which would be worse for King Romany, to be dead or to be helpless?

'One slightly worrying thing she said was that Olive's going out with a medical orderly.'

Betty was perplexed and slightly irritated by Kate's determination to always be anxious about someone or other. 'Why's that a problem?'

'I feel a bit responsible. I really should have taken more interest in her.'

'You've been too ill to look after her, and you're not fully recovered yet. Anyway, she's an employee. What she does after work's nothing to do with you, is it?'

'No, I suppose not.' Kate looked unsure. 'Have

you seen him?'

'Only fleeting glimpses and I don't often see her either.' There was no point in telling Kate that she heard Olive taking someone into her room at night – she'd only get more worried.

They drank tea together, and then, after promising to walk slowly and take several rests on the way, Kate departed for home.

When Olive entered the kitchen at midday three days later, Betty was surprised and asked if she had finished work early.

'I said I had a headache.'

'I could get you some feverfew, it works really...'

'No, I wanted to talk to you. I didn't have the courage the other day.' Olive stepped forward and grabbed her hand. 'I need your help.'

Oh no! There was only one reason for a young woman to say that.

'I've tried hot baths and gin.'

'I'm a midwife.'

'But you must know what to do. People use a knitting needle, don't they?'

'I'm sorry, Olive, I don't know anything about that.'

'You blinked then. You're lying.'

'I can't help you.' Of course she was lying, but there was too much at stake. If known to have done such a thing she would never work as a midwife again.

'What about the plants then? You're quick enough with the stuff for headaches, isn't there something I could take?'

Remembering the consequences of a similar request long ago, she shook her head. She could take neither the risk of being charged with procuring an illegal abortion like her grandmother, nor of being gossiped about like her sister.

'You're not listening to me, Betty. I'm desperate.'

'I'm sorry, truly sorry for you. I'm a midwife, there's nothing I can do.'

'You mean, miserable cow! Just 'cos your baby died doesn't mean you shouldn't care about other people.'

She must stay calm and resolute. 'I do care. I just can't help you.'

'You mean won't.'

There were too many worries to cope with. She knew what this poor girl was going through and could do nothing. It happened every day to hundreds like her. There was one far away who had fallen in love with Billy too. The fact that King Romany was married became suddenly too much to bear and she ran out of the house and up to the oak tree in Hankeys Land.

Sitting in the place where they had held councils of war against the invading armies and talked of smiting infidels with their mighty swords, she imagined him before her, astride the bough with scabby knees projecting out of the baggy short trousers handed down from his older brother. His golden eyes would be bright with excitement as, running grubby hands through his unruly mop of coppery hair, he deployed their troops. And, not knowing whether it was for Olive, or for Billy, or for herself, she wept.

Chapter Twenty-six

The common fern, known as bracken, is a strong purgative and should never be taken in pregnancy.

It had been a long night and the euphoria she always felt after a successful delivery was wearing off as she walked through the glory-hole and into the kitchen.

Kate, who was standing by the table, greeted her then said, 'I was looking to see if Olive left a note.'

'Why would she do that?'

'She didn't turn up for milking this morning so I came to see if she's ill, but there's no sign of her. There's nothing left in her room. She must've done a bunk last night.'

'I'm so tired I can hardly think straight.' Betty yawned, went to the dresser and selected a ration book from the pile on the lower shelf then waved it at her sister. 'She forgot this.'

'She'll go hungry without that.'

'I expect she'll write and ask me to send it on to her.'

'Maybe the chap at The Grange will know something. I'll go and see if he's there.' Kate looked at the ceiling despairingly. 'God knows what Charlie will say when he hears she's gone!'

When her sister had left, Betty sat at the kitchen table feeling miserable. Olive had had a frightened, haunted look since begging for help two weeks earlier – might she have gone to get an abortion in Bristol?

Kate returned half an hour later, shaking her head. 'No, the young man hasn't seen her today. He was surprised she'd gone without saying anything to him.' She bit her lip. 'I hope she'll be alright. You don't think she was in trouble, do you?'

Betty admitted she was, adding, 'She looked so desperate. I wanted to help her, but I couldn't take the risk.'

'You did the right thing, sweetheart, you know you did.'

Seeing the stricken look on her sister's face, Betty asked, 'Are you worried she'd do something to harm herself?'

'I hope she won't. She's probably at home in Birmingham by now. Actually, I was thinking how unfair it all is. There she is desperate to get rid of a baby and here I am wishing I could have one – well, wishing I could have a daughter.'

Betty touched the small mitten in her pocket and ached for her own little girl. Then, struggling to suppress a yawn, said she must get some sleep.

Kate kissed her and enquired, 'Shall we see you for lunch tomorrow?'

'Yes, it's my day off.'

'By the way, I met Alice at The Grange, she said Billy's wounded. She doesn't know how badly.'

Albert hummed all the way next day as he walked behind her along the path to the farm for their Sunday lunch and, on arrival, immediately sat at the table, awaiting the meal.

Betty looked over Peter's shoulder at the magazine he was reading and gasped at the picture of people searching through the rubble of devastated houses. 'My God. It's getting worse!'

Peter said, 'It says here the doodlebugs are terrorising the cities.'

Johnny asked, 'What's terryrising?'

Without looking up from the saucepan of custard she was stirring on the stove, Kate responded, 'Frightening them.'

'Why?'

Peter gave an exasperated sigh. ''Cos the Nazis want us to give in and let them invade us, of course!' He stood up and marched around the room with stiff legs, then stopped beside Albert, clicked his heels and raised his right arm. 'Heil Hitler!'

The old man looked askance without stopping his humming of 'Eternal Father, strong to save'.

Johnny giggled and then Albert gave a rare and beautiful laugh at which Betty exchanged smiles with her sister then looked out of the window over the yard and fields beyond. The Germans had been sending flying bombs to London for the past ten days and thousands of people were dead or injured. Kate was well enough to cope without her now. Maybe she should go back and help care for those poor people being bombarded in their homes while she was safe here in the country.

Peter returned to his seat and picked up the magazine. 'There's a picture here of the king visiting troops in Normandy.'

Johnny opened his eyes wide. 'D'you think he'll go and see Billy in hospital?'

'Don't be daft.'

The boy's lip quivered and Kate left the range and put her arm around him. 'The king went to France because we've got it back from the Germans. I expect he'll go and see Billy if he can.'

Charles put down the newspaper he had been reading and asked, 'Is there any more news of him?'

'His mother had a telegram saying he was in hospital with head injuries.' Kate looked anxiously at Johnny. 'It's good news really. It means he's out of the fighting.'

'Absolutely!' Charles agreed, then said, 'There's still no news of Olive. I went to the police and asked what one did in this situation. They're not worried. They contacted the parents and warned them she'd left, but she's almost twenty-one and after that they're only bound to do something if we think she's come to some harm.' He frowned. 'We don't actually know something bad has happened do we?'

'No, of course we don't.'

'Maybe she's gone to join up.' Peter wrinkled his nose. 'I wouldn't be in the Land Army if I could be in the real thing.'

'Yes,' Kate agreed. 'She probably decided the country life wasn't her style.' Turning from the stove she announced, 'Come and sit at table everyone. There's a chicken in the oven.'

Johnny said, 'I couldn't find Henny-Penny this morning.'

Peter pointed to the stove and opened his

mouth, saw his mother raise her hand and wag a finger at him, and closed it again.

Charles said, 'If she doesn't come back in a day or two I'll have to get a replacement.'

Peter grinned. 'Henny-Penny, d'you mean?'

Charles laughingly replied, 'Olive. You oaf!'

Kate reminded the boys they would soon be going to the cinema and staying the night afterwards at Old Myrtles which successfully diverted Johnny's attention while they ate the chicken.

When Betty prepared to depart, leaving her uncle asleep in a chair, Kate suggested walking back to the cottage with her and, once they were out of earshot, asked if they could go into the cave again, to which she eagerly agreed.

When they were sitting on the rocks beside the tomb, Betty held the piece of wood and closed her eyes.

'I have the cave well stocked with provender for the winter to come. It will be hard and long and there'll be a baby born to Myrtle at the end of it. There be three good cheeses and two small pieces of salted pig all given in thanks for the birthing of babies or the saving of them from the summer sickness. Six skins of elderberries and blackberries I collected be fermenting with honey. There be baskets of nuts, dried fungi and all manner of dried leaves and roots ready for when local women come seeking my aid for their ailments and those of their children and menfolk.

'At dawn this day I went out collecting withies to strengthen the roof for it will not withstand the winds to come after the shortest day. I walked along the riverbank well away from where I knew my daughter

to be and began cutting the reeds with my knife. Whilst remembering the kindly friar who had helped me mend the roof, all those years ago, I looked up and saw Myrtle watching me from the other bank. Her young face was distraught with grief. Her hands were spread open with despair.

'I waded across and held my child while her wept most piteously. Then we walked together along the riverbank to where the water ran fast and deep. The bent poles of his shelter and the ashes from his fire were still there, but his horse and cart, his stock of trinkets, pots and knives, and the beautiful young man himself were all gone.'

Opening her eyes she said, 'The girl does look awfully young to have a child, but I suppose that's how it was in the twelfth century.'

Two days later Betty stood by her uncle, who was sitting silently in his chair and said, 'You like the Marx brothers, and...' She tried to think of other films he had been persuaded to see.

'The Chinaman,' Peter suggested, 'you liked him, Uncle Albert.'

'Yes,' Johnny said, 'Charlie Chan, remember?'

The old man looked longingly at the wireless and then at his box of whittling wood.

Remembering her unwillingness to include him in similar outings when she was young, she held out her hand to him, saying, 'Come on, Uncle, we'll miss the bus if we don't hurry.'

A momentary flash of surprise showed in the old man's blue eyes before he grasped her fingers and allowed her to lead him out into the garden.

When they reached the gate he released his grip to close the latch and then walked alongside her to the village green where several people were waiting.

A woman told her companion that her son had written assuring her the war would soon be over and an elderly man who had overheard her attempted to square his shoulders before saying, 'Them Krauts can't keep it up much longer. We're letting 'em have it in Italy!'

Betty was standing with her hands on Johnny's shoulders as he leaned against her when she had a sudden mental picture of Billy's head wrapped in bloody bandages and flinched.

The boy squirmed and whined, 'You're hurting me, Auntie Bee.'

'Sorry, love.' She eased her grip on his collarbone.

The conversation about the war continued on the bus and she attempted to divert the boys' attention by encouraging them to tell her their jokes, all of which she had heard many times before.

After falling asleep during the first film, Betty was awakened by the cockerel loudly heralding the newsreel in which soldiers waved at the camera as they filed up the gangway of a ship. She sat upright when the Prime Minister, followed closely by Gerald Mottram, emerged from 10 Downing Street and made a V for victory sign with his fingers. Although still handsome, Gerry looked haggard and deep lines were now etched either side of his mouth.

Running her forefinger over the scar from the corner of her left eye across the forehead and up

335

into her scalp, she gave a wry smile. What would the people in this audience say if they knew that a few years ago she had been injured in his car and, not only that, had once straddled the respected politician while wearing her fur jacket inside out?

When the lights came on she gazed around her through the haze of cigarette smoke, and, looking at the eclectic mix of styles, sighed for the young self who had been so entranced when she first came here with Ernie. Turning to Johnny she smiled into his happy face. 'Enjoying it?'

'Yeah, it's wizard!'

After the interval the scarlet curtains opened, the lights dimmed and the buzz of voices diminished until *The Sea Hawk* appeared on the screen, and the audience fell silent. Betty tried to enjoy watching Queen Elizabeth the First encourage her dashing Captain to rob the Spanish, but, although becoming interested for a few minutes from time to time, mainly when Errol Flynn fought off the opposition single handed, the image of Olive's pretty face distorted by anger and contempt kept filling her mind.

Afterwards they and several other villagers who had also opted to miss the last bus in order to see the end of the film walked home along the moonlit lanes with Albert humming quietly whilst the boys fought duels with shouts of 'Have at thee, knave!' and 'Thy time has come, Spanish scoundrel!'

On arrival at the cottage everyone was very tired. She was relieved when the boys needed no prompting to take their candles upstairs to their room and she also could go to bed. Laying her head on the pillow she knew that, although exhausted, she would spend several hours agonising about Olive's problem and remembering when she had been in that same predicament seven years earlier.

Chapter Twenty-seven

Garlic may help with colds and treating worms in children.

Albert was restless. He walked up and down the kitchen humming a few bars of his mother's favourite hymn, to which Betty was adding the words in her head. 'Thy hand oh God has guided, thy flock from age to age. The wondrous tale is written full clear on every page.' Then, as he changed tune without drawing breath she found herself suddenly singing, 'God save our gracious King, long live our noble King. Long to reign over us, God save our King.'

Leaving the old man to his agitated pacing, she walked out into the garden, and, breathing in the delicious air, knew she would remember this bright May morning for the rest of her life.

Hearing voices on the bank at the back of the house, she called out, 'Here they are, Uncle,' then ran to the path behind the washing line and watched as first Peter, then Johnny, then their parents came down the steep rocky steps.

'We wanted to be with you,' Kate said breathlessly.

'I knew you'd come.' She took her sister's arm. 'Uncle Albert's in a state and it's my fault. I told him yesterday it would all be over at one minute past midnight and I don't think either of us has slept a wink all night.'

They hurried into the kitchen where the old man was now sitting in his chair rocking back and forth whilst pulling at his hair and humming the first few bars of 'Land of Hope and Glory'.

'Damn!' Kate muttered, then, sitting on the chair close by the old man, she gently explained that the Germans had surrendered and the war was over.

Charles looked tired and old as he sank on the green sofa, pulling Johnny close to him, while Peter turned the knob on the wireless and adjusted the sound of a brass band playing a brisk march.

Betty was wondering if she could to go to work a bit early in order to escape from Albert's incessant humming when the old man heard the national anthem begin and stood to attention. Johnny then imitated him with arms rigidly down his sides and so did Peter. Kate went and pulled Charles out of the sofa and Betty, feeling overwhelmed with love for them all, especially Albert, rose to her feet also.

She heard the announcer say 'Good morning on Tuesday the eighth of May 1945...' and heard him declare that war in Europe was officially over then found she was weeping and laughing at the same time as they all cheered and hugged one another.

When they had all quietened down and Kate

was making a pot of tea, Charles said, 'I wonder how long the rest of it will keep going.'

'D'you think it could go on for a long time?' Betty asked.

He shrugged. 'Who knows? The Japs might keep it going for years.'

She looked at her watch. 'I really must be going. Babies don't listen to the news, I'm afraid.'

Charles nodded. 'Nor do sheep and cows and I've told Irene she can have the day off as soon as I get back.' He walked to the door. 'It's strange we never heard about the other Land Girl. I wrote and asked her parents to let me know when she contacted them. I felt responsible for her in a way.'

'And she hasn't turned up?'

'Not yet. I told them how you'd done the same thing and had come home eventually.'

Betty gave her sister a pleading look whilst saying, 'I did send a card every Christmas.'

'Yes, that's true,' Kate agreed, 'and I was so grateful for that. These poor people have heard nothing from Olive, and Alice said the medical orderly she was going out with left The Grange soon after she went.'

'The conclusion must be they ran off together.' Charles sighed. 'I expect he was married and couldn't get a divorce.'

Betty felt relieved. 'I hadn't heard the chap went too.' She looked at her watch. 'I must go. Could you walk to the gate with me, Kate?'

When they were out of earshot she quickly explained, 'Knowing they went together is good news as far as I'm concerned. I'd been imagining her going to some sleazy back street abortionist and maybe getting caught or dying of septicaemia.'

'It's still worrying, isn't it?'

'Oh yes, but look at you and Charles. You've had two children out of wedlock, haven't you?'

'That's true, but it hasn't been easy at times.' Kate's eyes shone, whilst adding, 'But I've never regretted it for an instant.'

'And Olive's family might not be able to cope with the disgrace. She might think they're better off not knowing.'

'I suppose so.'

'She'll probably contact them eventually.'

'I hope so, sweetheart, I do hope so.'

Matron walked into the restroom and said, 'That was an election day we'll never forget. If you hadn't dealt with the cord like that we'd have lost the baby.'

Betty touched the brooch beneath her uniform and gave silent thanks to her grandmother.

'Did you get to vote?'

She yawned and explained she had been the first to arrive at the polling station on her way to work early in the day.

'You look exhausted. I really think you deserve to go home now, Nurse Barnes.'

'But there's no one else on duty, Matron. Nurse Hobson is not due in until the morning. She was expecting her son home on leave, if you recall.' She stifled another yawn. 'I can stay until she comes, Matron.'

'In that case put your feet up. I'll call if anyone

needs you.'

She sank down into the armchair and fell asleep.

Awakening with a start, she saw the ball of light expand into a zigzag...

Through the mist she saw a small room where the little girl was curled up on a bed talking quietly to a toy dog. 'My tummy still hurts. Mummy said I'd been a pig and eaten too many fairy cakes at the party in the street 'cos the war's over and she didn't have any sympathy, that's what she said. I never did, I told her so and she sent me to bed. I did like the sausage rolls. I did eat two of them.'

Betty leaned forward, longing to kiss the soft cheek...

'It's a good thing you stayed, Nurse Barnes.'

Blinking in the moonlight shining through the window, she exclaimed, 'Good heavens! I must have dropped off. What time is it?'

The matron smiled. 'Just after midnight. I'm afraid we have a new arrival and she's well on the way.'

Standing up, she stretched and looked in the mirror, then tucked a stray curl of fair hair under the white headdress and smoothed her starched apron. A new life was about to arrive in the world. How wonderful!

Mrs Hobson walked into the restroom, hung her cardigan on the back of a chair and stood with hands on hips as she announced, 'The country's gone to the dogs, if you ask me!' She sniffed disapprovingly. 'Mr Churchill brought us through the war. And now less than three months after we've won – look what the country's done to him!'

Betty unpinned her headdress. 'I'm really tired. I must go home.'

'I want to know who voted for these people. I mean, who could possibly want this hair-brained scheme they're talking about, the National Hospital Service?'

'Health Service,' Betty said wearily.

'Whatever it is. What's going to happen to the likes of us?'

'That's what I'm wondering.' Matron stood in the doorway. 'I've just heard the news on the wireless. I don't want some socialist coming here telling me how to run things.'

'Couldn't we be part of the new system?' Betty asked.

'You might, not me. I'm too old to change now.'

'And me.' Mrs Hobson's mouth tightened. 'I don't believe in people getting something for nothing. They don't appreciate it. There's people as would take advantage, mark my words, you'll see!'

Feeling too exhausted to argue with them, Betty walked out into the bright morning light and fetched her bicycle. She'd voted for the Labour candidate after reading a manifesto that had filled her with optimism and enthusiasm. Now, pedalling along the lane between drifts of cow parsley and red campion, she wondered if the matron might be right to worry because, whilst her establishment was usually kept scrupulously clean, there had been occasions when it might not have passed an inspection for the standards of hygiene required in hospitals, and also she would probably be unwilling to be inspected in the first place.

One certainty was that babies would go on arriving no matter who was running the country. In fact, now the troops were returning home and being reunited with their wives, an obvious result would be even more being born. She was determined to support the new health service no matter what happened at Melfont. All women deserved the safe delivery of their babies, not just the ones who could afford to pay for a nursing home or had a friend to pay for them as Fay so generously had for her. Suddenly thinking of Gerry and the possibility he had lost his seat in the election, she wondered what the Honourable Gerald Mottram would say if he knew that silly young Foxy had grown up and was thinking about such things and even voted against his party!

On reaching the cottage, she found Kate standing by the back door and asked her if she had heard the news.

'Yes, let's hope they can do all they promise.'

'Matron at Melfont's not very happy.'

'The doctor in Wells has his doubts too.' Kate shrugged. 'I can't see what's wrong with giving everyone equal chances. We were lucky we could afford the doctor's bills when I needed my hysterectomy.' She picked up her shopping basket. 'I came to let you know there's an open day at The Grange tomorrow and see if you'd like to come with us.'

'I'd love to. I'm not on duty until the evening.'

She saw Kate hesitate and her green eyes flicker. 'Are you thinking what I'm thinking?'

Kate nodded and fetched an oil lamp and they walked together to the cave and knelt before the waterfall, looking up into the implacable face in the rock. After scooping up some water from the red pool, they drank it and sat beside the tomb.

Taking the sliver of wood from the ledge, Betty breathed a deep sigh, then closed her eyes...

'Though her ravaged face spoke of a broken heart, my sweet daughter Myrtle uttered no word against him who planted the seed in her swelling belly. Throughout the dark days of winter we waited patiently for the new generation in the stream of life, the child to be born of the child who was born of me.

'When spring came and every footstep meant avoiding primrose, violet or windflower and the malodorous but beautiful white ransoms were vying with the sweet scented bluebell in the woods, the travail began.

'Many birthings have I seen. Some have ended in death 'tis true, for that is the way of it, but this was long, much, much too long and though she did cry most piteously at first, she made not a murmur at the end. The baby, when he came at last, was strong and yelled lustily for life while my beautiful daughter lay still as stone. No herb, no berry, no cure I know could bring back the life that slipped so quietly away.

'The pain of grief was like a searing burn to my heart, mind and soul. A mother should not bury her child. Surely this could not be God's will? My own corpse should be the next to join the others; not that of a lovely young woman newly emerged from child-hood.

'I went into the inner cave and placed the lighted torch by the tomb. When I slid the slab of rock to open it I could see bones gleaming in the flickering light and knew them to be the remains of the drunken miller whose life I took long ago. I fetched the body of my daughter and held her over the chasm, kissed her and let her go to lie on top of him who murdered my mother and violated me. Then, having asked the ancestors to understand and forgive me, I fetched the tiny baby and, kneeling before the waterfall, I bathed him in the pool as red as blood and named him for his grandfather.

'Jerome will live and, though not a girl, in time will take my place, for the line must go on. A child may die; an old woman may die; in the end there be only death. We be a finite part of a stream of life that is infinite. We all die. 'Tis the only certainty in life.

'My heart still aches with the memory of that quiet death but I do love...'

A strange scrabbling and scuffling interrupted the dream. Something was scraping on the rocks in the far corner of the cavern. A muffled voice said something that sounded like 'Hell's teeth!'

Kate hurriedly extinguished the lamp. They both turned their heads and looked at a tiny chink of light in the rocks to their right. Further scrabbling followed and they were in complete darkness with no sound other than the water trickling over crystals and down into the pool.

Sitting in the absolute, thick and disorienting blackness, she felt Kate's hand find hers and hold it. They remained silent for what seemed a long time until, whispering that she must get ready for work, Betty lit the lamp and they hurriedly left the cave.

As they walked back to the cottage, Kate said, 'I've always feared Jim Hall would come back.'

'The archaeologist who wanted to marry you?'

Kate nodded.

'The voice did sound familiar.'

'I know. But it wasn't clear and, after fourteen years, I can't be sure.' Kate groaned, 'Oh God! Whatever are we going to do?'

'I don't think we can do anything except block up the hole in case he comes back again. It's just possible he didn't see our light but we have to make sure he won't do so another time.'

'I suppose he must have got through from the witches cave.'

'What!' Betty exclaimed.

'That's what everybody calls it since they found the bones.'

'And you call it that too?'

'I have to. I can't very well say I object because I think it was me who was murdered and thrown in there, can I?'

'I suppose not.' She looked at her watch. 'I must get ready for work.'

Kate walked to the front gate and looked back. 'I think the sooner we can fill the gap the better.'

'Let's do it tomorrow, after we've been to the open day at The Grange.'

The following day when Kate arrived in the cottage she looked out of the window at Peter who was swinging Johnny round by his arms, saying, 'They're impatient to get going, sweetheart. They've not seen where Charles used to live before.'

On leaving the house they were soon ambushed by the boys who then ran excitedly ahead of them along the lane jumping up from time to time to try and look over the high wall around The Grange's boundary. Eventually, after finding they could see nothing other than the thick and tangled woods merging upwards into the hillside above Old Myrtles, they slowed down and approached the wide wrought-iron gates as though they were soldiers taking control with imaginary hand grenades and machine guns.

Once inside the entrance, and having been reprimanded by their mother, the boys were silent, until after following the curving line of yew hedge, they rounded the end of it and gasped at the beautiful stone house festooned with Virginia creeper on each side and wisteria dripping from a long balcony at the front.

'Did our dad really live there, Mum?' Peter asked.

'He did.'

Johnny frowned. 'Why doesn't he live there now?'

'He, well, he wasn't rich enough to stay there so he came to live in the cottage with me and then we went up to the farm.'

The boys had stopped listening and were waving at a family with three children standing by the large round pond.

Kate gestured at the garden. 'It looks the same, apart from those men in beds on the terrace and the nurses, of course. I expect the rooms have been made into wards for the patients now. It used to be so beautiful. There was an enormous sitting room overlooking the garden with a carved stone fireplace and all sorts of elegant furniture and magnificent Persian rugs, d'you remember?'

Betty shook her head. 'I only went in the kitchen. Cook used to have a soft spot for Billy and give us delicious cake and lemonade.'

'Look.' Peter pointed to tables on the lawn. 'There's hoopla and games and things. Come on, Johnny. Let's have a go.' They ran off towards them.

Betty said, 'I remember watching Billy's father prune the vine. We could go and see if it's still there.' She led the way along the gravelled drive beside the old coach house and stables until, on reaching the kitchen garden, they followed the narrow path to the greenhouse and went inside.

A man emerged from behind the greenery nearby.

'Billy!' both sisters exclaimed.

He greeted them warmly then held out his hand towards the woman approaching them and smiled proudly. 'My sister Mary and I are having a reunion. It's the first time she's been back for years.'

Betty asked if she could still cross her eyes and untie knots in bootlaces and Mary laughingly affirmed she could. They chatted about the family for a few minutes and, on hearing that their younger sister Daisy was now farming on the other side of the Mendips with her husband and two small daughters, she touched the cameo brooch pinned to her blouse, remembering how she had cured a wart all those years earlier. Then, seeing a gold ring on the third finger of Billy's left hand, she said, 'I hope I'll meet your wife.'

'Not yet I'm afraid,' he replied, 'she's in New Zealand with the baby. I'm waiting to hear when they're due to come here.' He explained that he had arrived home the day before and hoped he might visit the farm very soon.

Kate patted the ornate cast-iron pump with a long wooden handle just inside the door, saying, 'That's a beautiful old contraption.'

'Yes, it's used to pump the water up from the tank underneath the ground where all the water from the gutters collects. Dad was really proud of it. He said the garden could always be watered even in a drought.' He grinned at Betty. 'I remember how you drenched my feet. My mum was furious with me when I went home.'

Kate leaned slightly on the handle and gasped in horror as water spurted out onto Billy's shoes.

'Hell's teeth!' he exclaimed and roared with laughter.

The sisters stared at each other for a moment. Then Kate made elaborate apologies and Billy insisted his feet were quite comfortable despite the squelching sound as he walked. Seeing Betty looking at the wire leading from the breast pocket of his jacket to his left ear, he gave a rueful grimace. 'Bomb damage, I'm afraid.'

She ached inside while saying how sorry she was.

Kate looked embarrassed, then asked, 'Where's the water tank you were talking about?'

Billy pointed outside and they all stepped through the nearby open door. Betty then looked around the concrete. 'It's under here, I think. I remember Mr Nelson lifting something.' Seeing a metal ring set into a slab she stepped forward to point it out and the ground came towards her in a spinning circle of silvery grey...

The man's voice was low and tense. 'I can't stay long, Olive. There'll be hell to pay if I'm caught off the ward.'

'I had to talk to you.'

'Keep your voice down. Have you done it?'

'Not yet. I will, I promise. You do love me, don't you?'

'You said she'd do it soon.'

'She won't. I'll have to find another way.'

'What d'you mean, won't?'

'I thought she would, but ... you're hurting me.'

'You said she'd know.'

'Ron, please...'

'Shut up!'

'But...'

'Bitch! I know your game. Lying little bitch.'

'Help! Help!'

'Shut up! Shut up!'

A myriad of stars exploded then vanished into the darkness. Opening her eyes Betty found Billy kneeling on the concrete beside her. 'You're alright,' he said, 'you fainted.'

Mary bent over her. 'Shall I call a doctor?'

Kate's voice sounded higher than usual. 'Yes, she may be concussed.'

Betty sat up. 'No there's no need, I'm alright. I'm so sorry. So sorry.' The intense cold was rising up from beneath her. 'I have to tell you. It's Olive. I think she's down there.'

Kate muttered, 'Oh my God!'

Billy groaned and went very pale.

When, an hour later, the four of them emerged from the medical director's office, Betty thanked Mary for persuading him to allow the tank to be emptied the following day under the pretext it was being cleaned and then went home to prepare for work.

Whilst cycling to Melfont, she went over the recent events in her mind. Suppose she'd got it wrong? Maybe it was all in her imagination, and in which case, would anyone ever believe her again? Indeed, would she ever trust herself? And also, what was Billy doing in the cave?

The following morning, on being awakened by loud knocking on the front door, she grabbed her dressing gown and ran downstairs to find Billy, his sister and a policeman standing by the porch.

After being invited inside, Mary said, 'You were right, Betty.'

She sank onto a chair. 'In a way I was hoping I'd made a mistake.'

'No mistake, Miss,' the policeman said, 'there's human remains in that tank alright. Our chaps will take over now. I just came to ask if you'd give us some information on the possible identity of the deceased. Could you call at the police station tomorrow, perhaps?'

'I don't want any publicity, you understand?'

'Of course. We'll behave exactly as though they were found by chance when Mr Nelson went to look for the pocket watch he dropped down the hole.'

Betty thanked all three of them.

After the policeman had departed the others sat sitting drinking tea and discussing recent events. Mary was describing the moment of discovery when Billy, who had been very quiet since his arrival, stood up with sweat glistening on his pale forehead and ran out of the house holding his mouth. Mary followed saying she would escort him home.

A short while later Albert returned from lunch at the farm, accompanied by Kate and the two boys who rushed in eager to relate the news.

Johnny said, 'We saw a police car in the lane and an ambulance.'

Peter was pink with excitement. 'We've just met a nurse from The Grange. She said Billy Nelson dropped his watch down a hole yesterday and when they went looking for it in this water tank thing, you'll never guess what they found, Aunty Bee!'

Johnny made a face. 'It's really, really horrible!'

Albert groaned and sank into his chair then began rocking backwards and forwards.

Kate said firmly, 'They don't know who it is yet.' She looked at the wireless and then at the old man in the corner. 'It'll be Music Night later on.'

Betty said, 'Uncle Albert likes that. Don't you, Uncle dear?'

Peter played an imaginary violin. 'With the Palm Court Orchestra playing a selection from *The Merry Widow* and *The White Horse Inn* as usual.' Then, going to sit with Albert, he began asking him about the woodcarving he had in hand.

The terrible fact that Olive had been murdered suddenly became too much for Betty to bear and she felt uncontrollable tears running down her face. 'It's no good, I can't cope...'

Kate led her into the garden, down the path to the rock seat close to the cave.

Betty said, 'It's my fault, if I'd helped her she'd still be alive.'

'You can't take responsibility for what happened.' Kate put an arm around her. 'You did absolutely the right thing and when you tell the police they'll say so too.'

'Oh God! It'll all come out at the inquest and be in the newspapers. Then if they find the man...'

'Hush! All that can be reported, you can't stop it. The main thing is they've all agreed not to mention the real reason they investigated the tank. Billy even deliberately dropped a watch down the hole so they wouldn't have to tell a lie.' Kate gave a sad smile. 'He's such a nice fellow. Alice came here this morning and told me that his wife's waiting to come here. She went back to New Zealand to have the baby after she was stuck in Alexandria and couldn't get transport to England. She took the opportunity to get back there when she was offered it, but it's been really difficult getting a passage out again. The good news is that Mr Hayes wants to buy The Grange. He's got some idea of making a family hotel, and the best thing of all is that he's offered Billy a job.'

'But it's a hospital.'

'Not for long, apparently. Now the war's over, the patients can be moved to a special home near London.'

'Hell's teeth!'

'Pardon?'

Betty sighed. 'We know he's the man in the cave.'

'So Mr Hayes must've been showing it to him. That must mean he intends opening it to the public.'

'It would be an extra attraction for the hotel. The caves at Cheddar are very popular.'

They stared gloomily at one another until Betty said, 'We forgot to block up that gap in the rock yesterday. Come on, let's do it now.'

Once inside the inner cave, Kate held the lamp while Betty climbed up and investigated the spot where she had seen the light, and, running her hand along the line of rock, she soon found a horizontal gap a few inches long and deep enough to squeeze her fingers through. They then collected small stones, which she jammed into the space and placed larger ones on a ledge below to form a second cover, then, returning to stand looking up at her handiwork, said, 'Let's hope that's good enough.' Then, turning to face the figure in the rocks, she went on, 'I suppose most people would think we're odd keeping this place secret.'

'Because we could make money from it, d'you mean?'

'Exactly.'

'But then we'd be breaking the pledge our

ancestor made.'

'Of course. I wouldn't want to do it myself. I was simply saying what other people might think.'

Kate went and stood beside the flat rock covering the tomb. 'I wonder how many generations of women are buried in there.'

'It depends on how long ago they thought it was under threat of desecration from invaders. The Romans took over lots of sacred wells and dedicated them to their gods, like in Bath for example.'

'And then the Christians came along and named them after their saints.' Kate frowned. 'I think it would have been earlier than either of them, although I've no idea who they were and when they came. Jim Hall said those big humps on the farm were very old barrows and Gran called that area Prince's Grave Field. She said the name was left off the new map of eighteen twenty-two and they were just marked as burial mounds after that. I wonder if the people who built them were foreigners who made their tombs to look like the caves they would have used in their native land. It's possible that if they'd known about this cave they would have taken it over and buried their chiefs in it, and that's why it was kept secret.'

Betty dipped her fingers into the red pool. 'I'd like to know if there are other grottos like this hidden away.' She grinned. 'But if I did they wouldn't be secret any more, would they?'

Chapter Twenty-eight

A tea made with feverfew may help cure a headache.

Mrs Hobson threw open the door and said breathlessly, 'Matron wants to see us. And, guess what! The Japs've surrendered!'

Betty looked down at the tiny baby in her arms. 'It's all over. Thank God!' Whilst placing the little girl in her mother's arms she added, 'She's not a war baby – isn't that wonderful?'

The woman nodded wearily. 'I'll call her Hope.'

As they walked along the corridor the other midwife said, 'It was the enormous bombs the Yanks dropped on them; that's why they gave in.'

Betty yawned. 'It's over. It's over. I just want to keep saying it – it's over.'

'Yes, all those poor men stuck out east can come home at last.' Mrs Hobson knocked on the office door and they walked inside.

The matron's pale lips hardly moved as she said, 'I've decided to close down.' She sniffed. 'I've read through the letter about this new health scheme and I don't see where we fit into the grand plan.'

'What is the plan?' Mrs Hobson asked.

'All women would be entitled to either a free hospital delivery or a home delivery with a trained midwife employed by the County Council.' She swallowed and took a deep breath. 'So you see; we

356

won't be needed soon.'

'How soon?'

'The Act will be passed this year and be operational in two years from now on–' she looked at the leaflet on her desk '–July fifth nineteen forty-eight.'

Mrs Hobson shrugged. 'That's the end of me, then.' She turned to Betty and added, 'You'll be alright; you're qualified.'

Feeling uncomfortable, she replied, 'Maybe they'll need places for people to convalesce after being in hospital. You know, like sanatoriums for TB, only they wouldn't need to stay so long.'

'I suppose that's a possibility.' The matron looked doubtful. 'I could enquire. I suppose that would be better than nothing.' She gave a small, tight smile. 'I'll give you a reference if you want to apply for a hospital job.'

While thanking her she touched the cameo brooch and knew she wanted to deliver babies to women in their own homes. Then, leaving the two women commiserating, she went home and slept until Kate and Johnny arrived at four o'clock with the local newspaper.

'Mystery body in tank identified,' she read aloud. 'The remains found two weeks ago in an underground water tank at The Grange in Oakey Vale on Monday thirtieth of July.' Looking up she asked, 'it was Sunday, wasn't it?'

'I suppose the police actually removed the remains on the Monday and anyway I expect there'd have been complaints about not respecting the Sabbath.'

'Mmm, I see.' She continued to read, 'Have

been identified as being those of a young woman named Olive Dean, who had been employed as a Land Army girl until her disappearance in June of last year.' A ball of light flashed into view. 'Damn!' She struggled to keep upright and held onto the edge of the table as the light in the room dimmed and her sister receded into the gloom.

Kate said, 'You look awfully pale, sweetheart.'

'I do feel rather queer,' she replied. Then, as the light began flashing, added feebly, 'I'll be alright in a minute.'

'Why don't you go and lie down?'

The light expanded into a circular zigzag. 'But what about Albert's rabbit pie?'

'I'll deal with that. Off you go, I'll bring you some feverfew tea in a minute.'

Feeling increasingly frail and queasy, Betty walked slowly up the stairs to her room and, taking the mitten out of her pocket, lay down on the bed holding it. The zigzag moved outwards to the periphery of her line of vision and disappeared.

The smell of soap and soda and the overriding antiseptic was so strong she could taste it. As her eyes adjusted to the gloom she could see a child lying in the bed with a bandage around her head. The nurse sitting beside her was leaning forward holding the toy dog.

The little girl's eyelids fluttered, then opening them she whispered, 'Hello, Bonzo. Me and Cyril were having an adventure. He said his dad was working at Oakwood so we went there, but we couldn't find him so we walked back a different way and saw a lake like the one near us only with more trees, then we saw this

358

sort of hut where he said his brother did scouts and we couldn't find him either so we mucked about around there and played He.We were having such fun, such a good game! He was chasing me and I climbed the wall and ran along it, it was so exciting!'

The nurse said, 'I'll go and tell Sister you're awake, Victoria.'

Betty opened her eyes and, seeing Johnny standing beside her, pushed the mitten under her pillow.

'You won't die will you, Auntie Bee?'

'No, Johnny love. I'm not ready for heaven yet.' Taking his hand, she added, 'I wasn't feeling very well, but now I'm much better. In fact I'm going to come down and have breakfast, I'm starving!'

He laughed. 'Me and Uncle Albert's just had tea!' He pulled at her hand. 'We've got something to show you, come and see.'

The old man was smiling up at her as she walked into the kitchen.

'Look, look!' Johnny urged her, pointing at a piece of wood on the table.

Staring in amazement she picked up the small carving of a man and woman intertwined. 'Oh, Uncle Albert, is this really for me?'

He nodded.

'I'll get a blade from the ironmonger's tomorrow. This is such a lovely surprise, a special knife of my own just like Gran's and Kate's. Thank you.'

The old man mumbled something ending in, 'Dinnum', and smiled before humming 'Eternal Father Strong to Save', as he began rearranging the contents of a box beside his chair.

Kate ran her forefinger over the smooth wood. 'Gran said her grandmother had one like this and so did all the women back into the long ago. The village Wise Woman's knife would have been her most important possession; she probably cut everything from herbs to goatskins to umbilical cords, all with the one tool.'

Betty looked at Albert sharpening a small chisel. 'I feel he's really accepted me now, and, more than that, it's like I'm part of the story, I'm one of the line.'

Kate smiled. 'I'm so glad, so very glad, and I hope one day...' She left the sentence unfinished and began preparing to leave.

Later, when lying in bed, Betty thought of all the women who had lived their lives close to the cave and guarded its secret. Some would have died in childbirth and others of pestilence and famine, and yet somehow they carried on the line and kept their vigil. One thing they would have all had in common was their knife, their most precious possession, without which they could not have survived. She now had her knife, but, would she do as Kate wished and provide the next generation to follow on? Could she ever bear another child as perfect as Myrtle?

Walking into the farmhouse kitchen two days later she kissed Kate, who was standing by the range stirring the gravy and, after chatting about the weather for a few moments, said, 'I've been to see the solicitor about that endowment Gran left me. I'll be entitled to it next birthday in March.'

Kate chuckled. 'I remember you thought you

wouldn't live long enough to see it.'

'It was hard to imagine being twenty-nine when I was twelve.'

'So have you got plans for spending it?'

'I'm going to London to do some more training first.'

Kate looked anxious. 'You'll come and visit, won't you?'

'I'm only going for three months or so and then I'll come back and buy a car so I can drive around to deliver babies at home. The main problem will be Uncle Albert. D'you think you could look after him while I'm away?'

Kate frowned, then reassured her, 'Don't worry, sweetheart, I'll work something out.'

The door was pushed open and Charles and the two boys came in, sniffing the aroma of roasting meat.

When Kate had told them of Betty's plan, she added, 'Alice called by earlier and told me some news. Apparently Mrs Nelson's really upset because Mr Hayes is having second thoughts about buying The Grange and so Billy's gone to London to work for a friend of his.'

Johnny looked beseechingly at his mother. 'What's for pudding, Mum?'

'Wait and see.'

'Not again. That's what we have every Sunday!'

That evening, when Albert was ensconced in his corner listening to the Palm Court Orchestra on the wireless, Betty walked down the garden and sat on the rock outside the cave. Why was she so disappointed when she heard Billy had left the village? He was nothing to her now. She had no right to want him here. He had a wife and baby who were probably on a ship sailing to England. A sob formed in her throat. She was lonely, that was all, and still grieving for her baby. Suddenly gripped by a longing to see the lady in the rocks above the pool, she ran to the house and fetched an oil lamp, then went into the cave.

After sitting watching the water trickling down into the pool for several minutes and feeling calmed and comforted by the beauty of her surroundings, she reached out and took hold of the tiny sliver of wood...

Goatskins lay all around the dwelling, drying in the sun. Wood was stacked against the rockface and beside the animal pen. With careful management of the stores and the occasional slaughter of a goat they would have food enough for the coming winter. She straightened and eased her aching back. Many seasons had passed since she had come back here to live after leaving the convent. She had borne a child who had herself given birth and now she was old, of that there was no doubt. Whatever the tally of her life was in years, she had to keep going whilst the child needed her. She must not allow aches and pains to stop her from the task in hand. Only when Jerome was capable of fending for himself could she give way to time and go to join those who had gone before. Laying down the knife with which she had been cutting a goatskin into shapes that would make strong shoes for herself and the child, she inspected the dwelling built up against the cliff of rock. She must collect withies from the river to strengthen the thatch before the weather broke, but otherwise all was well.

Looking down she gazed at the little boy who was sitting on the grass gurgling and cooing. He was playing with some dried white bones and from time to time held one in his mouth and gnawed upon it. He had been fretful in the night, which was unusual, for he was of a quieter and less demanding temperament than his mother. Thoughts of Myrtle chilled her heart for a moment. Her beautiful daughter was in the cave before her time having paid the price of Eve; she had loved the handsome young tinker and died giving birth to the fruit of their coupling.

She knelt beside the baby and kissed his red cheek. 'There, there, my little Jerome, that tooth will serve thee well when it comes through.' The child leaned against her, gurgling contentedly. 'I named thee for the man who fathered thy mother. Such a fine handsome squire he was, no doubt long since dead.' She held the baby close, revelling in the warmth of his body. 'And though never a fine gentleman dressed in silk like him, thee shall learn from me to read and write as he did.'

When the stranger appeared through the trees, leading a large chestnut mare, she was apprehensive. Women came often to see her seeking herbs and cures for their ailments or a little withy doll, but men of the area rarely entered the valley, even the young tinker who beguiled her daughter had no doubt taken care to avoid her and moved on before she could curse him.

As the man approached she thought he might be the Bishop's Steward, checking on his master's nearby estate and, putting the child down on the ground beside her, she stood up to greet him. She had taken nothing of his and therefore had nothing to fear As he came closer, silhouetted against the sun, she saw he was sombrely but richly dressed in black. Clerics in the cathedral looked similar, but there was a different, unusual air to him. His velvet hat was of a shape she had not seen before and his shoes had longer toes than those of the merchants in Wells. His features, above a greying golden beard, were dark and indistinct as she shaded her eyes and peered at him.

'Caitlin?' he enquired.

Knowing him by his voice, she exclaimed, 'Jerome!'

They laughed in unison, before both standing in awkward silence.

She looked at his fine woollen tunic and fingered the coarse linen of her skirt. When he tethered the horse to a tree she saw a gold ring flash in the sunlight and put her dirty hands behind her back.

'I stayed last night at Glastonbury.' He scuffed the ground with his leather shoe. 'I went to the nuns and asked if they had word of thee.'

Her heart leapt and, forgetting her ugly hands, she reached towards him. 'Was Sister Marie there? I have not had word of her for many seasons.'

He nodded. 'She sends her love, and bade me say thee'll always be welcome.'

'My dear, dear friend.'

'Much time has passed since I left this place.'

'Aye.'

He looked around anxiously. 'Art thou alone?'

'Not entirely.'

'A man to share your hearth?'

She shook her head. 'Nay.'

He beamed at her. 'A child?'

'Aye.'

'The sisters were not mistaken! They hear of thee from travellers and pilgrims passing through.' He bit his lip. 'They were sure there was a child born to thee.'

'Aye.'

He stood upright, shoulders back and thumbs inside the leather belt around his hips. 'Sired by...?'

'No man has joined with me since thy departure.'

His eyes shone. 'Where is he?'

'Our daughter died last summer'

'Died? A daughter?'

'Aye.'

He sighed. 'A daughter.'

The baby, who had fallen asleep in the grass, awoke and sat up rubbing his eyes.

Jerome looked at the child and frowned.

Her heart was proud. 'He is named for thee.'

'For me?' he asked, then his face relaxed and looked young again. 'Is this the child of our child?'

'Aye. He is the very light of my life. The joy of my heart and soul. He is my reason for living.'

'What of his father? Does he not claim him?'

'Nay, he was up and away with his wagon knowing nothing of what he left behind.'

'He is a strong boy, is he not?'

'Aye, he'll make old bones, I'm sure of that.' She went to the child and picked him up. 'Come, young Jerome, and meet thy grandsire.'

The baby reached out and touched the greying beard in which strands the colour of oak leaves in autumn could be seen.

She felt her heart leap as when he had stood before her long ago. Catching her breath, she said, 'The fish are plentiful. I could catch some for us to eat.'

'Aye, I should like to taste it again.' His eyes held hers.

She remembered making love whilst the fish cooked on the fire and looked away. 'Come, little Jerome,' she said, 'let us go down to the river.'

They walked along the path to the place where she had laid her traps made of withies. She placed the baby on the bank and rather than remove her skirt as she did when alone, she waded in holding it above her knees, then on reaching the conical traps, had to let go of it in order to take out her catch and kill it with her knife. On returning to the bank carrying three large fish, she was pleased to find the baby in his grand-father's arms. Jerome looked at the sodden fabric hanging heavily around her legs and grinned. 'We shall need a good fire to dry thee, Caitlin.'

He carried the baby back to the dwelling and sat playing with him whilst she rekindled the fire and placed the fish to cook. 'I often think of thy fine berry juice,' he said.

She went to the cave and fetched a skin of brew from the previous season. 'It may be a little too sweet,' she said, pouring some into a goatskin vessel, 'I make it to barter for barley and rarely drink it myself.'

He took one sip, then another, and another. 'It is perfect,' he said, 'fit for a king. Here, take some of thy nectar.'

Their hands touched as she took it from him. Her heart was thumping as she nervously swallowed a mouthful. As the warm glow spread through her she giggled. 'Those sisters know what they're about!'

'They taught thee how to make the wine?'

'Aye.' She took another draught. ''Tis greatly liked hereabouts.' She handed him the cup. 'And what of *thee, Jerome, how have thee prospered?'*

'After I left all those years ago I lived in fear of capture for many days. A wool merchant from the lowlands took pity on me and I went with him to his country where I stayed and worked for him.'

She knew this explained his foreign hat and shoes, also the fineness of his garb. There were other questions she longed to ask. Was this the first time he had returned? Was there a wife in that far country? Did he have many sons with golden hair? But she kept silent; there would be time enough tomorrow for him to tell her all these things. For the moment she felt warm and content.

They ate the fish and drank more wine.

She gave the child goat's milk to drink and when he fell asleep she placed him on his bed. Then, feeling uncomfortably aware of Jerome's eyes on her, she took a stick and poked at the fire.

'Leave that and sit by me,' he said.

Fear made her hesitate. She had yearned for his embrace in cold nights and lonely days. For many years after he left she had often awoken weeping and pining for his touch.

He rose and put his arms around her.

Her body craved him. She ached to feel him thrust inside her again. Keeping her eyes on the fire, she said, 'It has been so long.'

'Far, far too long.' He drew her away and down onto her bed. Then caressing her face, he whispered, 'All these years I have thought of thy beauty.'

'I am old now.'

He kissed her neck. 'But still the most desirable woman I have ever known.'

The need was too great and his attraction too power-

367

ful. She responded eagerly to his embraces, longing to smell him, taste him and feel his manhood inside her. He brought her to ecstasy many times until, roaring in triumph, he sowed his seed.

At dawn she awoke and reached out for him. The place beside her was empty and cold. She knew he was gone and wept with rage at her own weakness.

The birds were making their usual great celebratory din. There was work to do and the child would soon awaken and need her attention. She rolled onto her back and stretched her limbs. No matter how foolish she had been, regardless of how hurt she might feel, the darling of her heart needed her.

It was unusual for the baby to sleep so long; he must have been exhausted by the excitement. He too was unused to company and he had so enjoyed playing with his grandsire. She held her breath, feeling the silence. There were no sounds within the dwelling; no small snuffling noises, nor steady intakes of breath. She sat up, looked at the empty space and screamed aloud. Jerome had taken the child!

Without pausing to eat or drink, she ran out from the dwelling into drizzling rain and followed the horse's tracks in the mud to the path leading to the moors. The rain grew steadily heavier and soon she found no hoof marks to guide her. He had spoken of visiting the convent when looking for her. Perhaps he would call there on his way back in order to get food for the child.

She pressed on for hours across the moors, paying no heed to her sodden clothes or disintegrating shoes; feeling only the agony of her loss and Jerome's treachery until at last she stood before the convent door. Then, becoming suddenly aware of the bodily pain she *had not allowed into her mind until this moment, she faltered and, losing her balance, fell into oblivion.*

Awakening and seeing she was in the infirmary with a nun sitting close by she grabbed the sister's veil. 'Did he come here again, did thee see him?' she screamed, but the sound that emerged from her mouth was a cracked echo of her voice.

The nun murmured, 'There, there. Drink this, it will ease thy pain.'

'Marie.' This time the word was clearly audible.

'Our blessed Virgin will hear thy prayer.'

'No, no. I need Marie.'

'Hush now, sleep. Rest and heal thy wounds.'

Her eyelids grew heavier and her body leaden with exhaustion. She fought to keep conscious, desperate to speak with Marie. 'My friend, she will help me…'

A strange chant with a chirruping descant awakened her. The closer sound was birds singing outside, further away in the chapel, the nuns were singing. For a moment the two sounds mingled, separated again and were then clearly different from each other. The familiar sound of early morning devotion meant she had slept for a long time, much too long if she was to catch up with Jerome. She eased herself up on one elbow and looked around the infirmary. All the other patients were asleep and one was snoring in the rhythmic way that presaged death. A nun entered and moved slowly between the low, straw-covered beds. She stopped by one and, after a few moments, covered the head with a sheet. As she passed the snoring form, which, as the dawn light increased, could be seen to be rising and falling in relation to the sound like bellows, she shook her head and crossed herself.

369

There was a certain way she moved, a turn of the head and set of her shoulders that had not changed. This was the very person she sought. 'Marie, my friend.'

Turning around the nun looked down and cried, 'Caitlin! Ma chère. Whatever has brought thee to such a pass?'

'Oh, Marie, my sister, my friend. Jerome, the father of my dear daughter, has taken her son from me.'

'My sister, my friend. How can I help in this matter?'

'He said he came here on his way to me. I was hoping he called again, might be staying with thee and together we could persuade him to return the child.'

The nun sank to her knees. 'My dear friend, I have prayed for thee every day since thy parting from us all those years ago. I can heal thy wounds, I can ease the pain in thy body, but I can do nothing to cure thy heartache.' She took her hand. 'There was a man who called about a sennight ago, he did indeed ask for news of thee and we gladly told all we knew. I heard from travellers of a child born to thee and how men feared thy magical powers. That was all I knew. He seemed so desperate for news, I thought we did good in the telling and would be thanked for it by thee.' She fingered the cross hanging at her waist. 'He was most generous. We did not know. We had no understanding he was not welcome.'

'Did he not come here again?'

'Nay, my friend, we have not seen him since.'

'He took the child. How can I get him back?'

'I do not know.'

'I fear he has taken him to the low countries where he now lives.' Fierce and murderous hatred filled her

being. 'I shall follow the path he has taken. Every step he took I shall shadow and when I find him I shall cut out his heart and...'

'Was he not the father of thy child?'

'Aye, but he has taken her baby from me. I shall never forgive him.'

'Never is a long time, my friend. Look at thy raw and bleeding feet; how will they carry thee to the sea? Have thee money for a passage on a boat? Where would he be in the low countries? Did he name a city or a place in which he dwelt?'

'I can find him. I can follow where he went. There will be those who saw him. He is a memorable man.'

'And if he be found, my friend. What then? To kill him would endanger thy immortal soul. Let him go, Caitlin. Come here and live with us. Pray for deliverance from earthly passion and learn to love our Lord with that same fervour felt for Jerome.'

She closed her eyes, lay back on the sweet-smelling straw and waited for death. The man who had once stolen her heart had returned to take her heart's delight. There was no reason to live.

Awakening to find she was lying on the ground having evidently fainted, Betty slowly rose and picked up the lamp then walked sadly back to the house, aching for that earlier self who had known the same grief but also burned with hatred for the man who had stolen her grandson. How fortunate she was, in this present lifetime, for, unlike that poor woman, long ago, she was looking forward – she was going to London for more training and on her return would be a peripatetic midwife, delivering women in their own homes.

371

Chapter Twenty-nine

Lavender tea may help with headaches and the digestion.

Her bags were packed, the house was clean and tidy, she had an hour to spare before Charles was due to drive her to the station – there was enough time for a visit to the cave before leaving. Whilst picking up an oil lamp she was regretting that Kate could not be with her because she had a cold, then, hearing the old man humming outside, her heart sank. Forcing a smile on her face, she opened the back door, saying, 'Hello, Uncle, have you forgotten you're staying at the farm for a while?'

With a shake of his head and muttering a string of words ending in 'Didnum', he walked purposefully to the chimney, reached into the space beside the range and pulled out the canvas bag. Then, taking out the little doll his mother had made of him he stuffed it in his pocket and beamed at her before walking out of the house, still humming his favourite hymn.

Feeling relieved to know he had settled in at the farm so well, Betty hurriedly carried the lamp to the cave and reached for the piece of wood...

'I mun leave thee, for I am with child.' Seeing the unspoken question in Marie's eyes she added, 'I lay

with Jerome.'

'How could this be so?'

'I foolishly thought he had come to find me again, not to seek the child he had fathered.' She wrung her hands then placed them over her belly. 'Now I am filled with another child of him who has taken my grandson, my only joy.'

'Did our Mother say thee must leave?'

'Nay. Her said I may stay, but I shall go back to my valley tomorrow. 'Tis where I belong.'

Tears coursed down the nun's pale cheeks as she pleaded, 'Stay and give birth here. I beg thee.'

'Nay, I dare not. First 'twill be "rest awhile, Caitlin" then 'twill be "summer be almost gone and thee must stay through the winter" and on and on. Oh Marie, my sister, my friend, I love being here, but I made my choice long ago. I am not a bride of Christ and have no right to stay.'

'Send word if in need of me and I will come.' Marie attempted a reassuring smile. 'There is daily traffic between the cathedral church being built in Wells and the Abbey here in Glastonbury. Word could be sent to the monks who would inform us here at the convent.'

'I shall ask for thy help, I swear.' She looked into her friend's eyes. 'It may be my daughter who needs thee.'

''Tis a girl?'

'Aye. Shall I name her for thee and the mother of our Lord?'

'Nay, give her the name of thy first daughter.' The nun smiled. 'Myrtle shall be as my own in her time of need.'

'We shall meet again, I know we shall.' She kissed the nun's pale cheek. 'Goodbye, dear sister.'

373

Having left the convent the following dawn with food and a change of shoes in her basket, she walked steadily towards the hills. And so, with frequent rests because of her aching back, she was in the valley before the day died.

The thatch had suffered in one corner from winter gales, but otherwise the dwelling was sound. By the time the sun sank into the western horizon she had found enough dry leaves, kindling and logs to make fire with flint and stone. She ate some food the nuns had given her and looked around her small home which, apart from the damp area where the wind had lifted the thatch, was as she had left it five moons earlier.

Remembering the morning she had rushed towards Glastonbury, ill-shod and without food, she clenched her fists and struggled with her hatred of Jerome. Marie had spent many hours persuading her to let go of her grandson and forgive the man who had taken him. She had prayed for strength to overcome her longing for revenge, had begged the Virgin Mary to help her and had done penance many times to no avail. Despite all her efforts, if the father of her unborn child were to stand before her now, she would thrust her knife into his heart.

Reaching to pick up a log to add to the fire, she felt the child within her stir. Although fearful of giving birth alone and at such an advanced age, she felt a sudden surge of joy. The baby would be born when the sun was high and the days long. If her own milk did not suffice then the goats would provide nourishment, as they had for little Jerome. The land would give its fruit and the river its fish. On the morrow she would visit the cave to see how much of the provender stored in the autumn remained edible and after that she would seek her goats on the hillside. She would have enough food to live until the birth, and after that, if they both survived, then she might know happiness again!

Opening her eyes, Betty wiped the tears from her cheeks and wished Kate had been able to share this dream memory with her.

A moment later she dropped the little piece of wood and felt panic rising as she scrabbled around for it. When finally her fingers felt its warmth on the cold rock floor, her heart was pounding erratically and, sitting still for a moment to calm herself, she admitted how much it had shrunk in the years since first finding it. Then, remembering this was her last visit to the cave before departing to London and there was a train to catch, she hurried out of the cave and found Charles waiting to drive her to the station.

An hour later, the guard had already closed the carriage door when Billy opened it, threw his suitcase in and jumped in behind it. 'That was a close shave!' He smiled down at her. 'Happy New Year, Your Majesty. May I join Your Grace?'

'Of course.' She smiled brightly despite her earlier hope of keeping the carriage to herself and having already undone her shoes in readiness for removing them and putting her feet up on the seat once they were under way. 'Of course, Your Highness, please do.'

Doors banged and the guard blew his whistle.

'I ran into Charles and he told me he'd just seen you off.' He put his suitcase on the rack and sat down opposite her. 'I've been staying with Mum. She's had a bad dose of shingles, so I didn't like to leave her and go visiting friends. I had to come by train 'cos the car's in dock.'

'I heard you were in London.'

'I'm working for a friend. He's set up a company mending holes in the road and I go round touting for business for him.' He grinned. 'All the roads were neglected during the war so there's plenty of work for us.' Then, as the train moved out of the station, he took out a newspaper and began to read.

Sitting back, she closed her eyes. She had to go on this course and was longing to see Fay and Twankey, but nevertheless leaving Oakey Vale had been surprisingly difficult and she was already looking forward to her return.

Billy folded the newspaper and said, 'I heard Melfont Maternity Home is closed.'

'Yes, times are changing.'

'I should say so! The coal industry's going be nationalised and the railways. The National Health Service sounds like a wonderful idea to me.'

'Yes, I'm hoping to be part of it, that's why I'm going on a training course.'

'You're not leaving the village are you?'

'No, I've realised now it's where I belong.'

He looked out of the window while responding, 'We can't always do as we like can we?'

'What would you like to do?'

He turned to face her again. 'I'd like to have

worked for Mr Hayes at The Grange, but now it's officially for sale the price is more than he's prepared to pay and so it looks like the Holiday Association Centre won't happen.'

'What would you have done there?'

'Create a guest house and activity centre for people who like walking on the Mendips.' He leaned forward, his golden eyes shining with enthusiasm. 'I'd like to aim at offering expeditions going pot-holing and rock-climbing in the gorge.'

She wanted to ask if he had been climbing the rocks in the cave, but said instead, 'There's room for a swimming pool and a children's playground, unless that's not quite the thing...'

'Yes, it's absolutely the thing, you've got the idea. I don't want a smart hotel for the gentry. I think people are going to need holidays when we've got back on our feet after the war.'

'It sounds a marvellous plan. I expect your wife is excited too, isn't she?'

'I'm hoping she will be, er ... when she gets here.' He stared out of the window again for a few moments before adding, 'It's taking longer than I expected.'

'I suppose it's a long way to come.'

'Exactly so. It was impossible for months. Then recently there've been problems with my daughter's health, she's not strong you see.'

'I'm sorry to hear that.'

After sitting in silence for a while, he said, 'I was so impressed when you knew what had happened to that poor girl.'

'I was very grateful to you and your sister. Without your help I doubt if she'd have been found.' She shrugged. 'Not that they've caught the wretched chap. Apparently he's vanished off the face of the earth.'

'Yes, a rum do, that. But it was good they found her wasn't it? For her parents' sake, I mean.'

'Poor things, I suppose it's best for them to know what happened.' They had seen Olive grow up and no doubt they watched her leave for the adventure in Somerset with aching hearts. Now they had only memories and grief for the rest of their lives.

'You'd understand how they felt, I mean.' He spread his hands in the air. 'Having lost a child like that.'

'And you would too.'

'I suppose so. Although I've never seen my little girl.' His golden eyes clouded. 'Anna went home to New Zealand before she was born. She was a nurse. We met in Alexandria when I was on leave before we went to Italy.' He shook his head. 'I can't believe how long it's been.' He produced a wallet from his pocket, took out a photograph and handed it to her. 'There they are.'

Looking at the young woman with dark curly hair framing her pretty face as she smiled down at the chubby little baby on her knee, Betty said, 'They're both beautiful. I do hope they come home soon.'

Billy swallowed nervously. 'D'you see the future as well as the past?'

'I usually suggest people ask Kate about that. She's really good with the tea leaves.' The flash of disappointment on his face made him look ten years old for a moment. She weakened and said, 'I do owe you a debt of gratitude, after all you backed me that day at The Grange. And for old times' sake too. Here–' she held out her hand '–give me your wristwatch.'

He unfastened the strap and handed it to her.

Closing her eyes, she saw him lying on the ground covered in dust. 'I smell burning.' The scene changed and he was slumped by a wall with his head wrapped in bloody bandages, exactly as she had seen when waiting for a bus with the boys.

'The tank was hit. I was thrown clear.' He swallowed. 'Two chaps were killed and my friend was badly burned. So you see, I–' he touched the rectangular box in his breast pocket and fingered the wire leading from it to his left ear '–got off lightly.'

Seeing the picture change again, she said, 'You're by a tree; it looks like the big oak on Hankeys Land. There's a young girl, with dark curly hair, she's wearing navy blue shorts and a red blouse. I can't see her face because she's climbing the tree. You watch to make sure she reaches the branch above, then you turn and smile. You have a streak of white in your hair. You laugh and point upwards, you look very happy...' Opening her eyes and seeing his astonished expression, she grinned at him.

'I don't suppose you saw anyone else by the tree, did you?'

'No, just the girl, but I saw your face clearly, you were smiling and waving to someone and you were very pleased to see whoever it was, I'm sure of that.'

They chatted from time to time during the remainder of the journey and did the crossword puzzle in his newspaper together. Then, as the train was approaching Paddington, Billy asked, 'Will you be staying in digs?'

'I hope to get a room in the nurses' hostel, but to begin with I'll stay with a friend in Chiswick who'd be very offended if I didn't visit her.'

'I'm in a similar position with an elderly great aunt in Kingston. She's a real darling and won't accept rent from me so I can save as much money as possible for when Anna and the baby come.' He rolled his eyes while adding, 'So it's hot cocoa and early nights for me.'

'I'm afraid I'll be getting late nights and bawdy company in a theatrical boarding house. The Laurels in Hardy Road is an appropriate address for it, don't you think?'

He laughingly agreed it was, adding, 'Another fine mess you've got me into! Did you see them in *Blockheads?*'

'I certainly did. I'll never forget Stan Laurel guarding that trench for twenty years 'cos nobody'd told him the Great War was over.'

'I saw it just after the second one had started and that made it rather poignant, but I still laughed my socks off.'

'He we are, back in the Smoke.' She pulled on her overcoat and wrapped a scarf around her neck. 'I hope Fay's got plenty of coal, we're in for a cold couple of months.'

He took her suitcase down off the rack. 'How d'you know that?'

She paused to wonder. How did she know? There were more berries on the holly than last year, it was true, but the knowledge had no tangible, obvious signs. 'I just know, that's all, and next winter's going to be even worse.'

They walked to the underground station together and, finding they were both going on the Piccadilly Line, took the same train. Sitting looking up at the long map of the stations, she said, 'I love to see the strange names. Arsenal, I suppose that's a store of arms, Turnpike Lane, were there soldiers there? Arnos Grove, that's nice, d'you think there was a chap called Arno who lived amongst some ancient trees? And, Oakwood–Crikey-blimey!'

'What's the matter?'

'Nothing. It's a coincidence. Someone mentioned that name.' The little girl had said, 'Cyril's dad was working at Oakwood so we went there but we couldn't find him so we walked back a different way and saw a lake like the one near us only with more trees.' In her mind she'd seen a forest, not an underground station. It was a coincidence, that's all!

'Turnham Green.'

'Oh goodness! I must get off.'

Billy placed her suitcase on the platform. 'Thanks for your company.'

'I hope your wife comes home–' the doors slid closed '–soon.'

On her arrival at The Laurels, Fay greeted her like an excited child. 'What a pity you wasn't here ter see the New Year in. We had a fine old shindig I can tell yer. We was all Brahms and Liszt, the neighbours came ter complain and ended up doing the Lambeth Walk with us. I've made a cake, eggless of course and I've saved some bacon, but it's mainly Spam fritters...'

She said, 'I like Spam, I love Spam, I adore Spam,' then, sinking onto a chair in the kitchen, added, 'I've brought my ration book, a packet of tea, a pound of sugar, some marge, a tin of sausages, half a pound of lard and eleven eggs.'

'Gordon Bennett! There can't be many clothes in yer case, Foxy!'

'I don't really have many clothes left to bring and I'll be spending most of my time in uniform.' She looked around her at the cluttered room. 'It's so good to be here after all this time.'

'Nearly two years.' Fay poured a cup of tea. 'Here, get some Rosie Lee inside yer.'

Betty put her feet on the Ideal boiler and enquired, 'Have you got plenty of coke for this thing and coal for the fires?'

'I'm getting a bit low, why d'yer ask?'

''Cos it's going to be very cold.'

'How d'yer know that?'

'I just do. And it's going to be even worse next winter. Worse weather than we've had for years. Will you remember that?'

'I suppose it's best ter Adam and Eve yer. I'll get onto the coalman in the morning. I've got the telephone connected at last so I can give him a bell.' Fay lit a cigarette then asked, 'Been telling any fortunes, have yer?'

'As a matter of fact I told one on the train. That was the first since I left here.'

The door opened. Twankey walked in and, on

seeing her, called out, 'Come and meet Foxy, everyone.' He clasped her to him and kissed her on both cheeks. 'Darling, you look wonderful!'

Four people joined them and were introduced. 'Frankie and Jimmy, comedy act. Frankie's the woman. Evie, conjuror's beautiful assistant and The Great Howdini, commonly known to us as Bert.'

'Hello, can I join the party?'

She looked round and smiled at the attractive young man in the doorway.

'Come on in, Donald,' Fay said proudly, 'come and meet our Foxy.'

'I've been admiring your picture in the bar. How d'you do?'

Betty smiled tightly and shook hands. She'd tried asking Fay to remove the pictures of her from the Gentlemen's Relish and found her failure to do so very irritating.

'We're on our way to work,' Donald said, 'p'raps we'll see you when we get back?'

She explained that she had an interview the following morning and would therefore be getting an early night and then they all departed, apart from Twankey and Fay.

'Lovely feller,' Fay said.

'Lovely,' Twankey agreed, 'and nice with it.'

'You could stay up just a little while tonight, couldn't yer, Foxy? I mean, we don't see yer very often, do we?'

'I have to see Sister Tutor at nine o'clock.' She looked at the two forlorn faces across the kitchen table and wavered. 'I suppose I could join you just for a few minutes.'

'Jolly good!'

'Smashin'!'

At one o'clock in the morning, when Fay had sung 'Roses are shining in Picardy' for the third time, Betty did try to leave the party, but was persuaded to stay and listen to Donald sing just one song. Feeling loath to offend the young man, she accepted another glass of British port wine and waited politely for him to sit at the piano. From the moment he ran his fingers over the keys she was entranced by his beautiful voice and professional presentation.

'I told yer,' Fay said, topping up the glass. 'He's a star. Good as Bing Crosby if yer asks me. Told yer, didn't I?' Without waiting for a reply she called out, 'Give us me favourite, Donald!'

With a dazzling smile, the young man played an introduction and began to sing 'Smoke Gets in Your Eyes'.

He was very attractive and he obviously liked her. Betty tried to feel something in return, but there was no flutter of excitement, no quickening of the pulse. She looked away and gazed at the floor.

'I think you're a bit Brahms and Liszt,' Fay said confidentially, as, swaying slightly, she refilled her glass. Turning to the others, she demanded, 'Who wants ter hear "The Boy I Love is up in the Gallery"?'

The following morning at twenty-five minutes past nine a small, grey-haired woman looked over her spectacles and said 'That will be all, Nurse Barnes.'

'Yes, I er … thank you, Sister.' The chair made a painful noise as Betty pushed it backwards on the tiled floor. This was the worst hangover of her life. She must never drink alcohol, not ever, ever again. The door seemed a long way off as she took a step towards it.

'Training will begin tomorrow. This will give you time to settle into the staff accommodation today. The next twelve weeks will be very intensive and we'll all be needing early nights and quiet living, won't we?'

Betty solemnly agreed and left the room. Then, standing in the corridor she leaned against the wall and rubbed her throbbing temples.

'Got a headache, old fruit?'

Turning to the nurse who had appeared beside her she gave a slight and sickening nod of her head.

'My name's Daphne. I'm here to show you the accommodation. Follow me.' She led the way out of the hospital along a path through gardens and into the nurses' hostel. On reaching a small room on the second floor she opened the door and ushered her inside. 'Usual rules apply. No men, no noise and none of what you were drinking last night.'

'Oh heavens! D'you think Sister Tutor knew?'

'Definitely. It's plain as a pikestaff that you were on the razzle with a capital R.'

'I assure you I don't normally drink. In fact I'm never going to take alcohol again in my whole life.'

'Where've I heard that before, I ask myself?' Daphne grinned. 'Where's your stuff?'

'At a friend's house in Chiswick.'

'I could drive you there this afternoon to fetch it if you like. I've got some petrol coupons.'

She gaped at her in disbelief. 'You have a car?'

'Yes, spoiled brat I'm afraid. Daddy's convinced I'm safer in his old Ford than I am waiting for buses.' She laughed. 'I haven't told him about the prangs or the wrestling matches.'

The headache made listening to every word an effort and she closed her eyes while asking, 'Pardon?'

'Medical students are the worst, wanting to practise, you know?'

'What? Oh, yes, I see what you mean.'

On arrival at three o'clock they found all the residents of The Laurels in the kitchen wearing dressing gowns. Fay, who was standing at the stove with two frying pans cooking simultaneously, greeted her with, 'That's an 'angover if ever I saw one.' Reaching up she grasped a bottle of aspirin from amongst a collection of salt and pepper pots then handed it to Betty, adding, 'Take two of them and eat some breakfast.'

When she had consumed four Spam fritters, three cups of tea and the two pills, Betty smiled and said she was feeling much improved.

'I knew you was Brahms and Liszt. I told yer, didn't I?'

'Those were your very words, Fay.'

'We was hoping Jane and Dave would get to see yer, but the younger one's got mumps. We'd even got some free tickets for the show tonight.'

Donald gave Daphne a leering smile. 'Perhaps

these two ladies could be persuaded to come instead.'

Betty shook her head. 'I really think we...'

'Yes,' Daphne interrupted, 'we'd love to come.'

'So long as we leave immediately afterwards.' Betty gave her an imploring look. 'We have to be on duty early in the morning and I've blotted my copybook once already.'

Chapter Thirty

A poultice of self-heal leaves may disinfect and heal minor cuts and wounds.

Daphne looked up from the newspaper and said, 'There's going to be a big celebration on the eighth of June. Victory Day, it'll be called. We'll really get lit up that night, Betty!'

'I'll be back in Somerset by then. I expect we'll have a street party in the village, for the children.'

Daphne chuckled. 'Sounds like you really know how to enjoy yourselves in the country. What about coming to Chiswick this weekend and having a more grown-up sort of bash?'

'Actually, I think I'd rather stay in and catch up on my notes.'

'Okay. So long as you won't be too lonely here without me. I'll probably come back early Monday morning.'

'I'll be perfectly alright.' She looked at the calendar on the wall. 'Today's the fifteenth of

February, so it's six weeks until the exam on the fourth of April.'

'Did you get a Valentine yesterday?'

'No, I haven't had one for ages.' She remembered the cards Billy had sent for a few years and gave a slight frown.

'Donald says you give "No Entry" signals to men.'

'Really?'

'Mmm. You must know you're doing it, surely?'

Of course she knew. 'I really don't want the bother and...'

'The risk of being hurt?'

'Something like that.' Something exactly like that! Emotional involvement had seemed to be part of a distant, separate world since Myrtle died.

'You could bring all your books and boring stuff with you and we could check each other's knowledge during the matinee tomorrow afternoon. Go on, Betty, we'll be on the ward from next week. This might be the last chance of a weekend together.' Daphne gazed imploringly into her eyes. 'Please say you'll come. You don't have to get rat-arsed and have a hangover on Monday like me. You know Fay would be thrilled to see you. She loves you so much, and you haven't been to see her for weeks. Please.'

'Well, I suppose...'

'Good, that's settled! We'll have to leave as soon as classes finish. I've put a shovel and a bag of salt in the boot in case it snows. The tank's full of petrol and my mother sent a tin of corned beef and a pound of butter she got on the black market. We'll have such a lovely time!'

On their arrival Twankey opened the door saying, 'Talk about brass monkey weather!'

Daphne ran upstairs to Donald's room and Betty went into the kitchen where Fay, who was sitting with her feet close to the grey enamel Ideal boiler greeted her with a delighted smile and suggested they should have a cup of tea.

Twankey filled the kettle with water and put it onto the stove. Fidgeting with his necktie he then said hesitantly, 'Foxy, er, I've never asked before. While there's no one else around, I was wondering if, well–' he shifted his weight from one foot to the other '–the thing is I'd like you to tell my fortune.'

Betty sighed.

Twankey looked at the floor. 'If you'd really rather not...'

This was the man who had walked along the towpath patiently encouraging her to pour out her grief. He had been a good kind friend. He had cut the remains of henna from her hair. Extending her hand towards him, she smiled, saying, 'Of course I will. Give me something of yours to hold.'

He removed a gold ring from his right hand and gave it to her.

A small child sat by a stream. 'I see you reach out to touch an animal. It looks like a rat! You jump up, I think – yes, it's bitten you.'

Twankey's jaw dropped open.

Fay warned, 'Don't say nothing, it puts her off.'

'You're in bed. A woman sits beside you reading; I think she does this a lot because you're ill for a long, long time.'

The scene changed. 'You're older, in your teens I think. I see you embracing a young man about the same age. You're both weeping. You stand by a wrought-iron gate and watch him walk away.'

Several images inside a hospital followed. 'I think you're visiting someone who's lying in bed. You're distraught.' She paused and then seeing him in a theatre, went on, 'Now I see you on stage and you look as you did when I first met you, your hair is bright orange and you're dressed as a dame in the pantomime. You play the fool to seem happy, but you're very sad and lonely.' When the scene changed again, she said, 'I see you looking much happier. There's a man you talk to. I see him in the shadows as you drive the ambulance alongside a building. He's there, he's waiting. Twankey, he loves you!'

Fay gulped. 'Gordon Bennett! Foxy, that was bloody fantastic!'

Twankey shook his head. 'When we first met I said I'd get him tickets for the panto when the war was over, but it's gone on too long for me to go back on the boards. I've lost my nerve, and I can't tell him I'm not in it any more.'

Betty touched his hand. 'I don't think he cares about that.'

'You'd be able to sit with him and explain the story, Twanks.' Fay lit a cigarette. 'Being Polish he might not know about Cinderella.'

'How d'you know he's a Pole?'

''Cos you've been telling me about this nice chap at Saint Tommies fer years, yer daft bugger!'

The door opened and Daphne said, 'I didn't

390

know you could do that, Betty. Will you do it for me?'

Fay frowned. 'I'm not keen on nosey parkers.'

'I don't promise to get it right, but I'll try.' Betty gladly held out her hand. This way of using her gift was suddenly proving to be a pleasure. 'Give me something to hold.'

Daphne took a gold cross and chain from around her neck and handed it to her.

'I see a big house in a beautiful garden. At school in your gymslip you run fast with a hockey stick. Now you're older, with your hair cut short and wearing an elegant linen frock as you stand on a balcony. There's a young man beside you, he has golden hair and a moustache. Now you're–' she hesitated on seeing Daphne lying on a bed weeping and punching the pillow '–very sad.'

The scene changed. 'I see you in a hospital ward. Now you're running along a corridor waving your arms in the air.' She was surprised at the next sight. 'You're wearing a large white hat and a very full skirt that sticks out and high-heeled shoes. I see you walking up the steps of a building made of grey stone. There's a man waiting in the doorway. He's in shadow, I can't see his face.'

'Gawd's truth!' Fay exclaimed and lit a cigarette. Then, hearing a knock at the front door, said, 'That's probably the Sally Army collecting old clothes for the refugees.'

Twankey went to open the door.

Fay called after him, 'They're in a heap under the stairs.'

'It's a gentleman to see Betty,' Twankey said, coming through the door.

Betty shook her head. 'No, that's not possible.'

'Yes, it is,' Billy said, standing in the doorway.

'Crikey-blimey!'

Fay gave her neighing laugh. 'She only says that for really special surprises.'

Billy grinned. 'I'm glad I caught you.' He held a large cardboard box towards her. 'Kate asked me to deliver this here in the hope you'd visit soon, she said to tell you there's perishable goods inside and the chicken...'

'What!' Fay shouted. 'We've got chicken for supper!' Then, on seeing Betty take the bird and place it on the table, screeched, 'Gordon Bennett! The flaming thing's still got its suit on!'

Betty explained she could deal with this and carried it to the sink.

Twankey offered Billy a chair which he refused, explaining that he had just driven up from Somerset and the roads were already freezing, then departed.

'Well I never did!' Fay exclaimed. 'He's a bit of alright, he is.'

Betty looked up from plucking the bird. 'We grew up together in Oakey Vale. I agree, he's nice. In fact he's very nice, but he has a wife and daughter.'

'In the village?'

'In New Zealand.'

'What are they doing there fer Gawd's sake?'

'That's her home. She was a nurse in Alexandria where they met. The transport was chaotic and she took the chance to go home because she was pregnant, but hasn't managed to get here yet.'

Fay gawped at her. 'The war's been over nearly a year!'

Betty counted on her fingers. 'It's only seven months since the Japs surrendered. It would be difficult to get a passage on a ship, wouldn't it? Unless you were rich or important, I mean. I had a sight of him watching his daughter climb the oak tree in Hankeys Land so I'm sure it will all work out.'

Donald walked into the room and, putting his arms around Daphne, said he had tickets for everyone. When Betty protested she would be studying, the others all booed and told her she was boring, so, reluctantly, in order to keep the peace, she agreed to go to the Chiswick Empire that night.

The theatre was crowded and noisy with the babble of chatter. The cigarette smoke wafting across her face was making her eyes water and her head ached. The mitten in her pocket felt warm and, anticipating the usual ball of light, she closed her eyes, then, when it formed and expanded into a curved zigzag, eagerly awaited what it would reveal.

The little girl was sitting on a bed talking to her toy dog while tying a grubby handkerchief around its front leg. Indicating with her head towards the bandage on her left shin, she said, 'The doctor said it will heal now with this special magic ointment. Mum said I should've been more careful and not run around like a wild animal in Hadley Woods when a nice lady like

Mrs Simpson is kind enough to take me out, then we wouldn't have had all this trouble just when Uncle George's coming to stay.' She held the dog's face close to hers. 'How was I to know there was horrible spiky wire tied round a tree?' She waved it from side to side. 'That's right, Bonzo. They shouldn't put the beastly horrid stuff where children want to play hide-and-seek.

'Adrian said it was there in case the prisoners escape and then they'd get cut like me. We saw them playing football. They had long hair and when I asked Adrian's mummy if all Germans looked like that, she laughed like that was funny and said maybe they were waiting for the barber to visit. She told Adrian off for shouting 'Krauts' at them. She said that was very rude and if he did it again she'd tell Mr Perrin and Adrian made a face 'cos Mr Perrin twists the boys' ears when they're naughty. When she wasn't listening Adrian said he didn't care what a silly old headmaster said and he didn't care if the war's over now and anyway that's what his dad calls the Germans, so there!'

She looked pensive for a few moments and then her lower lip jutted out as she held the dog close and asked it, 'We don't like Uncle George, do we, Bonzo?'

Awakening to see a man wearing a green uniform and pillbox hat standing on the stage beside a pretty girl in a ragged dress, she looked around her and saw the audience gazing up at the pair, obviously enthralled by them. This was the pantomime and Buttons was singing to Cinderella, only he wasn't actually doing that; his eyes were fixed on Daphne as he crooned, 'The way you wear your hat, the way you sip your tea, the memory of

394

all that, no, no they can't take that away from me.'
He really did seem besotted. Maybe he was the
man in the shadows at the top of the grey stone
steps?

Chapter Thirty-one

*A tea made with dried periwinkle may help with
menstrual problems.*

Straightening her back after placing a tiny baby
into a cot, Betty sighed with relief. The training
course was over and she had passed with several
complimentary remarks on her report. Tomorrow
she would visit Fay and the day after that could go
home to Oakey Vale, where the woods would be
filled with the scent of bluebells, or, in some
damp places, the pungent odour of wild garlic.
Primroses, wood anemones, periwinkle and
violets would be in every hedgerow and the
blackthorn would be adorned with creamy blos-
som. The special bright green of spring would be
showing on bushes and trees and the countryside
would be bursting into exuberant life – soon she
would be there, back where she belonged.

Walking out of the nursery into the corridor, she
stood by the window watching a gardener plant-
ing seedlings in neatly regulated lines around a
flowerbed and felt impatient to be in the unkempt
garden of the cottage. Hearing footsteps, she
turned round, and, seeing Daphne running to-

wards her waving a piece of paper, moaned, 'Oh no!'

'You won't believe this. They say I've missed too many days and I should retake the course at a later date.'

What could she say? Her friend had often been absent, preferring a day in bed with Donald to studying and, on many of the occasions when she had attended, she'd been suffering from the after-effects of too much alcohol. She'd hoped that Daphne was a good practical nurse and therefore had come to life on the ward and in the delivery room, but it was now evident she had not done so. Feeling very sorry for her she asked, 'Will you try again?'

'I dunno.' Daphne shrugged. 'I really do find the whole thing isn't my cup of tea.'

'What would you like to do?'

'Just be a wife and mother, that's all.' She brightened. 'Never mind, at least I've got a nice boyfriend waiting for me at Fay's. You'll come this evening, won't you?'

'Of course. Fay's expecting me.'

'Your friend Billy's going to the show tonight.'

'That's nice.'

'Donald gave him some tickets last time he came to see Fay.'

'Last time?'

'Yes, you've missed some good parties recently.'

Why did she feel so aggrieved? Billy Nelson was nothing to her. He'd probably be taking his wife to the show, she'd have arrived by now, and they were starting a new life together. Soon he would bring his family to visit his mother in Oakey Vale and one day his daughter would climb the oak tree. All would be well.

Fay was lightly dusted with flour when she opened the door. 'It's the last night of the panto. I'm making a huge great cheese flan and a sherry trifle with condensed milk. What d'yer reckon ter that?'

'Sounds perfect,' she replied.

'So yer all ready ter work for this new health set up, are yer?'

'Fully trained and raring to go.'

'Twankey and Baron are bringing some bottles of beer.'

'Baron?'

'The Polish geezer. Twankey and him have got together at last thanks ter you. He's got one of them unpronounceable monikers ending in "ovsky" so everyone calls him Baron. I can manage that, but what I do find drives me round the twist is all them people expecting me ter call them sunnink different, like you not wanting ter be Foxy no more and now Twankey thinks I should call him Julian. Fat chance he's got of that!'

'I hear Billy and his wife are coming.'

'I don't know nothing about a trouble and strife but Billy's coming alright. He brought a friend last time...' The doorbell rang and she went to answer it.

Betty heard Billy's voice and Fay's neighing laugh. The room darkened. She looked out of the window, wondering if a storm was due and saw that although the sun was low in the sky, the garden was still brightly lit. A ball of light flashed into view and began expanding. Oh, no! This wasn't a good moment for the little girl to appear. She struggled to ignore the circular zigzag forming before her eyes.

'Here's Billy and his friend.'

Turning round she could see two figures silhouetted in the gloom.

Billy said, 'This is Giles, he's an old chum of mine.'

She shook the proffered hand encased in a black leather glove.

Giles said, 'We were brothers in arms.'

Betty endeavoured to concentrate despite everything around her being distorted and shrouded in gloom whilst the zigzag opened out to the periphery of her vision. She could hear Fay asking them about their time together in the Eighth Army. Their voices were muted and far away; occasional words pierced her mind, landmine, inferno, lucky.

Making an intense effort she heard Giles chuckle and say, 'They called me "Hands" in rehab.'

Unable to fight any longer, she relaxed, let go and saw the little girl sitting on the floor of a small bedroom holding the toy dog.

Her face was blotched and swollen. 'I don't want a new daddy. We were alright before he came. Mummy said I mustn't sulk and be jealous of him and I mustn't be selfish and she deserves some happiness and she's given her life to looking after me since my daddy died in the war. But I don't like Uncle George. He smells horrid and I don't like him touching me down there like he does.' She looked searchingly into Bonzo's face. 'You don't want to go to Australia with him do you?' She shook the toy from side to side and nodded while continuing, *'I didn't think you did. Mummy wants to go so she doesn't have to live in a council flat and be a dinner lady any more.'*

'I'll find you. Don't worry.' Betty opened her eyes and found Billy kneeling on the floor beside her.

Fay exclaimed, 'Gawd's truth, Foxy, you give us the fright of our lives!'

Giles said, 'I thought you'd had a heart attack, but Billy insists you've been in a sort of trance.'

'Yes, something like that.' Her head ached, but mercifully the flashing zigzags had gone and she could see the kitchen clearly and the people beside her. She stood up and apologised for causing a fuss.

Billy asked, 'Who d'you need to find?'

'A little girl who's in trouble. She's in a terrible state, poor thing. I can hear her but she can't hear me. I have a few clues, but I don't know exactly where she lives.'

Daphne came into the kitchen. 'It's time we were going, everyone.'

'You carry on,' Billy said, 'I'll stay and keep Betty company.'

When the others had gone she explained what had happened.

'That's abominable!' Billy exclaimed.

'I have to find her.'

'Of course.' He took a fountain pen out of his pocket and picked up an envelope from the table. 'I could make a note of all the clues you can think of. Oakwood's a station on the Piccadilly Line, that's top of the list.'

'The girl said, "There's a lake somewhere near that's like ours." Her mother's a dinner lady, and they live in a council flat.'

'That's three good clues.' Billy wrote them down and then looked thoughtful. 'That incident when she hurt her leg was interesting. There can't be many places where you'd see Germans playing football.'

'That's true. I suppose one could find the names of any places where prisoners of war are kept. I'm afraid I don't remember the name of the woods she said they were in. I do remember the boy was called Adrian and his mother was Mrs Simpson. She said the headmaster twisted boys' ears. I think he was called Mr Perring or something like that. I've just remembered something about the time she was in hospital, the nurse called her Victoria, and, come to think of it, so did the teacher in the school.' She scanned the list. 'There's enough clues here for me to take the tube to Oakwood tomorrow and make some enquiries.'

'Indeed. I'd, er ... I'd really like to come with you. I could drive you there, what d'you think?'

She hesitated. 'I really don't want to trouble you.' Then, seeing his anxious look, she nodded. 'Yes, I think having a man with me would be a great help if I have to face Uncle George.' Glancing sideways, she saw Billy's hands resting on the table. Fay had admired them, and his eyes too, she was right, he was an attractive man, but there was no point in thinking such thoughts, he was also a married one. She smiled at him. 'I've been so preoccupied with my own problem I haven't asked how you're getting on.'

'I'm not sure what to do. Mr Hayes is buying The Grange after all and is negotiating a takeover date. He's waiting for me to decide if I want to work for him. He's agreed to wait until the last few patients have been moved to The Star and Garter Home in Richmond and then once that's happened I'll have to give a definite answer. If I don't take the job he'll find someone else.'

'I thought you wanted to do it.'

'I do, very much.'

'Why is there any doubt?'

'My wife says she wants to live in London because she has a friend from New Zealand working at Great Ormond Street Hospital and she'd like to work there as well when the baby's older.'

'So she's back then?'

'No.' He screwed the cap on the fountain pen and put it in his pocket. 'Actually, Giles thinks she wants a divorce but dare not admit it in writing in case I use that against her.'

'I don't quite follow. Why would he think that?'

'I showed him her letters. They're kind of polite and impersonal – almost businesslike, not at all affectionate or seeming very keen to come here. He thinks she's banking on me finding someone else and then asking her to set me free, that way I'd give her grounds for suing me for adultery and she'd be the innocent party.'

'She's said she's willing to live in London?'

He nodded. 'After I told her I didn't want to be there.' For a moment, he looked the same as he had at the age of twelve when telling her of his sister Mary's sudden departure from home, before adding, 'I wrote a long letter explaining about The Grange and describing the village and the Mendips and...' He looked sadly at the wall and swallowed. 'Maybe I overdid it and made it sound too rural and unsophisticated. I felt so strongly that Oakey Vale would be a good place for my daughter to grow up in, I'm afraid I didn't think what Anna would want.'

She thought of the girl climbing the oak tree and said, 'I'm sure it will come right in the end.'

That night seemed very long. As the cool light of dawn showed through the gap between the curtains, she knew there was no more hope of sleep. Gerald Mottram had danced in her dreams and memories of him tormented her wakeful mind. What a silly fool she'd been, such an idiot! On the other hand, if she'd been sensible she wouldn't have had those few short months with her darling baby.

When the sun beamed a line of bright light onto the windowsill, she thought of the little girl sitting on her bedroom floor looking desolate. Was the child merely a spectre born of her own desperate mourning and longing for Myrtle? She would probably be taking Billy on a wild goose chase and making a fool of herself yet again.

Hearing voices downstairs, she quickly dressed and ran down to the kitchen where Twankey was frying bread and Baron making tea while Giles, Billy and Fay were sitting at the table.

Looking up as she entered the room, Giles said, 'I've spoken to a chum of mine who said there's

402

a small unit for German prisoners at an old house in Hadley Woods and the nearest tube station to it is Cockfosters, which is the next stop along from Oakwood.'

Billy punched the air. 'That's it then!'

Sinking into a chair, she felt overwhelmed by kindness and doubt. If this was just a figment of her imagination these kind people would all have wasted so much time and effort on her behalf, but unable to admit this, she sat mute whilst Fay, Twankey and Baron fussed around her, persuading her to eat a piece of crispy bread and offering ideas on how Victoria could be found. Fay wanted to call the police. Twankey thought they should locate all the local schools and then visit them on Monday. Baron looked anxious and agreed with whatever his friend suggested.

'The question is,' Giles said, 'if you do find her, what can you do then?'

Deciding the best strategy was to continue despite her doubts, she replied, 'My priority is to save the child from this dreadful man. I'm sure any normal mother would be horrified if she knew her fiancé was molesting her daughter, so I've decided to speak to her and hope that will sort it out.'

The others all looked thoughtful.

Seeing Fay and Twankey exchange glances, she blurted out, 'I'm really worried about getting you all involved. The thing is, it could all be just a dream, a sort of wishful thinking, couldn't it?'

No one replied.

'I know you must be thinking that. Maybe we should call it off now?'

Giles said, 'Billy told me about the land girl.'

Fay and Twankey looked quizzically at Billy and he explained how the young woman's body was found in the water tank.

'But I can't promise I'm right this time,' Betty wailed.

Billy shrugged. 'I don't mind if you're not. If we found the child existed and was in no danger then that would be a relief, wouldn't it?' He looked around the room and, when everyone nodded, continued, 'If we found she didn't exist, then the bad headaches and worrying dreams might stop and even if they didn't, you'd feel less upset by them. Either way I feel we should investigate.'

'But it's your time and...'

'And mine,' Giles said, 'I've got nothing on this weekend. I'd like to come too.'

Betty gazed at the two men. Billy with his beautiful, kindly eyes was as gentle as he looked. Giles was probably equally so, but being more heavily built might look threatening to an unpleasant child molester. 'Thank you, that sounds wonderful.'

Giles said, 'I've spoken to my cousin's husband who's something at Scotland Yard, I can call on him any time for advice...'

Betty was doubtful. 'I really think we should wait and see what's going on before getting police involved.'

Daphne came into the room wearing her overcoat. 'I'll be off now.' She looked down at the floor. 'I ... um, I may not see you all for a while.'

Seeing her friend's red-rimmed eyes Betty exchanged glances with Fay, who said, 'Have a cuppa before you go.'

Daphne sat down.

Fay related what was being planned whilst pouring the tea and handing it to her.

Having listened attentively, with the occasional exclamation of surprise, Daphne asked, 'Can I come too?'

Guessing there had been a row with Donald, Betty looked upwards and then raised one eyebrow questioningly at her.

Giving a small shake of the head, Daphne bit her lip and concentrated on her teacup.

'I must warn you,' Betty said, 'we might be going on a wild goose chase. It's possible the child doesn't exist.'

Daphne shrugged. 'You think she does. That's good enough for me.'

Betty fell asleep in the car for an hour and, on waking up, was pleased to hear Daphne had obviously forgotten her disappointment with Donald and was chatting animatedly to Giles.

When they arrived at a parade of shops close to Oakwood underground station, everyone agreed they were hungry, and, while Billy went to a newsagent's in search of a map, the others walked into the small café three doors away and sat at a table in the window. Daphne picked up the envelope on which a list of known facts was written and read aloud, 'Oakwood station. Lake like ours. Scout hut with wall. Mother dinner lady and engaged to be married. Name Victoria. Headmaster Mr Perring. Friend Adrian and mother Mrs Simpson. Lives in council flat.' She looked up. 'That's plenty of clues. If I pretended to be looking for my long-lost cousin who was bombed out in the Blitz and all I know is she went to live in North London – no, that's no good, we don't know the name of the mother.'

Billy arrived and opened a map. 'They don't have a large-scale ordnance survey of the area, but even on this one I can see there's a small lake quite close to here and another about–' he measured with his thumb '–two to three miles away.'

'Well!' Daphne picked up the menu. 'We're definitely in the right place. Oakwood station is a few minutes' walk away and the two lakes have been located, so, do we walk from one to the other looking for clues?'

Billy suggested they might drive to the other one further away because the girl had called it 'our lake' and then walk around looking for a council estate.

Feeling light-headed and separate from her surroundings, Betty agreed.

'I'm starving!' Daphne declared. 'I'll have the stew and dumplings.' She looked at the other diners finishing their meals. 'We're a bit late. I bet most things are off.'

Giles nodded. 'I suspect they've had a hard time keeping it going during the war. Being in a small shopping parade like this it wouldn't have a large clientele.'

'Mmm,' Daphne agreed. 'It's a bit like the place my father goes to every day for lunch.'

'What does he do?'

'He's a solicitor. He meets up with his cronies, you know, the local bank manager, the estate agent, the manager of Woolworths... Of course!'

She looked at the others with a beaming smile. 'There's an estate agent's a few doors up, they'll know where the schools are and they'll probably have a large-scale map too.' She turned to Giles. 'I think this would be an ideal place to live, don't you?'

He nodded cautiously.

'Here we are; close to London, not the West side, admittedly, but we don't have to mention that's where you work at present and anyway the roads round here are bound to need mending like everywhere else. The tube station is near by, there's this very good row of shops with everything one could need including a café. All we need is a school for the children we've left with Grandma and we start looking at houses.'

Betty stopped listening to the conversation. The clatter of crockery when the kitchen door opened was so familiar; if she closed her eyes she could be in Edie's café. Looking up at a framed print of *The Haywain* by Constable, she thought of 'Bubbles' and wondered how many women had named their babies after that painting of a small boy advertising Pears soap.

'Is that alright with you, Betty?'

'Pardon?' They were all looking expectantly at her. Seeing the tall, thin woman wearing a black frock, white apron and a white band threaded with black ribbon across her forehead, she blinked. Why did waitresses dress like parlour-maids? 'Er, I'm sorry, I was miles away.'

Billy pointed to the menu. 'There's only the pasties left, will that do?'

'Yes—' she smiled up into the woman's anxious

face '–that would be lovely, thank you.'

When they had eaten the tasteless food, Giles lit a cigarette and enquired, 'So shall Daphne and me go to the estate agent's and pretend we're married?'

Billy frowned. 'Can't we come too?'

Giles held up his gloved hand. 'Sorry, old chap. If I'm going to keep a straight face, I need to be alone–' he indicated towards Daphne '–with my dear lady wife.'

Watching them leave together and walk along the pavement arm in arm, Billy looked thoughtful. 'They appear rather too convincing for comfort. What's happened with Donald?'

'I think they've parted company.' Betty shrugged. 'He had the look and the lifestyle of a rolling stone in my opinion.'

'I'm rather fond of old Giles and wouldn't want him hurt.' Billy lit a cigarette. 'He's in a vulnerable state at present, his fiancée has finally pulled out after shilly-shallying for months. She can't cope with his hands I'm afraid.'

'Does he wear the gloves to protect them or hide them?'

'Both.'

'Daphne may not be a natural midwife, but she's done some basic nursing and seen a lot worse than badly burned hands.'

'I've got some burn scars on my legs and they're absolutely hideous. I've warned Anna. I had to, it was only fair.' He tapped the hearing aid in his left ear. 'And this.'

'I really don't think that matters.' She was back sitting on a branch of the magic tree looking into his twelve-year-old face – King Romania needed support from his queen. Leaning forward and touching his hand she said, 'She's a nurse, too. And, anyway, if she loved you she wouldn't care, would she?'

'I don't know.' He swallowed. 'I don't know what to think any more.'

'Maybe Mohammed could go to the mountain?'

'That would take most of my savings.'

'You might like New Zealand. I've heard it's really beautiful. You could start a new life together.' She looked at the hard pastry crust left on the side of her plate. 'The food can't be any worse than here.'

He attempted a smile. 'You're right about that.' Then added, 'I really want to be in Oakey Vale, it's the nicest place I've ever known.'

She knew he was right, of course, but he needed reassurance. 'Maybe you'll find somewhere on the other side of the world you like even better. Whatever the outcome, you'd have tried your best.'

'Maybe.' He bit his lip. 'There's something else I should mention. I was in the cave with Mr Hayes one time.'

'Oh my God!' So he had seen her.

'We were looking at it when discussing our plans for The Grange. It would be part of the project, a sort of interesting feature for people to visit. I saw a little chink of light high up above me and climbed up the rocks and when I looked through the gap...'

'You saw me?'

He nodded. 'It looked like a very special place. I just want you to know, I told Mr Hayes I'd been mistaken and what I had thought was a light had merely been a bit of quartz shining in the beam of my torch.'

No sound came from her throat as she mouthed her thanks.

Giles tapped on the window and they went out onto the pavement where Daphne was bouncing up and down with excitement. 'We've located the school. It's called Merryleas and the headmaster's name, should we wish to make an appointment to see it is–' she grabbed Betty's hands and held them tight '–his name is Mister Perrin.'

'How did you find that out?'

'The agent's son is a pupil there.'

'And there's a small old cottage for sale that's been standing empty, and–' Giles paused for effect '–it's next to a small council estate within a short walk of both the school and the lake.'

Betty grasped Daphne's arm to steady herself.

Billy looked at the women walking past with shopping baskets over their arms and said, 'One of them might be the mother.'

Everyone climbed into the car and, following Giles' instructions, Billy drove through tree-lined roads of semi-detached houses until they reached open fields on the left and a stretch of glistening water on their right. Betty whispered, 'Our lake.' Then, as they followed the curving road round the edge of reeds and rough ground, past a large copse, she saw the group of grey buildings.

They drove around the small estate until Billy drew the car to a standstill beside a dilapidated

410

cottage, whereupon a cluster of children who were playing in the road ran to them and gathered round the car. A boy clutching an ancient tennis racquet with several broken strings indicated the small house and asked, 'You gonner buy it, mister?'

'I might do,' Billy replied, 'I need to look at it first.'

A girl flicked her brown plaits behind her head. 'It's got big mushrooms growing in the outside lav.'

A boy said, 'My dad says I mustn't go in it no more 'cos it's falling down.'

As they walked through the gateway into the overgrown garden, Billy asked quietly, 'Any luck?'

'No, none of them is Victoria.' Betty pushed her hand into her pocket and clasped the mitten, then held her breath as the ball of light flashed in her eyes and opened out to reveal the child and her toy dog.

'She's never smacked me before, Bonzo. I don't know what to do. I love my mummy; I promise you I do, but he's so horrid and disgusting. I don't like him touching me like that. She says I've got to call him Daddy and we're all going to be a happy little family. They've gone to the big shops up West to buy a special outfit for her to get married in. D'you think we should run away?'

As the image faded Betty said, 'She's been left on her own. I've got to find her.'

Daphne walked to the children who were playing cricket with the tennis racquet and spoke to them before returning with a triumphant smile on her face. 'Come along, we need to visit the maisonettes in Lavender Close. There's a girl called Vicky living at number twenty-two who sounds just like your little girl.'

They walked around the corner followed by the gang of children. As they passed the grey pebble-dashed buildings, net curtains moved in the windows of both the ground and first floors. On reaching number twenty-two, everyone stopped and the group were debating their next move when the door marked twenty-four opened and a woman wearing an overall and a headscarf tied like a turban over her curlers shouted, 'What d'yer want?'

Betty said, 'I'm looking for Victoria.'

Giles took out his cigarettes and, seeing the woman's eyes upon him, stepped towards her and offered her one.

'I don't mind if I do.' She took one from the packet, leaned forward as he lit it for her, then, having inhaled deeply and exhaled the smoke, asked, 'Vicky yer mean?'

'Yes.'

'Lives upstairs. I saw Gertie go out early on with her–' she hesitated '–her friend.'

'My mum says it's disgusting what goes on.' The girl with pigtails made a face. 'He stays the night he does.'

'We'll knock on the door,' Billy said, 'just in case she's at home.'

A boy shouted, 'There she is!'

'Vicky, open the door!'

'Yeah, open up!'

Betty saw the small, pale face at the first-floor window and stepped forwards.

'What's going on here?' a familiar voice suddenly boomed in her ear.

Turning round she saw a small, neatly dressed woman with dark hair and blue eyes and, in a blast of icy shock, knew the truth she had not dared to imagine.

The woman tilted her head. 'If you're the Jehovah's witness people we're not interested.'

Betty stared at the balding middle-aged man who was carrying two large carrier bags and felt her fingers bend into claws capable of grasping his windpipe and squeezing the life out of him. Taking a deep breath she looked at Billy, Giles and Daphne who were all standing by the gate, and at the children clustered on the pavement giggling with excitement. Then, returning her gaze to the woman standing on the path with head on one side and hands on hips, she unclenched her fists and, pulling back her hair to reveal the scar on her forehead, said, 'You've lost a lot of weight since I last saw you, Edie.'

Putting up her arm as if to fend off an attacker, the woman teetered backwards, banging against the man who stared at her open-mouthed as she sank to the ground.

Betty stood still, unable to move her leaden legs and hearing only the loud thump of her heart as she watched Daphne rush to the unconscious figure and kneel down. Then, seeing the man drop the carrier bags and turn as if to leave, she screamed, 'I know what you've been doing to that little girl. You wicked devil!' Adding, as a dark patch formed on the front of his trousers, 'You filthy, disgusting pervert!'

When the sound of blood pulsing through her temples had receded, she became aware of the neighbour taking a key from under a flower pot and opening the door. A moment later, seeing the small figure in the doorway holding a toy dog, she stepped hesitantly forwards, saying, 'I'm afraid your mummy's not well.' She held out her hand. 'I'm pleased to meet Bonzo at last.' Then, seeing the object tied to its neck with blue ribbon, she exclaimed, 'Oh, Myrtle, darling, you've still got the carving!'

Chapter Thirty-two

Meadowsweet tea may ease diarrhoea in children.

Somerset, May 1947

'Can I get down, please?' Johnny asked, already half off the chair and balanced on one foot.

Charles replied with exaggerated solemnity, 'You look quite capable to me.'

His son gave a despairing look at the ceiling. 'Please may I leave the table?'

'You may.' Charles watched the boy run to the window and turned to wink at Kate.

Seeing the anxiety in Myrtle's eyes, Betty smiled reassuringly across the table at her. Sunday lunch at the farm had become a regular habit since she had brought her home and now, after a year of experiencing the interaction of a

414

loving family, the little girl had settled in and become one of them – almost, but not quite. She still seemed withdrawn from time to time and looked troubled when Charles reprimanded the boys, no matter how lighthearted his tone.

'It's pissing down,' Johnny said, looking out onto the yard.

Peter sniggered and made a face at Myrtle, who blushed and again looked at Betty.

Kate stood up. 'That will do, Johnny.'

'It's what Peter says.'

'Never mind what your brother says, I'm telling you not to say it.'

'So can I say it when I've got long trousers like him?'

'Not in my kitchen, no you can't.'

Peter groaned, stood up and left the room.

Johnny looked outraged. 'He didn't ask to leave the table.'

Kate held her head for a moment before replying. 'You're quite right. I'll remind him of his manners when he comes back. Now–' she smiled brightly '–when you children have helped clear the table I'll give you some paper and crayons to draw with.'

A bustle of activity followed as plates and cutlery were carried to the sink by Johnny, Myrtle and the two women. Albert, meanwhile, retired to his chair in the corner and, humming happily, picked up a piece of wood and a knife and began carving. Charles looked out of the window at the rain, yawned, picked up a newspaper off the dresser and sank into an armchair then immediately fell asleep.

When the children were sitting at the table engrossed in their drawing and the two sisters were washing the dishes, Kate said quietly, 'They get on so well you'd think they were brother and sister, although–' she gave a wry smile '–judging by the way my boys carry on, maybe not.'

'I'm doing a wedding,' Myrtle said. 'Like the one I went to with my other mummy.'

Johnny sang, 'Here comes the bride, all fat and wide. Couldn't get through the doorway. Had to be married outside!' They both screeched with laughter and then returned to their drawing.

Betty scrubbed vigorously at the roasting tin, keeping her head down to hide the tears welling up in her eyes. Whenever she heard Myrtle speak of her 'other mummy' the intense pain caught her unawares. She could never forgive Edie for taking her child and stealing those precious years of childhood from her. Feeling Kate's hand on her arm and knowing she understood her suffering, she turned and gave a reassuring smile. 'I'm alright,' she whispered and then added in a louder voice, 'this is really difficult to get clean.'

When all the dishes were washed, dried and put away, Kate suggested to Betty that they could go to her bedroom and look at the hat she had offered to lend her. Once there, she asked, 'Are you looking forward to going to London?'

'In one way I am, but I'm dreading it as well. I'm longing to see Daphne and Giles get married but I'm wondering if it was wise to say I'd take Myrtle to see Edie's grave.'

'I'm sure it's good for her to understand Edie's dead even though it's hard for you. After all, she believed Edie was her mother until you found her, didn't she?'

Betty nodded, then tried on the hat and, remembering the many small creations with little veils worn at a stylish angle on her long red hair in the Foxy days, she smiled. 'This will do very well. All mine are pre-war and look so old fashioned now. And, most importantly–' she grinned '–this is smaller than the bride's.'

'How d'you know that?'

'Last year I saw her in a New Look outfit standing on some stone steps.'

'Did you see Giles?'

'No, just Daphne.'

Kate's green eyes were milky for a moment before she asked, 'And Billy, will he be there?'

'I don't know, I haven't heard from him lately. Daphne said in her letter she hoped he'd be back from New Zealand in time to be Best Man.'

'So he's definitely coming home?'

'I really have no idea what he's doing. I can't ask his mother if she's heard from him because she's gone to stay with her daughter Mary in Liverpool for a month – Billy will be pleased about that, and anyway she still doesn't speak to me apart from responding when I say good morning and Alice has gone to live with her new husband in Cardiff so I don't get the gossip from her.'

Kate nodded. 'Old ladies like her have long memories, but at least she's reconciled with her daughter. By the way, while we're alone, d'you think we could go to the cave before you leave?'

They agreed to meet at Old Myrtles the following morning and then returned to the kitchen where Kate went to the table and admired the children's pictures. 'That's a wonderful aeroplane, Johnny,' she said, then, on looking over Myrtle's shoulder, gasped, 'Good heavens! That's quite extraordinary!' Turning to Betty she added, 'Look at this, it's just like Gran.'

Whilst taking the three steps across the stone flags to reach the table, she saw Myrtle's eyes widen with fear. 'It's alright, darling–' she took the child's hand '–I only want to see your picture.' Then, looking down, she understood. There on the page, with heads out of proportion to their bodies, but nevertheless recognisable, were the unmistakable images of Albert sitting in his chair and, standing behind him with her hands resting on his shoulders, was the rounded figure of a woman.

'I'm sorry.' Myrtle's lower lip quivered as tears slid down her cheeks.

'But this is wonderful!' Kate exclaimed.

'Yes, darling, it's nothing to apologise for. We're pleased – proud even!'

Myrtle sniffed and accepted a handkerchief from Kate. 'But you won't tell on me, will you? I don't want to go to the loony bin.'

'Is that–' Betty shuddered '–what your other mummy told you?'

'She said I mustn't ever let on I see people what nobody else sees 'cos that's mad.' Myrtle gripped Betty's arm. 'Please don't tell.'

Kate took Johnny's hand. 'We can keep a secret.'

The boy ran his right forefinger across his neck. 'I swear. Cut my throat and hope to die.'

Seeing Myrtle look anxiously towards the old man engrossed in his carving and humming 'All things bright and beautiful, Kate said, 'Don't worry, Uncle Albert won't say anything.'

Hearing his name, he looked perplexed and muttered a few words ending in 'Dinnum?' then shrugged and held up the wooden spoon he had made.

Kate smiled. 'It's lovely, Uncle. That'll fetch five bob at the church bazaar.' When he had returned to his work she turned to Myrtle and said, 'I think you can see an old lady standing behind him, is that right?'

'Yes.'

'I expect you see other people sometimes too?'

'You promised.'

'We won't tell anyone. We'd just like to know, that's all. Actually–' Kate smiled at her sister '–we'd love to be able to do it ourselves.'

Myrtle looked up at Betty, 'It's a bit like when I used to see you only I don't talk to them or anything. They're just there.'

'As though they're visiting people?'

'Mmm, that's right.'

Kate looked lovingly towards the space behind the old man's chair. 'We'll call them visitors, shall we?'

An hour later, on reaching Hankeys Land whilst walking along the path from the farm towards the cottage in the valley below, Betty saw the majestic oak before them and stopped to gaze at it. 'Do you see anyone, any visitors here, Myrtle?'

'Only the usual.'

'What's that?'

'Oh, just a few men dancing around with a sack. They look really silly. Johnny says they're just drunk so we don't take any notice of them.'

'So he knew all about the visitors already?'

'Mmm, he's my best friend.'

'And he's absolutely right, darling.' Feeling suddenly aglow with happiness Betty grasped her daughter's hand as they walked on through the clearing.

Standing in the cave the next day, Kate stroked the slab of stone with her hand and said, 'There was a time when I thought I'd be lying under that by now.'

'I know.' Betty linked arms with her. 'I'm so glad you're not.'

They both turned and gazed silently at the figure above them for several minutes.

Kate sighed. 'It's such a relief to know we have Myrtle to follow on.' Then, with a smile she asked, 'D'you think you could hold the piece of wood and tell me what's happening again?'

'I'll try.' Reaching up and feeling on the ledge, she picked up the tiny splinter of wood and, on sitting down, found herself sitting outside the dwelling with the baby lying on the ground close by. Leaning over she saw the little face light up with a smile then, aware of Kate waiting for her to speak, said, *The babies be dying of the squit fever again and the women come to me too late as usual. I give them the plant to ease it but I know 'twill not save them. 'Tis always at this time when the sun is hot and the days long. I tell them 'tis the water and they say, "That cannot be so. How could God's precious*

420

gift be poison?"

'I weary of telling them. "Look at my child," I say "Look at her and do as I did. Heat water on the fire until it gives off steam and let it cool. Let the child drink only water that has been treated so," I say, but to no avail.

'"Give the child goats' milk if thine own be weak or dried up," I say, for that is how I kept my darling from dying. Smaller than the first Myrtle her be and though marked with a red line from the centre of her forehead to the bridge of her nose and having a twisted foot, her be the most wondrous creature. Some may say her be touched by the devil and be afeared – so much the better for her, for they will leave her be when I die. I thank God for the affliction that shall be her protection.

'I have lost a daughter and lost her son, but now I have the greatest prize of all...'

Opening her eyes, Betty looked down into her hand and saw only dust. 'It's gone,' she said, 'the link with the past has gone. I was so sure it was the wooden handle of a knife, you know, like the ones Albert made for us.'

Kate squeezed her arm in sympathy. 'I'm sure it was too, but nothing lasts for ever.' She stood looking up at the implacable face in the rock before leading the way through the gap into the outer cave.

When they had parted the ivy curtain and stepped into the sunlight, they then sat on the rock together and Kate said, 'I met Mr Hayes on my way here. He was smiling like a Cheshire cat. He's finally bought The Grange at last and is really pleased with himself.'

'And about time too, that's been going on for absolutely ages!'

'Yes, he told me delays on moving some of the seriously ill patients held them up. He said there'll be months of painting and decorating before the centre could be operational. And, I'm sorry to say, he also said he'll be opening the cave and charging people to go and see it. I tried not to show my feelings and just asked whether he'd be putting electric lights in there when the power is brought into the village next year and he said yes he would. I confess I'm really worried he'll discover our secret.'

'I don't see how he can now we've filled in the gap, and anyway that cave is lower than ours so no one can see in unless they're on a ladder. Also, don't forget, Billy's promised not to give us away.'

'You're right,' Kate agreed, 'I'm probably worrying unnecessarily. I just feel we'd be betraying Gran and all the others if they found it and opened it to the public with the other cave.'

'And there's the small matter of embarrassing questions about the tomb.'

'A very big matter I'm afraid. The funny thing is I recall Jim saying it was common practice long ago.'

Feeling the guilty blush colour her face at the mention of the archaeologist she had wanted her sister to marry because he had offered to send her to a select private school, Betty said, 'I read in a book about either Spain or Greece, can't remember which, that people bury their dead in caves there, and I seem to recall Jesus was buried in a cave too, the trouble is it's just not done here.'

'Not any longer, but there are places where it used to be. I still think the long barrows are made to look like caves. There was an article about them in the local paper recently. Which reminds me, I heard that some things which have been stored since before the war are going to be put on display at the local museum. Amongst them were some finds from the cave at Oakey Vale.'

'The bones!'

'Yes, and also the knife blade and the quartz ball. Just think, sweetheart–' Kate's green eyes sparkled '–you might be able to get messages from them.'

'The ball,' Betty murmured, 'if only I could hold that! I think she dropped her knife which was found by the man who looked after Caitlin and he took it to the Holy Land then gave it to her, but the ball must have been in a pouch at her waist when she died.'

They sat in silence for a few minutes until Kate looked at the washing hanging on the line and asked, 'Getting ready for tomorrow?'

'Just doing a few of my things. Myrtle's packed and ready to go. Well, almost, I'll add Bonzo at the last minute; we can't go without him.'

'It's not going to be an easy week, Betty.'

'I know. I'm dreading going to Edie's grave even more now I know how she frightened Myrtle about seeing the ghosts.'

'I suppose she didn't want the child attracting attention of any kind in case they looked into her background. I mean she must have forged some documents to change her identity like that.'

'Yes, quite clever, really. Billy went to Somerset

House and discovered Gertrude Simms and her son Victor had died in the early days of the Blitz. She took the woman's name and turned Victor into Victoria. I saw a baby in blue rompers the first time I held the mitten and then a toddler in a sailor suit. I'm sure she was already pretending the baby was a boy in case any one was looking for her. When I think how she almost got away with it, the anger rises up and–' She broke off, swallowing her tears.

Kate hugged her. 'I know, I know, but you did get Myrtle back and she's such a delightful child, so creative and imaginative. We all love her, and she's settled in so well and Johnny and she have had such a happy time together. She's convinced him the oak tree is like a magic carpet and they go on imaginary journeys – he'd never have done that without her.'

'I was worried about her seeing the ghosts of the hanging in the tree, but when I asked if she saw any visitors there, she just said she saw some drunk men carrying a sack.'

Kate exclaimed, 'Oh my God!'

'I really don't think we should worry too much. If we make an issue of it she won't want to play there and that would be such a shame.'

'I agree. The ghosts are a normal part of her life because she's always been aware of them.' Kate shook her head. 'It's a great pity Edie told her people would lock her up if she ever admitted to seeing them.'

'If you hadn't recognised Gran standing by Uncle Albert we might never have discovered she had such an amazing gift. Fancy her seeing the old lady in the kitchen every evening for weeks like that and never saying a word to anyone!'

'I was really encouraging her drawing because I thought she was unusually talented, I had no idea she was so gifted in another way. Actually I think your inspiration of calling them "visitors" saved the situation.'

'True,' Betty agreed, 'but she's still worried we might tell other people. I have to keep reassuring her we'll both keep it secret. I gritted my teeth and said Edie didn't mean to scare her, it was just that she couldn't see them herself and so didn't understand. When she's older I can tell her the whole story and then I think she'll see that Edie was worried about her own crime being discovered and not about Myrtle being thought to be mad.'

'I'm glad you're thinking of Myrtle's good rather than vengeance against Edie–' Kate kissed her cheek '–that's so much better for both of you.' She picked up her shopping basket and departed.

Betty leaned back against the ivy. Tomorrow they would travel to Chiswick, where Fay would be eagerly looking forward to the wedding the following day. She would talk loudly during the tube journey to Caxton Hall about the 'good old days' and at the reception she'd get tipsy and confide in everyone that she was Brahms and Liszt and sing for them whether they wanted her to or not. 'They don't write songs like that no more, Foxy,' she would say and Betty would agree, thankful they didn't, but feeling overwhelming love for her friend nevertheless.

'Mummy, look what I've got!'

Shading her dazzled eyes she waved at the shimmering figure beside the roses. 'What's that, darling?' Then, seeing Myrtle hold something above her head, she walked up the path towards her.

'It's the most beautiful blouse you've ever seen. Mrs Hayes has just given it to me. She said it's real silk, and she'd been keeping it for somebody from abroad, but they're not coming now so she thought I'd like it.'

'That's really kind.' On getting close, Betty squinted at the scarlet fabric. 'I see what you mean, it's lovely.'

'She said she'd bought it just before the war and never worn it 'cos it was too small and it'll be a bit big for me but I'll grow into it.'

Betty stroked the soft dark curls, savouring the delight of having her daughter close – this was the most beautiful, beloved child in the world. 'That will suit you very well, darling.'

'That's what she said. I'll go and try it on.' After taking a few steps, Myrtle stopped in the doorway. 'Miss Thompson had a visitor in the classroom today.'

'How nice!' Her heart quickened with joy. If the child was to relax and confide in her she must not overreact or be too excited – she must remain calm but interested. Reaching out and picking a white rose from the cascade of blooms hanging over the porch, she clasped it to her heart and asked, 'What did he look like?'

'A soldier with a beret.'

'I heard her brother died in the war, I expect it was him.'

426

'Mmm, 'spect so, he had nice big teeth like hers. You won't tell anyone else, will you, promise?'

'I promise.'

'I'll go and get changed now.' Myrtle turned and ran up the stairs.

She went into the scullery, and, whilst filling the kettle with water, wondered for a jealous moment if Edie's spirit ever came to the cottage, then immediately smiled at the irony of such a visitation when it was Edie who had told the child that people who admitted seeing ghosts were sent to the lunatic asylum.

Having put the kettle onto the range, she wondered what to make for tea, then, hearing the clatter of footsteps down the stairs, and knowing her daughter's liking for eggs, she turned and enquired, 'Which would you prefer, darling, poached or... Crikey!'

'What's the matter?' Myrtle looked down at her navy blue shorts. 'Don't they look right with it?'

Feeling her pulse quicken, she remembered holding Billy's wristwatch whilst sitting in a railway carriage with him. She'd seen him standing under the oak tree in Hankeys Land watching a girl in red and blue pulling herself up into the branches above him. 'Nothing's wrong, darling, I'm just impressed by how very beautiful you look.'

'I said I'd meet Johnny at The Magic Tree. We're going to see King Arthur and the Knights of the Round Table.'

She blew her a kiss. 'Have a nice time in Camelot.'

Sitting back onto a chair, she laughed aloud.

Billy had promised to keep silent about the secret cave, he had shared her joy on finding Myrtle and spent hours uncovering Edie's deception, and, when he came to say goodbye before leaving for New Zealand, she'd kissed him on the cheek with gratitude and friendly affection. Now, with a sudden gush of emotion, she knew that one day soon she would walk towards the oak tree in Hankeys Land and see him standing beside the enormous trunk whilst Myrtle reached for the branch overhead. He would have splatters of white paint on his overalls and a splodge of it in his hair, and he would smile in a special way as she walked along the path towards him. She had not only seen his future that day in the train, she had also glimpsed her own.

This Large Print Book for the partially sighted, who cannot read normal print, is published under the auspices of

THE ULVERSCROFT FOUNDATION

THE ULVERSCROFT FOUNDATION

... we hope that you have enjoyed this Large Print Book. Please think for a moment about those people who have worse eyesight problems than you ... and are unable to even read or enjoy Large Print, without great difficulty.

You can help them by sending a donation, large or small to:

**The Ulverscroft Foundation,
1, The Green, Bradgate Road,
Anstey, Leicestershire, LE7 7FU,
England.**
or request a copy of our brochure for more details.

The Foundation will use all your help to assist those people who are handicapped by various sight problems and need special attention.

Thank you very much for your help.